His Co...
Woman

She was his convenient woman…
to have and to hold!

Three passionate novels!

In May 2007 Mills & Boon bring back
two of their classic collections, each
featuring three favourite romances
by our bestselling authors…

HIS CONVENIENT WOMAN
His Convenient Wife by Diana Hamilton
His Convenient Mistress
by Cathy Williams
His Convenient Fiancée
by Barbara McMahon

AUSTRALIAN AFFAIRS
The Outback Doctor by Lucy Clark
The Surgeon's Proposal by Lilian Darcy
Outback Surgeon by Leah Martyn

His Convenient Woman

HIS CONVENIENT WIFE
by
Diana Hamilton

HIS CONVENIENT MISTRESS
by
Cathy Williams

HIS CONVENIENT FIANCÉE
by
Barbara McMahon

MILLS & BOON®

*MILLS & BOON and MILLS & BOON with the Rose Device
are registered trademarks of the publisher.*
Harlequin Mills & Boon Limited,
Eton House, 18-24 Paradise Road, Richmond, Surrey, TW9 1SR

HIS CONVENIENT WOMAN
© by Harlequin Enterprises II B.V. 2007

His Convenient Wife, His Convenient Mistress and *His Convenient
Fiancée* were first published in Great Britain by Harlequin Mills
& Boon Limited in separate, single volumes.

His Convenient Wife © Diana Hamilton 2002
His Convenient Mistress © Cathy Williams 2003
His Convenient Fiancée © Barbara McMahon 2003

ISBN: 978 0 263 85515 9

05-0507

*Printed and bound in Spain
by Litografía Rosés S.A., Barcelona*

HIS CONVENIENT WIFE

by

Diana Hamilton

Diana Hamilton is a true romantic and fell in love with her husband at first sight. They still live in the fairytale Tudor house where they raised their three children. Now the idyll is shared with eight rescued cats and a puppy. But despite an often chaotic lifestyle, ever since she learned to read and write Diana has had her nose in a book – either reading or writing one – and plans to go on doing just that for a very long time to come.

PROLOGUE

'YOU can't be serious! Are you actually suggesting I marry this Aldo Patrucco character?' Cat's green eyes flashed withering scorn in her grandfather's direction. She pulled herself up to her full five feet nine inches, towering above him, her patrician nostrils pinched with a mix of disbelief and outrage.

Gramps looked oddly shrunken, his clothes suddenly seeming too big for his frail bones as he sat in his favourite armchair. She felt sorry for him, of course she did, very sorry, and she loved him dearly, but no way would she fall in with the insane suggestion he'd just thrown at her.

'Listen to yourself, won't you?' she pushed out through her teeth. 'You're asking me to sell myself— it's positively medieval!'

'And you are overreacting as usual, Caterina,' Domenico Patrucco objected flatly, his black eyes immediately softening in his lined face as he went on to ask gently, 'Why don't you pour the tea and then we can sit and have a civilised discussion? Without shouting.'

Cat let out a long, pent-up breath. It would cost her nothing to humour him, would it? Poor old Gramps had had a tough time recently. He had lost both his

5

sister Silvana and his beloved wife Alice in the space of three months. She and Gramps were still grieving for Alice, so she knew how he felt. She'd never met her Italian great-aunt Silvana, of course, but she knew how much Gramps had looked forward to those long, gossipy letters which had told him of the doings of the Italian side of the family he had split from all those long years ago.

He was all alone now apart from Bonnie, who had been housekeeper here from the year dot. It had been Bonnie who had waddled over to the converted barn in what had once been the stack yard, where Cat had her workshop beneath her living quarters, to announce that her grandfather wished her to join him for afternoon tea.

As she dealt with the tea things Cat wondered if she should offer to move back into the farmhouse to keep the old man company. To stop him brooding and being too lonely. The farmland had been sold off years ago, when he'd retired, and the poor old guy had nothing to do with his time but come up with manic suggestions.

She owed him big time. He and Gran had brought her up since his only child, her mother, had been killed with Cat's father in a road accident when she had been little more than a baby. Their love and care had been unstinting.

Two years ago when she'd left college with a degree in jewellery and silversmithing her grandparents had offered her the use of the barn as a workshop and had reluctantly agreed to her plan to move out of the main house and convert the barn's upper storey into a self-contained flat. She'd been twenty-one and eager to have her own space where she could work or relax, entertain her friends, as the mood took her, be independent.

Keeping him company, keeping an eye on him for a few months, just until he was more himself, wouldn't hurt her. It was, she supposed, the least she could do after all he and Gran had done for her.

The tea poured, she handed him a delicate china cup and saucer and flopped down on the opposite side of the hearth to where he was sitting, her long jeans-clad legs stretched out in front of her, and offered brightly, 'Why don't I move back in here for a month or two? We could spend time together.'

She could sub-let her booth in the craft centre for three months and put her work on hold, she mentally sacrificed, and because that was not the best idea in the world as far as her career was concerned she flashed him a brilliant, Gramps-deluding smile. 'We could take days out together; I'll drive you wherever you want to go—'

'And give me a heart attack!' he interrupted drily. 'The way you drive is as flamboyant and erratic as the way you dress!' And, seeing the way her vivid, animated and lovely features went blank, her wide mouth compressing, he amended gently, 'I thank you for your concern, but I assure you I am not in need of such a sacrifice. What you can do to make me a happy man is give serious consideration to my suggestion.'

So they were back to that, were they? Cat ground her teeth together. Her diversionary tactics hadn't worked, so the only way to handle this was to get it all out in the open, force him to see that his intention to marry her off to his great-nephew was a complete non-starter.

'If your suggestion had been remotely sane I might have done that,' she came back carefully, tenaciously holding on to her patience. 'But I'm willing to listen while you try to say something sensible on the subject; that's all I can promise.'

Leaning back in her chair, she pushed her untameable mane of chestnut hair away from her face. The room was unbearably warm. It was only mid-September but a huge log fire was burning in the hearth. Her grandfather had lived in cool, misty England for many years but his Italian blood still craved warmth.

His heavily hooded eyes held hers but he said nothing for long moments. Trying to find a form of words that would make something crazy sound completely sensible, she guessed. Well, it wouldn't work, however he dressed it up.

'Family,' he said at last. 'It all comes down to family. Forget the shares for the moment; they are important but not as important as closing the circle.'

Cat could have asked him what he meant by that

but didn't bother. And as for the shares she would happily forget them. Forever.

Growing up she'd heard the story so many times it bored her socks off. How her grandfather had been incensed, hurt in his pride, as he put it, when his older married brother had inherited seventy per cent of the shares in the Patrucco family business while he had received a mere miserable thirty. Marcantonio had had the upper hand, made all the decisions, told him what to do. Had control. So the younger and disgruntled Domenico had just upped and left. America first stop, where, hot-headed and determined to show Marcantonio that he didn't need him or the olive plantations and the vineyards, he got into trouble over something to do with a parcel of land.

England next, to seek his fortune. What he had found was love. His Alice.

The only child of farming parents, Alice Mayhew had fallen head over heels with her handsome Italian suitor and after their marriage he'd helped out on the Shropshire farm; the income from the shares that had caused his permanent split from his brother had purchased more land, updated equipment and renovated the down-at-heel farmhouse.

However much he had despised the insulting smallness of his holding in the Italian business he had never sold those shares. And now, according to the healthy state of his bank balance, they were paying huge dividends.

'You didn't think family was important when you

upped and left Italy and broke off all contact,' Cat reminded him gently when she guessed by his continuing silence he had run out of things to say.

'That was pride. The pride of a man is stiff, unyielding.' He lifted his shoulders in a fatalistic shrug, but defended, 'I kept contact through our sister Silvana. She told me of Marcantonio's success in expanding the business, of the birth of his son, my nephew Astorre. Of my brother's death ten years after Astorre's marriage into a super-wealthy Roman family and the arrival of my great-nephew Aldo. Through her I know that Astorre has retired to Amalfi with his grand Roman wife and that Aldo now holds the business reins and has expanded into luxury holiday villas and apartments.'

Cat could almost feel sorry for him. A seventy-nine-year-old man indulging in pipedreams. She saw the relevance of that 'closing the circle' bit now. Sweep past resentments and quarrels aside, marry his granddaughter to his great-nephew and make everything right and whole again.

In his dreams!

'And through the photographs Silvana sent me—' a slow pause, a smile that might, if she were to be uncharitable, be described as sly '—I know that Aldo is a fine figure of Italian manhood—at thirty years of age he has a truly astute business brain and is the owner of a villa in Tuscany, a town house in Florence and an apartment in Portofino—*che bello*! You could do far worse! That I know all that is important to know about my lost family I explained to Aldo when I spoke to him on the phone a fortnight ago and suggested that a marriage between you two young things might be arranged to reunite the family.'

A beat of appalled silence. Cat felt her face colour hotly. 'You did *what*? I do not *believe* this!' Then the cool and welcome slide of common sense effectively stopped her exploding with outrage. 'And he quite rightly told you where to put your interfering "suggestion". Right?'

'Far from it. He accepted my invitation to come and meet you. To discuss the matter further. As I said, he has an astute brain. Which brings us to my shares.' He held out his cup and saucer. 'Would you?'

Rising, Cat poured his second cup of tea, her hands shaking. She would not let her temper rip. Her grandfather was seventy-nine years old; he was grieving for his Alice. His sister was also, sadly, gone. He couldn't make his peace with his older brother—he had died many years ago. He wanted to heal the family rift through his granddaughter and his great-nephew. She had to keep reminding herself of the facts to stop herself throttling him!

So she wouldn't storm out of here as every instinct urged her to. She really didn't want to upset him. Besides, no one on this earth could make her marry a man she didn't know, quite possibly wouldn't even like and certainly wouldn't love.

Reassured, she handed him his tea and asked, 'So when does this paragon arrive?'

'Any time now. I didn't tell you what I had in mind earlier. You would have suddenly expressed the wish to take a walking holiday in Scotland or go climbing in the Andes!'

Cat dipped her head, acknowledging his correct reading of her character. She recalled a note appended to one of her end-of-term reports. 'Caterina is stubborn and headstrong. She won't be led and she won't be pushed.'

Bolshie, in other words.

She preferred to think of herself as strong-minded. She knew what she wanted and that wasn't having to endure being looked over by some Italian big shot like a heifer at market!

'Why aren't you shouting at me, Caterina?'

The thread of amusement in his voice brought her attention back to her grandfather. She gave a slight, dismissive shrug and walked to the window to look out at the tail end of the afternoon. The days were shortening and the turning leaves of the damson tree mimicked the promise of hazy sunshine breaking through the warm and heavy early-autumn mist.

'The timing of Aldo's arrival is irrelevant. He is wasting his time coming here at all.' She turned back to face him, the russet colour of the heavy-duty smock she usually wore when she was working emphasising the burnished glow of her chestnut hair, making her skin look paler, her eyes a deeper emerald. She spread her long-fingered artist's hands expressively. 'I can't understand why he's bothering. The guy's obviously loaded and unless he looks like a cross between Quasimodo and a pot-bellied pig he could take his own pick of women.'

'As no doubt he has,' Domenico remarked drily. 'But when it comes to taking a wife there is much to be considered. Family honour demands that a man marries wisely and well and not merely because he has lustful desires for a particular pretty woman.'

'Your shares in his business,' Cat deduced in a flat voice. This Aldo creep was obviously the pits. Popular culture marked the Italian male as being passionate, hot-blooded and fiery but this distant relative of hers had to be anything but if he could contemplate, even for one moment, marrying a woman he had yet to meet for the sake of clawing back a parcel of shares.

Verifying that conclusion, Domenico dipped his head. 'My thirty-per-cent holding in his business, plus everything that is mine will one day come to you.' He stirred his tea reflectively. 'You are young, you are beautiful and when I am gone you will be all alone. If you were safely married to a man such as Aldo your future would be secure. You would be part of a family, cared for and pampered. I do not make this suggestion because I am crazy but because I love you and worry about your future.'

'There's no need,' Cat said gruffly, her throat thickening. On the one hand she wanted to give him a verbal lashing. He was like something out of the ark! In his outdated opinion women couldn't stand on their own feet; they needed a member of that superior race—a man—to look after them. And when he was no longer around to perform that duty he wanted to pass her over to someone he thought he could trust! He was living back in the nineteenth century—and, what was worse, an Italian nineteenth century!

On the other hand, she knew he loved her, cared about her, and that made her want to fling her arms around him and tell him she loved him, too.

She did neither. She said, relatively calmly, 'I'm a big girl; I can look after myself. And if we really must have to anticipate events—which is not what I want to do—then I have a business of my own, remember. I could sell those shares to invest in it,' she pointed out. 'I could buy more and better equipment, hire staff, open a proper high-street shop instead of trading from a craft centre. I have no intention of tying myself to a cold-fish business brain for the sake of a life of idle luxury!' She turned to the door, telling him, 'You'd better start thinking of how to apologise to the guy for bringing him over here on a wild-goose chase.'

'Wait.' Domenico's voice was smooth as cream. 'Marriage is by no means certain. Though I know Aldo wouldn't have agreed to this meeting if he hadn't thought the idea viable. And I warn you, if he does propose and you turn him down for no good reason but pigheadedness—going against my wishes and your own best interests—then the shares, everything I have, will go to him.'

For several long seconds Cat couldn't move. A heavy ache balled in her chest and her eyes flooded with tears. Gramps had said he loved her but he was quite happy to blackmail her. It hurt more than he would ever know.

The loss of her inheritance paled into insignificance. It would be tough, but she'd manage. When the time came she would have to find new living and working premises to rent, work all hours in order to keep her tiny business viable, and maybe not make it.

But that was nothing beside the knowledge that he was prepared to disinherit her if she didn't toe the line. He couldn't care for her at all, or not as much as he cared for what he called family honour.

When she could get her feet to move she walked out of the room and exactly one hour later she saw Aldo Patrucco arrive from the vantage point of her kitchen window above the cobbled stack yard.

He exited from the back of a dark saloon. He was tall, wearing a beautiful dark grey overcoat and a white silk scarf, and that was all she could see because the mist that had been hanging around all day had thickened in the autumn evening.

The uniformed chauffeur took a single leather suitcase from the boot and moments later drove away. So the big shot must have hired the package, Cat deduced as the main door was opened by Bonnie to admit the Italian.

Cat shuddered, her mouth clamped decisively shut.

Only ten minutes ago Bonnie had called from the bottom of the stairs that led up from her work-room, telling her that her grandfather expected her to take dinner with him and his guest. Eight o'clock sharp.

She could refuse to put in an appearance. Or she could turn up in her shabbiest work clothes, display disgraceful table manners and vile personal habits, and put the guy off the idea of having anything at all to do with her.

The latter idea was tempting but she had too much pride to let herself act with such immaturity. She would go. She would be dignified. Not speak until spoken to. And spend her time trying to calculate if the amount in her bank balance would fund the renting of new premises if her grandfather threw her out as soon as Aldo Patrucco had left England, his proposal of marriage—if he made it—rejected with the scorn it deserved.

CHAPTER ONE

MARRYING Aldo Patrucco had been the biggest mistake of her life, Cat told herself for the millionth time as she stood in front of the tall window at the top of the villa, staring out at the rolling Tuscan hills shimmering in the haze of afternoon heat.

The panoramic view might once have entranced her. But the gentle purple hills, silver olive groves and scattered ochre-coloured farmhouses, the ubiquitous punctuation marks of the cypress trees merely emphasised her isolation, her frustration and misery.

The villa—every luxury provided…well, that went without saying in a Patrucco residence—reputedly built for the Medici family way back in the middle ages, had been her prison for two long months, since shortly after her miscarriage back in June.

Apart from his twice-weekly dutiful phone calls she'd had no contact with Aldo; he'd used his excuse of 'Rest and Recuperation' to get her away from the house in Florence, out of his sight, masking his disappointment in her failure to carry his heir to full term with an unconvincing display of polite concern for her well-being.

Leaving him free to be with his mistress.

He was cold. Heartless. Unreachable. Except…

17

Except she'd once been so sure he hadn't been like
that at all, that she could somehow reach his heart.

But he hadn't got a heart, had he? Just an efficient
machine, like a calculator.

As it too often did, her mind slid back with humiliating ease to that fatal night when she'd first met
him. Only eleven months ago but it seemed like a
lifetime now.

Dinner at eight. True to her intention to grit her
teeth and make an appearance, to present a dignified
front, she'd dressed in the soberest garment she
owned. A peacock-green crêpe shift that skimmed her
generously curved body and left her arms bare. Her
make-up discreet, her unmanageable hair somehow
tamed, drawn back from her face and painstakingly
secured with a black velvet bow at her nape.

'Caterina—' There'd been such a note of pride in
her grandfather's voice as he'd risen from a leather
club chair in the study as she'd walked into the room
with her head high, but his introduction was lost on
her as Aldo Patrucco got to his feet.

Over six feet of superbly dressed Italian male, a
strong, harshly handsome face, his features shimmering out of focus because it was the look in those bitter-chocolate eyes that entrapped her.

She'd seen that look in men's eyes before and had
uninterestedly ignored it. Her one and only short-lived
affair with Josh, a fellow student, in her final year at
college had fizzled out with no regret on either side,
and since then she hadn't been remotely tempted.

But this hot, sultry branding held her as she'd never been held before, and her lips parted on a breathless gasp as his hard mouth curved in a slight, lazy smile just before he greeted her with easy Italian panache, his hands resting lightly on her shoulders, a light kiss on her forehead, another just above the corner of her mouth.

Just the softest brush of his lips against her skin, but it was enough to make her shake, make her breathless, disorientated.

'Ciao, Caterina.' His voice slid over her like warm dark honey. She mumbled something and turned away to hide the heat that suddenly flared over her face. She preferred to be called Cat—it sounded sharper, definite, more like the self she knew herself to be—but Caterina, on his lips, sounded like magic.

Charm, she told herself, making no attempt to join in the ensuing conversation, which was being conducted in part Italian, part English. He could turn charm on like a tap. Obviously. So why was she feeling hot and bothered, overpowered, when she had to know that the way he had looked at her, as if he wanted to bed her right here and now, was just the stock-in-trade of a man who knew what he wanted and how to get it? A man who was fully aware of his power over other people and used it.

The physical presence of the man filled the book-lined room with a dangerous sexual threat. A combination of a lean, powerful six-foot frame clothed in sheer Italian elegance, and that closely cropped black hair framing hard tanned features, that tough jawline and a mouth that could soften into a wicked, explicit promise whenever he looked her way made a tense, fluttery excitement curl in the pit of her stomach.

Cat rose with a sense of relief when Bonnie poked her head round the door to announce that dinner was ready, a relief that quickly turned into deep trepidation when Aldo rose to escort her, the palm of his long, lean hand hot against the small of her back, burning her. Burning her up with a sheet of wildfire that sizzled through her veins and made her feel lightheaded.

No other man had ever affected her this way. She'd sort of fallen into her brief affair with Josh because he fancied her, was easy on the eye, and had been amusing company. And it had seemed to her that she was the only girl in her peer group not in a relationship. But this feeling was entirely different. It was immediate, insistent. Shattering.

Seated opposite him, Cat didn't know where to put herself, and Bonnie's meal, beautifully cooked and presented as usual, was untouched on her plate. But the champagne Gramps had insisted on eventually loosened her tongue and Aldo's dark eyes locked on to her soft mouth as he murmured, 'You speak fluent Italian.'

'I was brought up on it—my grandparents insisted.' She drained her glass, feeling reckless, feeling more like herself. The situation was weird, like something out of an old and rather silly novel, but undoubtedly exciting. What woman wouldn't be feeling as if she were permanently plugged into a conduit for live electricity when face to face with such a breathtakingly sexy, brain-blowingly gorgeous male who was here with the express intent of looking her over, deciding whether she was suitable wife material?

'Caterina has always been made aware of her heritage,' Domenico put in with an undertow of satisfaction, like a breeder demonstrating the finer points of his bloodstock to a possible purchaser.

Far from experiencing all that earlier outrage, Cat giggled softly as she watched the bubbles rise in the crystal flute as Aldo helped her to yet more champagne. 'I have far more English blood in my veins than Italian,' she argued softly, feeling those bitter-chocolate eyes on her and secretly wallowing in the sensation of feeling more truly alive than she had ever done before.

Aldo leaned back in his chair, his eyes hooded now as they roamed from the crown of her glossy chestnut head, over her milky white skin and down to the lushly rounded breasts beneath the soft covering of fine fabric, the explicit shafts of golden light in the veiled depths making her blush as he murmured, 'With your colouring, your grace, you could be *Veneziana*, and I hear from Zio Domenico that your temperament is fiery, pure *Italiana*, with nothing of the phlegmatic English.'

'And could you cope with that, *signor*?' she dared, green eyes sparkling through a thick sweep of dark lashes as she thrust the agenda out into the open, wondering if such exposure would wrong-foot this supremely self-assured male, unprepared for and wantonly excited by his softly drawled comeback, the slow and decidedly rakish grin that made her pulse flutter.

'I am quite sure I could. With much pleasure.'

His purring, silken response filled her head with X-rated images. Married to him, enjoying him. His mouth on hers, giving her the heaven it had so far only promised, his hard, honed naked body covering hers, demanding, taking, possessing... It would be criminally easy to give him exactly what his eyes told her he wanted and then ask him for more!

She couldn't tear her eyes away from his; he mesmerised her, turned her blood to fire, filled her with aching need. And her breathing was going haywire, her pulse throbbing as Domenico rose to his feet, satisfaction in his voice after following their exchange as he announced softly, 'You must excuse me. I am an old man and retire early. Caterina, why don't you show Aldo where you work and give him coffee?'

Which was what she needed, yet didn't need at all. She wanted to be alone with him and yet the prospect scared her witless. She didn't trust herself around this man, she didn't trust herself at all and yet the prospect was heady, electrifying, disturbingly exciting.

Aldo stood and turned to speak to her grandfather, his voice low-pitched. Cat wasn't listening and she didn't look at him either. It wasn't safe.

Looking at him, drowning in that warm, honeyed voice short-circuited her brain. She needed to come down out of fantasy land and plant her feet firmly on the ground, put her brain in gear and tell him she knew exactly why he was here.

Tell him he didn't need to waste any more of his doubtlessly precious time looking her over because the idea of their marriage was a non-starter.

And yet...

Angrily, she squashed the treacherous beginnings of a mental veer in the opposite direction, the shafting thought that it would be much too easy to fall helplessly in love with this man, that marriage to him would be a challenge, exciting, endlessly rewarding.

Indulging in wild fantasies was alien to her, alien, unwanted and unnecessary. It was time she did something about it, put a stop to all this nonsense. Laying down her napkin, she, too, got to her feet and said stiltedly, 'Bonnie will bring coffee, *signor*; I'll ask her on my way out. So I'll say goodnight, too, Grandfather. I'm sure your guest has no desire to see a workshop.'

'I have every desire, Caterina.' The silken stroke of his voice made every muscle in her body tighten. His stress on that word 'desire' left her in no doubt that he wasn't referring to her work benches and tools. And the gleam in his eyes as he let them drift lazily over her taut body terrified her. Already she had a violently insane need to get closer, to loop her arms around those wide, immaculately clad shoulders and submit the soft, melting femininity of her body to his hard domination.

She had to be losing her mind! Resisting the impulse to cover her burning face with her shaking hands, Cat made a strenuous mental effort to pull herself together.

She was free, she was independent, she had her work and she loved it. She was passionate about everything she had, and had no intention of accepting a hand-picked husband, selected and presented in cold blood.

It was her misfortune that the man in question was sexier than any man had a right to be. What she was experiencing was lust, she reminded herself tartly. Just lust. All the more shattering because she'd been celibate for a long time, ever since she and Josh had broken up before the end of their final year at college.

Having been left with no other option, Cat led the way over the cobbled yard, picking her way carefully on the uneven surface. The security lights were on but she was used to striding around in flat shoes and jeans or flowing, colourful skirts, and the skirt of the dress she was wearing was narrow and tight and her heels, although restrainedly elegant, were too high.

She more than half expected him to slide an intimate hand around her waist on the pretext of steadying her slow and tottery progress but he did nothing of the sort. She didn't know whether to feel glad about that or strangely deprived. Whatever, her heart was beating so violently she was sure it would burst out of her chest.

As always, the double doors opened easily at her touch and as she depressed the light switch Aldo remarked coolly, 'You don't lock your premises?'

Cat shrugged slim shoulders. 'Sometimes. If I'm out for any length of time. Does it matter?' Which was her way of saying, Is it any of your business?

'It shows carelessness.'

Wow! His mood had changed quicker than she could bat an eyelash! Watching the lean grace of his beautifully clad body as he ignored her and walked further into the studio, the way his long hands slid carefully over the thin sheets of silver laid out on one of the work benches, she felt sick with disappointment.

Oh, grow up! she snapped at herself. She couldn't really want to fight a losing battle with him if he had brought that earlier covert seduction out into the open. Of course not. She should be deeply relieved that, away from her grandfather's watchful eyes, he had reverted to what he truly was—cold and calculating.

He held up the garnet ear droppers she had been working on earlier, switching on the desk lamp and turning them to the light, examining the moulded silver settings before laying them carefully down again and going to stand in front of the open sketch book displaying her designs for future projects.

'You have a certain talent.' He turned to her, his hands on the narrow span of his hips. And then he lifted his impressive shoulders in a dismissive shrug. 'Your grandfather tells me you sell your creations from a stall in a draughty, redundant church. You barely scrape a living.'

'Don't knock it!' Cat's eyes narrowed. How dared he dish out such a put-down? Her fingers curled into the palms of her hands, biting into the tender skin. Earlier she had wanted to kiss him; now she wanted to kill him! The effort of holding her temper in check made her words come out bitingly fast. 'Everyone has to start somewhere. We're not all lucky enough to be handed a ready-made thriving business empire at birth. One day I'll have my own shop premises, a hand-picked team of craftsmen and women—'

'When you get your hands on your inheritance?' he slid in with insulting silkiness.

Cat's face closed up. Had Gramps told him about her recklessly defensive message about selling those precious family shares to fund her own small business, thoughtlessly tossed out to stop him boring on about his wretched idea for an arranged marriage? Or had it been an astute guess?

Whatever, she had no intention of defending herself to this patronising monster. She didn't want to get her hands on her inheritance, as he had callously put it, because it would mean that her beloved Gramps was no longer around and she couldn't bear the thought of that.

Her green eyes glittering with emotion, she spiked out, 'Please leave. Now!'

'So soon?' The indolent tilt of one dark brow, his aura of sophisticated and total command, was probably meant to intimidate her. It might have done, had she let it. She didn't.

'Can't be soon enough! You know where the door is.'

Unnervingly, his dark eyes gleamed with amusement. 'I also know I'm not leaving until we've thoroughly discussed your grandfather's wishes. He is an old man, far from the country of his birth, estranged from his family. The least we can do is discuss the pros and cons of his suggestion. Even if we think it's mad. Over coffee. This way?'

His dark head dipped towards the steep flight of wooden stairs that led to her living quarters. Cat ignored him. She bit her tongue to stop herself hurling verbal abuse at him as he mounted the stairs, arrogant self-confidence in every movement of his strong, supple body, then launched after him, kicking off her shoes and hiking her narrow, restrictive skirt above her knees.

Did he, too, think her grandfather's scheme was crazy? Had he come all this way to humour a distant relative he had never met out of respect? Italians went a bundle on respect, didn't they?

But the question flew out of her head as he reached the apartment well ahead of her, despite her best efforts in the scampering department. The door opened directly into her living room. She had left a table lamp burning and the room just looked like comfortable chaos. But when he found the main light switch and depressed it the room looked like a squalid hovel.

And Aldo, standing in the middle of the muddle, was so beautifully groomed and immaculate. The contrast made her cheeks flame with embarrassment. The velvet bow that had held her hair in check fell off. She heard it hit the floor behind her just before the riotous chestnut tangle tumbled around her shoulders. And she was still holding her skirt above her knees. She dropped the hem immediately and said starkly, 'Coffee?' and picked her barefoot way through to the tiny kitchen, avoiding the piles of trade magazines and glossies, the pile of curtains she'd laundered but hadn't got around to re-hanging and the heap of work clothes she'd got out of before going through to shower and change earlier this evening.

When she was working, deeply engrossed in a new project, she forgot to be tidy, forgot everything. But no way would she explain or make excuses to this so obviously superior being, who probably had an army of servants to keep everything around him picture perfect plus one in reserve just to iron his shoelaces.

Thankfully, he didn't follow her to the kitchen to sneer at the empty baked-bean tin with the spoon still in it. There'd been nothing else for breakfast because she'd forgotten to shop and the Belfast sink was overflowing with unwashed dishes, but at least she did have decent coffee.

When she carried the tray through he had his back to her. He was studying the framed prints that broke

the severity of the white-painted walls. Nudging aside
a bowl of wilting roses, she set the tray down on the
low table that fronted the burnt-orange-upholstered
small sofa then stood very straight, dragging in a deep
breath.

Time to get the show on the road. Throw Gramps's
stupid idea straight out of play and get on with the
rest of her life. The old man would be deeply disappointed, she knew that, and would probably carry
through his threat to disinherit her, but she could handle that.

'So you think my grandfather's idea of an arranged
marriage is mad,' she stated for starters, carefully
keeping her voice level, non-confrontational as she
waited for his robust confirmation of what he'd said
earlier. And watched him turn, very slowly.

'Not necessarily.' His lean features betrayed nothing. 'It was idle supposition on my part—on your
behalf. Do you really think I would have come this
far if I'd thought the idea had no merit?' He strolled
with an appallingly fluid grace to where she was
standing. 'Shall I pour, or will you?'

The question didn't register. Cat's mouth ran dry,
her lips parted. She gasped for air; she felt she was
being suffocated. From his attitude since they'd taken
leave of her grandfather she'd drawn the conclusion
that he'd been humouring the old man, had as little
intention as she did of entering into an arranged marriage. Now it seemed the game was back on. It was
a deeply terrifying prospect.

Though why that should be she couldn't work out. No one could force her to marry anyone!

'Your silence tells me you don't care either way. About who should pour the coffee.' A strange satisfaction threaded through his voice and curved his lips. Cat's eyes went very wide as they locked on to that sinfully sexy mouth. Her own lips felt suddenly desperately needy and she was hot, much too hot; she could spontaneously combust at any moment!

The silence was stinging; it gathered her up and enclosed her with him, very tightly, and there was no escape. Her flurried gasp of relief was completely involuntary when he finally broke the awful tension and turned to pour the coffee.

Taking his own cup, he angled his lean body into one corner of the sofa, long legs stretched out in front of him, the sleek fabric caressing the taut muscles of his thighs like the touch of a lover.

Cat gulped thickly. Her thoughts were so wicked! She had to blank them, and when he glanced at the vacant space beside him and invited softly, 'Shall we talk?' she shied away, wrapping her arms around her trembling body, and had to force herself to say, 'There's nothing to talk about,' because the temptation to join him, sit intimately close, was enormous.

And very, very dangerous!

'No? No opinions?' he queried softly, his honeyed tone giving her goose bumps. The look in his eyes as they fastened on her hectically coloured face made her stop breathing. 'Then I'll give you mine, shall I?'

Cat forced herself to move, to give a slight, careless
shrug before she picked her way over to a vaguely
throne-like chair she'd picked up one Sunday afternoon at a car-boot sale. It's slightly vulgar ostentation
had amused her but it was supremely uncomfortable.

Aldo was watching her, his eyes hooded, looking
smoky. Seated, Cat kept her eyes firmly on her bare
toes. He could spout opinions all night but that didn't
mean she needed take the slightest notice of them.

But her heart was beating uncomfortably fast as he
raised his arms and laced his hands behind his head
and told her, 'I have nothing against arranged marriages, all things being equal. Up until now I've been
too busy to consider marrying. I confess to never having been in love, and unlike most of my compatriots,'
he added drily, 'I consider the condition to be vastly
overrated. It dresses the basic human need to procre-
ate in romantic flummery.'

Cat's eyes shot up from the anodyne contemplation
of her toes to lock with his. 'So you don't believe in
love,' she challenged. Her eyes gleamed. 'Bully for
you! I bet you a dime to a king's ransom the right
woman could teach you differently!'

Brilliant dark eyes sparked with pinpricks of
golden light at her husky outburst but his voice was
cool when he continued as if she hadn't spoken, 'As
far as I'm concerned, marriage is a serious matter. An
heir is necessary. Any wife I choose would have to
be intelligent, good to look at, have her feet firmly
on the ground—no girlish claims to be madly in love

with me because such emotional demands would merely make life difficult. Besides all this, I would need her to bring something of substance to the marriage. Family honour as well as sound financial sense demands that much.' He brought his hands down, his beautifully cut jacket settling back against his upper body with exquisite, unruffled elegance. 'I think you qualify on all counts.'

'Especially Grandfather's shares,' she said on a dry snap. 'Couldn't you offer to buy them off him—twist his arm or something? You could save yourself a whole heap of trouble.' If what he'd been saying was supposed to be a proposal then it was the coldest, most calculating one any woman was ever likely to hear. It deserved her utmost contempt. It showed in the green glitter of her eyes, in the tight downturn of her generous mouth.

Water off a duck's back as far as Aldo was concerned, apparently. He expanded his argument fluidly. 'Perhaps Domenico would agree to sell; perhaps not. But I have no intention of going down that road. Why should I when I can kill three birds with one stone? One,' he ticked off on his long, tanned fingers, 'I secure those possibly rogue shares for the family, where they belong. Two, I get a beautiful and intelligent wife, and three, I get an heir. And as far as you're concerned, you get a pampered lifestyle, more financial security than you've ever dreamed of—'

'I don't need it!' Distraught, Cat shot to her feet, her breasts heaving. Listening to this man—this…this sex-on-legs—talking of marriage as if it were a cold business arrangement was the last thing she wanted. 'I don't want your empty wealthy lifestyle—I want my own life, warts and all. I'm a big girl, *signor*; I can stand on my own feet, or hadn't you noticed?'

'Oh, I noticed,' he countered, smooth as cream. He rose to his feet and sauntered towards her and she gritted her teeth. He had too much style. He was too much altogether. And this close she could see those intriguing golden lights deep within his eyes, breathe in the elusive male scent of him, and her mouth fell open on a trembling gasp as he whispered seductively, 'You truly are a big girl.' His eyes slid down and lingered on her breasts, which annoyingly responded to this devastating no-touching slide of seduction. 'But only, I assure you, in all the most enticing places.'

'Don't!' Cat's command came out on a tortured whisper. When he turned on the sex, flooded his voice with it, she went to pieces.

He was lethal!

'Why not? It's a bonus.' Another movement, a step closer.

His black eyes looked drugged as he lifted them slowly from her shamelessly peaking breasts and fastened them on her softly trembling mouth as she muttered defensively, 'I don't know what you're talking about!'

'Yes, you do.'

The tension was making her shake, making the fine

hairs on the back of her neck stand to attention. The sheer sexual power of the man overwhelmed her. She wanted to fight it but didn't know how.

'A wife who would excite me in bed would be a bonus. Yes?' The soft huskiness of his voice was an unbearable intimacy; it made the blood pound in her ears and her whole body burn. He was much too close. She stared at him wildly. She had to put more space between them. At any moment she could find herself grabbing him, pulling his head down to discover if the promise of that so sensual mouth was capable of delivery.

Cat tried to move but her legs were so weak she could only sway. Aldo's hand slid to her shoulder to steady her and an electric storm fizzled through every cell in her body and her eyelids closed helplessly as his knowing fingers stroked the heated skin of her naked shoulder before it brushed with wicked intimacy over the tingling peaks of her aching breasts.

'And you would be excited, too. We would be dynamite together. I feel it and so do you. Yes?' His hands curved over her hips as he gently tugged the span of her against the hardness of him and the shattering excitement that flooded her produced a ragged sound, halfway between a gasp and a moan. As he lowered his sleek dark head to stifle the sound at source, her arms snaked around his neck, and her last coherent, triumphant thought as he plundered her avidly responsive mouth was a repetition of what she'd

said to him earlier—I bet you a dime to a king's ransom the right woman could teach you differently!

The sounds of a muted commotion in the courtyard
far below brought Cat out of her thoughts of the past.
Blinking the film of moisture from her eyes, she
peered down. At the sight of Aldo's silver Ferrari her
heart leapt and twisted like a landed fish then dropped
with heavy lifelessness to the soles of her bare feet
as he exited, and walked round to the passenger side
to hand out his mistress.

Three members of staff were milling around in excited welcome at their beloved master's unexpected
arrival. Cat willed him to look up to where she was
standing, to appear remotely interested in her where-
abouts. But he didn't glance towards the villa. His
attention was all for Iolanda Cardinale, who was
clinging to his arm, her sleek, elegantly clothed body
leaning possessively into his, her ripe lips parted with
sultry promise.

Fighting nausea, Cat forced herself to creep down
the spiral staircase to her suite of rooms. She was
going to have to act her socks off if she was going
to be able to pretend she could accept the situation.

Pride wouldn't allow her to let either of them see
how desperate she was. Love and sexual fidelity
hadn't been part of the bargain on his part, had it?

As her English grandmother would have said,
'You've made your bed, girl. Now you must lie
on it.'

CHAPTER TWO

REACHING her rooms and closing the bedroom door behind her, Cat leaned back weakly against the carved wood. She was going to have to face him. Them.

Why had he chosen to arrive unannounced? Why had he brought Iolanda Cardinale with him?

Because he was cruel.

Or simply because this sort of thing went on in the elevated circles in which he moved and he didn't consider it to be even slightly unusual?

And how long were they staying? Overnight? Would he share this room with her?

Grimly, she thought not. He hadn't bothered to visit during her exile and he hadn't so much as touched her since she'd told him—dewy-eyed and stupid with love for him—of the confirmation of her pregnancy.

Besides, he wouldn't even think about sharing her bed when he had his mistress draped all over him!

On that draining thought she levered herself tiredly away from the door and walked further into the lovely room. Apart from the gilded four-poster bed the furnishings and decorations were a dreamy medley of white and creams, gauzy drapes fluttering at the tall windows that looked out over the sun-drenched landscape, over the silver olive groves and purple hills.

36

She would have to prepare herself, put on the camouflage of warpaint and chic designer armour, and as if on cue Rosa came bouncing in after a decidedly hysterical rap on the door.

'*Il padrone* has arrived! So unexpected—everyone's running round in circles! Did you know? Why didn't you tell us to make ready? Come, I will help you dress, make yourself beautiful for him!'

Cat forced a thin smile. Rosa, assigned as her personal maid on her arrival here two months ago, had become her dresser, her nanny, her arbiter of correct behaviour and her friend. Unlike the other members of staff Rosa wasn't painfully deferential and she didn't whisper behind her hands when she thought she was out of earshot. And no, Aldo hadn't said anything about finally deigning to visit her the last time he'd phoned her.

'You have already bathed?' Rosa didn't wait for an answer, bustling towards the huge hanging cupboard that almost filled one wall, tutting disapprovingly as her eyes fell on the untouched breakfast tray. 'You must eat, *signora*. You lose too much weight already.' She pulled out one of the fitted drawers and handed Cat her selection of underwear, filmy, lacy pale cream briefs and bra, her kind eyes softening. 'I understand how you feel about losing your baby; it was a terrible thing to happen, but an accident of nature and nothing to blame yourself for. There will be other babies for you.'

Nothing to blame herself for? She knew differently.

Removing her wrap and dressing in the understated chic of the smoky-grey sleeveless shirt-shift Rosa had put out for her, Cat shivered as the cool silk whispered against her body. She'd been assured at the private clinic where she'd been taken on that dreadful night that the early miscarriage had been nature's way of coping when everything was not as it should be.

She had said nothing to oppose the well-meaning platitudes but she'd known that if she hadn't been so tense and anxious she wouldn't have lost her baby.

Aldo had politely and coolly distanced himself from her when he'd heard of the coming baby. Overjoyed at the news of her pregnancy, of course, and very solicitous.

Too solicitous, she'd felt smothered. Her eager explorations of the beautiful old city with her husband as her attentive guide had been firmly vetoed and he'd given orders to his staff at their Florence home that she was to rest, take a little gentle exercise in the cool of the day with Beppe, an ancient retainer who could walk no faster than a snail, as her companion.

And Aldo himself had been away more often than he'd been at home, catching up on the business responsibilities he'd neglected since their marriage, or so he'd said, and worst of all moving out to another bedroom.

'You are carrying my child,' he told her gently when she'd protested. 'If I share your bed I will make love to you; I will not be able to help myself. And our loving is fierce, truly passionate. Yes? I will do nothing to harm you or the tiny life you carry.'

In view of the way he'd ordered everyone to treat her as if she were made from the finest of brittle spun glass, she might have believed him. She might have lovingly teased him about being over-protective if Iolanda Cardinale hadn't dripped all that poison into her ears.

She'd refused to believe a word of what the hateful woman had said but the change in Aldo's attitude towards her when he'd learned of her pregnancy had forced her to acknowledge that Iolanda could have been telling the truth. Her tortured thoughts, her aching anxiety had to be responsible for that miscarriage.

Dutifully seating herself in front of the long mirror in its ornate gilded frame, she watched Rosa working on her hair, brushing it back from her face and securing it neatly in a French pleat.

It had been the first grand dinner party Aldo had thrown on their return from honeymoon, she remembered with a stab of the usual pain. Mainly for the benefit of business associates and friends who hadn't been able to attend the wedding and be introduced to his new bride at the lavish reception.

Iolanda, as Aldo's executive PA, had been there, oozing the understated chic Italians were so good at. Her svelte, cool loveliness had made Cat feel gaudy and overdressed in her swirly skirted, bootlace-strapped confection in her favourite shade of vibrant scarlet.

Wandering out onto the terrace to catch a breath of the cool evening air, Iolanda had joined her. As the only unpartnered guest at the gathering Cat had made a point of drawing Iolanda into the conversation around the dinner table so she wouldn't feel left out. So her smile was wide as she acknowledged the other woman.

'I would like to talk to you,' Iolanda said.

'That's nice! It's getting rather stuffy inside, isn't it?' Perhaps, being on her own, the other woman was feeling a bit out of things now that dinner was over and the guests circulating, forming chattering groups. 'Shall we find somewhere to sit? There are seats—'

'No.' The other woman cut across her, a note of impatience in her drawl. 'This will only take moments. In view of the situation I thought we ought to be properly introduced.'

'I thought we had been.' Cat smiled, puzzled, wondering if she'd missed something. Iolanda shook her head slowly, her smooth, raven-dark hair gleaming in the overflow of light from the main salon, her answering smile slight, tight and superior.

'Not really. You are Aldo's wife. I am Aldo's mistress. Ordinarily, we would of course know of each other's existence but we would not meet. Discretion in such matters is important—that is understood. But as Aldo and I work so closely together our occasional meetings cannot be avoided. I thought we should understand our positions. Suspicions and speculations only make life uncomfortable, as I'm sure you would

grow to learn when you have done your duty and
given him an heir and he begins to spend more time
away from you than with you and you wonder why.'

Again that hateful, superior little smile that left Cat
speechless with a mixture of rage and disbelief at
what she was hearing. 'That being said, I would
strongly advise you against making a fuss about a
situation which a man in Aldo's position regards as
being absolutely normal. An hysterical fuss would
only serve to estrange him from you entirely and do
you no good at all.'

'There—all done.' Rosa stepped back, surveying
the neat outcome of her ministrations with satisfaction. 'I'll leave you to do your make-up. Be sure you
cover up those dark circles round your eyes and put
some colour on your cheeks!'

Cat watched her reflection with no enthusiasm at
all. She no longer looked like herself. Her exuberant
hair had been flattened and tamed, her mouth drooped
and her eyes looked haunted.

She'd been stunned, knocked speechless by what
Iolanda had said, but she hadn't believed a word of
it. She'd refused to let herself believe it. The woman
was obviously a raving idiot! Iolanda wanted Aldo
for herself and was out to make mischief.

Having every intention of telling Aldo of his assistant's crazed lies, she'd changed her mind when as
soon as the last guest had departed he'd swept her up
in his arms and carried her up the sweeping staircase.

'I don't know how I've managed to keep my hands

off you!' he breathed rawly. 'All evening long I've wanted to rip your clothes off, bury myself inside you and make endless, endless love to you!'

And he'd done just that, she remembered with a fierce stab of pain. He'd ripped the scarlet dress right from the dipping neckline to the swirly-flirty hem, the wild, fiery passion of his lovemaking making a complete nonsense of Iolanda's wicked lies. Mentioning what the other woman had said would be a mistake. He would think she was only asking for reassurance, didn't trust him, and would resent it. Far more sensible to dismiss the distasteful episode from her mind.

But later, listening to the soft sound of his regular breathing, the first uncomfortable pinpricks of doubt had crept in as she'd wondered why the only real closeness they ever achieved was between the sheets, and why he always turned his back on her and immediately fell asleep after making love with her.

Having sex, she tiredly corrected. The only time he'd mentioned the word love had been when he'd confessed that he didn't believe in the condition. And had he only completely ruined her dress because he'd thought that was all the gaudy thing was fit for? Would he have treated Iolanda's elegant, wildly expensive black sheath with the same total lack of respect?

Turning on her side, she'd watched the first light of dawn filter through the partly closed window blinds. Perhaps there was a useful lesson she could learn. When in Rome, etc...

And so she'd set about turning herself into the type of woman Aldo would most respect and admire. If she couldn't have his love she could at least do her best to earn his respect.

Her still vibrant enthusiasm for every new project she took on board had ensured that her clothes were now the last word in unmistakable, understated Italian chic, her unmanageable mane of chestnut hair shortened and skillfully layered, *'Molto elegante!'* her horrendously expensive hairdresser had assured her, and she always wore spindly high heels to make sure her free-swinging stride was a thing of the past.

But her rapid transformation hadn't made a scrap of difference. He'd remained almost painfully polite and considerate, but distant. His eyes never smiled into hers, reminding her of shared intimacies the way lovers did; he never touched her except in bed.

When her pregnancy had been confirmed, her by then rapidly dwindling hope that things could be different between them soared high. That they had changed but not in the way she had wanted was something she hadn't foreseen, not in her worst nightmares.

Iolanda's words had come back to haunt her. 'You'll understand when you've done your duty and given him an heir and he starts to spend more time away from you than with you.' She hadn't given him an heir, she'd lost the precious baby she'd been longing for, but the signs had been there for anyone to see. As soon as he'd known of her pregnancy he'd wanted little more to do with her, his only concern the well-being of the child she was carrying.

Her stomach churning sickeningly at the memories that seemed to confirm everything that venomous woman had told her, Cat stood up from the dressing table, smoothing the silk of her dress over hips which were not as snake-like as Iolanda's, but getting there. Rosa was right—since she'd been banished after her miscarriage she had lost a lot of weight.

Facing her husband and his mistress with some semblance of dignity was the only thing she must make herself concentrate on right now, she decided with a welcome resurgence of the determination that had been absent for a long time.

But it drained away the moment the bedroom door swung open, revealing Aldo. He had the same unnerving impact on her as he'd had the very first time she'd set eyes on him. He took her breath away.

His dark business suit fitted his lean body to perfection and the crisp white shirt emphasised the bronzed skin of his austerely beautiful features. Cat veiled her eyes quickly. He was so unfairly gorgeous she couldn't bear to look at him.

'Caterina…' His voice was harsh; he had never directed that tone towards her before. His politeness had been the hallmark of their relationship.

Her puzzled eyes flickered upwards and met the glittering darkness of his. There were lines of strain on his face. She'd never noticed them before. 'You came here to recuperate, to regain your strength,' he condemned. 'What have you been doing to yourself?'

The heavy thumping of her heart quietened, subdued and regulated by an unexpected layer of heavy ice. How dared he criticise her, look at her as if her appearance offended him? She'd spent time and effort turning her exuberant self into what she'd hoped he'd appreciate—a model of Italian chic. And so what if she'd lost weight? Iolanda didn't exactly billow, did she? Or did fashion decree that Italian mistresses look like stick insects while Italian wives bulge comfortably in all directions?

Glacially, she held his darkly frowning eyes and intoned coldly, 'Since you haven't bothered to come and see what I've been "doing to myself",' she parodied his condemnatory tone, 'I'll tell you. Grieving,' she stressed tightly and inwardly flinched as lines of pain bracketed his stern mouth as her lashing remarks hit home.

'For our baby,' Aldo conceded with a softness that made her heart stand still. He took a step towards her. Cat retreated by a few rapid paces. If he belatedly remembered his abandoned husbandly role and tried to fold her in his arms to comfort her she would, quite simply, go to pieces and embarrass herself, and him, by blurting out all the sources of her present misery.

Turning back to the dressing table, she made a pretence of checking her appearance in the gilded mirror, replying, 'What else?'

She could have added, For the death of our marriage, for the loss of all hope that you'll ever learn to love me, but held her tongue because, to be fair to him, love hadn't been part of the bargain, just silly wishful thinking on her part.

But a mistress hadn't been part of the bargain either, she reflected trenchantly, and asked him brittly, 'Shall we go down? Had you let me know to expect you I'd have been waiting to greet you and your companion.' She swung towards the door, aware of his dark eyes boring into her back. 'What have you done with her, by the way?'

Aldo caught up with her as she opened the door, a lean, tanned hand snaking out to fasten disconcertingly on her shoulder. Desperately, Cat tried to control her weak body's electric reaction to his touch, to the effect of those bitter-chocolate eyes scorching into her own.

She dug her fingernails into the palms of her hands, using the resultant sharp sting of pain as an antidote to the overwhelming need to reach up her hands to touch that harshly handsome face, to beg him to open his heart to her, to love her, and only her.

But she wasn't so far sunk in physical and emotional weakness to let herself make such a fool of herself, was she? Some remnant of the old Cat surfaced from where it had been hiding and allowed her to meet those searching eyes with a flash of chilly disdain, and if Aldo had intended to say something then he obviously thought better of it, dropped his hand and made an after-you gesture towards the corridor outside her door.

Wordlessly, Cat preceded him, her back ramrod stiff, the only sounds that of their footsteps on the polished boarded floors, on the smooth stone steps of the wide staircase. There was so much to say, and yet nothing worth saying. Accusing him of neglect, of having a mistress, ranting and raving, would get her precisely nowhere. It would be water off a duck's back. He would simply give that insultingly insouciant shrug of his and continue doing exactly what he wanted.

With a hand on the small of her back, he guided her into a small sitting room at the rear of the villa, overlooking the beautifully tended gardens. Her entire system went into spasm. She didn't want him touching her. The resulting electric charge, the meltdown of her bones would remind her of the way things had been in the darkness of the night when he'd made love to her as if she were the only woman in the world for him.

She didn't want reminding, she wanted to forget. She jerked away, stepping sideways, and Aldo said, 'You worry me, Caterina. Your doctor assured me you were making steady progress.'

'So you bothered to check up?' Good, just enough scorn to bring his black brows together.

'Naturally. Every week, after his visit to you. You are my wife; of course I was concerned.'

'But not concerned enough to visit me yourself, to

stay with me.' The accusation came out smoothly, as if it wasn't really important to her. She had her pride and she was clinging on to it just as hard as she could. Let go of it and she'd start shouting and screaming at him and end up crying like a baby. To hide the sudden pulse of moisture in her eyes she walked to one of the windows and stared out, her vision blurred.

But her cool, almost uninterested words must have touched a nerve because she felt him moving closer, nearer to where she was standing, and heard him say gruffly, 'Ah, yes, I see. But I am with you now; everything has been put in order—'

What had been put in order was something she was destined not to know because the door opened and Iolanda trilled, 'Oh, I feel so much better! Please tell me I look better!'

'Much,' Cat heard Aldo say drily. She turned reluctantly, making her face expressionless. Iolanda was doing the classic exhibitionist's twirl, her slender arms outstretched. Her hair fell down her back like a waterfall of jet and she was wearing palazzo pants in a soft green chiffony fabric and a matching skimpy tunic top. Cat could see her nipples through the filmy fabric.

Coming to rest, the other woman sank gracefully onto a cream silk-covered sofa, her scarlet lips pouting. 'I hope you don't mind, but I asked one of the servants to take my luggage to a spare room. I needed more than a quick freshen-up. I had a divine shower and changed into fresh clothes—I was so hot and sticky after that long drive. Do tell me I have not abused your hospitality!'

'Of course not. I should have thought of it myself; it is I who should apologise.'

Aldo spoke with smooth urbanity but Cat knew from the rigid line of his shoulders, the firm set of his sensual mouth, that he was far from pleased. In his rarefied world wives and mistresses were kept in separate boxes, each satisfying different needs, never meeting each other and making life uncomfortable for him; that was the way the game was played.

Perversely, Iolanda's discomforting performance gave Cat a stab of bitter-sweet pleasure. Serve him right! And she could have applauded when the other woman leaned further back into the soft cushions and draped an arm along the back of the sofa, ensuring that her skimpy top rode up to display a couple of inches of taut, smooth-skinned midriff, her black eyes smouldering at him. Instead she asked coolly, 'May I offer you coffee, *signorina*?'

Dead silence, then a breathy little gasp coming from Iolanda. She shot an apologetic glance at Aldo between thick lashes. '*Signora*—I hadn't noticed you. What must you think of me?'

That you're a clever, dissembling little cow, Cat thought with uncharacteristic viciousness. Pretending you hadn't noticed me while confirming your position in my husband's life!

Or had she really been invisible with her pale, wan face and her melt-into-the-background smoky-grey dress? The thought produced a stab of hot anger. Before her ill-fated marriage she had been vibrant, outgoing, her flamboyant appearance drawing unwanted yet ego-boosting wolf-whistles when she walked down the street from the car park to the craft centre.

'Coffee?' Cat reiterated, feeling Aldo's brooding eyes on her and ignoring him.

'Oh, please—don't go to any trouble on my account. You should be resting, not trying to look after me,' Iolanda objected prettily. 'Aldo can do that in recompense for all the hard work I've put in for the company—you're obviously still unwell.'

Cat found a chair and sat on it. Miss Butterwouldn't-melt wasn't going to get rid of her so easily. And went hot with temper when after a barely discernible shrug Iolanda turned her now limpid eyes to Aldo. 'I think we deserve champagne, don't you? To celebrate our wonderful—successes?'

Directing a sweet smile towards Cat, she elaborated, 'You probably don't know much about your husband's business but we've been simply everywhere! Checking on all ends—grain, olives, grapes... you name it, we've checked it! I have been slave-driven! But it's been such fun, especially the acquisition of an almost intact castle on Sicily. It is run as an hotel, a shabby one. Such a pity! But in our hands it will be transformed into superb luxury holiday apartments. That was the best time.'

She gave a dreamy sigh. Her eyes were modestly

downcast but her smile was feline. 'We have been living in each other's pockets, travelling the length and breadth of the country for nearly two months, and now I am exhausted. I am so thankful I have the whole weekend before I need show my face in the Florence office.'

'I'm sure,' Cat responded drily, noting the frown line between Aldo's eyes as he turned and stalked out of the room, presumably to ask someone to put the champagne his mistress had demanded on ice.

Aldo Patrucco was definitely displeased!

The way Iolanda had flaunted herself, glanced at him with those come-bed-me eyes in front of his spare-wheel wife had annoyed him. It simply wasn't done in the sophisticated circles he moved in. The fact that she was now trying to make amends by turning all her attention on the wife wasn't cutting much ice, apparently.

Cat felt cold all over and then very hot. She wanted to take Iolanda by the scruff of her neck and throw her out. Her fingers curled into the palms of her hands as she fought to get her emotions under control. It was time she started fighting back. She wasn't a wimp and should stop behaving like one.

Aldo had only married her to get his hands on those wretched shares and she'd been one huge fool to think she could teach him to love her. But she was his wife—for the time being, she decided bitterly—and she deserved some respect. That he had brought his mistress here, to what was her home, or one of them, showed he had none.

It was time to forget she was stupid enough to love him and fight him as well!

She didn't know how, but she'd think of something!

'You are displeasing my husband.' Cat took the first battle to Iolanda, mentally and finally accepting that Iolanda had been telling the truth when she'd almost casually mentioned her mistress status. If she'd had any doubts before they'd gone now. Instead of being with her, comforting her over the loss of their baby, he had been with his mistress. 'Your attitude, the way you're dressed. I imagine he would expect you to know your place and behave, in my presence, like a mere employee. You are upsetting the status quo, jumping out of your box. Aren't you afraid he'll give you your marching orders? If you're not then perhaps you should be.'

If she'd been expecting embarrassment or fury Cat got neither. Iolanda merely hid a tiny yawn behind her long fingers, remarking, 'Oh, I don't think so. He finds me too irresistible—always has. Marriage was out of the question; I have nothing apart from what I earn and we all know why he did his duty and married you—my position in the company made it ridiculously easy to find that out. It's me he wants—oh, he'll make a show of wanting you, he'll shut his eyes, have sex, and think of his heir—and as for the way I'm dressed, Aldo will understand I need to be cool.

It is so very hot and we have been driving since dawn. We broke our journey by an overnight stay in Rome. It was more perfect than you can imagine...' She broke off as Aldo re-entered the room, and imparted brightly and untruthfully, 'I was just telling Signora Patrucco of a wonderful beautician I have heard of in Florence—apparently, she can work wonders, especially with women who have been dragged low by illness. I think the *signora* deserves such a tonic. I will be happy to find the telephone number for you.'

Thankfully, Cat was saved the indignity of leaping up and slapping the hateful creature by the arrival of the housekeeper with a tray of coffee. She blinked rapidly to dispel the red mist of rage as Iolanda rose gracefully to her feet.

'I will pour, shall I?' She addressed her limpid remark to Aldo, who regarded her unsmilingly from his vastly superior height. 'The *signora* must not exert herself.'

If she was disappointed by the non-appearance of the champagne she had as good as demanded, she certainly didn't show it as she dispensed coffee as if she were mistress of all she surveyed.

And when Aldo, pacing the room, his coffee-cup ignored, glanced at the slim gold watch on his wrist, Iolanda said demurely with a sly sideways glance at Cat, 'Aldo, I know you said you would have one of your staff drive me back to Florence after lunch, but would you reconsider?' She let her fabulous lashes droop. 'If it's not too much trouble, could I spend the night? I wasn't joking when I said I'm exhausted and we could spend the evening going over the facts and figures and making sure I've got everything right. I wouldn't want to make a mistake.'

She was making a huge one right now, Cat noted with dour satisfaction. Aldo's shoulders had gone rigid, and one dark brow elevated warningly. Iolanda might be his mistress, his irresistible mistress, but she was clearly stepping over the demarcation line. She was embarrassing him and he wouldn't want her under the same roof when he went to his wife's room, had sex for Italy, and tried to sire an heir in the place of the one she had lost.

Leaping in smoothly before he could veto the suggestion, Cat stuck a big false smile on her face and gushed, 'But of course you must stay. For as long as you like. I'll instruct the housekeeper.' And swept from the room, sensing Aldo's frowning eyes upon the suddenly vulnerable-feeling back of her head, and went to find the housekeeper, her mouth grim and tight.

If her intervention had put him on the spot, made him uncomfortable, then that meant she was at last fighting back. He deserved to feel uncomfortable. And if he read his precious mistress the Riot Act and asked her what she thought she was playing at then she, Cat, would have won the moral high ground!

But, instead of giving her satisfaction, the thought left her feeling decidedly sick.

CHAPTER THREE

'CATERINA…'

Aldo emerged from the shadows just as Cat was approaching her bedroom door. He must have followed her immediately, using the main staircase to her tower rooms. Her stomach plunged to the soles of her shoes. She'd stated her need for an early night and left him and Iolanda on the terrace as Maria, the housekeeper, had brought through the after-dinner coffee. She'd thought she'd handled her exit neatly, but apparently not.

His crisp white shirt was open at the neck and she could see a pulse beating rapidly at the base of his tanned throat. He skimmed her a veiled glance, his dark eyes narrowed and unreadable, and Cat's heart jumped. He looked so incredibly sexy, and the warm, clean scent of him swamped her with erotic memories, achingly insistent memories of the passion of their nights when she'd foolishly believed that he was beginning to really care for her.

'What is it?' she asked thinly as he reached forward to open the bedroom door, his hand brushing against hers, making her flinch away from the tingling contact. Heat sizzled between them and the tight, spiralling shaft deep inside her was naked, raw desire. And that was a definite no-no; she had to fight it.

His irresistible sexuality had trapped her right from their first meeting, overwhelming her, changing her from an independent free spirit to a mass of rioting hormones, willing to do anything, be anything for the paradisical pleasures of the marital bed. It wasn't going to happen again—as far as she was concerned their marriage was as good as over.

She entered the room, her spine ramrod straight. The lamps were already lit, the sheets turned back on the four-poster bed, and Rosa had laid out a fresh oyster satin nightdress and wrap.

What little colour she did have drained from her tense features as he followed her and closed the door behind him. Her whole body was reacting to the mere presence of his, her flesh quivering, her blood racing. She didn't know how to counteract it. She adored him but he had broken her heart. She didn't want the unfaithful swine near her!

Tearing her eyes from the suddenly frowning concentration of his, she bit out with a snappish lack of politeness, 'What do you want?'

'To be alone with my wife.' A small smile that lingered on his incredibly sexy mouth, a minimal shrug of those elegant shoulders, an inquisitorial upwards tilt of one dark brow. Cat drew in a ragged breath.

So he remembered he had one, did he? Because he'd checked with Dottore Raffacani and been given the go-ahead? Iolanda's vile prediction was coming true. He would have sex with her, shut his eyes and think of an heir.

Rage beat at her temples but Cat knew she had to stay cool. If she allowed herself to get emotional he'd take advantage, move in for the kill. Arching one brow, she commented drily, 'So you finally remembered my existence. It took you long enough—two months by my reckoning.'

The infuriating smile that again curved his beautiful mouth was a mixture of satisfaction and patronising amusement, Cat noted with a savage punch of blistering fury. Man-like, he thought she was sulking because she was feeling neglected and one kind word from him, one touch, would have her melting in his arms, pathetically eager to help him along in his efforts to do his duty and get her pregnant again.

Well, she wasn't sulking and her days of melting were well and truly over and she wanted to strangle him. And boil him in oil as a finishing touch as he stepped closer, his voice a husky murmur.

'*Cara*—I admit my absence was regrettable, but it really was necessary if—'

'I'm sure it was,' she cut right across him, feeling her face go tight with suppressed rage. 'Business, was it? And talking of your so-called business, you are neglecting your guest. I'm sure she's finished her coffee—'

'*Your* guest, *cara*.' It was his turn to cut her off in mid-flow as he reached for her in one smooth, unexpected movement, his hands resting lightly on her hips. 'It was you who pressed her to stay on, remember? I had arranged for her to be driven back to her home. I wanted rid of her.'

The heat of his hands, the gentle yet insistent pressure of his long fingers, the snare of his dark, stunning eyes combined to swamp her with a crashing wave of unwanted physical excitement. A shiver rocketed down her spine and all the way back up again, and her efforts to fight the effect his slightest touch had always had on her made every muscle in her body tense.

'I wanted to be alone with you, but instead Iolanda's been playing gooseberry. Of course,' he defended, making Cat cynically decide that perhaps he did have a conscience over his two-timing behaviour, at least as far as Iolanda was concerned, 'she won't have realised that. She's brilliant at what she does but she can be insensitive. She says and does things without thinking; she doesn't mean any harm.'

The way a viper means no harm when it sinks its venomous fangs into your flesh! And exactly where did her 'brilliance' lie? In her work or between the sheets?

Silly question!

And he'd obviously been referring to Iolanda's sugary-sweet suggestion that his wife visit a beautician, sit down before she fell down—all that stuff. He wouldn't want the women in his life tearing each other's hair out, he'd want to keep them sweet and compliant in the roles he'd assigned them! And would he have defended her to his mistress, saying she was a brilliant wife?

Another silly question!

Cat took a wobbly step away from him but the pressure of his hands simply increased, bringing her closer to the hard arch of his pelvis. His body heat scorched her. Her heart thumped madly and she gasped as she tried to pull enough air into her starved lungs to enable her to tell him to stop this hateful pretence, but all that emerged from her parched lips was a tiny, despairing groan.

'Don't be sad, *cara*,' he said, obviously mistaking that distressed little sound for something else entirely. His voice was soft now, silken and husky at the same time, and his eyes were drenched with concern. It might be spurious but from where she was standing it looked bone-weakeningly real, she thought distractedly. 'I do know how you feel. I, too, grieve for our lost child.' He drew her gently within the circle of his arms, one hand easing her head into the accommodating breadth of his shoulder, the other stroking her rigid spine until against all common sense she felt her whole body relaxing into him.

Her eyes filled with hot tears and, almost hesitantly, her arms curved around him, the palms of her hands flat against his shoulder blades. However much she hated and despised him for the emotional turmoil he had put her through she loved the feel of him, the strength of bone, the perfectly honed muscles, the warm satin of his skin. He was addictive, like a drug, and she was hooked, she acknowledged shakily, despising herself far more than she had thought she despised him.

And as he murmured soft words of comfort in Italian, surely the most seductive language in the world, his clean, warm breath feathered against the long line of her neck and made her tremble.

He sounded so sincere she could almost believe he cared. Fool that she was, she wanted to believe, she needed to. She shifted slightly closer, she really couldn't help herself, feeling the inevitable pool of liquid heat between her thighs, feeling the answering, hardening response of him against the shimmering, needy fire that was building up inside her body.

She had never doubted that he'd been devastated when she'd lost their baby, that he genuinely mourned the tiny lost life. But now her mind was frantically grasping at straws, holding on to the belief that perhaps he really cared for her, too.

'There will be other babies for us,' he murmured deeply, and Cat shivered as she forced herself to take that in, her mind recoiling and then finally understanding.

How could she have forgotten the way things really were, clung on to the illusion of his concern and caring? She felt humiliated and deeply ashamed of herself. She pulled away from him, her movements stiff and clumsy, her eyes haunted in her pale face.

He meant to do his damnedest to get her pregnant

again and she, like a dutiful little wife, was meant to go along with it. That was what all this sickening pretence at closeness and caring had been about! Where had he been when she'd needed him most— touring the length and breadth of Italy, staying in glamorous top hotels and having a wonderful time— with his mistress!

'Leave me alone. Just go!'

Her face felt so tight she had to force the words out through her teeth. And she flinched as if he'd hit her when he gazed down at her with those bitter-chocolate eyes and soothed, 'You don't mean that. You are still understandably upset. Raffacani warned me your hormones could still be all over the place. But I am here now to help you overcome this.'

Oh, was he? Was he really? And none of this was his fault—of course not! Heaven forfend! It was all down to her and her hormones!

Cat snatched in a ragged breath and then exploded, 'I meant it—I want you to leave me alone! I had Maria make a bed up for you in the master suite. You'll find your things in there, too.'

She'd discovered them after lunch while Aldo and Iolanda had been closeted in the library, supposedly going over the facts and figures the wretched woman had keyed in on her laptop. Cat's need to clear both him and his clothes out of her space had been violent and immediate.

Her wishes hadn't been consulted; he'd simply taken it for granted that he would share her bed. Like any normal husband. But he wasn't a normal husband, was he?

And the way a wash of hot, dull colour spread over his hard, high cheekbones, his stiffly polite, 'As you wish,' as he swung on his heel and strode out, cut no ice with her. She watched his exit through narrowed, glittering eyes then wondered why her throat seized up and a torrent of tears ran down her cheeks.

How she could be expected to sleep when her mind kept running round in circles, Cat didn't know. Grumpily, when a squinting look at the tiny gilded bedside clock told her it was past three o'clock, she gave up the attempt and slid out of bed, padding over to one of the tall windows to gaze out at the purity of the moonlit landscape, trying to calm her mind.

But it would keep churning, homing in on memories, presenting each in vivid Technicolor before skittering on to the next.

Their fairy-tale wedding in Florence. A besotted bride in a beautiful cream silk dress. Aldo tall and impossibly handsome in his morning suit, looking for all the world as if he was truly in love with the woman he had decided to make his wife. And Gramps, pleased as punch, acquainting himself with his nephew Astorre and his grand Roman wife— Aldo's parents—happy to be welcomed back into the bosom of his Italian family.

Cat pressed her fingertips to her throbbing temples. She wished Gramps were still here, so that she could turn to him for advice and comfort. Wished he hadn't insisted—despite all offers to the contrary—on returning to England, Bonnie and the memories of his Alice and Anna, her mother, the daughter they had so tragically lost all those long years ago.

Cat wanted her mother. And her father. She had been too young when they'd died to remember either of them. But she wanted them now. She, who had always been so independent, wanted someone to lean on. Loving Aldo had turned her into a wreck. And she hated the feeling!

And still the unwanted memories came, mind pictures she couldn't dispel, no matter how hard she tried to shut them out...

The honeymoon in the house above Portofino, the vine-covered mountains as a backdrop, the fabulous view over the spectacular coastline. The long, shatteringly intimate nights, the sun-drenched days, wandering hand in hand down to the yacht-filled harbour, past the pretty, pastel-coloured houses set in gardens filled with a riot of blossoms, eating locally prepared delicacies, toasting each other with crisp Ligurian wine...

And the way it had begun. Begun as soon as she'd set eyes on him. The sexual chemistry had been mind-boggling. But she could have handled that, written it off as the entirely natural reaction of a young, healthy, celibate female to a superb specimen of manhood. A specimen whose eyes had promised paradise.

But she hadn't been able to write off what had

happened in her studio apartment. From the moment
he'd taken her in his arms and kissed her she'd been
lost. She had kissed him back, it had been hot and
torrid, hands everywhere, breathing fast and fevered,
and she'd been lost in abandonment, his for the taking, and he had tasted of heaven, of desire, and she
had sunk into him, offering all that she was, all that
she had, and afterwards, towards dawn at the end of
that long, shatteringly ecstatic night, she had known
with every fibre of her love-drenched, expertly rav-
ished body that she could teach him to love her.
Given time and patience.

It had been her secret weapon. Secret because he
had said he wouldn't marry a woman who claimed to
be madly in love with him because emotional demands such as that would complicate his life.

So she had never let him know that she adored the
very ground he walked on. She had matched his
greedy passion of the night and never even hinted at
the dagger of hurt deep within her heart when he
acted like a polite, considerate stranger away from the
earth-shattering magic of the bedroom.

Telling herself she was in for the long haul—such
a self-controlled, self-confident individual wouldn't
be quick to admit he'd been wrong, admit he could
fall in love—she had held her tongue, hidden her feelings and set about turning herself into the type of wife
she guessed he wanted. Cool, in control, chic and sophisticated. Almost the complete opposite of who and
what she really was.

And she could have handled it. If it hadn't been for the drip of poison.

Iolanda's poison.

Cat ground her teeth together. Her whole body was in pain. She paced the floor, her movements savage, until she snapped to a halt in mid-turn.

What if it wasn't true? What if none of it was true?

Was Iolanda spiteful enough to make up such terrible lies?

You bet she was!

To begin with, Cat had refused to believe a word of what the poisonous woman had said. But events had forced her to change her opinion. What if those telling events—his moving to another bedroom as soon as her pregnancy had been confirmed, his increasing absences from their home, his complete absence after her miscarriage—had been mere coincidences?

He hadn't wanted to make love to her and put their child at risk, or so he'd said. A very unenlightened belief, but one he could genuinely have held perhaps? And his prolonged business trek with his executive assistant—well, that could have been genuine too.

He had business interests all over Italy, huge responsibilities. He had once told her that he insisted on taking complete control over every area and delegated very little, confessing wryly that he had become something of a workaholic.

And he hadn't neglected her entirely during the past eight weeks, had he? He'd phoned her twice, sometimes three times a week, and sent postcards from each area he'd visited—usually with some humorous comment. And once, by special messenger, a pair of fabulous emerald earrings with the scrawled comment, 'You don't have to make your own now! Enjoy!'

She was weakening. And muddled. And the only way to clear up the mess was to ask him outright, demand the absolute truth.

Was Iolanda his mistress?

If he categorically denied it and fired his executive assistant for telling lies and making mischief then she would do her utmost to make a go of their marriage, even though it didn't seem likely that he'd change his entrenched opinion that falling in love was for idiots, because at least she would know that he had enough respect for her to stay faithful.

She should have asked him earlier, when he'd followed her to her bedroom, she acknowledged as she slipped into her wrap and tied the belt around her narrow waist. But pride had stopped her, not to mention despair and the out-and-out hurting of her battered heart.

It was the early hours of the morning and he'd be sound asleep but she was going to have to wake him. Now that the need to know had finally and with much effort burst through her tight-lipped, brooding suffering she couldn't wait another second.

The suite of rooms she had banished him to was about as far as it was possible to be from her tower rooms and she took the long, thickly carpeted corridor that branched from the main staircase and was pretty sure the mad beating of her heart would suffocate her long before she reached her destination.

Wall sconces, placed at intervals between the closed doors along the silent corridors that now seemed never-ending, threw muted pools of welcome light and as she reached the last corner, the final stretch, the door to Aldo's suite opened quietly and Iolanda, clad in something revealingly diaphanous and skimpy, slipped out, her lovely face flushed.

Cat's bare feet came to an abrupt full stop, everything inside her curling up in a painful, icy knot with the horror of what she was seeing. And after a momentary hesitation when the other woman looked as if she had been turned into stone, Iolanda's mouth curved in a cat's-got-the-cream smile as she clutched the tiny packet she was holding between her pert little breasts.

No need to ask what she was doing, or what that packet contained, Cat thought jaggedly as her stomach lurched over nauseously and her knees turned to water, wobbling alarmingly as Iolanda, putting on that definitely superior smile again, advised, 'I wouldn't bother if I were you. You can take my word for it, Aldo definitely won't be able to accommodate you right now.'

And swept past her, heading for her own room, trailing wafts of heavy perfume, her low, husky laugh more than Cat could possibly bear.

She was shaking, sick with shock as she forced her rubbery legs to carry her very slowly back to her own rooms, making it to the bathroom just in time before she was violently and wretchedly sick.

At least her question was now answered, she told herself as she rinsed her mouth out with cold water. She'd had all the confirmation she needed without having to ask her rotten husband if he was being unfaithful, and inadvertently revealing how deeply and permanently she'd fallen in love with him on that fatal night when he'd made love to her for the first time.

She'd been spared that ultimate indignity, which was the only thing that could be said for the horror of what she'd witnessed.

Slowly, she made it back into the bedroom and coldly smoothed out the bundle of hot chaos that was her brain.

She would make him pay for breaking her heart. She would make him pay in spades!

CHAPTER FOUR

'THAT colour always suited you. I like it,' Aldo approved warmly as Cat finally presented herself at the breakfast table in front of the open French windows later that morning.

The last morning she would be sharing anything with him, she reminded herself hollowly as she poured coffee from the pot and took it with her to the edge of the terrace that overlooked the tumbling, flower-packed gardens.

Devious, lying, rotten creep! She reinforced her rock-bottom opinion of the wretched man who called himself her husband. How dared he pay empty compliments when he'd spent the best part of last night having wild sex with his mistress?

She didn't trust herself to speak to him, let alone sit at the table with him. At least Iolanda didn't seem to have surfaced yet. Catching up on the beauty sleep she'd missed last night, was she?

And as soon as she'd had her much-needed shot of caffeine she'd tell him what she'd decided.

And of course he didn't like the in-your-face vivid scarlet of her short cotton skirt and matching sleeveless cropped top; that was partly why she'd chosen it.

It wasn't chic, understated or even remotely sophisticated! And the long, searingly yellow chiffon scarf she'd tied tightly around her waist to keep the now too-large skirt from dropping round her ankles would be viewed as an affront to his impeccable good taste. Even now he was probably squinting, reaching for his shades.

Which was precisely why she'd delved into the depths of the huge hanging cupboard to find what she could of her pre-transformation clothes and had been already dressed in the most flamboyant things she could find when Rosa arrived with the tray of morning tea.

Ignoring the other woman's tut of disapproval, Cat had dismissed her. Never again would she allow her hair to be sculptured and tortured into sleek submission or dress in the sort of classic gear designed for the seriously sophisticated. From now on Aldo could look to Iolanda for his idea of female perfection. She was reverting to type! She was her own woman again, not his!

'Aren't you eating?' The soft, dark-honey voice that came from directly behind her now was threaded through with what Cat supposed was meant to convey husbandly concern and she guessed that it wasn't entirely manufactured. He'd want her fit and healthy when he got her pregnant—that was the main consideration and she'd do well to remember it.

Apart from that he had little interest in her.

As witness what had happened last night, she thought on a renewed spurt of crushing anger. His

wife had as good as booted him out of her bedroom
so he'd merely shrugged those impressive shoulders
and arranged for his mistress to share his banishment.
No skin off his arrogant nose!

'Where is she?' Cat ignored his question and replaced her cup on its saucer. It rattled alarmingly. She
put it smartly down on the stone balustrading, out of
harm's way.

Aldo, moving closer, asked with ominous smoothness, 'Who is "she"?'

Cat took a long, hopefully calming breath. The air
was hot and arid and scented with the wild thyme and
fennel that grew on the stony hillside. 'The Cardinale
woman,' she managed frigidly. No way, no way
would she let him know how very much he'd hurt
her. If he knew how deeply she'd loved him it would
be the final ignominy. She'd suffered enough, hadn't
she?

Aldo stepped into her line of vision. Cat shivered
despite the hot August sun on her bare arms. Dressed
in light fawn chinos and a casual coffee-coloured
lawn shirt, he looked monumentally devastating, his
dark eyes veiled by the thick, curving sweep of lashes
that failed to completely hide the hard golden glitter
of biting impatience.

She tipped her head, presenting him with her profile as he voiced his displeasure. 'Iolanda left an hour
ago. I arranged for Sergio to drive her back to
Florence.' His tone became glacial. 'Iolanda is a
highly valued business colleague as well as a friend.

I expect you to remember that and show some respect.'

Unable to respond to that without blowing her top
explosively, Cat ignored his more conciliatory invitation, 'Why don't we start the morning again and
have breakfast together?' swung round on her heels
and sailed back through the French windows, resolutely bypassing the white linen-covered table set
with rolls and honey and a huge bowl of fresh fruit.

'I'm leaving you,' she said clearly so there could
be no mistake. 'I want a divorce.'

A tiny pulse of utter silence, then, 'What did you
say?' he delivered in a tone of utter dryness and Cat
paused in her dignified retreat, and that was a huge
mistake, she recognised sickly as his overwhelmingly
masculine and coldly furious body suddenly appeared
in front of her, blocking her path.

'You are not going deaf, as far as I know,' she cast
at him brittly, her chin up, her eyes narrowed with
emerald disdain as she fiercely reminded herself that
she could handle the two-timing brute. 'You heard
me. I want a divorce.'

'Why?' His mouth was set in a hard, enraged line,
but a genuine query drew a line between his eyes.
Was he shocked to discover, probably for the very
first time in his life, that what he wanted was not
always what he got?

'Because I don't like our marriage,' she answered
flatly.

She was desperately hanging on to her by now precarious cool. Start to tell him that she knew of his affair with Iolanda, display her hurt and jealousy, and she would end up raving, going to pieces right in front of him. Her closely guarded secret would be out, laid raw and bleeding in front of him.

The realisation that she loved him, had since she'd first laid eyes on him, would make her look a fool and give him the ammunition he needed to sweet-talk her into staying with him. Making promises he had no intention of keeping to get what he wanted: financial assets to add to masses he already had, a dutiful and gullible wife, children. That was never going to happen; she wouldn't let it. She would make sure her secret was safe.

Disconcertingly, he stood aside to let her pass unhindered. And tears stung her eyes as she took the stairs to her tower rooms. Was he prepared to let her go so easily? Had their marriage meant so little to him? Had she?

Obviously.

Well, she already knew that, didn't she? Senseless to get in a state about it. She hadn't really wanted him to try to talk her out of her decision—surely she hadn't! Besides, she'd be free of him before too long, she reminded herself. Back in England, able to get on with the rest of her life.

Gramps would be furious with her, that went without saying, but surely when he knew the full story he would be firmly on her side, she consoled herself as she dug the clothes she'd brought to Italy with her from where Rosa had consigned them to the far depths of the wardrobe. She wanted no reminders of her life here; she'd leave all the expensive designer gear behind.

Just as she'd leave her heart behind? a nasty little voice enquired inside her head. She blotted it out vehemently. She hated Aldo now. Falling in love with him had been a highly costly mistake in emotional terms. And as long as she lived she would never repeat it.

Aldo's attitude was the right one. Falling in love was for fools.

Her passport was somewhere. She couldn't get back to England without it. Maybe she'd put it in one of the dressing-table drawers, or Rosa had. She really couldn't remember. She'd been in a state of shock and utter misery when she and the luggage Aldo had personally insisted on packing for her had arrived here shortly after her miscarriage, not really aware of, or caring about, what was going on around her.

'Looking for something?'

The shock of hearing his voice froze her fingers as they scrabbled through the contents of her underwear drawer. Cat felt her colour come and go and her spine prickled with tension. Somehow she had to control herself, stay cool. She had to!

Turning slowly, she said very precisely, 'My passport.' She pushed a wayward strand of copper-coloured hair away from her forehead with the back of her hand, praying she looked calm and collected even though she was churning with anger, jealousy and the sense of bitter betrayal. 'When Sergio returns I want him to drive me to Pisa Airport,' she stated with a coolness that quietly amazed her.

And was even more amazed when he answered her demand by pacing right up to her, his smile gentle but with a definite touch of the predator about it.

What he found to smile about in this ghastly situation she couldn't imagine but soon found out when he said with cool warning, 'No one will drive you anywhere and your passport is in the safe in Florence, along with mine and our wedding certificate. You are my wife, and what is mine I keep. Always remember that, Caterina.'

He was still smiling, that was the worst part. Even worse than the problem of getting herself back to Florence to pick up her passport. She wished he wasn't standing so close to her, close enough for her to inhale his cool, lemony aftershave, to feel his body heat. It was physically unsettling.

But she wouldn't retreat, not by a single inch. He mustn't know how threatened she felt by his nearness, how he made her whole body tingle, every cell going on red alert, every nerve-end screaming a warning.

Cat stood her ground so firmly she was proud of herself, her words sounding harsh as she pushed them through her teeth. 'You can't keep me where I don't want to be. Short of chaining me to the bedpost.'

'Now, there's an idea!' he came back softly, his smile widening to a grin. A grin which slid into wicked sultriness as his bitter-chocolate eyes imprisoned her gaze with blatant sensuality. He had hypnotic eyes, she thought with a deep shudder. She couldn't look away, even though her tired brain told her she must. She felt as if she were drowning. She felt her lips part as she struggled to pull air into her starving lungs.

'But I don't need to use chains, do I?' A hand came up to touch the dimple at the side of her mouth, lingering for one tummy-clenching moment before dropping away. 'There are much more pleasant ways of keeping you with me. Yes?' A lean hand reached for the trailing ends of the long yellow scarf. And tugged.

Cat's body was on fire. Now a mere whisper away from the lean masculinity of his, she didn't know what to do with herself, couldn't have stepped away even if she could summon the will-power to want to. He had her trapped, as much by her own deeply regrettable lack of defences against him as by his far superior strength. And when he'd spoken there had been a strand of powerful satisfaction in his voice, so something about her must have betrayed her.

She made a tiny sound of humiliation at the back of her throat and Aldo dipped his darkly handsome head closer and warned softly, 'But to cover all contingencies, even if you do manage to hike the five miles down to the village you will get no further. One phone call from me will make sure that no one, but no one, will be willing to drive you anywhere.'

Another tug on the yellow scarf around her waist

brought them into direct contact. The thrust of his pelvis, the hard wall of his chest pressing against her breasts, his thighs against her thighs. Her mouth went dry and the old familiar throbbing started up deep inside her.

Desperately, Cat tried to mentally gather the knowledge that he was a despicable, unfaithful, uncaring rat but her brain was spinning so dizzily she couldn't hold a single Aldo-damning thought in her head for longer than a nanosecond.

'You are mine and you stay mine.' He dropped the scarf and clamped his hands on either side of her narrow waist in one smooth, authoritative movement, pulling her weakly unresistant body hard against his, his gorgeous mouth so close to hers that his warm, clean breath feathered over her lips, making them tremble and feel almost unbearably sensitive. 'And you go nowhere until I know what you meant when you said you didn't like our marriage. But for now there are things I know you do like, *cara*.'

His hands slid up her ribcage and curved over her aching breasts as he slowly explored the outline of her engorged nipples. Sultry heat spread through her entire body, converging hectically on what his clever hands were doing to her. 'You can explain what displeases you later and I will remedy it,' he promised with husky-voiced male arrogance, his eyes dropping to watch the movement of his fingers as he began the task of slipping the buttons down the front of her top from their moorings.

He was going to make love to her, Cat knew that. She could stop it by flinging his infidelity in his face. Or she could let it happen, take what her feeble body was yearning for. It was her choice.

Or no choice at all. She gave a harsh inhalation of breath as he parted the fabric, exposing the hedonistic invitation of her peaking breasts. An invitation he took with an avidity that swept her to dizzy heights of ecstasy and pushed her mental flailings for autonomy right out of existence.

This need for him was elemental, raw and passionate. It had been her undoing from the first moment she'd set eyes on him. That was her last coherent thought as he gave each breast individual and tormenting attention. And then, as so many times in the past, she was actively helping him, her fingers undoing his shirt buttons, her concentration feverish and intense.

As she exposed his perfectly honed naked torso to her drugged eyes and ran her fingers over the sleek, bronzed skin Cat moaned softly and he bent forward, taking her breath into his mouth as he enforced with soft determination, 'You are mine,' before plundering her lips with a hot, hungry urgency that had her reeling, responding with her own feverish demands, her hips echoing the blindingly erotic movement of his, her fingernails digging into the taut, heated skin of his firmly muscled back as he walked her backwards to the huge bed.

The last of their clothing was jettisoned in a flurry

of impatient hands, the bed covers flung to the floor as their bodies writhed, mouths clinging together, and their lovemaking was savage, almost, Cat thought with a wild, exultant cry, as if they needed to punish each other.

But later, and after, it was gentle, dreamy, slow and thoughtful, and as Cat drifted into an exhausted sleep she wondered if she would experience anything so out of this world and perfect ever again.

It was very far from perfect, was Cat's immediate thought when she woke abruptly. Letting Aldo seduce her senseless all over again had been nothing but a self-destructive mistake.

From the angle of the sun as it flooded the room with soft light she could tell it was late afternoon. They had been in bed together all day—she could just imagine the staff's knowing smiles when neither of them had been seen, not even for lunch. Her face went red with embarrassment and shame for the weakness of her will.

She had planned on being out of here by this time on the first leg of her journey back to England.

Only Aldo had insisted she wasn't going anywhere. He'd move heaven and earth to stop her.

Cat shifted gingerly. The last thing she wanted to do was wake him. For the first time ever he'd held her close to him after they were both too sated to do anything other than fall into a deep and drugging sleep. Normally he turned his back on her, shutting her out.

Ironic, really, she decided grimly as she carefully extricated herself from the imprisonment of his arms. Once she would have rejoiced, taken the way he held her as an indication that he wanted a close, intimate contact beyond the act of sex itself.

Now she saw it for what it was. Imprisonment. Exactly that.

'You are mine. What is mine I keep.' His earlier words echoed sharply in her head.

But why? He certainly didn't love her. She was a mere convenience, one that could easily be replaced. He couldn't even feel affection for her, let alone respect. Carrying on with his mistress was evidence of that!

As she moved out of the room her bare feet hit the cool white marble of the *en suite* floor and she paused, pressing her fingertips against her burning forehead. Why would he be so adamant about holding on to an unloved wife who had categorically stated that she wanted a divorce?

She would have staked her life on him letting her go with about as much regret as he'd wipe a smear of mud from the sole of one of his hand-crafted shoes. His pride and arrogance would have demanded nothing less.

Under normal circumstances she would have opted for a long soak in a warm, scented bath to soothe away the little aches and stiffnesses occasioned by long hours of intense lovemaking, but this afternoon she really needed to get a move-on, clear her head and plan her way out of the stranglehold Aldo had on her.

Never mind Aldo's feudal power over the local villagers, it wasn't beyond her ingenuity to look further afield, find a taxi firm which would be willing to send a driver out here—preferably with someone riding shotgun!

The stinging needles of the icy-cold shower took her breath away but it helped the penny to finally drop and gave her the stark answer to the questions she'd asked herself earlier.

Of course! It was obvious when she looked at it from his viewpoint. A divorce would mean she could claim a large chunk of his assets and, as far as he knew, the loss of those shares and the inheritance that would eventually come to her.

What was his he kept; he'd never said a truer word! She mentally derided her slow mental processes as she dried herself briskly to get her circulation moving again after nearly freezing under that prolonged douche of icy water. She should have cottoned on immediately.

Aldo Patrucco, head of a huge and highly successful business empire, had married for purely mercenary reasons, as many of his ancestors before him had done. Fact.

His avarice meant he would do anything to keep her and the assets she came with—even to the extent of expending all that energy making love to her, proving that he could turn her on with just one look. Fact.

Well, she didn't aim to be the captive of his avarice, she told herself staunchly as she blow-dried her hair until it stood away from her face like a wild and crinkly halo. And she could have saved herself a whole heap of heartbreak and anguish if she'd turned down his marriage proposal and told him not to worry. Her inheritance would go to him, lock, stock, barrel and wretched shares. Gramps had been very firm about what he intended to do if she'd refused to go along with his mad idea.

She would bet her last bent farthing that had he had that information Aldo would have made good and sure she didn't accept him, most definitely would not have turned on all that considerable sex appeal and seduced her into saying yes. He would have taken her refusal and turned thankfully on his heels, safe in the knowledge that he would eventually get back those shares without going to the bother of marrying anyone!

He could have carried on his nasty affair—with the vile Iolanda and who knew how many others?—without the fear of being found out by a jealous wife!

Aware that her blood pressure was threatening to blow the top of her head off, Cat told herself to cool it. There was a way out of this mess; of course there was.

All she had to do was be very adult about it. Tell her two-timing husband that if he agreed to a divorce, to let her go, she would ask for nothing from him. She needed only assure him that she would sign any document agreeing to that to have him moving heaven and earth to get her on the first available flight back to England. After she'd signed on the dotted line, of course!

Remember, too, to assure him that Gramps would see the break-up of their marriage as being all her fault. He'd certainly been more interested in closing the family circle after the rift of his own creating than he had been in her future welfare or happiness, so he'd view the divorce as just as reprehensible, if not worse, than an initial refusal to marry the man of his choice and disinherit her in favour of Aldo as he had threatened.

That still had the power to hurt. Badly. Her eyes glinted with tears and there was a lump the size of a house in her throat as she crept quietly back into the bedroom. She swallowed noisily and then, panic-stricken, held her breath.

But thankfully Aldo seemed to be still asleep. Sprawled out on his back, stark naked. Cat dragged her eyes away. He was stunning. Her throat closed up as the lingering intimate ache at the juncture of her thighs suddenly and sharply intensified.

She could throttle him for having this power over her and she had to get dressed as quickly and quietly as possible. Naked, she felt spectacularly vulnerable. As she acknowledged with a huge feeling of shame, he only had to look at her, say one word, to have her weakly giving in to the desire he had brought to scorching life.

One look at her nakedness with those dark, sexy eyes, one velvet word—

'*Cara,* what are you doing?'

Cat froze, her heart tumbling about inside her chest. That slow, honeyed tone made every sensitised inch of her skin burn and prickle with unwanted, shameful excitement. She hated herself for what her louse of a husband could do to her!

And he could see what she was doing, she thought dementedly. Hopping about on one foot trying to get her knickers on!

Arms flailing wildly, she lost her balance and one of Aldo's hands snaked out to steady her, to drag her onto the rumpled bed with him, her white satin briefs round her ankles.

'You don't need these.' He disentangled the scrap of fabric and dropped it to the carpet, his big naked body partly covering hers as she lay spreadeagled against the pillows. His gorgeous face was a mere inch or two away from her own; she could see the tiny golden lights deep in his dark-as-sin eyes and stopped breathing.

One strong hand held both of hers above her head and one hair-roughened thigh imprisoned her slender lower limbs. 'I intend, my little darling—' a lightly provocative brush of his mouth against her parted lips '—to keep you in bed—' another kiss, as light as a butterfly's wings, on the tip of her neat nose '—na-

ked. Until—' his long, sensual mouth found the point
of her jaw just below the lobe of her ear '—you tell
me—' and trailed a line of shimmering fire down the
taut line of her throat '—why you had a tantrum and
said you didn't like our marriage.'

Tantrum! How dared he speak to her as if she were
a simpering child? Her treacherous body, which had
been on the point of melting completely and shame-
fully beneath the seductive onslaught of his mouth,
bristled, a bundle of furious energy prepared to fight
him off every inch of the way.

Aldo shifted, presumably sensing a battle he had
no intention of losing, Cat thought agitatedly, everything inside her going haywire as she felt his erection
against the quivering flesh of her tummy. Heat pooled
through the centre of her femininity, began to pulse,
and, desperation fuelling her, she tried to clamp her
thighs together but the domineering strength of his
thigh prevented any defensive movement at all.

And then she found she didn't want to move at all
as his tantalising mouth moved lower, finding the val-
ley between her breasts, his voice a wicked seduction
in itself as he covered her unbearably sensitised skin
with kisses and murmured throatily, 'For me, our
marriage is good. You are so beautiful, *cara*. And for
you, you have me, you live in luxury, you will never
want for anything. What is there not to like about
that? You have everything I promised you when we
agreed to marry. And the sex is the greatest. Yes?'

As if to prove his point he slid a hand down to the

soft copper curls at the apex of her sex and, as if satisfied by her wriggle of immediate and unconquerable response, he whispered, 'We have shared a sadness in the loss of our baby but I am with you now, as I planned it, and I promise to make everything perfect.'

Make another baby! That was what the unfaithful wretch meant!

That finally got through to her, galvanised her treacherously weak body into raging action. He would have sex with her until he was sure she was pregnant again—and then take off! That was his vile plan!

Languid, nerveless hands became tight fists, fists to punch holes in those wide, dominating shoulders; the body that had been supine, aching for his, squirmed like an eel, taking him by surprise as she slithered off the bed, snatching up a long-discarded sheet and wrapping it tightly around her tense body.

There would be nothing adult or calm about what she threw at this...this monster now! Of course he was content with this marriage—a dutiful wife, kept in pampered luxury, responsive to his dutiful attentions, expected to turn a blind eye to his sordid, on-going affair!

And pushing his immense wealth, the luxuries she was supposed to be grateful for, under her nose was the very last straw. If he'd loved her then she would have been happy to dress in rags, share a cardboard box with him and wash in a bucket!

'I have something to say to you,' she hissed at him,

all fired up to let him have both barrels—his infidelity, the divorce, everything—hardly hearing her own words through the violent roar of her own thoughts that was drowning out everything else.

She could see, though, see the frowning intensity of his eyes as they stabbed into her own. See the way he had swung upright and was sitting on the edge of the bed, his face shadowed and grim as if he couldn't understand what was going on here.

See the way he reached out one hand to her, his mouth parting as though he was about to say something then clamping shut again, his frown deepening alarmingly as he looked towards the door.

He bit out, 'Yes?' his voice blistering, and Cat turned. If Rosa had knocked before entering she hadn't heard her through the angry roar of blood in her brain.

'I'm sorry, *signor.*' Rosa went red, obviously embarrassed by her employer's naked state. She was holding one of the cordless phones. She held it out to Cat. 'A message for the *signora*; I think it's important. Otherwise I wouldn't have dreamed of—'

'Forget it.' Aldo's injunction was tersely impatient. He rose to his feet, magnificently male, magnificently unembarrassed as he strode through to the bathroom, leaving Rosa to scuttle away and Cat to give her attention to the slim, silver-coloured instrument in her hand.

It was Bonnie. Her grandfather's housekeeper sounded at the end of her tether.

'You must come—he'd want you to. They've just taken him to hospital and—'

'Who?' Cat suddenly went icily cold, the blistering heat of her anger towards her errant husband washed away with a swamping wave of fear. She already knew the answer.

'Your grandfather. The ambulance. I phoned them. It's a heart attack. There were these paramedics. They said he would be fine but it looked very bad to me. He was asking for you. He wanted to tell you something; I knew it was bothering him and—'

'Bonnie,' Cat's voice was firm even though her whole body was trembling with reaction, 'I'll be with you just as soon as I can. Hire a taxi—anything—just go and see him and tell him that. And Bonnie...' her voice cracked '...tell him I love him.'

CHAPTER FIVE

AS THE Patrucco company jet began its descent to Birmingham International Aldo took Cat's clenched hands and gently straightened out her white-knuckled fingers.

'Try to relax. A hired car is waiting. If the traffic is kind you will be with your grandfather in a little over an hour. Maybe an hour and a half.'

Cat gave him a wan smile and made no attempt to pull her hands away from the comforting strength of his. She knew she shouldn't need her unfaithful, self-seeking husband, not in any capacity, but to be brutally honest with herself she did. She didn't know what she would have done without him today—run around like a headless chicken, she supposed glumly.

Aldo had taken over the phone, making three or four terse, authoritative calls, packed for them both and almost before she'd had time to draw breath he was driving them to Pisa.

Someone from his company had been waiting at the airport with the passports he'd obviously been instructed to collect from the house in Florence. Every single thing had gone like well-oiled clockwork. She hadn't had to do a thing except get herself dressed and notify the staff of their imminent departure.

She would always be deeply grateful for the way he'd calmly taken charge, organised everything with no fuss whatsoever and not a second's waste of precious time, endlessly grateful for his quiet reassurances, his immediate understanding of how frightened and nerve-rackingly anxious she was feeling.

If only things were different, she thought wretchedly as the transfer from the jet to the waiting car was accomplished with a smooth lack of delay. If only he'd given Iolanda her marching orders before they'd married and stayed faithful to her she would have loved this man until her dying breath, lived for him, for his pleasure, even though she knew he would never really love her. She would have settled for affection, fidelity and respect. As it was she had none of these things.

Tears were glittering on the tips of her long, sweeping lashes as he settled in the driving seat beside her and leaned over to check her seat belt.

'Don't,' he pleaded thickly as he brushed the drops away with the tips of his fingers. 'I can't bear to see you cry. We have no way of knowing how severe Domenico's attack was until we speak to his consultant. Until then we must be optimistic. He is in good hands, remember, and these days, *cara*, miracles can be worked.'

Cat nodded mutely as, with a final intent appraisal of her drawn features, he fastened his own seat belt and turned the key in the ignition. Her tears, that time, had been for the ending of their marriage, but he wasn't to know that. By unspoken agreement they had put everything on hold, not mentioned her demand for a divorce since the news about Gramps's heart attack had come through.

Late at night the motorway was relatively quiet and the powerful saloon simply ate up the miles, and Aldo invited, 'Tell me about your grandfather's house-keeper—Bonnie, isn't it?'

'Ellen Boniface,' Cat supplied, leaning back against the leather headrest and closing her eyes. 'Why? What about her?'

'Is she a fixture?'

'As fixed as they come.'

He couldn't really want to be regaled with infor-mation about Bonnie but probably thought that get-ting her to talk about the elderly housekeeper would shift her mind away from her worries about Gramps. In many ways Aldo was a fine man, but in the most important way, as far as she was concerned, he was deeply flawed.

But she didn't want to think about that, either, so she pushed it to the back of her mind to be brought out later when she'd truly satisfied herself that Gramps was going to be OK.

'No family of her own?'

For her sake he was still trying to draw her out on a subject he could have no real interest in, so she'd do him the courtesy of going along with it, even though it was an effort to talk at all.

'Apparently not. Bonnie never married and, initially, my grandparents hired her to help look after me after my parents were killed. I was only a baby. When I got less of a handful—'

'I can't imagine you ever being anything other than a handful!' he commented with dry amusement. 'I can imagine you as a complete tomboy and spoiled rotten.'

'I saw a fair bit of action,' she concurred readily, remembering the scrapes she'd got into while she'd been growing up and the whole of the countryside had been her playground, casting a glancing look at the darkened austerity of his profile as she told him tremulously, 'I don't know about being spoiled rotten, but I do know I was loved.'

Her throat closed up; she couldn't say any more. She'd been surrounded by love in her childhood but Gran was gone now and Gramps had demonstrated that healing the rift with his Italian relatives counted for more with him than she did and that had left a wound that would take a long time to heal over.

And Aldo had never loved her at all.

But she couldn't blame him for that, she counselled herself with painful honesty. He had never once tried to fool her; he'd told her quite openly that he didn't believe in the condition. The fault was all hers for naïvely believing she could change his mind and make him fall in love with her.

The warm pressure of his hand as it briefly and comfortingly closed over hers startled her then filled her with a deep and yearning ache. He was being too kind; she couldn't bear it! And she had to swallow hard and pull in a harsh breath to enable her to answer at all when he continued to question lightly, 'I guess your Bonnie grew into your family?'

'Absolutely.' Her voice sounded choked, but she soldiered on. 'My grandparents relied on her and she on them. After Gran died Bonnie and Gramps got even more dependent on each other.' She frowned and chewed on the corner of her lip. 'I haven't given her a single thought for hours—she'll be rattling around in that big house on her own, worried out of her wits.'

'Then contact her now. I should have thought about it sooner,' he admitted tersely. 'She'll be glad to hear we're well on our way.' He produced a slim mobile phone from the inside pocket of the fawn linen jacket he was wearing. 'And tell her to get some sleep. We're booked into an hotel near the hospital so she won't have to wait up for us, or worry about feeding us.' And at Cat's sharp intake of breath he added, 'I thought it best for you to be a few hundred yards away rather than fifteen or so miles.'

Cat's throat was achingly tight as she dialled. She wished he wouldn't be so damned thoughtful and considerate! It only made her love him more and she really couldn't afford to!

Bonnie answered on the first ring. Her voice tearful, she explained that she hadn't been allowed to visit, but she had asked the person she'd spoken to to pass on Cat's earlier messages, and when the call ended after five minutes of gentle reassurances from Cat, who was feeling far from reassured herself, the elderly housekeeper sounded more relaxed.

'Not long now,' Aldo commented as the call ended, his voice gruff. 'Thankfully, the hospital's signed on every intersection.'

Cat nodded mutely, her hands twisting together in her lap. He'd been brilliant—since leaving the motorway he'd only once asked her to consult the road map. It was just a pity that he couldn't be as good at being a husband as he was at everything else!

But that anguished thought, together with everything else, flew right out of her head as they entered the hospital environs. Her stomach clenched in a sickening knot of dread.

And only Aldo's strong arm around her waist kept her upright as they made their way to the Intensive Care Unit and only will-power kept her from bursting into tears when the door was unlocked and she was admitted alone with strict instructions not to make a fuss, or a noise, and only stay for two minutes.

Gramps looked so frail and shrunken, his face a distressing shade of grey. He was hooked to a monitor, a drip, and was being fed oxygen, and the humming of machines in the otherwise utter silence seemed unearthly.

She snagged in a breath. He was sleeping. Wanting to transfer some of her strength to him, she touched his hand and willed him to get better. And as his eyelids fluttered open she leant forward and kissed his forehead and whispered, 'Love you, Gramps. Rest now and I'll see you in the morning.' And saw him smile before closing his eyes again and slipping back into sleep.

Released back into the corridor, Cat fell into Aldo's waiting arms. He was offering comfort and right now she needed it, she excused herself as his arms tightened around her and she buried her bright head into the wide angle of his shoulder.

Tomorrow, when she was over the shock of everything that had happened today, things would be very different. He would no longer be needed and she'd be able to stand on her own feet.

But when he brushed the tangle of hair away from her face and murmured, 'I've been talking to the senior nurse on duty. Preliminary tests show the attack was not too severe. There are more results to come in, of course, but we'll be able to talk to his consultant tomorrow and get a clearer picture,' she was not so sure, and clung to him weakly, needing his strength.

Only when they'd been shown to their hotel suite ten minutes later did Cat get a grip. Thankfully, there were two single beds, but even so the enforced intimacy made her spine go stiff.

She had told him she wanted a divorce and he had countered by telling her that she was his and he kept what was his, and had gone on to demonstrate just how effortlessly he could sublimate her will in his.

Sharing a room with him would be like going on a strict diet and having a plate of luxuriously wicked cream cakes dangled under your nose! she thought agitatedly.

A state of mind that markedly increased when he shrugged out of his jacket and loosened his tie just after a waiter had delivered a selection of sandwiches and an opened bottle of wine.

'Sit down and relax,' he told her gently, his bitter-chocolate eyes soft with compassion. 'We both need to eat and a glass of wine will help you sleep. The hospital has my mobile number. You will be called if you're needed, but I honestly think the possibility of that happening is very remote.'

Cat sank down onto one of the pair of brocade-covered chairs that flanked a low table, and when he gave her a glass of wine her hand shook. And her eyes were haunted as she watched him move about the room, unpacking for them both. Toiletries into the *en suite*; one of her nightdresses laid out on one of the beds. He had chosen her favourite, the pale aqua silk with the delicate creamy lace inserts, she noted with a violent stab of misery.

She remembered him buying it for her, and the matching wrap, when they were on that magical honeymoon in Portofino. His strong, lean hands had been so gentle as he'd taken it from the tissue wrappings, holding it in front of her and telling her huskily, 'I long to see you wearing this for me almost as much as I long to peel it off you.'

It seemed more than a lifetime away and the look of what she had only been able to describe as adoration in his dark eyes when she'd appeared in it later had been nothing more romantic and meaningful than the practised seducer's knack and the need to get an heir, she reminded herself forcefully.

She had believed that their marriage could work out beautifully. Now she knew differently, that it had never stood a chance.

'You must eat something,' Aldo instructed as he joined her and piled a selection of tiny triangular sandwiches on a plate and put it down on the table in front of her, before dropping fluidly into the other chair and lounging back, his long legs stretched out in front of him.

For a moment his eyes closed and Cat felt dreadful when she really looked at him and saw the lines of strain that bracketed his beautiful mouth, the shadows of fatigue that painted dark rings around his eyes.

He had had a dreadful day, too. Starting off with hearing his wife tell him she wanted a divorce. He might thoroughly deserve it, but at the same time it would have come as a shock. As far as he knew he would see his hopes of regaining those shares flying out of the window and that had to be a severe blow.

But, despite all that, if she tried from now until the next millennium she wouldn't be able to fault his care, his concern for her, or the ultra-efficient way he'd taken care of the travel arrangements.

Feeling guilty for so far only thinking of herself and what she had been going through since she'd seen Iolanda coming from his suite last night, and totally forgetting that he was flesh and blood, she managed gently, even though she felt her heart was breaking all over again, 'I'll eat if you will.'

'A done deal!' His heavy lashes lifted and his stunning eyes smiled into hers, the lines of fatigue washed away like magic as he sat upright, selected a sandwich and held it in his lean fingers. 'You first!'

His sinfully sexy eyes threw out a glinting challenge and Cat shivered with immediate response. She was looking at the man she had fallen so cataclysmically in love with and every last one of her senses reacted to him as shatteringly as they always did.

'I'm waiting—do you want me to die of starvation?' His mouth curved in the wicked smile that sent little electric sparks racing up and down her spine, and she answered with the first real smile she'd given him in what felt like ages. She took a bite and watched him pop the whole of his smoked-salmon-filled tiny triangle into his mouth with a feeling that she was shocked to analyse as melting tenderness.

She still really cared about him, she recognised with drenching dismay. In spite of what had happened she still cared deeply. She despaired of herself, she really did, she thought tetchily as she ate what she could and watched him polish off the remainder and help her to more wine, only sipping sparingly at his own barely half-filled glass.

She had to get a grip, keep firmly in mind what he was really like, protect herself from the insanity of loving him. And her voice was harsher, harder than

she'd intended, despite the supposedly mellowing influence of all that wine, when she told him, 'You
might as well go back to Italy tomorrow. I can manage on my own now.'

'Do you have to try to pick a fight?' Aldo's dark
brows clenched in a swift-as-lightning frown, his eyes
going bleak. 'I am your husband,' he reminded with
unnecessary forcefulness. 'My place is here with
you.'

'No.' Cat dragged air into her suddenly starving
lungs. For the whole period of their marriage he had
called all the shots while she had stayed wherever
she'd been pushed, dutifully trying to turn herself into
the type of wife she'd believed he'd wanted, always
there, willing, eager and responsive when he'd needed
her, keeping her misery and complaints to herself
when he took himself off to be with—as she now
knew—his mistress. 'No,' she enunciated more
clearly. 'I know—who better?—how busy you always
are. You don't have to stay on, because we don't have
a marriage left worth talking of.'

Cat put her empty glass down on the plate which
held the curling remains of her second, nibbled-at
sandwich and tried to stare him down. But his black
eyes ensnared her and made her mouth run dry.

'And I still don't know why you think that way,'
he countered with the chilling smoothness of polished
black ice. He got to his feet with the innate masculine
grace that was so typical of him. Then he stood over
her, incredibly still, his voice low and intense as he

warned, 'I don't want to discuss it. Now is not the time. For the time being we present a united front, for Domenico's sake. Remember his condition and behave yourself. We will discuss the subject fully at a time of my choosing. Now,' he gave her the benefit of a glacially polite smile, 'Will you use the bathroom first?'

Stumbling to her feet, Cat snatched her nightdress from the bed and locked herself in the bathroom. Her head was pounding with the strain of everything that had happened since Aldo had walked into the villa with the triumphant Iolanda.

And nothing had been settled about the divorce and it wouldn't be until Gramps was fully fit again. Aldo, as always, was right, she acknowledged with a seething fury that did her pounding head no good at all as she struggled out of her clothes.

They would have to pretend they were the perfect couple and she wasn't at all sure she could carry it off.

CHAPTER SIX

CAT woke feeling like a week-old corpse. As she forced her eyes open Aldo padded into her fuddled viewing range. He was wearing a towel slung rakishly around his narrow hips, his naked torso all sleek, power-packed muscles covered by silky golden skin.

Muttering a string of grumbling imprecations, Cat burrowed her head back into the pillow and pulled the sheet over her head, but with one lean hand Aldo twitched it away again and with the other placed a cup of steaming tea on the night table beside her lonely little bed.

'Drink this and you might feel more human.'

Annoyingly he sounded amused and, what was infinitely worse, he looked fresh as a daisy, full of his usual boundless energy as if this were another typical day which he could effortlessly sail through, his innate easy arrogance bending everything and everyone before him to his will.

While she felt as if she'd been buried for days and then dug up again. She hadn't slept until dawn, when she'd crashed into a sleep which had been peopled by spectacularly awful nightmares.

While he had instantly fallen into a deep and peaceful slumber, she had tossed and turned, wondering how her grandfather was doing, her ears standing to attention in case Aldo's mobile rang with bad news from the hospital, and all the time half expecting Aldo to wake, climb in with her and give her another lesson in his so easily achieved sexual mastery. Half dreading, half hoping. Needing him yet wishing he was half a world away.

Grumpily she hauled herself up against the pillows and tugged the sheet with a modest defiance up to her chin, ignoring the way he raised one mocking eyebrow before he turned and sauntered back to the bathroom, dropping the towel on the way.

Lordy, but he was so gorgeous! He exuded enough raw sexual charisma to turn the sanest woman silly. He would have no trouble at all when he came to choose a new wife. Someone who would stay besotted enough to look the other way when he strayed, his vast wealth providing a powerful anaesthetic.

Whoever she was, she was welcome to him. That type of sordid scenario wasn't for her, and the only thing she had to do to convince him that a divorce was the best idea since Creation was to assure him, no messing, that those wretched shares, the cause of all her present misery, would eventually belong to him.

The hot tea actually did help. She drank it in two thirsty gulps then scrambled off the bed and dived to the wardrobe to investigate the things Aldo had unpacked for her last night.

Selecting a pair of narrow dark grey trousers, a

silky white T-shirt and a light cotton jacket in dusky red, she draped them over her arm and plucked fresh underwear from one of the fitted drawers, listening for the sound of the shower to stop.

In happier times she would have joined him; now she just stood waiting, tense and simmeringly angry because she couldn't stop remembering just how it felt when his strong, clever hands soaped every inch of her body, every movement of his long fingers and curving palms intensely erotic.

Knowing what she did, she should be able to block all those memories from her mind, find him repulsive. But she was desperately weak where he was concerned, she acknowledged bitterly, thoroughly despising herself for the way her wretched body instinctively reacted to the very thought of him.

The opening of the bathroom door sent an electric jolt through her limbs to gather in a squirm-making burning knot deep inside her. He was freshly shaven, his dark hair clinging damply to his skull, his magnificent body entirely naked.

Her breath went, every inch of her skin tingling in that deeply regrettable response. With a small whimper of frustrated self-loathing she tore her eyes away from the cool, knowing mockery of his and dived past him, locking the door behind her. She wished she'd never met the self-serving, arrogant, unfaithful creature!

Cat took her time. She needed to find herself again, lose the lovelorn bundle of conflicting emotions she had become, the witless creature obsessed in every way there was by a man who would never love her, a man who would use his powerful sexual magnetism, his effortless charm to manipulate her for his own advantage.

Ready at last, she faced her reflection. The crinkly copper hair framed pale, serious features, the only colour the dark green of cold eyes, the defiant scarlet lipstick. Deliberately she compressed her mouth into a hard, narrow line, straightened her spine and walked through to the small sitting room.

Room Service had delivered breakfast. Aldo was sitting at the table beneath the window, pouring coffee into two cups. He barely glanced at her as she slid into the seat opposite, merely stated, 'Domenico had a good night and we may speak with his consultant at ten-thirty, after his visit.'

She accepted the cup and saucer. Her hands were steady, she approved. And said coolly, 'You preempted me. But thank you. I was going to phone the unit later.'

A barefaced lie! Too bound up in her own messy emotions, she'd unthinkingly left everything in Aldo's hands. But it would be for the last time, she thought, shaking her head as he offered her the toast rack, taking a ripe peach from the bowl in the centre of the beautifully laid table instead and slicing it into neatly precise portions on her white, gold-banded bone-china plate.

'You were right; we should present a united front

when we visit Gramps, at least for the time being,'
she conceded chillingly, unconsciously forming the
segments of fruit into a perfect circle. 'But away from
him we have to face reality. We can't pretend everything's normal.'

'Aren't you going to eat that? Or do you just want
to play with it?'

Detecting the thread of amusement, she raised cool
green eyes to him. He had finished eating and was
leaning back, one arm casually hooked over the back
of his chair. Seriously annoyed, Cat picked up her
fork and speared juicy fruit between her lips. A tiny
frown declared her perplexity. It wasn't like Aldo to
avoid hard facts, so why hadn't he taken her up on
her statement? It had been direct enough in all conscience.

Why didn't he want to face reality?

Lots of reasons!

Like gathering those shares back into his possession, like providing himself with an heir, like having
a dutiful doormat of a wife who was perfectly content
to be neglected while he enjoyed a life of hedonistic,
bachelor-type freedom!

Tossing her fork back down on the plate, she
reached for a linen napkin to wipe her mouth, did it,
then tossed it onto the mangled remains of her peach,
thrust her chair back from the table and stood up, all
in a series of tightly controlled movements.

'Face it,' she uttered, her voice low and clipped
with the effort of holding on to her temper. 'I want

out, and you know it. Yet you won't discuss it. You're so damned arrogant you don't even want to know why!'

'But I know why,' he countered mildly. But his eyes were strangely bleak as he, too, got to his feet. 'As I recall, you said you didn't like our marriage.' Two paces brought him to within a few inches of her space and despite all her good intentions her body began to overheat, her heartbeat quickening. 'And to the best of my recollection,' the dancing golden lights that now gleamed at her from those bitter-chocolate eyes did what they always did—melted her backbone—and the now sexily intimate tone he employed made her mouth go dry and her pulses race, 'I was able to prove that you liked it very much indeed.'

Sex. He was talking about sex. About his ability to seduce her out of her senses. There was no point in denying it and she wasn't stupid enough to try. The point was, 'There is more to marriage than having sex together—when you happen to be around.'

'Yes? Then why don't you show me? I am quick to learn, *bella mia*. But before you complete my education, we could consolidate on what we both know you *do* like.'

He lifted his hand, the movement so slow she had time to move if she wanted to. She knew what was coming, but he mesmerised her, and the atmosphere was so thick and heavy she could taste it. It sizzled on her tongue, spread through her veins and pooled hotly between her thighs.

A tiny, yearning whimper was forced from her throat as that hand finally made contact and slid beneath her jacket to touch the sensitive peak of her breast, linger for a tantalising moment and then, just as she was spilling into that hot, curving palm, withdrew and clamped around the back of her head, long fingers tangling in the tumbling curls as he drew her towards him.

His kiss was almost brutal, hot and possessive, taking her breath away, pushing her headlong into a losing battle for self-control. And only when she began to respond with fevered abandonment did he break it, black eyes glimmering down into pools of hazy green shame as he mocked, 'You want me, *cara*. I can prove it just like that.' Lean fingers snapped cynically. 'I have already told you that I will listen to your complaints at a more suitable time, so until then stop having tantrums and get ready to leave. We don't want to miss Domenico's consultant.'

'I hate you!' Cat whispered passionately as they stood in the small visitors' waiting room. She'd been seething furiously with bitter resentment since the humiliating aftermath following the primitive domination of that kiss, and it just had to come out before the consultant appeared.

'Calm yourself.' It was the voice of authority that had doubtlessly quelled unfortunate underlings who had failed to live up to his high expectations but Cat wasn't to be classed as an underling and her eyes narrowed further, spitting green fire in his direction.

He was wearing a dark grey suit in some beautifully structured, silky-sheened fabric, a pale grey shirt and a paler tie. He looked cool, remote, capable of controlling any situation.

Abruptly, Cat swung round to stare out of the single window that overlooked a dreary vista of roof tops. He was going to have to learn that he was no longer her puppet master. She had cut the strings.

Her rigid spine turned towards him, she heard the door open, heard his greeting. And turned back, her eyes fixed on the consultant, hanging on every word he said.

Ten minutes later her knees were sagging with relief. The attack had been minor, with no damage done. After a few more days of observation her grandfather would be able to go home. He would be given advice on diet and a mild exercise regime, and medication to lower his blood pressure.

'That's great news!' she breathed happily, her hatred for her husband temporarily forgotten as they walked the few paces to the unit and waited while the door was unlocked. She had been so desperately afraid that her grandfather wouldn't recover or, if he did, that he would have to spend the rest of his life as a semi-invalid. Despite his age, he had always been an active man. He would hate the restraints of chronic illness.

'Keep that smile on your face and you won't upset

Domenico,' Aldo advised with patronising smoothness as they were admitted. Cat totally ignored him
and swung towards the bed in the far corner.

'Gramps—you're looking so much better!' He was,
too, she thought as she hugged him gently. He had
lost that frightening grey colour, and although he was
still on a monitor he'd been taken off the drip and the
oxygen.

'I am a fraud,' Domenico admitted as Aldo brought
two chairs to the bedside. 'I am told I escaped lightly,
for which I am thankful, but I have dragged you both
here unnecessarily and I feel bad about that. I know
how busy you are, Aldo, my boy.' His brown eyes
glistened with weak tears. 'And you, my poor
Caterina, dragging you here and worrying you over
what turns out to be nothing but a warning when you
have had such trouble of your own—'

'Hush!' Cat took his hand, horribly aware that he
was upsetting himself, the news of her miscarriage
still recent in his mind, his longed-for great-
grandchild a hope dashed. 'I am fully recovered now,
truly.' Her fingers tightened around his. 'And as for
my busy husband—' the saccharine smile she turned
in his direction would fool her grandfather but it
wouldn't fool Aldo, not in a million years, and it
wasn't intended to '—now we know you will be fine
as long as you take proper care he can get back into
harness and I shall stay here and help Bonnie look
after you until you're really back on your feet again.

It will be a holiday for me, too, I promise you. So I don't want any arguments.'

'I have missed you,' he admitted gruffly. He returned the pressure of her fingers, his eyes misting over until a broad smile made them dance with all his old vigour as he turned to face Aldo. 'Caterina was always the stubborn one. Even as a toddler and learning to talk, she refused to call me Nonno and insisted on that ugly Gramps. So I won't waste my breath trying to make her change her mind, so long as you don't mind a short separation, my boy?'

He wouldn't have to mind, would he? Cat thought on a wave of heady triumph. He didn't have a leg to stand on when faced with Gramps's obvious pleasure at the thought of her being with him for the duration of his recuperation. And the short separation would become a long one, lasting a lifetime.

But, 'No separation will be required,' Aldo slid in smoothly.

Cat shot him a spearing glance. Her skin prickled in warning. He looked like a cat who had just swallowed a very fat canary!

He smiled at her, a slow, dangerous smile that chilled her to the bone. 'When Caterina became pregnant I started to reschedule my working life,' he explained to her grandfather. 'It necessitated much hard work. Then, sadly, our baby was lost and I used her recuperation to increase my efforts to visit and appraise every aspect of my business interests, to hand the reins over to employees who had earned my trust.

I freed myself up during the period of her recovery so that I could devote a great deal more of my time to my wife and, hopefully, my future family. My time is now largely my own. Happily I can be here too.'

Cat gulped away the sudden and unwelcome lump in her throat. Had he really been doing that? For her? If he'd bothered to explain all those absences she would have understood!

Then, Gullible idiot! she scolded herself. All that flannel was just to pull the wool over the older man's eyes, make him think what a wonderful, considerate and caring husband he was. When those absences had really been his opportunity to skive off with his vile mistress.

Once she was safely pregnant he had been free to swan off; unsafely unpregnant he'd had to return to do his duty all over again when the time was right, she reminded herself bitterly, and when she tuned in to the conversation again she went cold with horror.

'I have been thinking,' Aldo, lounging back, thoroughly at ease, was saying. 'When you get your doctor's go-ahead, Domenico, you might like to return to Italy with us. I know my parents are anxious to get to know you better. You are the missing part of our family; we all want to have you with us. And Caterina and I would love to give you a long, relaxing holiday. Bonnie must accompany you; that goes without saying. Apart from anything else I'm sure she has earned a rest. What do you say?'

If she'd been asked that question she would have

answered that he was a manipulative monster, Cat
bristled silently, trying to keep her face from con-
torting with the need to strangle him.

That was why he'd been asking questions about
Bonnie's situation, she recognised acidly, not because
he'd wanted to take her mind off what had lain ahead
at that time. He was trapping her with her love for
her grandfather for his own despicable and mercenary
ends.

Before he could reply she gave her grandfather's
hand a final squeeze and got to her feet. 'We must
go. We mustn't tire you.' How she managed to keep
her voice on an even keel, a smile on her face, she
would never know. She bent over to kiss him, promising to visit again in the evening, asking if he needed
anything, filling the few minutes with soothing chatter
until she was out in the silent corridor again, Aldo a
smugly self-satisfied presence right behind her.

She turned to face him, wanting to slap his bland
and blameless, too beautiful face. 'What did you do
that for?' she threw at him, the need for play-acting
over now they were outside the unit, the need to lash
out at him positively explosive.

He put his hands on her shoulders and turned her
round to face the lifts at the end of the corridor, his
expression still smack-worthily bland, as if he'd never
played a devious hand in his life. 'Do what?'

'You know what!' Cat's voice rose to a shriek of
fury but she clamped her mouth shut as the doors of
one of the lifts hissed open to reveal two nurses and

a cleaner with an industrial polisher coming out. Red-faced with embarrassment, fully deserving the half-humorous, half-curious looks she'd earned herself and with Aldo's hand firmly in the small of her back, she allowed herself to be propelled forwards into the empty waiting lift, and only when the doors had closed them into the small, downward-travelling space did she let rip.

'Why stay on when you know I want you to go?'

'Domenico's peace of mind?'

'Rubbish!' she spluttered rudely. 'And then, to cap it all, you invite him to stay with us in Italy when you know full well I won't be there!'

'Silenzio!' Hard hands reached for her, pulled her into close, intimate contact and silenced her with his mouth. He plundered her lips with a passion so raw and hungry it made her dizzy, breathless and out of it. Small fists pummelled at those wide, dominating shoulders but the battle was lost, and she knew it as his tongue probed with deepening intimacy and her legs went from under her.

She hated what he could do to her, what he could make her, yet her whole being craved him. She was hooked and she'd never get her rehabilitation under way if she gave in, just melted, every time he touched her!

The whimpers of protest had turned to ragged little gasps of pleasure, when a high-pitched giggle and an appreciative male 'Atta boy!' brought her crashing back to her senses.

The lift had come to rest, the doors sliding open. Doing her best to ignore their enthusiastic audience, Cat unravelled herself from where she'd got herself twined all over Aldo and shot out into the crowded hospital foyer, her face scarlet, her self-esteem somewhere under the floor.

And her infuriating husband was just behind her. She could feel his lazy, sardonic smile all the way down her spine.

CHAPTER SEVEN

'Oh—I'm that glad to see you!'

Bonnie was waiting at the open door of the former farmhouse, wreathed in the kind of smile that threatened to split her pleasantly round and wrinkled face into two quite separate pieces.

While Aldo was fetching their luggage from the boot of the hired saloon Cat returned the housekeeper's enthusiastic bear-hug. As he'd checked them out of the hotel after their visit to the hospital Cat had phoned to warn Bonnie of their imminent arrival. His suggestion, but she'd more than readily concurred.

If she couldn't talk him into going back to Italy, and it was now obvious that he wouldn't be budged— short of her having him kidnapped—then she'd be better off back in her own surroundings. She'd be more in control. Well, wouldn't she?

'And I'm that relieved your grandad's going to be all right I don't rightly know where to put myself!' the housekeeper cried. 'And your old flat isn't suitable, not for a couple, so I've made up the bed in the guest room. Much better than you staying in a nasty hotel, and I've put a batch of scones in the oven! You don't get good home cooking in hotels!'

Cat found a weary smile, said, 'Lovely,' and

couldn't be bothered to impart the information that the hotel had been very far from nasty and she couldn't eat a thing to save her life.

'*Buongiorno,* Bonnie—how nice to see you again, especially now the news of Domenico is so good. I do hope we're not imposing?'

The charm of Aldo's smile as he joined them, the smooth silk of his voice, set Bonnie fluttering, her face going decidedly pink, Cat noted with a quiver of disgust. He could charm his way out of hell itself, she decided morosely as Bonnie burbled eagerly, 'Not a bit of it, *signor*! Imposing, indeed! I'll be glad of the company. Now, let me take those up for you and then I'll make coffee.'

She reached for the cases but Aldo said warmly, 'Coffee would be most welcome, Bonnie, if you will share it with us? And I'll carry our luggage up. Caterina will tell me where we're to sleep. You've been through a rough time over the last day or two and we refuse to put you to any extra trouble.'

'This way,' Cat threw out and headed for the stairs. Any more of this and poor old Bonnie would be a simpering heap on the floor!

She had always viewed the guest room as being gloomy but this morning it looked positively sombre. Dense cloud cover had hidden the earlier late-August sunshine, making the panelled room look dark and heavy, and the carved oak four-poster with its muted tapestry hangings looked wildly uninviting.

'There's a bed in the dressing room.' Cat indicated

the connecting door in the carved oak panelling with a sharp dip of her bright head, letting him know she had no intention of sleeping with him, tonight or any other night for that matter. 'No *en suite*, I'm afraid, but there's a bathroom next door down the corridor. I'll unpack my stuff later. And we're going to have to discuss the divorce; you can't keep sweeping it under the carpet and pretending it isn't an issue,' she warned bleakly.

She swung on her heels and was saved from whatever he might have come back at her with by the ringing of his mobile, and she left as he was fishing the slim instrument from the breast pocket of his jacket and went down to have coffee with Bonnie.

Doing her best to force down a scone so as not to disappoint the woman who had been like a second surrogate mother to her for as long as she could remember, Cat listened to a much dramatised account of the trauma of Gramps's collapse and, pouring herself a second cup of coffee, eventually butted in with, 'You were wonderful; I dread to think what might have happened if you hadn't been here and kept your head—and you must be tired out. So why don't we have a simple salad for lunch? I'll throw one together. It's too hot and sticky to bother with anything cooked. And I won't be in for supper; I'll get something in town after I've been to visit Gramps. I don't know about my husband...' How that word stuck in her throat! 'You'll have to ask him.'

As if on cue, Aldo strode into the old-fashioned

farmhouse kitchen. Cat immediately shot to her feet. As Bonnie got up to make a fresh pot of coffee for him Cat told her in passing, 'I'll go and see what Dan's got to offer in the way of salad stuff,' and swept out, sparing Aldo the merest glance.

But that glance was enough to tell her that the phone call he'd received hadn't pleased him. Hoping it was a cry for help from the manager of one or other of his various business ventures, something only he could deal with, in person, this minute if not sooner, she left the house through the door in the utility room.

The midday heat was oppressive, but nevertheless Cat was glad of the breathing space. Her brain was apt to misbehave when she was around Aldo—she was either yelling at him or falling into his arms, and neither was in the least bit sensible.

Believing that a gentle amble around the garden, on familiar home territory, would help to settle her, she wandered along grassy paths between billowing herbacious borders glowing with rich, late-summer colour and through the clipped hornbeam tunnel. Coming at last to the round garden, she stared at the arching sprays of tiny white roses that surrounded the central sundial and her eyes filled with wretched tears.

It wasn't working. She felt like a displaced person. She was here in an English garden, part of her former life, part of her happy childhood, but her heart was stubbornly back in Tuscany. Maybe she had more Italian genes than she'd reckoned on.

Or was her heart really locked back in those few

short months when she'd truly believed the man she loved could and would begin to really care for her?

That kind of sloppy, sentimental line of thinking didn't deserve headroom—events had proved her wrong, with a vengeance—so she scrubbed her eyes with the back of her hand and headed purposefully on and found Dan in the potting shed.

He came in for a few hours each day, always had done for as long as she could remember, and he regarded the garden and everything in it as his own personal, jealously guarded property.

So she had to ask very politely and with a suitable note of deference, 'May I help myself to salad stuff?' If she'd gone to the kitchen garden and picked what she needed Dan would have sulked for days on end.

'You're back, then.' The elderly man's hands worked steadily on, placing salvia cuttings in pots of compost. ''Bout an hour ago Bonnie come down and told me your grandad's going to be all right; she didn't say nothing 'bout salads.'

'We've only just decided,' Cat explained, trying not to grin at his curmudgeonly tone. 'It's far too hot to cook lunch.'

'We're in for a storm.' It was as near as he would get to agreeing with anyone. About anything. The compost in the last pot tapped down to his satisfaction, he straightened his bent shoulders. 'I'll cut what's ready to be cut and take it up to the house. Should have asked sooner. I'll likely as not get a right soaking while I'm about it. So will you, if you don't hop it.'

Taking her dismissal gracefully, Cat stepped out into the humid air. Dan was a grumbler, he was famous for it, but what he didn't know about growing things wasn't worth knowing. Which was why everyone put up with him.

But he had a nice side, too, a side not many people got to see. He might dislike his fellow human beings, but watch him handle a seedling, or hear him give an encouraging pep talk to an ailing clematis, and he was like a tender father with a precious newborn!

The encounter had taken her mind off other things, cheered her in a funny sort of way, and far from taking Dan's advice she left the main garden and headed for the deep belt of trees that bordered the property on three sides.

There was a maze of narrow bark paths and they all eventually led to a secluded summer house. She would sit there and reflect on the way her life was going and get herself calm and collected before she had to face Aldo again and make him accept the fact that their doomed and unworkable marriage was over, and that taking her to bed to prove a point was unworthy.

And downright wicked, she grouched to herself as she felt her face go pink when she recalled how sinfully easily he had been able to do just that.

The first violent clap of thunder, sounding ominously close, had her momentarily frozen to the spot, and the almost simultaneous appearance of Aldo, heading her way from a different direction, had her practically leaping out of her skin.

Altogether she was in no fit state to voice any objections when he caught her hand and pulled her in the direction he had come from, and he sounded as if he was almost enjoying this, as if the storm dovetailed with his mood when he said, 'I just passed a round hut arrangement. We can sit this out.'

The open-fronted summer house—Cat recognised his description as the first heavy drops of rain penetrated the leaf canopy. They made it just before the heavens opened, penning them in with a solid curtain of water. He had taken time to change into narrow-fitting, worn jeans and a darker blue T-shirt and he looked absolutely spectacular, his staggeringly attractive lean features lit up by a blinding flash of lightning, the spiky black lashes adding a *frisson* of mystery to his dark, unreadable eyes.

'Alone at last, no interruptions, nowhere to go. Time to talk?' She heard the dry mockery in his voice and shivered. Cat knew exactly what he meant. This, at last, was the right time and place.

She had many precious, happy memories of this place. Alone or with her friends from school. The summer house had doubled as an enchanted castle, an ogre's cave, a fort to be defended from marauding Red Indians, a place for lavish picnics provided by Bonnie or, as she'd reached her teens, simply a place to sit alone and daydream.

It seemed a shame to spoil all those wonderful memories by adding a vile one that would smother and choke all the others. But, she reminded herself tartly, this was no time for sentimentality.

Feeling cold and strangely leaden, Cat sat in the middle of the bench seat that curved around the outer wall, stingingly aware of the suddenly intense way he was looking at her. Waiting.

She stared fixedly at the wall of rain.

Swallowing uncomfortably, her pulses racing as she took the plunge, she dragged in a deep breath and reminded him quietly, 'Neither of us pretended to be in love with each other when we married.'

She had to be fair about that. He had never been less than honest on that score. And for her part she had kept silent about the way she felt because he'd told her that he didn't want the emotional upheaval that would crash around his head if he married a woman who was in love with him because he would be unable to return it, and he didn't want that kind of complication.

'I could accept that,' she admitted heavily.

Accept it because, naïvely, she had really believed she could change it.

And now for the words that would force him to understand why their marriage was dead and couldn't be healed by the gift of a pretty jewel or his spectacularly passionate lovemaking. It would be an ending. Final. Her throat closed over the words. She felt empty.

Hugging her arms tightly around her body, as if she was defending herself against something unspeakably dreadful, she forced it out in a voice that was tense in the effort to hold her feelings back. 'As your wife I expected—deserved—your respect and fidelity. You gave me neither. As soon as you knew I was pregnant, you took off with your mistress.'

She heard the sharp tug of his breath and slid in quickly because she knew her carefully contained control would shatter into a million screaming pieces if he tried to lie his way out of this—and, God help her, she might let herself be fooled into believing him! 'Do you remember that dinner party you gave soon after our honeymoon?'

He didn't answer that; she hadn't expected him to. This wasn't a normal conversation. She tried to look relaxed and made a conscious effort to fold her hands loosely together in her lap.

He settled himself on the bench at her side but made no attempt to touch her, and she couldn't bear to look at him although she could feel those bitter-chocolate eyes on her stoically expressionless features.

She couldn't afford to betray herself, let him know how much she was hurting inside. She had to keep all those rioting emotions firmly at bay, pretend she was talking to a stranger about something not particularly important. Cool, matter-of-fact statements delivered without bitterness or anger was the way to play this.

'Iolanda told me she was your mistress. She was quite civilised about it, of course, and explained that such an arrangement was considered normal and acceptable by men such as yourself. Men who marry for dynastic reasons.'

The quality of his watchfulness had changed, hardened. She had felt it as soon as she'd mentioned the other woman's name. He'd been caught out and naturally enough he didn't like it and was going on the defensive. So be it. She sighed softly, even though she hadn't meant to.

'I didn't find it at all acceptable. I guess I'm not sophisticated enough to take that sort of behaviour in my stride. But I didn't believe her, not then, even though you started to treat me like a house guest in daylight and at night time like a whore.

'Then things really changed. Everything began to slot together. I got pregnant. You moved to another room. You stayed away for days on end. You'd done your duty as you saw it. Then the miscarriage. I got hidden away...'

Her voice had wavered; she swallowed sharply, annoyed with herself for allowing even a hint of emotion to show through, and retrieved her former even tone. 'And while I was kicking my heels in luxurious isolation you and Iolanda had a couple of months together—until it was time for you to come back and try to get me pregnant again.'

She pulled in a deep breath. Her fingers, she noted, were knotted tightly together, a sure sign of inner tension. She straightened them out, kept them clasped loosely together in her lap again and wondered why he was just sitting there as if he'd been turned to stone, saying nothing.

And told him, 'Even then I wasn't absolutely sure. I had no real proof that she'd been telling the truth until that night. I couldn't sleep. It was the early hours of the morning by the time I decided that I had to ask you for the truth. She was coming from your room. She left me in no possible doubt about what you'd both been doing. As your wife, I believe I deserved more respect, better treatment than that.'

She had done it, Cat congratulated herself bitterly. He wouldn't have a clue how deeply and permanently he'd hurt her, how she'd bear the scars for years to come. She had, at least, salvaged her pride. But the victory was a great, hollow ache inside her and she wanted to vent all the pent-up pain and emotion in his direction but knew she couldn't do that and be able to walk away from this marriage with her head high.

There was a truly stark silence. Nothing but the now distant rumble of thunder, the rain hitting the canopy of the trees.

It was desperately unnerving. Cat had fully expected him to try to wriggle out of this. After all, those rogue shares were at stake—or so he believed. So why wasn't he telling her she'd got it wrong? Repeating the excuses he'd given to her grandfather for his long neglect of her, telling her that Iolanda had been lying, promising to punish his blabbermouth mistress by giving her the sack?

After all, willing mistresses would be ten a penny in his rarefied stratosphere. Wives who came packaged with a bunch of coveted shares weren't all that thick on the ground.

Cat ventured a sidelong glance. His bronzed skin was abnormally pale, his jaw rock-hard, and there was not a shred of warmth in those furiously narrowed black eyes. As if the turning of her head had sparked off some terrible rage inside him, he rose to his feet, shot her a look of compressed loathing and stalked out into the rain, his dark head high and proud, the atmosphere around him positively smouldering.

Pressing her fingers against her trembling mouth, Cat stopped herself from venting a cry of anguish. She started to shiver. Apart from lust she had just witnessed the first gut-wrenchingly real emotion Aldo had ever experienced for her.

Anger. Plain, old-fashioned, explosive anger.

In his eyes, she translated, she hadn't measured up. It was as simple as that. She was neither docile and cowed enough, nor sophisticated and blasé enough to shut her eyes to his extra-marital activities. She had made a fuss, demanded a divorce. That sort of reaction didn't fit with his idea of a marriage of convenience.

And the telling fact that he hadn't tried to shoot her accusations out of the water, convince her that Iolanda had been lying her socks off, invent a credible

excuse for the wretched woman's presence in his bedroom, only emphasised the truth. He wasn't going to
lie about his affair with Iolanda. She, Cat, simply
wasn't worth the indignity of his having to do that.

And the swamping waves of desolation that engulfed her as she wrapped her arms around her trembling body just went to show what an abject fool she
was.

She hadn't known it before, but she knew it now.
In her heart of hearts she had secretly hoped that he
would have moved heaven and earth to convince her
that he'd never had an unfaithful thought in his head,
much less acted on it.

Half an hour later Cat walked slowly back to the
house through what was now a steady drizzle.
Slipping in through the utility room, she found
Bonnie in the kitchen.

'Oh, there you are! Dan told me he'd warned you
a storm was coming.' She eyed Cat's damp clothes,
the copper curls that clung to her skull, with an expression more reminiscent of sorrow than of anger.
'At least you didn't get as drenched as the *signor*.
He's gone up to change. You'd better do the same
while I see to lunch.'

'Bonnie—' Cat thrust her own troubles to one side;
the older woman looked tired out, wisps of grey hair
had escaped from her normally neatly tight bun and
her shoulders drooped '—I'll do it. Why don't you
go to your room and catch up on some rest?' she

suggested softly. 'You must be bushed. I'll bring you a cup of tea in a couple of hours or so.'

'Well…' Bonnie looked doubtful, but did confess, 'I wouldn't mind putting my feet up for half an hour. I haven't been able to sleep for the worry.'

'There's nothing to worry about now; Gramps is going to be fine,' Cat affirmed gently. She put her arm round the housekeeper's sagging shoulders and walked her to the door. 'So you can catch up on all that lost sleep with a quiet mind.'

She would be needed here for several weeks, if not months, Cat recognised as she watched Bonnie slowly head for her room. The housekeeper was no longer young and Gramps would need lots of TLC when he came home. Aldo wouldn't want to stay around for an indefinite period and he wouldn't be able to insist she return to Italy, not under these circumstances.

Not that he would want to do either, she reminded herself dully as she headed slowly up to the guest room. The look he'd turned on her as he'd stalked out of the summer house left her in no doubt that he actually hated her.

As if the breakdown of their marriage was entirely her fault!

The knot of dread in the pit of her stomach tightened unbearably as she approached the guest room. Her heart was thumping as she pushed on the door, her head spinning dizzily at the thought of having to face him, encounter that anger head-on.

She had had enough, she thought wildly, pressing

the tips of her fingers against her throbbing temples. She couldn't cope with any more. The loss of her baby, Aldo's infidelity, the shock of Gramps's heart attack—she couldn't hope to handle the rank unfairness of being made to feel responsible for the breakdown of her marriage on top of all that!

The bedroom was empty, she noted with a strange sense of anticlimax, nothing to show signs of anyone having been here except for her unpacked suitcase at the foot of the looming four-poster.

And then he walked through the connecting door and her heart stood still for long, breath-depriving moments then raced on, tumbling about inside her chest. He had changed into a dark, beautifully cut business suit. He looked intimidatingly handsome, intimidatingly cold. He looked through her.

Cat's head started to spin. There was a roaring sound in her ears and her throat went so tight she felt she was being strangled by unseen, vicious hands. She swayed on legs that were suddenly the consistency of jelly, put out a hand seeking support and, finding nothing but thin air, she staggered.

Aldo gave an impatient hiss. '*Perfetto!*' he grated on a note of deep, sarcastic exasperation as he dropped the case he was carrying and covered the distance between them in three loping strides. Strong arms caught her, holding her upright. 'Trust a woman to pick her moment!' he gritted in a fierce undertone as he lifted her bodily and placed her with not too much reverence on the bed.

Hands on his lean hips, he stared down at her with impatient eyes. 'I have the jet on standby, I have to drive the hired car back to Birmingham and you pick this moment to stage a collapse! *Dio!* Just look at you!'

Cat's eyes were swimming with weak tears, so she couldn't be sure, but she thought she saw his black eyes suddenly soften with compassion. She only knew she didn't want him to go. Which was nothing if not perverse of her, she knew that much, but she couldn't do anything about the panicky feeling of loss that came out of nowhere and utterly overwhelmed her.

'Are you leaving?' Of course he was. But she had to be sure. Maybe she'd misheard him.

'Naturally,' he said flatly, his eyes turning to flint. 'It is what you say you want. And, since you are unable to give me what I need from this marriage, it is what I want also.'

What he needed! Her blessing on his extra-marital activities! A sob choked her and the tears escaped, pouring down her ashen cheeks.

Frowning down at her, he muttered something that sounded very rude and ground out, 'You need attention. I will ask Bonnie to come to you.'

'No!' Cat tried to get herself upright, failed in the attempt, and flopped weakly back against the pillows. 'Bonnie's resting,' she muttered, ashamed of her body's wimpish descent into feebleness. 'She's worn out. And I'm fine.'

'You are far from fine,' he uttered in a voice so

cold it sent shivers down her spine, his eyes narrowing as they swept over her. Then he made a sound like a man who had just received a hefty punch in the stomach. '*Dio!* What am I to do with you?'

He sat on the edge of the bed and took her icy hands between his, gently rubbing warmth back into them. A warmth that spread its seductive tendrils all through her body. There was a rough note in his voice as he murmured, 'Events have overtaken you. That is what has happened. One way and another, you've been through a lot, been so brave and strong, and now it has all caught up with you. It is to be expected.'

Brave and strong? Cat's eyes went wide as she tugged her hands from his. If she'd had any courage, any strength at all, she would have refused to marry him in the first place! She would have put the painful pangs of unrequited love down to experience and got right on with her life!

'Don't be stubborn,' Aldo chided gruffly, recapturing her hands and exerting a brief gentle pressure before lifting them and looping her arms around the back of his neck. 'Listen to your body; it is telling you that you need to rest and relax, take time out.'

It was telling her no such thing! Cat thought on a shudder of despair. It was telling her she still wanted this man, loved him in spite of everything.

She must have done something unforgivable in a previous existence to warrant this kind of punishment, she decided bleakly. And as her eyes drank in the masculine magic of his hard bone structure, the harsh lines around that long, sensual mouth that told of internal strain, the dark, dark eyes, her limp fingers took on a life of their own and slid eagerly into the warm luxury of his hair.

Briefly, his eyes swept down to fasten on her parted, tremulous lips and then he said tightly, 'Hang on to me; I will lift you. Then you will be able to get out of your wet clothes more easily.'

In one smooth movement he had lifted her to her feet, his hands clamped on either side of her waist. Her arms still looped tightly around his neck, she could feel his body heat through the damp layer of her clothing, inhale the fresh and tangy, enticing male scent of him and see every individual lash that so lushly framed those spectacular bitter-chocolate eyes.

A hopeless little cry was wrung from her as she pressed her weary body closer to his. Fully aware that she was being ridiculous, she could do nothing about the driving need to hold him for just one more time.

Their marriage was over and, for all she knew, she would never see him again, so was one final brief moment of closeness really too much to ask, if only for the sake of the sadness they had both shared when she'd lost the little life they had created together?

'Don't!' he commanded with harsh warning as he swiftly released her hands from their stranglehold around his neck. 'Don't cling. You may be hungry for the only thing I could ever give you but I have lost my appetite. Get out of those wet clothes,' he instructed tersely as she raised stricken green eyes to his. 'Or do I have to do it for you? And if you're really that incapable then I shall phone for a doctor before I go.'

'Shut up!' she snapped nastily, the import of what he'd been saying hitting her brain like a sledgehammer. Did the conceited so-and-so really think she'd been begging for sex? When all she'd wanted—silly, misguided, sentimental fool that she obviously was— was to hold him for one last time, mark their final parting with softness instead of bitterness. 'Just go; I don't need you hanging around like a wet weekend,' she blistered unfairly. 'I can look after myself.'

'You have made a swift recovery,' Aldo commented with withering dryness. He picked up his abandoned suitcase and glanced at the watch that graced his flat, bronzed wrist. 'I am running short of time. But before I go,' he said with flat finality, his cold black eyes making a swift inventory of her face and body, as if checking whether she was fit to be left on her own, 'I advise you to keep the news of our impending divorce from your grandfather, at least until he has made a full recovery. I will handle everything from my end. I'll phone now and then to check on his progress.'

And left. Just like that.

Left her staring at the space where he had been, harbouring the first thought, which was that she would never see him again. And then the second, which was that he obviously wasn't afraid of her laying claim to a great chunk of his assets and losing, as he imagined he would, those wretched shares. That package of losses had been the sole reason for that previous statement when he'd vowed that he didn't let go of what was his, and that included her.

Somewhere along the line something had changed. He wanted rid of her at any price!

She had no idea how long she'd been standing there when the sound of the telephone in the hallway below brought her out of her miserable trance-like state.

Bad news from the hospital about Gramps? Oh, no, dear heaven, don't let it be that, she howled inside her head as she flew down the stairs. And her voice came out in a breathless rush as she lifted the receiver and gave the number.

'Pass me on to Aldo, please.'

Iolanda's tinkly voice! That was all she darn well needed!

'I was expecting him to return my earlier call. I know how difficult things are for him right now but it's personal and important. I've tried his mobile, but it's switched off.'

'Get lost!' Cat growled and replaced the receiver with a satisfying crash, then dropped to the floor and cried as if she would never stop.

CHAPTER EIGHT

ALDO would be arriving in less than an hour! She didn't know how she was going to be able to handle it!

As Cat glanced at her bedside clock her stomach leapt. She felt drained and distinctly nauseous again and she flopped down on the four-poster, sitting right on the edge, staring at her feet while she waited for the unpleasant sensations to subside.

His phone call, two days ago, had come as a shock. Not the call itself, because over the past three months he'd phoned fairly regularly for the sake of appearances, but because of what he'd said.

He always asked for information on her grandfather's progress then left the rest of the not very long conversation down to her. Idle babbling into an uninterested silence that had broken her heart all over again, but necessary if the pretence of a stable marriage was to be kept up for the benefit of Gramps's sharp ears at this end of the line.

But this time he'd said, 'Expect me in two days. Around seven on Wednesday evening. It's been over three months and Domenico is now strong enough to be told about the divorce. This situation can't go on any longer and it's best if we tell him together.

Presenting a united and civilised front will hopefully take the edge off what will come as an unpleasant shock.'

His voice had been so hard and impersonal. Just thinking about it set up a shivery reaction all over her body, made her battered heart ache. Trying to block the way he'd sounded out of her aching mind, she shot to her feet and crossed the room to draw the heavy brocade curtains to shut out the dark, mid-December evening.

She should be changing, not sitting around feeling sorry for herself. Gramps had said, 'Run along and pretty-up. You haven't seen Aldo for months—far too long in my opinion. So wear something glamorous and remind him of what he's been missing!'

Glamorous was out. All her designer gear was back in Italy. And even if it weren't, her mood tended more towards sackcloth and ashes. Gramps didn't know it yet, but Aldo wouldn't have missed her at all. He was as anxious for the divorce as she was, but for entirely different reasons.

Plucking a garment at random out of the wardrobe and fresh underwear from one of the drawers, she carried them to the bathroom and ran hot water into the huge, claw-footed Edwardian tub. Perhaps a long soak would calm her nerves, although she seriously doubted it.

As always, Aldo was right, she thought frustratedly as she lowered herself into the scented water. The time had come.

In the early days of his convalescence Gramps had unquestioningly accepted the fiction of the sudden business crisis that had necessitated Aldo's immediate return to Italy. But as he'd grown stronger and fitter and late summer had turned into late autumn she was sure he was harbouring suspicions.

'There's really no need for you to stay on,' he'd stated briskly as she'd accompanied him on his prescribed morning walk a couple of weeks ago. 'Don't think I'm not grateful for all you've done. I am. Truly. Hiring Mrs Peterson from the village to do the cleaning and laundry was a brilliant idea of yours, too. I'm a selfish old man, Caterina. I hadn't stopped to think that Bonnie's getting older as well. So, now we're all settled—thanks to you—and I'm feeling better than I have done in years, it's time you got back to your husband.'

Her excuses for staying on had been pretty thin but he'd had no option but to swallow them, particularly the one about her need to tag along when he had his appointment with his consultant, although he had protested that he didn't need a nursemaid.

The appointment had been and gone and he'd been given a clean bill of health, and the approach of the Christmas season had brought more probing questions. Would Aldo be joining them here, or would she be returning to Italy? And as for the holiday Aldo had promised himself and Bonnie, well, he was hugely looking forward to it. Some time in the coming spring would be nice.

So yes, it was time.

But she wished she'd taken the matter into her own hands before now, not left it to Aldo to decide when the time was right. As always, it seemed, he was the one to take the lead, leaving her to tag along behind.

Many times over the past few weeks the news of the breakdown of her marriage had hovered on the tip of her tongue. But always she'd held back. Something had stopped her from actually spelling the situation out. Not only because she had known it would really upset her grandfather—her reluctance to actually say the words and make it all official went deeper than that. She was sure it did, but for the life of her couldn't exactly say why.

And now she could hit herself for the lost opportunities. It could all have been done and dusted by now and Aldo wouldn't be on his way here to break the news in person. She didn't want to have to see him again. It would bring her far too much pain.

Belatedly aware of the remorseless passage of time, Cat dressed in a hurry and only fully realised when she checked herself in the mirror back in her bedroom that the dress she'd plucked so haphazardly from the wardrobe was the one she'd worn at their first, fatal meeting.

Too late to change now. In any case, what did it matter? she asked herself snappishly, taking extra care as she applied her make-up because her hands were shaking so badly. He probably wouldn't remember.

Why should he? He had only been interested in her grandfather's business proposition, not in her.

He had never been interested in her, she reminded herself grittily. And when he'd seduced her, that very first night, he'd probably shut his eyes and pretended she was Iolanda!

Cursing herself roundly for letting her nerves get her into this hyper state, she scowled at herself in the mirror, tucking straying strands of curly copper hair behind her ears, turned sideways and surreptitiously viewed her body profile.

There was just the smallest hint of a bulge, but nothing anyone would notice. Not yet. Just a soft roundness where before her tummy had been concave. Her heart turned to warm treacle and a tiny smile erased the former tension from her features for a few short moments as she placed a near-reverent hand over the tiny new life.

Her secret. Her baby.

History wouldn't repeat itself, she vowed fiercely. It would not! She would carry this baby to full term. She was taking good care of herself and her GP had told her, during her last sneaked visit, that everything was fine. The first three months were the tricky ones and they were already behind her.

Everything would be fine.

The only decision she had to make was whether or not she would ever tell Aldo he had a son or daughter. But that could wait; she'd think about the implications at some later date.

Feeling more reassured and in charge of her life than she'd felt since she'd received the shock phone call that had sent her into a state bordering on panic, she cast one last probing look at her reflection then went down to see if Bonnie, who was cooking up a storm, needed help in the kitchen.

'That was a truly splendid meal!' Aldo complimented Bonnie as the last crumb of her famous apple pie disappeared. 'No, don't get up,' he instructed warmly as the elderly housekeeper, dimpling with pleasure at the praise, made to rise from the table. 'Caterina and I will clear away and make the coffee.'

They had eaten in the library, the cosy book-lined room, the open log fire a good choice if relaxation was on the menu.

But Cat couldn't relax; she felt like a too tightly strung-up chicken just waiting to be roasted. Since his arrival Aldo had been behaving normally—too normally. She didn't understand why. Surely it would be better to get everything out in the open straight away. Why prolong the painful charade?

Fortunately, she'd heard the crunch of his hired car's wheels on the gravel before anyone else had. She'd been listening for the first sounds of his arrival until her ears had ached.

She'd wanted to warn him that Bonnie had insisted on cooking the fatted calf in his honour and that if he wanted to avoid having to sit through several courses, feeling awkward because their bombshell was still unexploded, then they'd better say their piece right now and then he could leave.

As he'd walked in out of the darkness, wearing that beautiful cashmere coat, his lean face was taut, his sensual mouth compressed. And he was carrying a soft leather suitcase, not a small one, either, and her warning fled out of her head, replaced by, 'Surely you don't intend staying here overnight!'

The narrowed eyes that swept over her tense body were dark with something she couldn't put a name to and she heard the rough intake of his breath, yet his response of, 'I don't intend sleeping in the potting shed, if that's what you have in mind,' was flat and dry.

'Use your brain, can't you?' she hissed, appalled by the scenario that presented itself. 'If you hang around until the morning Gramps will make us sit up all night while he busts a gut trying to get us to change our minds! Do you really want that?'

'Not particularly.' The skin over his harshly sculpted cheekbones tightened. 'Which is why I came prepared to stay. It will give us the opportunity to talk things out, in private, before we hit him with the divorce.'

Things? What things? Cat hopped from one foot to the other in agitation as he put down the case and removed his coat. Then it hit her. Of course! The size of the settlement he was afraid her lawyers would demand from his.

As she opened her mouth to reassure the avaricious

streak in him that wouldn't want to part with a single
lire, tell him that she wanted nothing from him, the
words were snatched right out of her mouth by
Bonnie's, 'I thought I heard something! Did you have
a good journey, *signor*?'

Grinding her teeth with frustration at the lost opportunity that surely would have had Aldo smartly
revising his plans, Cat gave up and went to the
kitchen on leaden legs, leaving Bonnie to show him
through to the library, where the round tripod table
was already laid for a lavish supper and Gramps
would be waiting.

Now, as she followed Aldo through to the kitchen,
clutching a pile of dishes while he carried the piled-
up plates, Cat saw her chance.

Tell him she wanted nothing from him and would
sign any papers to that effect, then they could break
their news and he could disappear. Where to, exactly,
was his problem. She couldn't bear to have him
around much longer. In spite of what he'd done he
still had the power to turn her will to water, to make
her want him, love him, reducing her self-discipline
to thin air.

And if he stayed overnight Gramps would expect
them to share the same room. There was always the
dressing room, of course, but even so—

But again the housekeeper put paid to any hopes
of her making the speech that would have him showing a clean pair of heels!

'No man does dishes while I have breath in my

body!' she carolled, swooping on Aldo's pile of plates. 'Domenico has been so looking forward to seeing you, *signor*; go through and keep him company and I will make coffee.' She was already rinsing plates at the sink, prior to stacking them in the dishwasher. 'Domenico and I will not have any. We'll retire and leave you two young things together.'

Since when had Bonnie used her employer's first name? She'd obviously been at the wine bottle, Cat thought sourly, uncomfortably remembering the quirk of Aldo's darkly defined brow when she'd refused wine herself.

He couldn't suspect, of course he couldn't, Cat told herself staunchly as Bonnie shooed him out of the kitchen. Her tummy was only a little rounder and the only real pointer to her condition was the way her breasts had grown, well, quite a lot fuller, actually.

Hoping he wouldn't have noticed that interesting fact, even though every time she'd looked up from her barely touched meal she had found those dark, unreadable eyes on her, she plugged in the kettle to make coffee and tried to close her ears to Bonnie's chatter, which largely centred on how ecstatic she must be to have her so handsome husband with her again.

'So there you are—I was just coming to see if you'd got lost!' Gramps huffed when Cat finally arrived with the loaded coffee tray. She began to force a smile so that he wouldn't guess that she'd had to steel herself to come back here at all but it faded as

Aldo rose to take the tray from her, one dark brow sardonically raised, his mouth flat and ungiving.

'I was just telling Aldo that it was high time he came over here and fetched you, since you wouldn't budge no matter how hard I tried to push you.' He turned to the younger man. 'She seems to think she's got to molly-coddle me and all the time she's been pining for you! Picks at her food and looks half-dead every morning. And if that's not pining, I don't know what is.'

Cat could have throttled him—he made her so furious! As far as Aldo understood it, pining away for him would be the last thing she would be doing. She had been the one to insist on a divorce. Therefore—Oh, it didn't bear thinking about...

She swung herself away from the pair of them, sitting in the winged armchair, facing the fire, cutting out her view of the quizzical golden light in the depths of Aldo's darkly speculative eyes.

'If I've been looking frayed round the edges,' she muttered from the depths of the chair, 'then you can put it down to having to run round you, making sure you keep to the regime of diet and exercise you've been given; left to your own devices, you'd be pigging out on cream cakes and fry-ups.'

'*Touché.*'

Cat heard the grunt of humour in the old man's voice as Aldo came to stand in front of her, holding out a coffee-cup. Raising her eyes to him, she silently pleaded, Tell him now! and he must have been able to read her mind because he simply shook his head and her decision to take the matter into her own hands and tell him herself, put an end to this senseless charade, was only half-formulated when her grandfather ruffled her hair, said a gruff 'Goodnight, see you both in the morning', and disappeared.

The ensuing silence, broken only by the crackle of the fire and the moaning of the cold winter wind around the old house, sizzled with tension. Then Aldo made his move and Cat's hands clenched into tight fists in her lap.

'So.' He dropped into the chair on the opposite side of the brightly crackling fire. He rested his elbows on the arms and steepled his hands, the pads of his long fingers touching his mouth. 'Where to begin?'

His endless legs were stretched out, the soft fabric of the narrowly cut trousers of his dark business suit moulding tautly muscled thighs. Too intent on trying to fight the ravaging effect the wretch always had on her to conjure up a sensible reply, Cat glared into the dancing flames, denying herself the self-defeating and painful satisfaction of looking at him at all.

'Nothing to say? You have changed!' he commented drily. 'Too ashamed of your behaviour?'

She pulled in a sharp, sudden and desperately painful breath. 'What did you say?' Stung by the utterly unforgivable unfairness of that remark, she bristled straight back at him, having to glue herself to the chair to stop herself from jumping up and strangling him. 'You are the one who should be ashamed!'

'In some respects, yes,' he drawled levelly. 'Which is partly why I am here now. You accused me of unspeakable things,' he added in a tone that told her that the dominant Italian male expected any woman he had elevated to the position of his wife should have had enough sense to hold her tongue, close her eyes to his philandering and be grateful for the honour of bearing his name.

Cat's green eyes went dark and narrow as she glared at him and pointed out, 'You didn't deny them.'

'Why should I demean myself?' he asked with quelling cool. 'You angered me almost beyond my ability to contain myself. I bitterly resented your low opinion of me. What you accused me of made me out to be worse than an animal. So I decided there and then that if you wanted a divorce, you could have it. If you couldn't give me what I wanted from our marriage—your trust—then I wanted no part of it either.'

Her browline knotted in a scowl, Cat recognised his devious male tactics. He was turning the tables, putting all the guilt onto her. Well, he wasn't going to get away with it!

She made a conscious effort to smooth her forehead and manufacture a chilling little smile, and came smartly back with, 'I almost forgot—silly me!—but shortly after you left me the lovely Iolanda phoned. She was expecting you to call back on some important and personal matter, apparently. Though I expect you've managed to sort it out; you have been back with her for over three months.'

For a few short moments his shatteringly gorgeous features were blank, as if he didn't know what she was talking about, and then he dismissed edgily, 'Oh, that. She had phoned me earlier, saying there was some problem back at Head Office. I told her to deal with it; that was what she was paid handsomely to do.

'Which brings me back to what I had started to explain before I got sidetracked. After I got Iolanda to confess to everything she'd said to you I dismissed her immediately. Even so, it took me some time to recover from the injury you'd dealt me. Then I began to see how you might have come to believe her. You were still fragile, your hormones all over the place, after that miscarriage. You would have been easy prey for a malicious woman who was deeply jealous of you. Though how she could possibly imagine that I would ever have thought of her as anything other than a first-rate assistant, I can't think.'

'You're saying she *wasn't* your mistress?' Cat slotted in between trying to grasp what he was saying, wanting so very badly to believe him, yet not quite daring to.

'I am saying you should have been able to trust me.' He gave her a dark, condemning look. 'And I'm saying that, finally, I can forgive that lack in you, at that time, due to the prevailing circumstances. My being away so much can't have helped your state of mind.'

Was he implying she'd gone loopy? Did he have that much gall?

Cat sat very upright as he got to his feet with the fluid grace that always made her breath catch in her throat and her knees go weak. She hated him for his ability to do that to her, loathed him for the way he was trying to lay all the blame on her!

She registered the slight clink of the neck of the wine bottle against glass and unthinkingly shook her head when he handed one of the glasses to her, missing the slight tightening of his mouth as he replaced it on the dinner table and took up a looming, straddle-legged position in front of the hearth.

'I came here with the intention of giving you moral support when we told Domenico of our plan to divorce. But when I saw you again—my frame of mind had calmed sufficiently to make me wonder if I should ask you if we could try to make something of our marriage.' He targeted her muddled mind with the deadly accuracy of a cruise missile.

And it took long moments of his dark, unwavering, questioning scrutiny for her to emerge from the chaos of his making and come back with a cynical, 'I see. You'd rather put up with me than miss out on my grandfather's shares and have to shell out a considerable sum by way of a settlement.'

'Don't be so ridiculous!' he grated with formidable

fury, the cool he had maintained throughout this disappearing at the speed of light.

He slammed his wineglass down on a side-table and swung round to glare down at her. 'Before I even laid eyes on you, you idiot woman, Domenico told me that he had changed his will and that his shares would eventually come back to me, to the family, where they belonged, irrespective of whether we married or not. He also told me that you knew of this.

'I tried to change his mind because I considered that he was behaving like a barbarian, but he was adamant. Apparently, he felt ashamed for having cut loose all that time ago, taking his share of the profits without doing a stroke of work for the family business, and he wanted to make reparation. All this,' he blistered forcefully, 'because I had responded to his idea of a marriage of convenience with the doubts that any modern young woman would give such an archaic concept any headroom at all. He said he'd put the right kind of pressure on you; you would either have nothing, or everything. And when it comes to that, when have I ever been less than generous to you? A divorce settlement would not cause me to lose a wink of sleep.'

Stark incomprehension tightened his savagely beautiful bone structure. 'Is there any sin you won't happily accuse me of? *Madonna mia*—I am not a greedy man. I don't ask for your love, only for your trust, which you are patently unable to give! Do you have any idea at all how much I resent all this? How it makes what we did have together tawdry and worthless?'

Cat's brain was spinning out of control as she tried to put what he'd been saying into some kind of logical order. Who was really to blame for what had happened? She could no longer be sure. Was that what this was all about? The steady stream of counter-accusations, designed to make her feel humble and guilty? And why on earth did he want to keep their marriage intact if—?

'But I have changed my mind; you will not be consulted on the subject.' He interrupted her frantic thought processes with a voice that was now as cool as ice. 'There is no question of a divorce. You are pregnant.'

Filled with horror, Cat felt her body shrink into the chair. How could he possibly know? It was the last thing she needed. She hadn't yet decided whether to eventually let him know he was to become a father or not. Was even this to be taken out of her hands?

'What do you mean?' she managed with what felt like the last feeble breath in her body.

'Pregnant? How to explain it?' He made an insulting pretence of sinking into deep thought. 'Having conceived. With child. Will that do?' he asked with a lazy drawl that made her heart clench with a greedy need to slap his handsome, arrogant face.

'I know what it means—don't treat me like a fool!' She snatched at what little composure she had left.

'What I meant was, why would you think I'm pregnant?'

'Oh, this and that.' He rocked on his heels, thrusting his hands into his trouser pockets. 'I remember how it was for you for the two months you carried our first baby. The bouts of nausea in the early mornings, your commendable insistence on avoiding all alcohol. And you have gained weight.'

'Eating too much.' She tried to dismiss that with an airiness that didn't quite come off and solidified into a lump of dismay in her chest when he reminded her,

'According to Domenico you merely pick at your food, so that won't wash.' His following and utterly scathing, 'With your history you should be constantly monitored. I don't suppose you've even bothered to see your local GP.'

'I have!' Stung by the implication that she was uncaring enough to neglect any aspect of the welfare of the precious child she was carrying, she sprang to her feet, her eyes blazing in the parchment pallor of her face. 'I have!' she repeated furiously. 'And everything's just fine!'

The swift flash of triumph in the depths of those stunning eyes had her shaking like a leaf. She had just unthinkingly given him the truth, all the leverage he needed.

The hard curving of his sensual mouth made her knees wobble and confirmed her opinion even before he said with derisive contempt, 'I will not do you the dishonour of suggesting the child you carry is not mine. And as its father I insist we stay married. My child deserves both mother and father. And be warned, if you persist in starting divorce proceedings I will move heaven and earth to have custody.'

Tears fell then, sliding down her cheeks. And she was too numb with the shock of what he'd said to avoid the hand he raised to gently brush the moisture away. 'Go to bed,' he advised softly. 'I won't disturb you when I come up. Tomorrow we will talk again.'

He dropped a light kiss on her forehead, a kiss that actually shocked her because she had expected nothing remotely caring from him. 'Go now. Sleep.' And she went, heavily, like a very old woman. She didn't know what she felt. Just that, as before, she was a captive wife.

Held captive in the beginning by her hope that he would grow to love her as she loved him.

Now she was to be held captive by their coming child.

CHAPTER NINE

WRIGGLING irritably, Cat made yet another determined effort to get comfortable, but the Jacobean four-poster bed seemed to have sprouted lumpy rocks and jagged hollows all over the place.

By her reckoning several hours must have passed since, with her head buried under the elaborately quilted bed cover, she'd heard Aldo walk quietly through and firmly close the dressing-room door behind him.

He was only a matter of yards away, separated by a panelling wall and an unlocked door. If she listened hard, would she hear him breathing?

Jerkily, she pushed at the quilt and soft woollen blankets. She was much too hot. She couldn't seem to breathe properly, either. And her brain wouldn't be quiet and let her get to sleep. Hazy plans that had hovered on the periphery of her mind ever since she'd learned of her pregnancy coalesced into startlingly vivid clarity now that it was all much too late.

She could have moved back into the flat above her workshop, created a comfy nest for herself and her baby, taken up her abandoned career. At least she could have designed and made the pieces and farmed them out for someone else to sell. Supported herself and her child—no domineering input from a husband who merely put up with her—and hopefully saved enough so that when the time came and she had to move out she could afford to rent half-decent premises somewhere.

But that wouldn't have been fair on either Aldo or their child, one of the conflicting, argumentative and sleep-denying voices that had taken up residence in her head reminded her starkly.

To deny him knowledge of his child would have been despicably selfish, she had to admit, she thought guiltily. If she lived to be a million years old she could never forget how ecstatic he'd been when after missing a period she'd done a home test, secretly had it confirmed and was able to announce that they were having a baby. Or his stark grief when she'd lost the little life they'd both held so precious at ten weeks.

She sat up amid the muddle of tangled bed covers and dragged her fingers through her already wildly rumpled hair. She'd had no right to think, even for one moment, that she could keep their baby's existence from him. As usual, he was right; a child needed both parents. And they could rub along fairly amicably, provided he didn't replace Iolanda with someone of her ilk.

So had he definitely not had an affair with Iolanda, then? That question still actually needed answering. All that anger at her lack of the trust that he said was so important to him could have been the natural reaction of a man who was stuffed full of arrogant

Italian pride. He would grind anyone who didn't consider him to be perfect to dust beneath his heel.

And yet—there were other aspects of what he'd said to her that needed clarifying. Aspects which, now she'd had time to properly think about them, offered a newly emerging green shoot of hope.

There was no time like the present. Get the clarification she needed and maybe, just maybe, she'd be able to get some sleep.

Slipping her feet to the floor, with her heart hammering away at the base of her throat, she dragged the quilt off the bed and covered her naked body and headed for the connecting door.

As she pushed on the smooth wood she cringed inside and she felt dizzy enough to lose her balance and fall in a heap. Was this really the right thing to do? Or would it be better to wait until the morning?

But there had been too many occasions when she had stubbornly held her tongue, her pride not allowing her to ask questions.

Too many occasions when he'd shut her out, made her feel surplus to requirements. If there was to be any hope of making their marriage work on any level at all she had to know if the tiny bubble of hope was worth harbouring and cosseting or whether a few terse words from him would prick it and reduce it to nothing.

Whatever, she needed answers, didn't she? And she needed them now!

With her breath lodged beneath her breast bone and

her legs feeling distinctly shaky she pushed the door
fully open. Aldo hadn't bothered to close the curtains
and moonlight fell directly onto the narrow bed.

He seemed to be soundly sleeping. Cat moved tentatively forward, the quilt dragging behind her, conscious that she was holding her breath.

He was facing her, moonlight emphasising the
planes and angles of his stunningly gorgeous features,
heightening the contrast between his dark hair, the
thick twin crescents of his lashes and the olive tones
of his skin.

One arm lay over the top of the down-filled duvet,
exposing a hard, muscled shoulder. Cat took a deep
breath, reached out and gently shook it, and caught
in another breath, more ragged than the first, as the
contact between her skin and his had the all-too-
familiar electrifying effect.

'You want something?' He sounded fully alert, his
black eyes immediately opening, pinning her with
lancing intensity.

Cat withdrew her hand as if she'd been scalded and
backed off a pace. He must have been awake all the
time, watching her tentative approach through the
thick screen of his black lashes, waiting while she
plucked up the courage to lean over and touch him.

He was proving himself to be a dab hand at putting
her at a disadvantage, she thought, not knowing
whether to laugh or to cry. She moistened her dry-as-
desert-sand lips, swallowed the strange lump in her
throat and answered, 'To talk?' and it came out as a

quavery question and nothing at all like the impera-
tive she had intended.

'Sure. Why not?' he drawled lazily, hoisting himself up against the pillows and shifting over. 'Sit
down—unless you'd like to climb in with me. It's a
bit narrow, but we'd manage.'

Manage what? Cat wondered hysterically, her eyes
glued to his hard, muscular torso. To have sex?
They'd always managed that, no problem!

'I'll sit,' she said in a prim, tight voice and hoped
the cold wash of moonlight would bleach out the hectic colour that was making every inch of her skin
burn. She lowered herself gingerly to the very edge
of the bed, her legs getting tangled in the heavy folds
of the smothering quilt.

'This is not a social visit, I take it?'

'It's not funny,' she chided huffily. The undertone
of amusement she'd detected in his smooth drawl
wasn't making this any easier.

'Perhaps not. But it could be fun.'

'Don't!'

'Don't what?'

'Be so flippant.'

She watched his eyes narrow, felt the mental distance he now put between them, and when he asked
coldly, 'Then tell me how I'm supposed to react when
the woman who has literally accused me of being a
monster and tried to hide the fact that I am to be a
father pays a visit in the small hours,' she shuddered
as a wall of ice washed right the way down her spine.

This wasn't going to plan. She could almost hear the air hissing out of that brave little bubble of hope. He was making her out to be a really vile person, someone that any man in his right mind wouldn't want to know.

Averting her eyes, shrinking deeper into the smothering quilt, she finally got out what she'd found the courage to come and ask. 'Why did you marry me?'

One long, aching silence. Then, on a snap that sounded suspiciously defensive, 'You know why.'

'No, I only thought I did.' Cat ventured a sidelong glance at him. His arms were folded high over his impressive chest, his tough, shadowed jawline clenched. He looked very far from relaxed.

But this was too important a point to be merely shrugged aside; it could affect the whole of the rest of their lives together.

So she elaborated quietly, 'I thought,' she stressed gently, 'that you'd looked at what was on offer—the property and shares that would come to me eventually—and decided you were on to a good thing. You did tell me on that very first meeting of ours,' she reminded, in case he happened to have forgotten, 'that a man in your position looked for a wife who would bring something of substance to the marriage, that family honour and sound financial sense demanded it.'

She turned to face him fully, grabbing at the quilt that was sliding off one shoulder, and stated firmly, 'But I was wrong, wasn't I? Because before you so much as set eyes on me you knew you would get those shares, as well as everything else, because Gramps had already told you. You had no need to marry me to get what you wanted. You knew that, so why did you?'

Disconcerted wasn't in it. His narrowed, moody eyes flicked to her and away again and the skin tightened over his slashing cheekbones.

Cat shuffled just a little bit closer and, her skin dampening with the tension of wondering if maybe she'd got her wires crossed, pressed home this rare advantage. 'And apparently it wasn't because you'd taken one look at me and fallen madly in love. You're not into that sort of delusory nonsense, or so you were at pains to point out. Or did you change your mind on that score?'

She was actually coming out with it and asking if maybe, just maybe, he'd married her for love, and a million butterflies were whirling around inside her tummy as she waited for his response.

It came almost immediately. 'I took one look at you and wanted you naked and in my bed!' he sliced at her in a charged undertone. 'I wanted you like hell! Satisfied? Is that what you wanted to know?' he demanded rawly. 'You know exactly what I'm talking about because that night your eyes told me you felt the need, too.'

Dark colour stained his taut features as he told her grimly, 'I agreed to visit Domenico when he eventually contacted me after the deaths of his sister and his wife. It was obvious that he wanted to heal the rift with my side of the family and I guess I felt sorry for him and wanted to facilitate that. As for that proposed arranged marriage, well, I wrote that off as an old man's pipedream. But when I saw you I knew I had to have you whenever I wanted you, and if that meant agreeing to what I'd considered—right up until that moment—Domenico's lunatic idea of an arranged marriage, then so be it.'

'So you seduced me.' Cat's voice was flat. She hadn't liked the sound of what he'd said. He certainly hadn't given the answer she'd so desperately hoped for. That the sexual chemistry between them had been immediate and explosive wasn't in any doubt, but she had wanted—hoped—he might have confessed to something deeper.

With a harsh sigh Aldo admitted, 'I am not proud of myself for that. For the first time in my life my hormones got the better of my common sense,' he tossed out disgustedly. 'I behaved like a callow youth pumped full of testosterone.'

'Yet that night was the most wonderful experience of my life,' Cat said softly, gently reassuring, because it actually physically hurt her to hear him putting himself down. 'And it got better.'

'So it did.' He shot her an underbrow look, then, his hard mouth curling with a mixture of contempt and derision, 'Until you believed Iolanda's lies.'

Cat's soft mouth dropped open. He had finally admitted the foul woman had lied! That was good enough for her! She wanted to fling her arms around him, kiss him until he didn't have an ounce of breath left in his body.

Instead she contained herself with quivering difficulty and asked sympathetically, 'How did the lying harpy get herself into your room that night? What sort of excuse did she make up?'

His dark eyes found hers, held for long, sizzling moments before he huffed in a deep breath, expelled it on a slow sigh and asked gently, 'Does that remark mean you finally get to trust me?'

Cat nodded violently, too choked to utter a single word, despising herself for letting the malicious lies of a jealous woman poison their relationship. Her emerald eyes welled with emotional tears as he reached out and took her hand.

Then he shifted on the pillows and his face lit up with the type of grin that sent her heart soaring into orbit. 'I was already deeply annoyed with the wretched woman! For the way she'd spoken to you, the way she invited herself to stay—an invitation she would have had to take right back again if you hadn't jumped in and endorsed it.

'Then you'd tipped me out of your bedroom and the planned happy reunion with my wife was turning into a farce and I couldn't sleep for wanting you and wondering what was going wrong, and telling myself to give you more time because you obviously weren't over the loss of our baby, and in walks my personal assistant, as good as naked, bleating about being restless, having a headache. I told her to get the hell out, grabbed a pack of painkillers from the night-table drawer and threw them at her. I also told her to be ready to leave first thing in the morning.'

He lifted her hand to his lips and placed a kiss in the palm, not taking his eyes off her widening, watery gaze. 'I had no idea you'd seen her—how could I have if you didn't tell me? And as there's no way I'm going to let you turn your back on our marriage you're going to have to air any grievances—real or imagined—that might crop up in the future. Promise me?'

She nodded, the tears spilling over. She'd been such a fool, she castigated herself. If she hadn't bottled everything up inside her then none of this trauma would have happened. Their marriage hadn't been perfect and maybe she'd been greedy to expect that he would love her as she loved him. Which reminded her...

'Don't cry,' Aldo murmured gruffly, knocking her thought processes off line. 'There's nothing to be sad about. I forgive you,' he tacked on with an air of magnanimity that made Cat suppress an inner giggle and love him even more, warts and all. 'And now that's all out of the way, are we back on track?' he asked with what she could only describe as a suspiciously wolfish smile. 'If we are, I have no objections to you joining me, provided you get rid of whatever it is you're bundled up in. There's not room for it and us in here.'

The invitation was too tempting. Cat tried to resist for all of a full half-second then joyfully gave in, uninhibitedly dropping the quilt from around her naked body and sliding in beside him, every inch of her skin quivering helplessly as her body fused into the lean, hard length of his.

'There're just one or two more things.' She persisted in following her interrupted line of thought while she could still speak, arching her spine hedonistically as his arms came around her, fitting her more intimately against him, his mouth finding the tender hollow at the base of her throat while she struggled to find the words to complete what she'd started.

'If you hadn't tricked me into admitting I was pregnant, would you still have wanted to stay married to me?'

'But of course.' A soft line of kisses marked the delicate arch of her collar-bone. 'Why do you think I refused to listen when you kept rabbiting on about a divorce, and immediately changed my mind about giving you what you wanted when I saw you again and realised my damaged pride wasn't really worth sacrificing our marriage for? Discovering you were carrying my child gave me all the leverage I needed.'

Aldo hoisted himself up on one elbow, his eyes simmering down into hers, level and serious. 'The big question is,' with one gentle hand he brushed the tangled copper hair away from her forehead, 'we both made mistakes and put our marriage at risk. For my part, I've already forgotten them because I know you do now trust me. But are you happy to remain as my wife? No more talk of divorce?'

'Not unless you seriously annoy me!' She reached up and touched the unsmiling line of his mouth with delicate fingertips, but he didn't respond and she whispered, sincerity making her voice shake, 'Of course I want to stay with you! I wouldn't be here in this bed with you if I didn't.'

That verbal reminder of the way their naked bodies were practically welded together in the confined space sent each of her nerve-ends haywire. With a tiny gasp she fitted her hips into the cradle of his and wound her arms around his neck, dragging his head down, her full breasts pressed urgently against the broad expanse of his chest.

Cat felt his body shudder in response, but his mouth was a tight line still as she whispered against it, 'You said you weren't a greedy man. You didn't expect love in our marriage, but you did expect trust. Did that mean you wanted love, but weren't greedy enough to ask for it?'

Aldo's big body tensed. He unwound her hands from around his neck and dropped them. Hauling himself up against the pillows, he stared into space. He might have been turned to stone.

Cat held her breath, her heated flesh going cold. Had she got everything so very wrong?

She couldn't breathe for the dread of it until he said in a tone of deep aggravation, 'I gave myself away with that, didn't I just? *Madonna mia*—of course I wanted you to love me! I told myself I was marrying you because you were the first woman I'd ever wanted to own, to possess in every way possible. But, looking at you on our wedding day, I knew I felt something very different. Lust was a very small part of it. Love had crept up on me and hit me when I wasn't looking!'

'Why didn't you tell me?' Cat kept her voice suitably demure because the poor darling was obviously having a hard time right now and this wasn't the most sensitive moment to vent the ecstatic, triumphant shout that was bubbling up inside her.

'And make myself look ridiculous?' he questioned on a note of the male's savage impatience with the female's dim-wittedness. 'As far as you were concerned, you'd married me because otherwise you faced a rocky future. With no inheritance to count on to take your one-woman business into viability, you'd have to sink or swim on your own. So you took the sensible option. And let's face it, you knew the sex was good. Was I really expected to make a fool of myself and confess I was insanely in love with you?'

Cat could have made quite a few serious and highly voluble objections to that portrait of a woman who would sell her body for a life of idle luxury. And the bonus of great sex. But she wasn't going to argue the toss with him about anything. Not any more.

Instead she scrambled as upright as she could get without falling off the narrow bed, looked him straight in the eye and stated very firmly, 'I crashed headlong in love with you that first night. I knew I wanted to spend the rest of my life with you, loving you. You'd already said you didn't believe in the condition—' her wide mouth softened into a tender, understanding smile as she registered his involuntary flinch '—so I crossed my fingers and hoped you'd eventually change your mind about that chunk of masculine idiocy.' She leaned forward and put her lips against his shell-shocked mouth. 'I promise you, I'd have married you if you'd had no prospects and nothing but the clothes you stood up in.'

And then it happened. The golden gleam came back to those bitter-chocolate eyes, making the silvery wash of moonlight that surrounded them pale into insignificance. His strong arms wrapped lovingly around her as with one fluidly sexy movement he laid her back against the pillows and took her mouth with a kiss that was so achingly tender it made her want to weep with the total beauty of it.

She was weak with wanting him, with the insistent pulsing heat between her thighs. He was so beautiful, so hard, so sleek, so perfectly packaged. And he loved her, her heart sang ecstatically as she wrapped her legs around the hair-roughened length and strength of his and felt the needy, greedy response of him as his kiss deepened passionately and her body writhed feverishly against him.

'No! *Mi amore,* no!' With a harsh, driven cry, he put her gently away from him. 'What am I doing to you?' he uttered on a note of bitter self-castigation.

'We must remember our baby. Last time I was level-headed and unselfish and removed myself from temptation. Your gynaecologist had explained to me that sex was possible during the first three critical months but that it must not be—I think the word he used was excessive.'

He ran an unsteady yet infinitely loving hand from her temple to her jawline. 'I had no option but to move to another bedroom because our lovemaking has always been…excessive, *mia cara.*' He sighed with draining regret. 'You should return to your bed before I forget my good intentions. Yes?'

'No.' Cat trailed seductive fingers over hard, muscled flesh, following the line of crisp hair from his chest to the base of his sex, muting his raw groan of driven denial with her soft lips. 'The three months are already safely behind us and who knows how unexcessive we can be if we don't try? I promise you it will be all right,' she murmured as he shuddered in sharp response. 'If we take it nice and slowly.'

Nice was too insipid a word to describe his languorous and inevitable capitulation. It was something beyond heaven, Cat thought deliriously as Aldo covered her body with slow, luxurious, reverential kisses, and when he finally could contain himself no longer he entered her with slow, measured strokes that only intensified the almost unbearable pleasure, drawing it out until she exploded cataclysmically beneath him and afterwards, when their mingled sighs of draining satisfaction left them with breath to speak, he said proudly, 'I managed it, *mi amore*! I was not excessive and I think it was the most beautiful thing I have ever experienced. For you too, yes?'

'Oh, yes,' she breathed, still monumentally shaken by the whole loving experience, melting into boneless satiation as he enfolded her into his arms.

'How often I had wanted to hold you after making love with you. I never did quite dare because I knew that if I did I would end up revealing my true feelings for you.'

'Which are?' Cat mumbled through a deliciously sleepy smile, snuggling her head against his broad, accommodating chest.

'That I love you more than my life.' He nuzzled his cheek against the top of her head. 'And every day I will remind you of that, until you get sick of hearing it,' he warned.

Which will be never, Cat thought blissfully as she drifted off to sleep.

CHAPTER TEN

'YOU'RE spoiling me,' Cat said, smiling blearily through a tangle of copper curls as Aldo brought her late breakfast in bed.

'Just getting some practice in.' He gave her his wide, nerve-tingling grin as he settled the tray on her knees. 'I'm going to spoil you for the rest of my life, so get used to it.'

'Sounds good to me!'

Cat shifted slightly to make room for him to sit on the side of the narrow bed. As always, her gorgeous husband looked fantastic, good enough to eat, his lean, powerful body clad in a soft black cashmere sweater and a pair of beautifully cut stone-coloured chinos. Smooth, sophisticated, yet possessing a rawly lethal masculine sexuality and that air of natural command that set him head and shoulders above any other man she'd ever met and turned women's heads wherever he went.

And he was hers, and he loved her, he really loved her—life couldn't get any better!

'Is that all right?' He indicated the contents of the tray with a slight inclination of his glossy dark head. 'Bonnie and Domenico are out for a walk and the last I saw of the cleaning lady she was taking a flask of tea down to Dan in the greenhouse. There was no one around to ask what you managed to eat in the morning. Last time, I remember, you threw up at the sight of anything edible.'

Cat dimpled at the totally unprecedented note of hesitancy in her normally self-assured husband's voice. 'You've thought of everything,' she assured him, then burst out laughing when a flush of mortification spread over his unfairly handsome features as they surveyed his offerings together.

A glass of fruit juice, another of milk and yet another of bottled water. Two cups, a pot of coffee, a tiny pot of herbal tea, a single slice of toast and a boiled egg complete with a quilted cosy. A peeled and segmented orange in a glass dish.

Their eyes met and he joined her laughter. 'I might as well have added the kitchen sink,' he admitted as she wiped her eyes with the backs of her fingers, poured coffee for him and the herbal tea for herself.

'I haven't actually thrown up at all this time,' she confessed as she bit into the dry toast. 'I've sometimes felt a bit queasy in the mornings, and a bit down in the dumps—but that was more to do with the misery of facing another day, knowing everything had gone so dreadfully wrong for us.'

'I'm sorry, *mi amore*.' He reached out a hand and ran the backs of his fingers down the side of her face, regret deepening his husky voice. 'I should have been with you. I should have stayed and made sure we

thrashed the whole sorry subject out instead of leaving you alone, feeling betrayed and ill.'

'Not ill,' Cat assured him, melting under the sober
scrutiny of his darkly regretful eyes. 'Physically, I've
been feeling fine. Fit as a fiddle and as happy as a
lark now that we're together again and everything's
been sorted out.'

Well, not exactly everything, but the rest could wait
until later, she decided as he said, watching her with
eyes that were drenched with love again as she sliced
the top off her egg, 'You may feel fine, but we're
going to have to get you properly checked out. Does
Domenico know you're pregnant?'

'No, I haven't told anyone. And I have had a
check-up. I did tell you.'

Aldo brushed aside her input. 'Thoroughly checked
by your gynaecologist back in Florence. He knows
your history better than anyone.'

The authoritarian note was well and truly back in
evidence and Cat said meekly, 'Anything you say,'
and meant it because he had to be as concerned as
she was about their baby's continued safety, even
though, fingers crossed, she was pretty sure everything was going to be OK.

But later, as she was dressing, having sent Aldo
packing because time was racing by and his insistence
on running her bath, and soaping her all over, not to
mention patting every inch of her body dry, then
anointing every last pore of her skin with perfumed

body oil, had delayed things considerably, she wasn't quite so sure.

Sometimes the sheer terror of losing this baby came out of nowhere and sent her into a state of jibbering panic, despite the reassurances of the obstetrician she had seen privately when Gramps and Bonnie had thought she was on a shopping spree.

The waistband of the vivid scarlet needlecord jeans she had chosen soon wouldn't fasten round her middle. She laid a trembling hand over the small bulge, evidence of the precious new life that was growing inside her, and silently willed the unfounded dark pall of absolute terror to go away.

She had Aldo, had his love, and together they would see this through, Cat firmly reminded herself and felt immediately more secure and positive. She added a soft lambswool bright orange tunic top to give her back the courage she had momentarily lost, painted her lips a startling red and set off to find her hunky husband because being apart from him for ten minutes was proving to be ten minutes too long.

Her grandfather and Bonnie were taking their coats off in the hall as she walked down the stairs, their cheeks flushed with healthy colour from their walk in the fresh winter air.

Bonnie said, 'I'll go and make a start on lunch. Just a simple fish pie today.' She beamed cheerfully at Cat. 'Ask the *signor* if he'd like coffee. I'd ask him myself but he's just disappeared into the study with his mobile phone; I wouldn't want to disturb him.'

Another five minutes apart, Cat mourned, then sensibly decided she could just about manage that and said, 'I'm sure he'd like some. I'll help you, Bonnie.'

But Gramps said firmly, 'I want to talk to you in private, Caterina. I've been meaning to for some time now. The sitting room?'

Giving the housekeeper a wry, apologetic grin, Cat followed the remarkably spry figure of her grandfather into the sitting room, wondering what he needed to say that couldn't wait, and didn't find out because as soon as he'd settled himself in his favourite armchair at the side of the open fire Aldo walked into the cosy, chintzy room, his face lighting up with pleasure as his eyes homed in on her.

'I'll go and chase that coffee up,' the older man said tartly and unsettled himself again, stalking out of the room, and Aldo said, 'You are so bright and beautiful and I am so lucky.' And took her in his arms, wondering wryly, 'Was it something I did? Domenico is in a bad mood, yes?'

Nestling in the blissful comfort of his arms, Cat explained, 'It's nothing personal. He thinks you're Wonder Man with knobs on. He had something he wanted to say to me in private, but you walked in before he could come out with it.'

Unfazed, Aldo lifted her chin with a won't-take-no-for-an-answer forefinger and told her, 'If it's important we'll make sure he gets the privacy to get it off his chest before we have to leave,' and rained kisses on her eagerly responsive lips until she forgot all about it, and only when she remembered something else entirely did she pull away from him, look him straight in the eyes and tell him,

'Before we start on a new life together, I have a couple of conditions to make.'

'Conditions? You put conditions on the wonderful new life we are forging together?' His hands slid to her waist, pinioning her against him, his dark eyes gleaming with golden shafts of teasing light. 'I demand unconditional surrender!'

Gazing up into those laughter-filled eyes, the curving lines of his sensationally sexy mouth, Cat almost capitulated and vocalised the words of total surrender to his every whim that immediately sprang to mind.

Only when she had firmly reminded herself that now and then a woman—no matter how besotted she happened to be—had to show her man that she did have a mind of her own could she get out, 'I dress to please myself in future. I tried to look like a typically wealthy Italian's wife because I thought you'd expect it of me—tasteful designer gear in sophisticated, muted colours—and honestly it just wasn't me. I like bright things and—'

'You are the brightest thing in my life, *cara mia*,' he murmured softly. 'Whatever you wear you are beautiful. In fact,' still clasping her waist, he stepped back half a pace, his head tipped to one side as if in deep consideration, 'I definitely approve of those red trousers. Very sexy. And that orange top thing makes me very jealous.' His voice roughened hungrily. 'It touches your fabulous breasts. I want to change places with it.' His hands demonstrated his desire to do just that and Cat closed her hazy green eyes on a groan of uncontainable excitement, and when his mouth touched her parted lips she thought she might explode with the pleasure of what he could do to her.

Only reluctantly returning to reality when he stopped touching, stopped running tantalisingly soft kisses over her mouth and said wryly, 'Sadly, we must behave ourselves. You are tempting me to repeat our highly successful experiment of last night, *bella mia*! Think how we would embarrass your grandfather, and the estimable Bonnie would throw our coffee in the air and fall in a faint!'

He dropped one final kiss on the end of her nose and reminded her tenderly, 'Conditions, you said. Plural. So far you've only got around to talking about the way you intend to dress—which, by the way, I totally accede to.'

And whose fault was that? Taking a deep breath, Cat envied his control. She was still almost painfully aroused and she had to think really hard before she remembered what her other condition had been.

'You don't—' She stopped to clear the constriction in her throat then carried on a bit breathlessly. 'You don't leave me alone for weeks and weeks at a time. Oh, I do realise how hard you have to work,' she qualified rapidly, just in case he was thinking what a naggy, demanding wife she would turn out to be.

'And I appreciate that you made time to write funny postcards, and send gifts. But Aldo, I did miss you.'

She searched his gorgeous features for signs of male huffiness and found none, just frowning contrition.

He slapped a hand against the side of his head, and his voice was growly as he dragged her into his arms again, claiming rawly, 'I am an idiot! *Pazzo!* I had wanted to come to you and tell you I had put my working life in order, that I would be able to mostly conduct my business affairs by the touch of an electronic button from wherever we might happen to be. It was to be such a wonderful surprise!' he stated in a tone of sardonic self-deprecation.

He tilted her bright head back, his eyes dark and serious as they probed hers. 'You must have felt so neglected. I was too stupidly intent on what I was achieving to think of that! The way I saw it, I was working for a future that would allow us to spend all our time together, thinking you were getting all the pampering and luxury you needed after your miscarriage. Can you forgive me?' he pleaded. 'I had never been in love before. I was unused to conducting a love affair with my wife. I handled it very badly.'

He was asking her forgiveness!

Her mistakes had been far worse than his; he might have handled his 'surprise packet' badly but he'd had love in his heart, had been single-mindedly intent on achieving a closer future together for them both, while she had been crediting him with every sin she could think of!

Her eyes glistening with tears of contrition, Cat wound her arms around his neck and kissed him to stop him rubbing any more salt in the wound. And the kiss deepened to fiery passion and might have ended in goodness only knew what indiscretions had not Aldo ended it, alerted by her grandfather's unsubtle cough.

As always, Aldo kept his cool while Cat's head was still spinning wildly. At least Bonnie hadn't fainted! she thought, feeling her face go dark red as she hurriedly rearranged her clothing.

The coffee tray was safely deposited on a low table, and Aldo met the older man's twinkling eyes and said with smooth pride, 'You must excuse us. Cat has wonderful news. She is expecting our baby and we've never been happier!'

And wasn't that the truth! Cat thought mushily, her eyes fixed admiringly on his straight back and wide, rangy shoulders, on the arrogant way he held his perfectly shaped head, then felt herself drowning in the love that shone from his eyes as he turned back to her and took her hand.

And then they were both smothered in the warmest and sincerest congratulations, and champagne was produced to mark the occasion. Cat, contenting herself with a cup of weak coffee, wondered if there were any known cases of people actually exploding from sheer happiness.

It was all just a glorious blur until lunch was over and her grandfather said, just a little bit wistfully, 'Do you think you could both stay on until after Christmas? Bonnie and I would love to have you share it with us.'

'Cat?' Aldo turned to her, one dark brow slightly elevated.

He was leaving the decision down to her. But she knew what he wanted. And she knew Gramps would dearly love to have his family around him at this time of year and she would have loved to accommodate him—in spite of the way he'd disinherited her, whether she'd agreed to marry the man of his choice or not!

But, 'Sorry, Gramps. We need to get back to Florence. I need to arrange for regular check-ups, that sort of thing,' and was glad she'd made that decision when she saw the deep relief in Aldo's dark, dark eyes.

'Of course you must,' the old man agreed immediately. 'I was being selfish. Not thinking.' He reached over the table and patted her hand. 'Forget I mentioned it.'

'We want both you and Bonnie to be in Italy for the birth of our baby,' Aldo insisted. 'I'll make all the necessary travel arrangements—a car to collect you from here, the company's private jet. Early spring, if it suits you? Then you can enjoy the Italian sun, get to really know your family again and wait with us for the newest member to put in an appearance.'

They were due to return to Italy at the end of the week. The days passed in a whirl of activity that Aldo tried to calm down without a great deal of success.

There were gifts to be chosen and carefully wrapped in shiny gold paper for Gramps, Bonnie and Dan—not forgetting the cleaning lady, because Mrs Peterson was proving herself to be a jewel beyond price. And there was her packing to be done, the sale of her equipment in the workshop to be arranged. The Christmas tree to be ordered as usual, and collected and set in the wide hallway. And decorated.

On the last afternoon Gramps was taking his usual snooze in front of the sitting-room fire, Aldo was helping Dan barrow the latest load of logs into the woodshed and Cat was taking a rare break, sprawled out on the chair on the other side of the hearth thinking cosy maternal thoughts, when her grandfather snored and woke himself up.

'I'll make you a cup of tea, shall I?' Cat bounced upright, knowing it was always the first thing he wanted when he woke from his after-lunch nap.

But he waved her offer aside with, 'Mrs Peterson always brings me a tray at four, just before she leaves, as you very well know. And at least I've got you to myself. There's something I want to say to you.'

He was beginning to look decidedly uncomfortable, Cat thought, and she guessed that whatever he wanted to say wouldn't be easy for him. She had never known her grandfather to be anything other than absolutely direct, never mincing his words if he thought that what he had to say was right.

Concerned, she padded over the hearth rug and sank down at his feet, laying her bright head against his knee. Just waiting.

'I don't want you to think badly of me, Caterina. What I did turned out for the best, didn't it? No, don't say anything,' he warned as she lifted her head, prepared to tell him she could never think badly of him. 'Just hear me out.'

He cleared his throat roughly then went quickly on, 'Ever since Aldo was a child my sister's letters were full of praise for his strong-minded character, his generosity and good humour. And the occasional photographs she let me have showed him to have the makings of a fine-looking man. I felt I knew him through and through.

'Then, after your dear grandmother died, I started thinking more and more often of my Italian family, to regret the irresponsible way I'd behaved as a young man. The ingratitude. The taking of handsome dividends I'd not lifted a finger to earn,' he sighed.

'I found myself with two definite aims. To make reparation and to hand your welfare and happiness over to the safekeeping of a man such as Aldo. I used blackmail. I'm not proud of it except in that it procured a happy result—I've never witnessed two people more obviously in love with each other than you and my great-nephew.

'What I do sincerely regret is having given you the impression that I was completely cutting you off without the proverbial shilling. It wasn't so. I always intended those shares and whatever is left from the unearned dividends to return to the Patrucco family business. But the rest—this house, your grandmother's jewellery—will be yours. Whatever had happened—if you'd turned Aldo down flat, for instance—I would never have left you with nothing. I wanted you to know that. It's been bothering me, and it's taken me too long to get round to it. But confessing my sins has never been my strong point!'

'Oh, Gramps!' Leaping to her feet, Cat leant over his chair and gave him a huge hug. 'You and Gran looked after me all my life. You were the only real parents I had and you gave me a happy, secure childhood.' A fond kiss on each cheek. 'I would have still loved you even if you'd thrown me out of the house without a rag to my name—and don't you ever forget it!' She grinned down at him. 'I might have been a bit snippy when you told me you'd picked out a husband for me. But believe me, it couldn't have turned out more beautifully!'

EPILOGUE

THE city of Florence sweltered beneath a sky so bright it hurt the eyes. The streets and squares were like ovens.

Fanning her face with a languid hand, Cat entered the nursery from the balcony, the full skirts of her pale cream-coloured fine-lawn dress whispering around her legs. A cluster of pale cream rosebuds nestled in her hair, just above one ear. She smiled widely. So many people today had told her she looked like a bride.

Her green eyes went dreamy as she checked the air-conditioning unit. The fact was, her gorgeous Aldo made her feel like a bride every day of her life!

And as for Gianluca Domenico Patrucco, well he was their precious bonus! Her lovely face wreathed in smiles, Cat quietly approached the carved-wood, lace-flounced crib which had been in the family for generations.

At just over two months old, her beautiful son bore a definite resemblance to his handsome father. All the doting attention he'd been receiving today had been lapped up with wide, gummy smiles and bubbly gurgles, but as soon as he'd realised he was hungry the assembled guests had been treated to his world-beating lusty bellow.

Retreating to the nursery with her fist-flailing, scarlet-faced precious bundle of noise, Cat had removed the two-hundred-year-old christening gown, changed and fed him, and now he was sleeping like the darling little cherub that he was.

'All quiet.' Aldo had approached silently to join the fan club. 'Looks like an angel, doesn't he? It always surprises me how much noise can come from someone so small.'

One cream-coloured light-jacketed arm pulled her against the leanly elegant length of him and Cat looked up at him, her eyes adoring, her temperature sizzling as he traced a line of kisses from the point of her jawbone, all the way down her throat to the point of the V-neckline of her floaty dress.

'Have I ever told you how much I love you?'

His voice was low and luxuriously sexy and Cat answered breathlessly, 'A million times and still counting, but not to worry, I can never hear those words often enough.' She caught a wandering, tanned, long-fingered hand between her own and placed tender kisses on each of his knuckles and reminded him, 'Our guests.'

'Gone. Our son broke the party up pretty effectively!' He captured her hands and looped them around his neck, his dark eyes flirting with hers. 'I thanked them all for coming and made your excuses. I think some of the stuffier ones thought you should

have handed our roaring offspring over to a hovering
nanny! They were too polite to say so, of course, so
I pointed out that we enjoy doing everything for him
ourselves.'

So they did. Cat had been adamant that no hired
nanny would take charge of her precious baby. And
between them, she and Aldo had discovered that, despite the odd sleepless night, it was an adventure they
wouldn't have missed for worlds.

Aware now that he was sneakily walking her towards their adjoining bedroom, Cat protested, definitely half-heartedly, 'Where are your parents?' She
was very fond of them both, and it was mutual and
she didn't want them to feel neglected on their final
day here in Florence.

Aldo easily put her mind at rest. 'Out on the loggia,
sitting in the shade with Domenico and Bonnie. My
father's trying to persuade your grandfather to settle
permanently near him in Amalfi. Bonnie, too. They
are so used to each other. You know him better than
anyone—do you think he's open to persuasion?'

'Maybe.' Cat couldn't think straight, not when her
body was welded to the length of him. 'They've both
been happy here in Italy, and I know Gramps feels as
if he's come home at last. We'll have to wait and
see.'

The bed was made of painted and gilded wood,
with carvings of exotic birds and fruits. And whether
the steamy heat was down to the ambient temperature

or the sizzle of sexual excitement that arced between them, Cat couldn't say.

'Florence is too hot in August,' Aldo murmured as he gently turned her around and began sliding down the fine zip fastening at the back of her dress. Parting the fabric, he ran his fingers over her shoulder blades and down to her neat little waist. 'Tomorrow, after Bonnie and Domenico have been safely put aboard the jet for England and my parents have left for Amalfi, we will make plans to revisit Portofino.'

His hands retraced their path to her shoulders and the dress pooled to the floor. 'We will take Isabella and Louisa,' he named two of the permanent staff here in the Florence town house, 'to look after the villa and babysit on the evenings when I wine and dine my beautiful wife.'

He turned her round. She was wearing just a lacy bra and the tiniest of matching briefs. 'And you are so beautiful, *mi amore*. I am the luckiest man on the planet.'

And she was the luckiest woman in the universe, Cat thought as he shrugged out of his elegant jacket. She began a determined assault on the buttons of his shirt.

Eleven months later the two-hundred-year-old christening robe was in use again. Little Silvana Caterina behaved perfectly, following the proceedings with her mother's vivid green eyes, copper-coloured curls peeping out beneath her enchanting lace-trimmed bonnet while Gianluca was stomping around on his sturdy little legs, falling into the furniture because he hadn't got used to this walking business yet, his smart new sailor suit smeared with chocolate because he often missed where his mouth was.

Aldo had been over the moon at the arrival of the miniature of the woman he adored. 'But enough is enough,' he'd stated firmly. 'Two babies to keep us awake at nights, to have to watch like hawks. I am a greedy man. I want you to myself. The family christening robe gets locked away.'

'Just as you say, *caro mio*,' Cat had replied demurely as she lay with her newborn in her arms. 'We'll lock it away but we won't lose the key!'

HIS CONVENIENT
MISTRESS

by

Cathy Williams

Cathy Williams is originally from Trinidad but has lived in England for a number of years. She currently has a house in Warwickshire which she shares with her husband Richard, her three daughters Charlotte, Olivia and Emma and their pet cat, Salem. She adores writing romantic fiction and would love one of her girls to become a writer, although at the moment she is happy enough if they do their homework and agree not to bicker with one another.

Don't miss Cathy Williams' exciting new novel, *Kept by the Spanish Billionaire*, out in June 2007 from Mills & Boon Modern Romance™

CHAPTER ONE

'YOU look tired, James. You work too hard. How many times have I told you that if you do not slow down, you will end up as another of those…those…?'

'Statistics?'

'And there you go. Making fun of me, an old woman who is only foolish enough to love you more than life itself.'

James's dark eyebrows flicked upwards in a teasing smile and he stretched out his long legs in front of him, crossing them at the ankles, cradling his glass of whisky with one hand.

Perfect. The perfect time of evening in the perfect place. The summer sun had turned into that warm amber glow that preceded the onset of twilight and outside was awash with the rise and fall of colour, every shade of green and yellow imaginable. This was wild Scotland at its most majestic. Through the massive windows, the landscape of the baronial estate unfolded into the horizon and the backdrop of mountains rose upwards into the sky like an implacable matriarch making sure that her feudal tenants kept to their place.

Ah, yes. Perfection. And, like all things perfect, it was really only palatable in small doses. A bit, James thought, like women. Too much of a good thing was guaranteed to dull the palate and bring on thoughts of boredom and restlessness.

'Are you listening to a word I'm saying, James Dalgleish?'

'With every ounce of attention, Mama.' He smiled lazily, sipped his whisky and focused on the handsome woman sitting on her upright chair by the fireplace, that was adorned, for summer, with a sumptuously large array of flowers, all hand-picked from the extensive gardens.

Maria Dalgleish, for all her talk about being an old woman, was an indomitable and youthful force, as untamed as the Scottish Highlands she adored, even after forty years of living in its towering purple shadows. The passion that coursed through her Italian veins had never quite abandoned her and she possessed a vitality he had never seen in a woman anywhere else in his life.

Perhaps, he thought idly, at the age of thirty-six he was a mama's boy, destined to become a cantankerous old man living alone in his sprawling mansion. But a cantankerous, *wise* old man, he thought, taking another appreciative sip of his drink. Wise enough to know from experience that women were drawn to money like moths to a flame. Better no woman than one of those. Although, better still, a series of women of conveniently abbreviated duration.

'Now, James, how long will this visit be? I hope you have not forgotten that you have duties here. Trevor wants to talk to you about some repair work to the roof and then there is the business of the summer party and there is no point grumbling about getting involved. It happens every year.'

'Did I say a word, Mama?'

'You do not have to. I can see the grumble in your expression.'

'I think I'll take a bit of a break this time, stay for a week or so before I fly to New York.'

'New York, New York. All this flying business every other day. It is no good for you. You are not a young man any more, you know.'

'I know, Mama.' He shook his head and adopted a penitent expression. 'I am ageing by the second and what I need to do is find a good woman to have a brood of babies and look after me.'

Maria huffed, tempted by the carrot offered to involve herself in one of those conversations dear to her heart, but it was getting late and she could tell from her son's expression that he was too relaxed to do anything other than humour her in that infuriatingly stubborn and relentlessly charming manner of his.

'Yes, well.' She clicked her tongue to imply that the subject would rear its head soon enough. 'Now, tomorrow evening the Campbells have asked us over for supper. Lucy is up from Edinburgh.'

'Oh, good heavens.'

'It will be very nice and you know how much everyone enjoys seeing you when you fly in.'

'I'm here to relax, Mama. Not get caught up in a hectic whirlwind of socialising.'

'Things are never hectic in this part of the world. And how will you ever meet a nice girl if you refuse to socialise?'

'I socialise in London. Too much, if you want to know.'

'But with the wrong sort of girl,' his mother muttered darkly, unperturbed by the impatient glitter in his eyes.

'Mama,' he warned, 'let's just leave this alone, shall we? Agree to differ? The girls I socialise with happen to be just what my jaded soul desires.'

'I will leave this alone, James, *for the moment,* although you are still too young to be jaded...it is late and besides...' Maria Dalgleish allowed her voice to trail off into speculative silence.

'Besides...what?'

'There is something you might be interested in...'

'It's…' James glanced at his sleek, expensive watch, and then looked drily at his mother '…nearly quarter to ten. Too late for mysterious guessing games.'

'Someone has moved into the Rectory.'

'What?' James sat up straighter, leaning forward to rest his elbows on his thighs. The lazy, indolent ease had been replaced by that watchful edge that his mother only occasionally glimpsed.

'Someone has moved into the Rectory,' Maria repeated, primly flicking invisible specks of dust from her flowered skirt.

'Who?'

'No one local. In fact, no one is quite certain…'

'Why didn't Macintosh tell me that the place had been sold? Dammit!' He stood up and began pacing the room, frowning as he contemplated his lawyer's crass inefficiency. He'd had his eye on the Rectory for the past three years, had used every ounce of his formidable persuasiveness to try and convince Freddie that he didn't need a place that big, that he would get way over the top if he chose to sell.

Freddie had always laughed, poured them both a whisky or three and explained that the lady was not up for grabs. That James's plans to convert the expansive Dalgleish estate into a first-rate hotel with his mother overseeing the details from the Rectory, which was ideally positioned alongside the estate, would just have to go on hold.

'I intend to live to a hundred,' he had said more than once, grinning wickedly at James's frustration, 'and when I do finally decide to go, maybe we can strike a deal. If you're still around, wee laddie. Though what I would do with the money is beyond me. I've no family to speak of to leave it to. Still, I'm not agin doing a favour for a neighbour. Especially one who is so desperate to bring jobs into this beautiful countryside of ours. Not to mention a bit of much needed glamour for our local lassies to get their bored teeth into.'

'Because it has not been sold,' Maria replied.

'I told the man a thousand times after Freddie died that I wanted the place. I'll have his hide for breakfast.' He paused to stare through the windows, frowning. Underneath all the bantering, Freddie had wanted him to have the place but, Freddie being Freddie, had died suddenly two months previously while driving his old banger to see if he could unearth something interesting at Loch Shiel and had left no will to indicate what he wanted done with the Rectory.

James had simply had to inform his solicitor in the town what *his* intentions were and it had not once crossed his mind that he would fail to get what he wanted once all the technicalities of the place had been sorted out. He had the money, could move with speed to tie up any annoying loose ends and would be doing a service to the community by converting his own rambling baronial manor into a hotel, not to mention taking care of his mother, who wasn't getting any younger and would be happier in the relative cosiness of the Rectory. Still close enough to keep a jaundiced eye on the manor, to argue with contractors and suppliers and employees, while not having to contend with the overwhelming size of the place. She didn't look her age, had still retained the pure bone structure of the model she had once been, but she was sixty-five and didn't need the worries of running a house the size of Dalgleish Manor with grounds to match, staff or no staff.

He was furious that his plans had been scuppered at the last minute. His mansion in the outer reaches of Scotland was there to soothe his harried spirits not harbour yet more stress that he could do without.

'Who's bought the place, then?' He spun round to look at his mother, switching on one of the table lamps to dispel the infernal duskiness that had settled in the room. 'Some speculator, I presume? Someone who wants to convert the place into a little bed and breakfast where he can fleece innocent tourists and hobnob with the local gentry?'

'You are not listening to what I have just told you, James.'

'Of course I'm listening! I've done nothing *but* listen since you dropped this little gem on me!'

'The place has not been *sold*,' Maria repeated emphatically.

'Not been sold? You just said...' He breathed a sigh of relief as his long-range plans began to once again take root in his head. He had already got Max, one of his top architects, to begin doing some preliminary work on the conversion of the manor, based on a series of photographs. Step two would be a trip to the place for a couple of weeks to see how viable his thoughts were.

'Well, if it's just a question of someone showing interest then that's fine. I was under the impression that the place was occupied.' He shrugged and shoved his hands into his pockets so that his trousers were dragged down slightly, the waistband dipping down the flat planes of his stomach. 'I can beat off any competitor.'

'Freddie left the Rectory to a relative,' Maria Dalgleish said bluntly.

'Freddie did...*what*?'

'Willed the place to a relative. Everyone was as surprised as you are.'

'He didn't have any living relatives.'

'Perhaps you could try telling that to the woman who moved in three days ago.'

'Woman?'

'I am not too sure what the relationship was. I do not even know what she looks like or how old she is. You can imagine that everyone is buzzing with curiosity.'

'*Woman?*' Why would a *woman* want to move to this part of Scotland? This was beautiful but rugged terrain, not the sort of place a woman would choose to make her home. His mother was one of the few women who had come to the area from afar and he knew from what she had told him smilingly over the years that she had arrived with a truckload of misgivings only to find that the rugged Highlands had suited her far more than she could ever have imagined. Jack Dalgleish had belonged to the place as much as the lochs and trees did and his happiness there had infected her—in fact had turned her into a pivotal member of the tightly knit community.

'No one is really even too sure what her name is.' Maria couldn't help savouring the mystery, even though she flushed sheepishly at her own nosiness. 'Valerie Ross happened to see the removal van heading out towards the Rectory and when she spoke to Graeme—you know Graeme—yesterday he told her that a woman would be moving in, but he couldn't speak. He was on his way out of the house to the airport and I am sure got a great deal of pleasure allowing Valerie to stew in her own curiosity.' Mother and son exchanged a split-second of mutual amusement at the accuracy of this surmise, then James was back to his frowning contemplation.

'A woman,' he murmured half to himself. 'Well, if she's decided to make this part of the world her bolt-hole, then she's either a sad little lady with no life to speak of, hoping to find one here, or else she's running away from something.'

'What nonsense.'

'Bad marriage, bad love affair, bad job.'

'And what will you do?' Maria looked at her son with a mixture of indulgence, down-to-earth cynicism and deep affection. 'Persuade her that it is in her best interests to sell the place to you?'

'Why not?' He hadn't realised, until this moment, how much he wanted to turn Dalgleish Manor into something, wanted the Rectory for his mother, wanted to invest some of his vast reserves of wealth and power in a project that was emotionally closer to home. His financial house, a place where deals and mergers were cemented and money made in sums only appreciative accountants could truly understand, kept him busy but it hadn't been enough. Wasn't that why he had trained his eyes on an ailing firm of architects and nurtured them into a multimillion-pound concern that now flourished throughout Europe? But the travel and privileges had done nothing for his soul. He *wanted* this project, wanted to watch it grow like a baby and delight in knowing that he would be doing what would eventually be right for his mother in the process. None of it would be possible without acquiring the Rectory. It was ideal.

A woman. He felt a slight stirring of interest at the prospect of getting what he wanted. A woman was a far different cry from Freddie or, for that matter, from someone looking to make a quick buck. A woman he could handle. Fairly, generously, magnanimously even.

'I think,' he said, stroking his chin thoughtfully, 'I might just pay a little visit to our new neighbour in the morning.'

'I hope you don't intend to intimidate anyone into doing anything,' his mother said sternly and he grinned at her, a devilishly winning grin.

'Now, now, Mama, would I?'

Intimidation would have been the sports car, garaged when he was away and pulled out whenever the weather put him in the mood to drive through the unsullied roads around the estate in a fast car with the top down.

Now, his old four-wheel-drive, on the other hand. Denim-blue, ten years old and still driving as sweetly as a nut. *That* wouldn't intimidate an agoraphobic spinster with a fetish for twitching net curtains. As he now thought of his mystery obstacle.

At ten o'clock the following morning he drove through his estate, breathing in the fine summer air wafting through the open windows, lush with the scents of grass and flowers and lochs, turned right when he hit the crossroads and took his time covering the short distance to the Rectory.

Sara heard the car long before she spotted it. Something to do with the utter absence of noise in the place, she supposed.

Yes, peace and silence had been things she had predicted weeks previously when she had sat at her glass kitchen table in her lavish apartment in Fulham, rereading the letter she had received from a solicitor whose name she had never heard, about a house in the wilds of nowhere willed to her by an uncle whose existence she had only dimly been aware of. Peace and silence that had seemed so alluring and were now proving to be unnerving, even after three days. Just something else unnerving to add to the list already mounting in the back of her mind. And unnerving was a kind way of putting it.

She waited by the kitchen window, watching the shimmering landscape and waiting to see the car that was almost certainly heading in her direction.

'Everyone will want to meet you,' she had been told slyly by Freddie's lawyer, when they had finally met face to face over a cappuccino in one of the trendy London cafés. 'They all pretty much expect the place to be sold.

As far as everyone was concerned, Freddie was alone in the world. No wife, no children, no family.'

Fool that she was, she had actually, six weeks ago, looked forward to the country life full of people who would know her name, had pleasantly anticipated walking into shops and chatting with the people inside them. Bliss, she had idiotically thought, after her time in London, where life had been lived at breakneck speed and smiling at the shop assistants was regarded as a form of lunacy.

Her three days of isolation and peace had put paid to her illusions. She hated it here, hated the lack of noise, hated the horizon-less countryside, hated the utter stillness and had avoided heading into the town with something approaching obsession.

Naturally, sooner or later, the town, she now thought, would come to meet her. One by one. And there, approaching in a blue vehicle, was visitor number one.

Oh, heavens, but she had made a dreadful mistake. She had dared to think that the grass was going to be greener on the other side, and greener it was here, yes. Literally. But that was as far as it went. *How on earth was she ever going to survive?*

The car trundled through the fields, wending a lazy and inexorable path towards the Rectory, and Sara fleetingly contemplated hiding.

Where was Simon? She listened, heard him in the snug across the landing from the kitchen, happy as a lark, setting up his bricks on the low wooden table no doubt, a handy, child-friendly piece of furniture, precious few of which had previously cluttered his life.

She only turned away from the window when the car was entering its final swing towards her circular courtyard. Then she breathed a little sigh of resignation, glanced briefly in the direction of the snug with an expression of longing and reluctantly opened the kitchen door.

She looked a mess. She knew that. In London, now a lifetime away, she had always been impeccably groomed. Had had to be, to compete in the heavily male-dominated world she had inhabited. Her long red hair had always been tamed away from her face, securely pinned up, her make-up had been the armour of the top businesswoman, as had her assortment of sober-coloured, extremely expensive designer suits. Snappy, fashionable, but not ostentatious. In the City, success was always subtly dressed.

Here, though, in the space of only a few days, her grooming had slowly but surely unravelled. No make-up for starters and certainly nothing approaching work clothes. Just jeans and T-shirts and flat loafers.

It was what she was wearing now. Faded jeans, snug-fitting dark green T-shirt that almost but not quite matched the colour of her eyes, and her brown loafers.

She stood by the kitchen door, squinting into the sun, barely able to make out the driver of the car.

Her hair was plaited back, one thick braid that fell almost to her waist, from which escaped the usual rebellious tendrils. An inelegant hairstyle but practical for the thousand and one jobs she had to do around the house.

Her visitor was a man. Sara shaded her eyes, waiting and watching as the man killed his engine, pushed open the door and emerged from his car in one easy movement.

He was tall. Very tall and dark. Her green eyes took him in with a quick stirring of surprise. He didn't look Scottish. His skin was olive and his hair was dark and thick, curling into the nape of his neck. Nothing about him looked local. From his physical appearance to the angular lines of his face that spoke of power, self-assurance and worldly-wise experience.

He looked like a city-dweller, she thought with a rush of disdain. The usual high-powered type she had spent years dealing with. A mover and a shaker who did deals and transformed the whole process of money-making into a number-one priority. She had spent many a long business lunch with types like this one, men in love with themselves and casually indifferent to anything that stood in the way of them getting what they wanted. In fact, she had made the irreparable mistake of actually doing more than just business with one of these types and look where that had got her.

It was only after an inordinately long time that she realised that the man was watching her watching him, his expression cool, calculating and utterly unruffled by her curiosity. Irritating, considering that he was on her property.

'Yes?' she asked, not moving, her hands still shading her face from the glare of the sun. 'May I help you?'

'Now, that's a big question,' the man drawled, slamming his car door and walking lazily towards her.

He was at least six feet three, Sara realised a little nervously. He towered over her in a way few men did. She was five-ten in bare feet and quite used to looking down on a great number of the men she had come into contact with over the years. There was also something a little scary about him. Was it the way he moved? Or his eyes? Deep blue, she could see now that he was closer, and strangely contained.

'Who are you and what do you want?' Sara demanded quickly, realising for the first time just how isolated this damned Rectory was.

Jumpy, James thought now that he had got over his astonishment at seeing the net-twitching spinster in the flesh. She was nothing like what he had expected. What the hell was a woman like this one doing out here? The mild curiosity he had experienced during the drive to the Rectory had crystallised into something pleasurably invigorating.

Jumpy and defensive. Why? Shouldn't she be flinging out the welcome mat and hustling to make tea for the friendly local visitor who had come to make her feel right at home and show her how warm her neighbours could be?

'So you're the new girl in town,' James drawled when he was finally standing in front of her. 'You picked the best month to move up here, I must say. June is usually kind. Lots of sun and blue skies.'

His blue eyes never left her face. Sara could feel his inspection and it was an uninvited intrusion into her space.

'You haven't told me your name,' she said flatly, edging slightly so that she was positioned in front of the kitchen door, making it quite clear that there was no automatic invitation to step inside.

'Nor have you told me yours. And I'm James Dalgleish.' He extended his hand and Sara found hers enclosed in long, strong fingers.

'Sara King.' She pulled her hand politely free and resisted the urge to massage it.

'Freddie's...niece perhaps?'

'That's right.'

'Funny, he never mentioned having any relatives,' James said thoughtfully, 'and I certainly don't recall any coming to visit.' He gave her a smile that didn't quite conceal the lazy challenge that seemed implicit in his comment.

Sara flushed and remained silently uncooperative. Did he, she wondered, think that she was some kind of opportunist? Would that be the general reaction of everyone in the town who had probably been discussing her furiously while she had holed herself up in her house and spent her time trying to work out why on earth she had come to this far-flung place?

'Mum!'

Her head whipped around at Simon's shout.

'My son,' she said, by way of explanation.

'You're married?'

'No.' She heard the scramble of footsteps heading towards the kitchen and gave a little sigh of irritation at her visitor, who continued to stand with implacable resolve by the door. 'Look, I'm rather busy at the moment.'

'I'm sure you are. Moving house is always a headache.' James watched as she raised one slender hand and pushed some flyaway red hair away from her face. 'You need to sit and relax. I'll make you a cup of coffee.'

'I—'

'Mum, I'm thirsty. Can you come and see my garage?'

'This is Simon,' Sara introduced reluctantly as her five-year-old son appeared next to her and proceeded to stare unblinkingly at their visitor. 'Simon, how many times have I told you that you should wear your slippers around the house?' By way of reply, he popped his thumb into his mouth and continued to inspect James curiously.

'Being barefoot is so much easier, isn't it?' James said, stooping down until he was on the same level as the boy.

What was the story here? he wondered. Having planned to call on this woman so that he could find out how serious she was about living in the Rectory and how much he would be prepared to give her to buy her out, had even planned on suggesting other parts of the town where she could live if she wanted, he now found himself holding back on stating the reason for his visit in preference to discovering more about the red-haired woman and her child.

'Um,' Simon agreed, still sucking on his thumb.

'So you've built a garage? Anything I would want to send my own cars to?'

'Do you have children, Mr Dalgleish?'

James glanced up at her. 'Child-free.'

Now, I wonder why I'm not surprised at that, Sara thought. Lord, but how long would it take for her to get over the bitterness that still burned the back of her throat at the thought of Simon's father?

'How about that cup of coffee?' He stood up with a questioning look and Sara felt a little shiver race along her spine. It was almost as though he could read her mind and was calmly determined to stay his ground in the face of her reluctance. And she had to stop being reluctant. She knew that. She would have to go into the town sooner rather than later, if only to buy provisions for herself and Simon, and she would have to meet her new neighbours. Hiding was not an option.

'Come in.' She smiled another tightly polite smile while he headed through the door with the familiarity of someone who knew the place.

As he would, she thought. In a place of this size, everyone would know everyone else. From the looks of him, he was probably the local professional. A banker or a lawyer of some sort who fancied himself a cut above the rest.

She poured juice for Simon, who hovered by the table and ignored his slippers, which were by the chair. His baggy, long shorts made his thin legs seem even thinner and she reminded herself that he was the reason she had moved up here.

'Now, shall I come and put on a video for you, Simes? Your favourite cartoon, perhaps?'

'Can you play with me?' he asked hopefully, and she shook her head with a grin.

'Nice try. I'm just going to have a quick cup of coffee with Mr Dalgleish and then maybe we can go out and do some gardening. I'll let you use the watering can.'

'The big one?'

'If you can handle it.'

'I have some soil.' Simon turned gravely to James. 'For planting vegetables.'

'Really?' He didn't know much about children but this boy was so serious and so *thin*. He looked as though one wisp of a Scottish breeze would blow him off his feet, never mind the harshness of winter. 'Any in particular?'

'Beans.'

'Would those be baked beans?' James grinned and for the first time Simon smiled, a wide smile that brought a light to his face.

'With sausages and chips,' he said, giggling.

Sara felt something uncomfortable tug inside her and she frowned at James. 'Come on, Simes. Let's go and see what video we can put on for you.' She held out her hand and curled her fingers around her son's little ones.

When she returned to the kitchen it was to find that coffee had been made and was waiting for her. James was sitting at the kitchen table, his body turned away from her as he looked out of the French doors, which were sprawled open on to the front garden that rolled down towards the lane at the bottom and open countryside beyond that.

It was funny, but the house had felt so damned hollow since she had moved in. Now his presence filled it, making her edgy and defensive and for the first time turning her thoughts away from herself and the enormity of the mistake she had made.

'There was no need for you to make the coffee.' Sara stepped through into the kitchen and he turned slowly in his chair until he was looking directly at her. Those eyes, she thought, a little confused. Midnight-blue and thickly fringed with black eyelashes. Seriously disconcerting eyes.

'No problem. It won't be the first time I've made coffee in this kitchen.'

'You knew my uncle.' She willed herself to get her legs together and moved towards the opposite end of the kitchen table, pouring herself some coffee from the percolator *en route*, and sat down, cradling the mug between both hands.

'Everyone knew Freddie.' He gave her a long, measured look. Feeling out the land, he thought. How long had it been since he had last done that with a woman? Or anyone, for that matter? 'He was something of a local character. As you might know...or do you?' He raised his cup to his lips, sipped some of the coffee and regarded her over the rim of the cup.

'Is that why you came here, Mr Dalgleish? To try and pry into my life and find out what I'm doing here?'

'The name is James. And of course that's why I came here.' That, amongst other things, though those can wait for the moment, James thought. 'So...what *are* you doing here?'

Blunt to the point of rude, Sara thought, but rude to the point of getting whatever answers he wanted, because he put her in a position from which to evade his questions would have seemed like unnecessary shiftiness. And if she was to make a go of things here, unlikely though that seemed at this moment in time, then she would probably be meeting him again. To kick off by creating a bad atmosphere was not going to help either her or Simon.

Still, something about the man addled her and made her want to skulk away behind her defences to a position of safety.

'I...' She raised her green eyes to look steadily at him.

'Well, I inherited this house. If you *must* know, I never knew Uncle Fred. He and my father had a bit of a falling-out years ago, before I was born, and they never really patched things up. Anyway, moving up here...well, I thought that it...that it would be a good idea,' she finished lamely.

'A good idea?'

Sara felt her hackles rise. His tone did a good job of implying that any such good idea could loosely be translated as stupidity.

'And where have you come from?' James asked without giving her time to expand. 'South somewhere?'

'Everywhere is south of here,' Sara informed him coldly.

'Touché. I was actually referring to London.'

'I *was* living in London, yes.'

'With a child?'

'People do.'

More puzzling by the minute, James thought, sipping some of the coffee, which had gone lukewarm. He allowed himself to savour the thought of unravelling Sara King, finding the chink that would give him the leverage he wanted that would enable him to persuade her to sell the Rectory to him. He would be fair, more than fair, he decided, but he would get what he wanted in the end. And, looking at her now with her red hair, that pale, flawless skin, those translucent green eyes that were doing their best to be guarded but could not help simmering with fire, he had a sudden, disconcerting feeling that he was going to enjoy his dealings with her.

Physically, she was far removed from the type of women he tended to be attracted to. She was too tall, too slender, too pale. But there was still something about her that carried the unexpected. Perhaps the hint of a sharp brain that did not conform to what was expected of it.

'Are you finished with your coffee?' Sara asked, rising to her feet, one hand already outstretched to take his cup. 'I hate to rush you away, but I really have a million things to do and Simon will start acting up in a minute if I don't go through.'

'Have you been to the town yet?' Of course she hadn't. She had managed to keep herself to herself. 'Met any of the locals?'

Sara was grateful to be able to look away from those penetrating eyes as she moved towards the kitchen sink with both their cups in her hands. 'Not yet, no.'

'Then I insist you come to a luncheon party my mother is having on Sunday.'

'I…'

'You might as well satisfy their curiosity,' he commented drily, 'or they will simply start fabricating half-truths about you. Why did you choose to live here if you are afraid of facing the people you will find yourself living amongst?'

'I'm not afraid of any such thing!'

'Twelve precisely. You can't miss the house. It's the one next to yours. First left.' He stood up and Sara followed him with her eyes as he walked towards the kitchen door, giving her a brief salute before disappearing outside towards his car.

CHAPTER TWO

'SO WHAT'S she like?'

'Red hair. Green eyes. Tall. Has a child, a boy.'

'No, James, I meant what is she *like*? You know. Chatty, sociable, boring, *what*?'

Good question, James thought. He looked down at Lucy Campbell and then absentmindedly out towards the direction of the Rectory. She hadn't shown up. It was now four in the afternoon, lunch had been served, a splendid buffet of cold meats and salads, which had been eaten on the sprawling back patio with its rich scent of flowers. Croquet had been played amateurishly by a handful of the guests. There had been some talk of lawn tennis, but this had fizzled out to nothing because most of the guests had had too much of the very fine white wine to drink and were disinclined to put themselves through the effort of running around trying to hit a tennis ball over a net.

'James?'

He focused on the woman in front of him. By any standards, she was a pretty girl. Petite, blonde-haired, blue-eyed, impeccably haute-coutured and with the regulation cut-glass voice. Unfortunately, she irritated the hell out of him, and she was irritating him now, gazing up at him with the expectant expression of someone looking forward to a bit of juicy gossip.

'She seems pleasant enough,' he expanded with a shrug. He sipped some of his wine and found his gaze straying again in the direction of the Rectory.

'Pleasant?'

'No obvious psychological problems that I could spot,' he said edgily. Just damned hostile, he thought to himself. Was that a reaction to *him* in particular, he wondered, or men in general? He had found himself thinking about her more than he had anticipated and the fact that he was thinking about her now annoyed him.

'Very droll, James.' Lucy smiled a coquettish little smile, a smile she had perfected over the years and one that usually had men melting. It didn't appear to be working now. 'That's one of the things I absolutely *adore* about you.'

'Sorry?'

'You were telling me all about your fascinating new neighbour.' She held on to the smile but with difficulty. 'So she's tall, has red hair and seems pleasant. Is that all? What about this son of hers? What do you think they're doing here? *Really?* Would you like to know what *we* think?'

James didn't have to ask her who the *we* were. He knew well enough. Her little clique of privileged friends, four of whom had trooped along with their parents to the luncheon.

'You can tell me if you feel inclined,' he said discouragingly.

'Well, *we* all think that she's a bit of a nobody who's suddenly found herself the owner of a pretty nice house, you must admit, and has decided to land herself up here on the off-chance of meeting some dashing man to pick up the bill for her and her child.' Lucy drained her glass of wine. Her eyes were sparkling, over-bright. She had had, James thought with distaste, too much to drink.

'Really.'

'So you'd better watch out.' The blue eyes hardened

even though the pink, half-opened mouth continued to smile invitingly. 'She'll be after you before you know it.'

'Oh, I shouldn't think so,' James drawled, but he had a sudden vision of her stripping off to reveal a slender, pale body. He imagined her high, pert breasts and that long hair hanging around her in a tousled mane. He shoved one hand in his trouser pocket and took another mouthful of wine. His last girlfriend had been small, voluptuous and dark-haired. A sexy little thing with a penchant for expensive presents and designer outfits. Very rewarding for a while until her conversation, or lack of it, had begun to make itself felt over and above her physical assets.

'Of course she will,' Lucy was saying, half in jest, half serious. 'She's probably eyed you up as a good catch and is plotting how she can net you. And you men are so gullible, you won't know what's coming until it's hit you like a freight train.'

'I think,' James lowered his head slightly, 'you must be talking about the men *you* sleep with, Lucy, because *I* certainly do not fit that particular description.' Just the opposite, he thought drily. He'd already had one collision with that particular type of freight train and he was in no danger of ever having another.

No wonder the woman had not been inclined to discover the charms of the locals. If she knew the rumours circulating about her, she would stay away for the rest of her natural life. Lucy and her friends might not be permanent residents of the place, choosing to work in Edinburgh and travel back home to their parents on the occasional weekend, but if they were discussing Sara King and her motives then he would bet his mansion on the fact that their parents were as well.

And he had to admit that the thought had crossed his own mind. Before he had met her.

If Lucy had been witness to his brief visit the day before then talk about motives and gold-digging and the search for a husband would not be figuring highly in her conversation, because Sara King had shown not the slightest interest in him as anything other than a nosy neighbour she wanted to get rid of as quickly as possible.

He wondered wryly if this wasn't the reason why he had been spending so much time thinking about her. The fact that he had so obviously failed to impress her when in fact wowing women had always been a talent he had taken utterly for granted.

His mother was calling him over, urging him to participate in a new game of croquet, with two teams competing for a bottle of champagne. It was simply too glorious a day for them to go inside, and croquet, she whispered into his ear with a smile, was a sedate enough game to accommodate old age and tipsiness.

'I'll play on one condition,' James said, *sotto voce*, 'and that's if I'm spared the company of Lucy Campbell. There's only so much of that girl's wittering a man can take.'

'I thought you liked her!' Maria said in surprise and her son gave her a look of dry disbelief. 'Or at least didn't mind her,' she amended.

'Reminds me too much of certain social climbers I meet in London,' he said dismissively. 'Young, rich and a little too much in love with themselves.' He placed one foot neatly on a mallet lying on the grass by him and flicked it up, catching it with one hand.

'In which case, it's a good thing I hadn't lined her up for you as a prospective wife,' Maria smiled.

'No need for you to line me up with anyone, Mama. According to our dear debutante Lucy,' he flicked his head in the general direction of the Rectory, 'someone is already lining herself up to fill the role.'

'Oh, yes?' Maria cocked her head to one side and looked interestedly at her son. 'And who might that be?'

'Don't pretend the innocent with me, Mama,' James said with a slow grin. 'This is the original nesting bed of the malicious rumour, and Lucy and her clique of friends have already begun circulating one.'

'Which is…?'

'That our new neighbour is a money-grabbing gold-digger on the look-out for a prospective husband.'

'You have met her. You do not agree, then?' Maria asked casually and James gave a snort of laughter. 'Perhaps they are right.' She stole a curious look at her son, who was staring grimly out towards the Rectory. He had invited the girl over and she had failed to appear. She, Maria, had made no comment on this, but she knew that her son had been unsurprisingly annoyed. It wasn't often that his orders, which they always were, however prettily he tried to package them, were ignored.

'Perhaps,' Maria mused speculatively, 'she *is* on the look-out for a nice, eligible, rich man…'

'In which case she's barking up the wrong tree. Anyway, I can spot an opportunist a mile off and I can't think of anyone less on the look-out,' he said, his head filling with the images of the dismissive look she had thrown at him when he had stepped out of his car and the impatient resignation with which she had greeted his offer to make her a cup of coffee. 'She struggled to invite me into the Rectory, for God's sake!'

'What a shame,' Maria murmured teasingly, 'and how did you cope with the shock of not being fawned upon by a woman?'

'Women do not fawn over me, Mama,' he denied vigorously, but he flushed at the accuracy of her dart. He was fully and cynically aware that he possessed just the right combination of attributes to make a woman's head turn. 'And this one certainly didn't.'

'So your plans to buy the Rectory have taken a nose-dive, am I right?'

'Oh, I wouldn't rush into assuming any such thing.' But he had no idea how he was going to persuade her to sell. She hadn't struck him as the sort of woman who could be talked into doing anything she didn't want to do.

'Well, if she does not like you, James, then she is hardly going to agree to selling something she has travelled hundreds of miles to possess.' Maria looked out to where several of the guests were already trying to decide who should be in what team. Constance Campbell, who usually shifted automatically into the role of organising everyone else, was having a hard time with guests who were tipsy enough to get a kick out of thwarting her.

But I could get to know her, couldn't I…? James reflected. Discover the chink in her armour. The Rectory was beautiful but frankly falling to bits. If he got to know her, well, he could just help her along the way to realising just how much needed doing to the place and how much easier it would be to shift the potential headache to someone else. Namely him. No good barging in when she still had her little head in the clouds, but a few carefully placed remarks might work wonders.

'Who knows?' he answered in a distracted voice. 'Anyway, shall we get on with this wretched game of croquet? You know I can't stand the sport.'

'I know.' She touched his cheek briefly and lovingly. 'Not vigorous enough for you. It is nice having you home here.'

'And it'll be even nicer when this lot depart. You know what they say about too much of a good thing.'

As it turned out, it was after six before the last of the guests left and after eight by the time a thoughtful James had eaten dinner, which was served informally in the breakfast room off the kitchen. His mother chatted inconsequentially about the luncheon party, amusing him with barbed remarks about village gossip and what was happening with whom and where. Normally, they would have retired to their favourite sitting area, the one which offered the most tantalising views. It would have provided a soothing and welcome end to a fairly hectic day, but James was in no mood to be soothed. His mother's voice drifted in calm waves over his head but he was thinking. Thinking about what she had said earlier, her throwaway remark that their Rectory neighbour might prove to be as stubborn as the uncle she had clearly never met.

The train of his thoughts made him edgy and he knitted his dark brows together in a frown, only realising his distraction when his mother said something which he was obliged to ask her to repeat.

'There is no need for the Rectory,' Maria sighed. 'Have I not told you this over and over? If the manor is converted to a hotel, I can simply live in a suite.'

'And share your dinner with the hotel guests?' He gave her a brooding frown that arrogantly denied his mother doing any such thing. 'Walk out into the garden so that you can join clusters of other people admiring the flowers? Have your evening drink brought to you by a waiter on his way to serve other people their evening drinks? I would rather,' he rasped, 'abort my ideas of converting this place than suffer you going through any of that.'

'Why do you think Miss King did not come to our little

lunch party?' Maria asked, to change the subject, and he shrugged.

'Perhaps the thought of socialising with us all filled her little soul with terror. Although,' he couldn't help but add, 'believe me, it would have been the other way around. *She* would have been the one filling *their* little souls with terror.'

'She made quite an impact on you, James, did she not?'

'I'll let you know tomorrow,' he said slowly, standing up and stretching. He raked his fingers through his hair and then turned to look at his mother.

'Why tomorrow?'

'Because I think I'll head across to Miss King and find out for myself why she did not appear when I specifically invited her.'

'You were piqued, weren't you?' Maria asked slyly.

'Hardly. It's simply that…I intend to buy her house and I won't be able to dangle money at the end of the carrot in an attempt to persuade her. Whatever brought her rushing up here, it wasn't poverty. From what I glimpsed of her possessions, at least the ones in the kitchen, she was not labouring under financial stress. So I shall simply have to dig deep into my reservoirs of persuasiveness to get what I want.'

'Does that not sound easy?' Maria murmured to herself, her dark eyes speculative.

'So I shall see you tomorrow, Mama.' He strolled to where she was sitting and kissed her once on each cheek, as he always had done ever since he was a boy, on his way back to boarding-school after the holidays, half longing to stay with his parents and enjoy his life in Scotland with the wide, open spaces around him, half longing to return to his friends with their boisterous camaraderie.

He was under no illusions as he later drove across to

the Rectory. Sara King wasn't going to welcome him in with open arms. She hadn't the first time round, and she was going to be even less enthusiastic this time. Especially as it was after nine and he would probably have to drag her out of bed with his banging on the kitchen door. Neither prospect was sufficient to put him off the matter at hand.

There were lights on, at least, when he pulled up outside and he killed the engine of the car, sitting inside for a few minutes before going out. Then he strode out, peered through one of the kitchen windows at the side just in case she was busying herself in there, and, not seeing her, banged on the knocker.

From upstairs, where she had just finished settling Simon, Sara heard the authoritative knock and immediately felt her spine straighten in irritation. It had been a hell of a day and seeing James Dalgleish was the last thing she needed, because she was certain that it was him. She had not gone to his wretched luncheon party and now he had come to check and find out why.

She half debated whether she should just ignore the banging on the door and then remembered the way he had continued standing there the previous day, not prepared to budge an inch until she had invited him in. He would just keep banging if she didn't answer until eventually Simon woke up.

There was no time to try and make herself remotely presentable. Her hair was loose, having been washed only an hour before, and it fell around her shoulders in untamed ringlets, still half-damp. Instead of her usual jeans, she was wearing a loose grey jersey skirt that fell almost to her ankles and a clingy ribbed grey top that ended just above the waistband of the skirt.

'All right!' she muttered irritably under her breath, hurrying down the stairs before he broke down the door in his attempts to be heard. 'Did it occur to you that I might have been sleeping?' she greeted him angrily as she pulled open the kitchen door.

Idiot that she was, she had forgotten how overpowering he was. She had so successfully managed to shove him into the same category as her ex-boyfriend and her son's father, the mere thought of whom was enough to fill her throat with sour bile, that to see James standing there against the backdrop of the sinking sun almost made the breath catch in her throat.

He was so awesomely good-looking. He possessed skin that reacted warmly to the sun, and even in the space of a mere day he seemed browner than she recalled. The top two buttons of his cream shirt were undone, exposing the same, magnificently coloured skin, and the sleeves were roughly rolled back, and as her eyes dropped she took in his lean, muscled arms, then she blinked and her head cleared.

'No.'

'It's after nine at night!' she snapped, a little annoyed with herself for being bowled over, if only for a few seconds, by his physical allure.

'And you normally go to bed at nine?'

'Why are you here, anyway?'

'I've now been here twice and both times you've given me a pretty hostile reception. Tell me, is it just me or is it the entire human race?' He looked at her with lazy speculation in his eyes, knowing that she was taken aback by his comment, and while she was still struggling to come up with an appropriate response he continued in the same musing voice, 'I think it's the human race. Hence your willingness to bury yourself here without even bothering to take the time out to meet the people in whose community you have chosen to bury yourself.'

'And I think that you should keep your opinions to yourself considering I haven't asked you to share them with me.'

'Where is your little boy?'

'Asleep.'

'My mother was disappointed that you didn't come. She was looking forward to meeting you.'

Sara flushed guiltily. She'd had no compunction about letting *him* down, but she hadn't considered that she might be letting anyone else down in the process.

James could read it all from her expression and from the delicate bloom of colour that crept into her cheeks.

'She wondered,' he carried on, elaborating on this piece of fiction without the slightest twinge of guilt, 'whether you had perhaps been taken ill. The Rectory is quite isolated and, as far as she knows, your telephone might well not have been connected as yet.'

'I…yes, the telephone is connected. With Simon…'

'Of course. Still…she was concerned.'

There was a short, awkward pause during which James wondered whether he had piled it on too thick. But if she was going to develop a habit of slamming doors in his face, then he certainly could not afford to develop a habit of allowing it. Not if he wanted to get the Rectory. And anyway, he was, by nature, incapable of allowing anyone to slam a door in his face.

'Look…I apologise for not coming to your party… but…'

'It's a little chilly out here. That's the thing with summers in Scotland. However fine the day is, the night always reminds you not to take the warmth for granted. I merely stopped by to make sure that you were all right.' He half

turned, curious to see whether the flush of guilt would be
sufficient for her to stop him and it was. She invited him
in. Not in the most gracious of voices and certainly with
no noticeable enthusiasm, but it was an invitation he discovered he had been quite looking forward to and was all
too keen to grasp.

'Tea?' she asked, once they were in the kitchen. 'Coffee? Something stronger?'

'Coffee would be fine.'

'I apologise for not coming to your mother's little
party,' Sara repeated, spooning coffee into cups, with her
back to him, 'but I couldn't. How was it? Did it go all
right?'

'Couldn't...?'

Sara didn't answer. She poured boiling water into the
cups, and a dash of milk straight from the long-life carton
in the fridge. The fresh milk she had casually tossed into
the cardboard box for the trip up had expired. The dreaded
trip to the shops could no longer be avoided, that much
was true. Nor could she allow her negative feelings about
the place to influence her response to the people who lived
there. If she did, then her life would be even more of a
nightmare than it already was.

'Simon wasn't very well, I'm afraid,' she said
brusquely, putting his cup down in front of him and taking
the chair on the opposite side of the table from which she
could observe him without that aura of his pervading her
senses.

'What was wrong?' Under the merciless glare of the
overhead light, he could see what he hadn't noticed before.
Her face was drawn and there were anxious shadows under
her eyes.

'He...suffers from recurrent chest infections. He's still
got one now and he was a bit poorly today.' She swal-

lowed a mouthful of coffee and shifted her eyes away from
the blue ones studying her face.

'Is he all right now? I know Tom Jenkins, the local
doctor. I could call him and get him out here to have a
look.'

'Thank you, but no. Simon's a bit better now. He's upstairs sleeping. Anyway, I couldn't come to your mother's
party because at twelve today I was busy dealing with his
wheezing and coughing.'

'You should have driven over. Got me.' Why had he
just said that? he wondered.

'Thanks, but I can deal with Simon on my own. I don't
need any knights in shining armour to help me out. I've
done it for the past five years and I'll carry on doing it.'

'I wasn't offering myself as a knight in shining armour.'
James's voice was a shade cooler. 'I was merely suggesting that at this point in time I happen to be the only person
you know in this town and as such, if you had needed
help, it would have made sense to have come to me.'

'I told you, I didn't need any help. Look, if you don't
mind, I haven't had anything to eat this evening. I'm going
to make myself a sandwich. I'm sure you have much better
things to do than hang around here watching me eat my
dinner.'

'Sit down.'

'What?' Sara flashed him a smile of cool incredulity at
the rasping command in his voice. 'For a minute there, I
thought I heard you tell me to sit down.'

'Which just goes to show how accurate your hearing is.'
Before she could stand up, which he knew she was going
to do, he stood up himself and moved swiftly to where she
was sitting, leaning over her with one hand splayed on the
arm of her pine chair and the other on the table.

'What do you think you're doing?' Sara demanded in a high-pitched, unsteady voice.

'I am making sure you do as I say. Sit down and I'll make the sandwich for you. Tell me what you want in it and point me in the direction of the bread.'

'I...'

'You look exhausted. You've obviously been through one helluva long day. Now do as I say.'

'Or else what?' Sara flung at him. Their eyes clashed and she was mortified to find that she couldn't seem to stop looking at him. Up close, she could smell the fresh, clean scent of him, mingled with the erotic tang of sheer masculinity. It filled her nostrils until she felt as if she was going to faint. Instead, she blinked and clung on rapaciously to her pride. She didn't need this. She didn't need some man, a perfect stranger, to waltz into her house and try and give her orders, even if those orders were issued for her own benefit. She had had to fend for herself from a young age and she had carried on having to do it right the way through pregnancy, childbirth and motherhood.

'Oh, all right,' she snapped, just to get him to move away from her.

'Good.' James pushed himself up but continued to look down at her. 'Now, where's the bread?' he repeated.

'Bread bin on the dresser.' The dresser had been Freddie's. Sara herself had not possessed any such thing when she had lived in London. The kitchen in her flat had been all chrome, granite and smooth cherry wood. An old pine dresser would have been ludicrously inappropriate, but she had since discovered that it was an extremely useful item of furniture. She had kept Freddie's mismatched crockery in place, stashing her own out of sight, and there was a growing pile of Simon's things on the surface, stray colours, bits of Lego, various action-hero dolls in strangely contorted positions.

'This bread's mouldy,' James said, holding up the plastic bag.

He looked so ridiculous that she had to stifle a smile that crept up from somewhere and threatened to chisel away at her defences.

'Do you *know* how to make a sandwich?' she asked curiously. 'Have you *ever* made a sandwich in your life before?' He just didn't look the sandwich-making type.

'I happen to be a very good cook, actually. You haven't eaten any of this today, have you? Is there another loaf somewhere? No? Then I'll just have to make do, and before you start protesting, my original order to sit down still applies.' He tossed the bread in the bin and did a swift inventory of the modest kitchen, noting the uneasy mingling of her own things amongst Freddie's.

'You really don't have to,' Sara said automatically, but lord, it felt good to take the weight off her feet and have someone else do something for her for a change. She rubbed her hand across her eyes and stretched out her long legs.

'Tell me about London,' James said, pulling out a chopping board and then gathering what vegetables he could muster from the basket by the dresser. Everything, he noticed with interest, was as Freddie had left it. Either she had possessed surprisingly little herself or else could not be bothered to install her own things. Which said what? he wondered. 'What did you do there?'

'Where did you learn to cook?'

James glanced over to her. She had rested her head back against the chair and her eyes were closed, as if she was simply too weary to keep them open, and for the first time since he'd arrived he felt a pang of guilt at having foisted

his company onto her at nine in the evening. Then he reminded himself that she would have had to eat anyway,
and she had actually done quite well from him considering
he was here cooking up a pasta dish for her, not an activity
he was known to do for any woman.

'At the hands of my mother during the school holidays,'
James informed her, allowing her change of topic to ride.
For the moment. 'She's Italian and prides herself on her
culinary skills. As soon as I could hold a sharp knife, I
was given things to chop.' His eyes flitted over to find that
she was staring at him, and for no logical reason, because
he was vastly accustomed to being on the receiving end
of women's stares, he felt himself stiffen in response. 'And
as soon as I was tall enough, I was taught how to use the
Aga.'

'Your mother was a chef?'

'My mother was a model from Naples who met my father in London. Much to her agency's disgust, he charmed
her into marrying him after a shockingly brief whirlwind
romance and removed her to the back of nowhere, where
she flourished. She relished breezing into the lives of all
the locals, who had never met a real Italian before and had
certainly never had one live in their midst. She held huge
parties in winter and taught the wives how to cook home-
made pasta. After a couple of years they were eating out
of her hand.'

Sara listened to the smile in his voice and felt her heart
contract. Whatever else she thought of him as a man, and
cooking her a meal would do nothing to alter her opinions,
he loved his mother deeply and that counted for a lot.

'Hence,' he told her, 'my cooking skills.'

'And I always thought that it was the other way around,'
Sara said, 'the woman stuck at home cooking the food
while the man just did whatever he damn well pleased.'

'Has that been your experience?' James asked casually, sliding his eyes over to her and taking in the way her body language altered and her face became watchful and closed.

The thought of drawing out whatever story she had to tell, finding out what the hell made her tick, coursed through his veins in a sudden, exhilarating rush. It was a sensation so alien to him that he belatedly reminded himself of the Rectory, which was, after all, the prize to be won.

'I never asked you whether you were married,' Sara said, surprised to find that she had automatically assumed that he wasn't when she should have assumed just the opposite. 'Would your wife be happy about your cooking food for me?' she continued slowly, trying to picture the sort of woman he would be married to. Beautiful, blonde and brainless, presumably. She had learnt over the years the better-looking and more powerful the man, the less they wanted a wife who could compete with them. Not restful enough.

'You insult me,' James said coldly. 'If I were married, I wouldn't be here. I would be with my woman.'

The way he said that, the casual male acceptance of possessing a woman the way he might possess a piece of furniture, should have had every liberated bone in her body rushing to form a picket line, but instead she felt a searing heat rip through her.

'Cooking for her?' Sara asked lightly, to stop herself from analysing her reaction which didn't make sense.

'Not necessarily,' he said with lazy amusement. 'I might find other things to do in a kitchen that don't necessarily involve food.'

Sara's stomach curled warmly at the blatant image he had casually tossed at her. 'Well,' she tried to gather her scattered wits and speak in a normal voice, 'at any rate, whatever you're cooking smells very good.'

'And it will taste even better,' he assured her, spooning pasta onto a plate and pouring sauce over it straight from the saucepan. It was a rich sauce which he had concocted using a handful of ingredients which hadn't appeared to be dead or in the process of dying, like the three tomatoes he had uncovered next to the onions.

He placed the plate in front of her. 'Now eat.'

'You like giving orders, don't you?' But her mouth was watering and she dived into the food with enthusiasm, not realising how hungry she had been until she saw the bottom of the plate.

'I prefer to see them as instructions.'

'And do you give instructions to all the locals?' she asked, scraping some of the fabulous tomato sauce onto her spoon and relishing it.

'To the locals? Why would I do that?'

'Because you live here?'

'I have a house here and my mother lives here.'

Sara looked at him over the rim of her spoon. 'And where do you live?'

'In London.'

'Ah. That makes sense.'

The shutters were back up, he saw. She carefully closed her fork and spoon and took her plate to the sink, offering him the unrevealing view of her back as she washed the crockery and placed it on the draining board next to her.

'And why does that *make sense*?'

She turned around and perched against the sink, supporting herself with her hands on either side of her, her fingers curled over the edge of the counter.

'I thought you were a little too urbane for around here,' she said. 'A little too sophisticated.'

'Should I take that as a compliment?'

'You can take it any way you want to, although it wasn't meant as one.'

'I presume you have something against urbane, sophisticated men?' James stood up and shoved his hands into his pockets. 'Has that got anything to do with Simon's father, by any chance?'

The silence stretched tautly between them until Sara forced herself to smile with tight politeness at him. After all, he *had* cooked her a meal.

'Thank you so much for cooking for me. It was delicious.'

'Most sincerely spoken.' James walked slowly towards her and the closer he got, the tenser she became, until he was standing inches away from her. Then he reached out and caged her in with his hands, leaning towards her so that their faces were only inches apart. 'But you haven't answered my question.'

'And I don't need to!' she flared angrily. 'My life is none of your business. I'm a very private person and I intend to stay that way.'

'Then, lady, you came to the wrong place. Because I, for one, intend to get right down to the bottom of you.'

He stood back and walked towards the kitchen door. 'We'll meet again.' And he meant every word of it. Without even realising it, she challenged him, and he had never been able to resist a challenge.

CHAPTER THREE

THERE was no need to drive to the nearest sizeable town for her shopping, even though she was sorely tempted to do just that, if only so that she could savour the anonymity which she now found that she perversely craved.

Nestled cosily against the vast backdrop of mountains was the local village. Sara, with one eye on the map next to her and the other on the twisty road, rounded a bend straight into suburbia.

From his car seat in the back, Simon was peering through the window in apparent fascination at the scenery. So fascinated, in fact, that his mouth was parted to accommodate a thumb he had forgotten to suck.

And yes, she had to admit that the scenery was spectacular. From the Rectory to the small town, there were times when the winding road almost seemed to be an insolent intrusion into Mother Nature. Every so often, a sudden bend in the road would offer a tantalising glimpse of flat, glassy water in the distance. She had no idea whether this was an estuary or a loch but, whatever it was, Simon had been enthralled. She, slightly less so. The more magnificent the landscape, the more she longed for the concrete jungle in which she had spent all of her twenty-six years. Noise pollution, air pollution and having to make do with window-boxes in place of a garden had never seemed more enticing.

'Houses!'

'At last,' Sara muttered. They had passed a few big old houses on the journey but these were real houses with real roads that did real things, like branch out in various directions. 'I was beginning to think that we had been transported into the Twilight Zone.'

'What's the Twilight Zone?'

'Should we just drive straight through here until we get to a proper town,' Sara mused aloud, 'or face it?'

'I'm thirsty.'

'Then I guess we'll face it.'

The local village turned out to be bigger than she had expected. Not quite the cluster of basic shops, leaning shoulder-to-shoulder against one another so that the owners could while away their time gossiping outside. The flat white fronts and grey stone façades of the houses, which sprang out from the main street, eventually gave way to small shops offering everything from fly-fishing equipment to guided tours. Further along Sara came to the central square, dominated by a statue of whose identity she had no idea, although his warrior-like bearing didn't suggest the local poet. Cars were neatly parked in slots in front of the monument and spreading around the square was a further assortment of shops, bigger and less picturesque than their counterparts further down the road.

She pulled into a parking space, manoeuvering her small black car until it was resting snugly between a four-wheel-drive on one side and weathered pick-up truck on the other.

'Right,' she said, fetching Simon out of the car and looking around her with some interest. 'We can get lost here.'

'Why would we want to get lost?' he asked in a bewildered voice, and she squeezed his hand gently.

'It's just a saying. Now, where first? Supermarket? Quaint craft shop with hand-knitted jumpers? Pharmacy to check out the medicines for you just in case you get another chest infection. Or maybe just an ice cream before we start doing anything at all?'

This wasn't going to be as bad as she had feared, Sara thought as they headed for the nearest tea shop. She wouldn't quite be able to lose herself here, but at least she wouldn't be singled out as the intruder who had gone to live at the Rectory. Perhaps, she told herself, she could see this as a sort of short holiday. Stay until the middle of August, perhaps, admit the mistake she had made and then head back down south with her tail between her legs. They wouldn't have to return to London. They could live somewhere just outside, somewhere as peaceful as this place without being quite as scarily remote.

She was so busy turning her thoughts over in her head that she failed to notice the significant hush that greeted her breezy entrance into the shop.

She focused and then saw what she had missed when she had first entered, with Simon jabbering away about what flavour ice cream he wanted while she frowningly chewed over thoughts of flight in her head.

All heads were turned in their direction. A table of six elderly women seemed particularly interested. Even the ruddy-cheeked, fresh-faced girl behind the counter had stopped what she had been doing to stare.

Sara ventured a weak smile, her eyes skittering away from the gang of six sitting by the window with their cups of tea and little delicate plates of scones and cream.

'A table?' she asked in a lame voice. 'For two?' She could hardly believe that she was the same assertive woman who had once been a powerful career woman.

'You must be the new girl at the Rectory!' The booming voice stopped her in her tracks and forced her to look across at the six women. 'We've all been dying to meet you! Have we not, ladies?'

'Come, my dear, and let us have a proper look at you and your delightful little boy!'

Sara helplessly looked at the girl behind the old-fashioned wooden counter, who shot her a sympathetic smile.

'I…I…' she stammered, making her way to the table.

'Naturally we were curious about this relative of Freddie's. The old rogue never breathed a word about having a niece. Did he, ladies?'

'You poor thing. Could you not get away from that big old place a little sooner? Heaven knows, you must have been up to your elbows in it! And you with a wee lad as well to look after.'

'Would that be why we haven't spied you in town before?'

'I…I…' Sara repeated weakly.

'And what's *your* name, child? I bet you've come here for an ice cream. This place makes the best ice creams in Scotland!'

'And you should know, Angela. You eat far too many of them for your own good.'

'Now, dear, why don't you pull up a chair and we can all have a cosy little chat.'

'I…well…' Sara licked her lips nervously, while Simon hesitantly accepted a teacake from one of the ladies and began chatting in his low, childish voice to her.

'You might be able to help us! We're trying to sort out the summer fête at the manor. Some fresh input might be just what is needed, would you not agree, ladies? And no, Valerie, we are *not* going to be accommodating your daughter's suggestion about a disco. For a start, Maria would go mad!'

'Well, well, well…' a familiar velvety voice drawled from behind her and Sara felt as though fingers had lightly slithered up her spine, making her pulses race. 'I see you've been caught by the local witches.' There was a wicked grin in his voice when he said that, and Sara didn't need to turn around to imagine the expression on his face. One of utter charm. She could see it in the way the six ladies tittered. 'Be warned, you may not escape this place in one piece.'

'Now, now, young man!'

'Where's your mother, James? She said she would be here by eleven. I'm very much afraid she's missed the first pot of tea.'

'Trouble with one of the gardeners. His daughter's been admitted into hospital, it would seem.'

'That would be young Emma. Baby's on its way, poor thing.'

One of the gardeners? Sara wondered whether she had heard wrong. She had gleaned that the man lived in a big house and was doubtless wealthy or else how could he have a place in London as well, but *how big was his house if he needed more than one gardener to control the lawn*?

Suddenly she didn't want to be here, didn't want to feel his breath against her averted face, because he was standing so close to her that she could. Nor did she want to find herself wondering about him. She already knew enough.

'I... If you don't mind, I have a thousand things to do before I go home, and...and...'

'You've frightened her,' he said on a low laugh, and Sara had the impression that in some peculiar way he was toying with her.

'Don't be ridiculous!' she snapped, whipping around to look at him. Her blazing eyes made little impact. He continued to smile in amusement and had not even been surprised into stepping back. She felt engulfed by his physical presence and hurriedly spun back round so that she was looking at the women, although she knew that her cheeks were burning.

'I really don't mean to be rude, but…but Simon, my son, is just getting over a chest infection and I wanted to try and make it to the pharmacy to buy a few things for him.'

'A chest infection? Oh, you poor wee thing.'

Looking down, Sara wryly observed how he puffed himself out in the face of all the sympathetic tittering from the old ladies.

'Is that one of the reasons that you came up here?' one of the ladies asked. 'They often say that clean air is good for respiratory conditions and we know you lived in London. Is that not a fact, Mary? Didn't your Eleanor have to leave London because her asthma began to get worse?'

'Well, as a matter of fact,' Sara mumbled, keenly aware of the man standing behind her and not really sure why allowing him access to this little sliver of personal information was so off-putting, 'it was one of the reasons.'

'Well, of course we must let you get on. Sandra, dear! Another pot of tea. I can see Maria on her way. If she can manage to get away from that old fool Jenkins. Now, my dear, I hope we'll be seeing a lot more of you!'

'And I'm sure,' James said, 'that the feeling is entirely reciprocated, isn't it? Sara?' His voice was like dark chocolate curling around her name and something hot and alive deep inside her kicked, unbidden, into life. It was something she didn't want to feel and she responded accordingly by pushing it away.

'Of course.' She managed a polite smile, eager to go now that she had established her excuse.

'Oh, good, because there's our little summer dance at the village hall…'

'You're more than welcome to help decorate…'

'On Friday evening. Barbecue if the weather permits…'

'And it will. If those weathermen are anything to go by, not that they usually are…'

'Friday,' Sara said lamely. 'I'd love to, but Simon—'

'I'm sure my mother would be more than happy to babysit,' James interjected, knowing full well where her protest was leading. He hadn't planned on staying quite as long as Friday, but the minute he had removed the objection from her mouth he was filled with an inexplicable urge to prolong his sojourn.

Get to know her, he argued to himself with every semblance of rationality. How else does one win ground unless one is fully aware of the layout?

And, irritating though the admission was, he still knew practically nothing about her and he wanted to find out more. It was a first for him. Hidden depths were not something that he particularly looked for, or for that matter had ever found, in any of the women he had dated. And he liked it that way. That way there was no room for nasty surprises.

'I couldn't possibly…' There was a hunted look in her eyes which he blithely ignored.

'You would be doing her a great favour. She adores children and would love nothing better than to spend the evening with Simon.'

'Well, Simon is very shy with—'

'You could even bring him up to our house. There's a room occupied solely by the most elaborate train set a child could ever hope to find…'

'Train set?' Simon's ears had pricked up, and with a sigh of frustrated resignation Sara conceded defeat.

'So…' he had followed her out of the café, out into the glare of the sun '…you came here because of Simon…why did you wait five years? Surely he would have been suffering from recurrent chest infections from birth?'

'Have you nothing better to do than tag along behind me?'

'Not at this point in time,' he informed her, proving, she thought, that he was every bit as thick-skinned as she had deduced from their first meeting.

Indeed, at this point in time, the business he had intended to do while his mother spent a pleasant couple of hours with her cronies had faded into the background. Right now, he could think of nothing better than glancing over to catch sight of that vibrant red hair that was today caught up in a tortoiseshell clip that barely contained its luxuriant waywardness, that creamy white skin, tinged pink at her discomfort at having to endure his presence.

'You never bought your ice cream,' he pointed out suddenly. 'I suppose our resident crew called you across before you could get to put in your order.' Everyone was curious, he reasoned, and so she would not be able to resist letting her natural curiosity have a wander, even though the determined tilt of her head told him that she would have liked nothing better.

'Who *are* they?' Sara asked, glancing into the windows of some of the shops they were strolling past, catching the occasional look in her direction and uncertain whether this was due to her or to curiosity about why the man at her side was with her.

'Supermarket?' he asked, leaving aside her question for the moment.

She wouldn't have immediately guessed. 'With travel brochures in its window?'

'That's Bill MacKenzie next door. Pays for some of the window space and Trevor never could resist a buck.'

The quaintness of the arrangement brought a smile to

her lips, a smile that he noticed, just as he noticed the reluctance behind it, as though it was dragged out of her.

'Look, why don't you go and get your shopping and I'll take Simon for that ice cream? We can meet you in the square in half an hour.'

'No!'

The vehemence of her response surprised him and he looked at her levelly, his eyebrows raised.

'What's the problem?' he murmured.

'There's no problem. I just don't want to accept your offer. Isn't that enough for you? I have a lot of things to do before I head back home and Simon…needs to be with me.'

And I won't allow my son to get close to a man who sees me as a little mystery he'd like to have fun trying to solve while he's killing a few days here.

Every protective bone in her body had reared up into action at the thought of that. Simon had had enough disappointments in his short life what with having to deal with a father who was not particularly interested in him, who had routinely made arrangements to take him somewhere only to break them at the very last minute because something more important had come up.

In the space of a few still seconds, the past five years unreeled themselves in her head like a series of cinematic clips which had been edited and fast-forwarded to encapsulate her ex-partner and the misery he had brought to her life.

The pregnancy, Simon, Phillip's lack of support because, as he had ruefully informed her, he wasn't the marrying kind, still less the paternal sort. He had seen Simon occasionally but his life had been moving onwards and upwards. There was no time to fit in a sickly son who was too thin, too small and got ill all the time.

The only thing that had ever mattered to Phillip, if only she had been able to see that from the word go, was his career and the ambition to get even further with it. And here was James Dalgleish, who seemed to be as ambitious and career-oriented as Phillip, pretending to take an interest in her son, an interest that was never going to get anywhere, but try telling that to a vulnerable five-year-old child without a father.

She could easily cope with the likes of James Dalgleish. She was immune to men like him. But ice cream in the village square with her son? Oh, no, she thought, *I don't think so.*

'What's the matter?' James's voice seemed to come from a long way away and the sharpness of it snapped her out of her memories. She blinked and focused on him. 'For a minute there you looked as though you were about to pass out.'

'Did I?' Sara asked coldly.

Her tight, closed expression mirrored the iciness of her voice. Whatever she wanted most right at this very moment, and he would bet on this, was for him to disappear. But he wasn't going to do her that favour.

'Now, why would that be, I wonder?'

Sara licked her lips nervously. Her body seemed to have broken out in a fine film of clammy perspiration and she didn't like the way he was looking at her, with that sort of curious interest that made her feel a bit like a specimen being observed by a very clever, very dangerous scientist.

She also didn't care for what he was doing to her body, because even though her brain was furiously seeing with perfect clarity all the danger signs that were going off like alarm bells in her head, her body was behaving with a life of its own. Her breasts felt as though they were pulsing and there was a treacherous warmth spreading through her that illogically made her even angrier with the man standing unperturbed in front of her, looking at her as though he could read every little strand of thought in her mind. And if he couldn't, then he intended to probe until he could.

'What's Simon's relationship with his father?'

Colour drained from her face. *How dared he?*

'That's no business of yours!'

'Is it a secret?' He had asked the wrong question, he could see that now. Somehow he had managed to dig into a wound that was still raw, but hell, he would go for broke now. 'What's *your* relationship with him?' he asked.

Sara reacted on impulse. There was no longer any Simon by her side, no shops around her, no pavements teeming with people all out doing their shopping in the fine weather. There was just him.

Her open palm stung as it made fierce contact with his face and the sound of flesh hitting flesh shocked her almost as much as it shocked him, but before she could turn and flee the unpleasant scene she felt his fingers circle her wrist and he was bending over her, his mouth thinned into a flat, angry line.

'Don't,' he said with silky menace, 'ever do that again.'

'Or else what?' Sara demanded through gritted teeth. 'What will you do to me? Throw me in prison? Chain me to a post in the village square?'

'Such antiquated ideas,' James said with soft intent. 'Punishment comes in many different packages.' He lowered his head and his mouth made contact with hers, driving her back slightly, and in that moment of unsteady surprise his tongue found a way to plunder her mouth. It was a hard, savage kiss that ended almost before it began and he couldn't have thought of a more brutally effective punishment because Sara could only stare at him in silent shock.

Her lips felt bruised but it was inside that was really doing a wild, terrifying roller-coaster ride. She couldn't have been more affected if an electric current had been driven into her. Her whole body ached and throbbed and wanted in a way that filled her with fright and dismay.

'And don't forget,' he reminded her in a perfectly level voice, 'that my mother will be babysitting for you on Friday.' His deeply sensual mouth parted into a humourless smile. 'And don't, likewise, imagine that you can wriggle out of it. It's a small town and tongues wag. If you want to be happy here with your son, then I am sure you see the necessity of kicking off to the right start.'

His accuracy of the size of the town and the wagging of tongues struck home later that evening when, over dinner, his mother carefully closed her knife and fork and gave him one of those shrewd looks that he knew from experience promised a serious conversation.

'I knew that you had met our new neighbour,' Maria Dalgleish said ruminatively, 'but I had no idea that you had become quite so intimate with her.'

'Now, how did I know that that was coming?' James tossed his white linen napkin next to his plate and sat back in the chair, pushing it away from the exquisitely polished table so that he could cross his legs.

'A passionate kiss in the middle of town, James?' Her eyes flashed with sudden amusement and she looked down at the tips of her fingers. 'Surely you must have known that such a thing would have had…' she searched to find the appropriate phrase in English '…fall-out.'

James's eyes were brooding and uncooperative. He had known full well what the so-called fall-out of his actions would be, had known it even as he had lowered his head towards her. The possibility of *him*, the most prominent man in the area, probably in the whole of Scotland for that matter, going unnoticed was zilch.

But he had been compelled to. He had looked into those fiery green eyes, looked lower to the angrily parted lips, perfectly defined petal-pink lips, and he had been unable to resist tasting them. Only the knowledge that they were in public and her son was staring up at them wide-eyed and curiously accepting, had made him pull back from her. Or he would have carried on kissing her and he had wanted more. Much more. Just thinking about it now made his body react in a pleasurable but utterly inappropriate way.

'Because there are too many idle women in this place,' he said irritably, 'with nothing better to do than talk about other people.'

'So,' Maria said briskly, 'is it tomorrow that you are off? Or Wednesday? I had planned a meeting with the girls for tomorrow to discuss this summer fête at the manor, but of course I can easily cancel that and we can maybe go somewhere for lunch.'

'No need.' He sat frowning and thinking, cursing himself for having given in to his ridiculous male impulse to kiss the damned woman and expose her unwittingly to gossip. 'I've decided to stay until at least the weekend.' He refocused on his mother and added drily, 'I at least have some duty to escort Sara King to the local ball, having sullied her image in the first place.' He imagined her standing hesitantly on her own by the door of the village hall, having been forced to attend an event she clearly had not wanted to, while everyone stopped what they had been doing to look covertly at her. 'Which reminds me, I told her that you'll babysit her son, Simon. I hope you don't mind.'

'Mind? I will enjoy every minute of it. You know how much I love children.'

'And don't even think it, Mama,' James said wryly, toying with the slender stem of his wine glass, watching the remnants of his white wine swirl around. 'I'm not about to get involved with her. She's as elusive as a shadow and you know I have only ever been attracted to the straightforward type.' But even as the words had been uttered, he had a compelling vision of a tall, slender creature, with creamy white skin, breasts pushing forward like ripe fruit to be tasted. He drained his wine and stood up, ready to take his leave.

And Maria Dalgleish was more than happy to let him. She couldn't think while he hovered there, and thinking was what she felt like doing tonight.

'I shall show him your father's train set, shall I?' she asked with a smile and he nodded with a little shrug.

'Why not? He's bound to love it. I did.' Now that he had decided not to leave, just yet, he had business to see to. Thank God for computers, faxes, e-mails and all the technology that would enable him to run his empire away from his offices, if only for a while.

He would stay at home, he thought, and work. His visits to the estate were so short that no one would question the fact that he was no longer around in the town and he would not risk bumping into Sara again.

He had frightened her with his questions, appeared to have utterly panicked her with his ill-thought-out kiss. He would give her time to recover and build up her defences.

But the mere thought of those defences going up was enough to fire him up at the thought of breaking them down.

But go back up they would. Less than a mile away, Sara was feverishly thinking the same thing. She had spent the

day in a state of charged confusion. Done her shopping
and hurried back to the Rectory with Simon. Normally,
being with him was always enough to take her mind off
her problems, but today her mind was caught in a trap
elsewhere, filled with images of James Dalgleish and the
kiss he had forced upon her as fair retribution for her having slapped his face.

He would never have had his face slapped by a woman
in his life before, she thought as she sat in the cosy snug
with the television providing muted sound in the background. That arrogant, devastatingly attractive face would
not have inspired anger in any woman he might have been
out with. It would have inspired *craving* because everything about him, from the way he looked to the way he
moved, was sexually mesmerising.

He had touched her and her body had shot up in flames,
hot flames that licked every part of her. It would almost
have been better if she could have put her response down
to the needs of a woman who had been celibate for the
past five years.

And they would be talking about her in the town. Their
kiss hadn't exactly been conducted in the privacy of four
walls.

But there were still some things that needed doing.
Someone to come and install an extra phone line for her
so that she could use the internet on her computer. Someone to come and link up her computer for goodness' sake,
get it up and running. She had never had to bother with
the nuts and bolts of the thing, but then in London she had
had a secretary to do all that for her, to get the appropriate
software technicians in when it was playing up. Even if
she only intended to stay put for a limited period of time,
she would still have to buy a book on computers, at least
so that she could learn some of the rudiments herself.

After all the effort she had made to get here, though, the thought of running back down south now seemed exhausting. More change for Simon. And if she returned south, then how long before the headhunters began? Life was frantic down there.

She shook her head wearily and decided that she had better check out schools, get Simon registered, just in case.

That, too, would need a visit to the town. Balking at the prospect of meeting yet another set of people who knew her business was not going to do her any good.

But, as it turned out, her trip in on the Thursday was less of an ordeal than she had imagined. And she found out, really without asking, that James had left to return to London. This piece of information came from a girl in her twenties whose young boy ended up playing with Simon in a little park on the edge of the town where Sara had taken him to see some ducks. She herself had ended up sitting on the bench with the girl, to discover that her mother was one of the dreaded six and that she, Fiona, was the local vet's assistant.

'You won't be over-popular with some of our girls who think that James Dalgleish is up for grabs,' Sara was told with a laugh, 'but you'll be very popular with the rest of us who find that little lot extremely annoying. *That kiss* has been the most exciting thing to have happened here in months!'

That kiss was not going to happen again, at any rate, Sara thought on the Friday as she nervously contemplated going to the village hall, an invitation which had been thrust upon her and one which she was morally obliged to meet.

Fiona, at least, would be there, she consoled herself. She would have an ally should she need one. And James Dalgleish was safely tucked hundreds of miles away.

On her last trip to the town he had been nowhere in sight, and his absence made sense. Powerful businessmen like him were incapable of staying away from their offices for too long. It would almost be easier for their bodies to defy gravity than it would for their minds to defy the pull of the top-level business meeting.

She got dressed, and by seven she was ready.

Lord, but it felt alien to be in proper clothes, after her daily uniform of jeans and T-shirts. She looked at the reflection staring back at her and remembered that this was the image that had been *her* only a matter of a few short weeks ago.

In fact, this was one of her favourite dresses. One she had worn on a number of occasions to see her friends or go to the cinema. Casual but not too casual, revealing, but not alarmingly so, just sufficient to show off the length and shapeliness of her legs. The dark green hues complemented her colouring and the fairly prim style was compensated for by the way the fabric clung to her curves. If she was going to go to this damned local dance, then she certainly wasn't going to hide behind something unshapely and dull.

She had already bathed and dressed Simon. She had spoken to Maria on the phone two days previously, had immediately felt comfortable, and the day before Maria had popped over to the Rectory on her way to town so that she could meet the little boy who would be her charge for two hours at the most.

Sara had almost asked her whether she could confirm that her son had gone but the question would have sounded odd and she had cravenly shied away from mentioning his name just in case *that kiss* had been reported back to his mother.

But she had liked what she had seen and so had Simon.

Maria Dalgleish was very much like James to look at, apart from the eyes, and she looked feisty enough, but there was none of the arrogance or the casually assumed self-assurance that sat on her son's shoulders like a cloak.

She had arranged to drive over and was curious to see what this manor looked like and exactly how extensive those gardens were, when the doorbell went.

She pulled open the door, a ready smile on her face, her mouth half-open to tell Maria that she shouldn't have come for Simon, that she was going to drop him off herself as arranged.

Her smile froze as did her thought processes as she took in the man standing in front of her.

James Dalgleish, the man who should safely be miles away in London, the man who had managed to do what no other man had since Simon had been born, namely destabilise her, reach behind the fortress she had erected around herself and touch a part of her that did not want to be touched.

Tall, so beautiful that it brought a gasp to her throat and every inch a man she did not need in her life, not in any way, shape or form.

CHAPTER FOUR

'YOU! What are *you* doing here! You should be in London!'

'Oh, should I?' Dark, winged eyebrows shot up in apparent surprise at this statement, but surprised he most certainly was not. She would have thought he was in London, at least if she had wandered into the town again, and she undoubtedly would have had to, just as she would undoubtedly have had to have seen someone who would have started chatting to her, trying to find out what was going on between him and her. And it wouldn't have taken her long to discover that, as far as everyone was concerned, he had done his usual vanishing trick, because that was what his mother had told her friends, who would have told everyone else.

He had only found out by accident, having volunteered to drive his mother into town to meet her cronies for their weekly game of bridge.

'Oh, no need,' his mother had responded with uncustomary vagueness. 'I may have mentioned that you were heading back to the City, and why see them again just yet if you do not have to? Hm? You know the questions you will be asked! They can be so forthright sometimes.'

'You *may* have mentioned it, *cara Mama*?'

'It is possible, *sì*. I do not know. I cannot quite remember. Such a small detail!'

But actually having her believe that he was not around, that he wouldn't threaten her by being at the dance, suited him perfectly. James Dalgleish was not a man who hid behind neatly contrived preconceptions. She challenged him and he wanted her. Before he had laid eyes on her, his one thought had been the swift acquisition of the Rectory, to which end he had been prepared to do anything. Pay over the odds, find the woman somewhere else to live even if it meant building a house for her. He had enough money to compensate her in any way she chose, financially. Then he met her and for a while he saw himself as simply a shrewd businessman who was prepared to get to know his quarry, find out exactly whether her plans to live at the Rectory were long-term, discover the weakness that would provide him with what he wanted.

But he hadn't kicked off with his plan to denigrate the house, had he? And now he acknowledged that he just wanted her. Wanted to take her to his bed and make love to her, watch her closed, defensive face open up before his eyes like a flower blooming under the rays of the sun. He wanted to hear her moan aloud with desire, desire for *him*, he wanted to watch her writhe on his bed and lose all her inhibitions. All thoughts of buying the Rectory had temporarily taken a back seat to urges that were stronger and far, far more irresistible.

So the accusation burning in her eyes now was hardly a shock to his system.

'I was under the impression that you had urgent work to attend to in London!'

James shrugged and gave her a helplessly apologetic grimace that did nothing to erase the dismay she felt at seeing him again. And every pulse in her body was racing. She looked around a little desperately for Simon and called him, turning away so that she didn't have to look at the man lounging in front of her.

He was dressed in pale cream chinos that accentuated the lithe narrowness of his hips and the length of his legs, and a dark grey short-sleeved shirt. Both reeked of immaculate and very pricey tailoring and neither did much to lessen the predatorial impact of his darkly handsome face and whipcord-lean body.

Now she felt hugely self-conscious in her get-up. She had dressed to make a positive statement when she confronted the people who were her neighbours, at least for the moment. If you're whispering about me behind my back, she wanted to imply, then you don't frighten me.

Instead, with those riveting dark blue eyes broodingly looking at her, all she could feel was the straining of the fine material of her dress against her breasts and the over-exposure of her legs, which weren't even protected with tights because the night was so balmy and she had predicted that it would be positively hot in the village hall.

She breathed a sigh of relief when she heard Simon's little feet pattering towards the kitchen.

'Did your mother send you to fetch me?' Sara asked in a stilted voice, clutching at the last straw that he might not actually be going to the wretched dance. She bent down to adjust her son's pyjama top and then ran her fingers through his fine hair. 'Because there was no need. I'm pretty sure I could find your house if it's next door to mine. In fact,' she continued, standing up and clutching Simon's hand in hers, 'it might be a good idea for me to follow you in my car. I want to have my own transport.' In the face of his silence, which was accompanied by a patient tilt of his head, as if he was listening carefully to what she was saying but not really paying a great deal of notice, Sara felt herself chattering on witlessly. She gave a nervous laugh. 'I wouldn't want to find that I had to walk home if I was having a rotten time! All this isolation stretching into infinity! I would get hopelessly lost!' Her voice faltered into silence and the silence continued for a few awkward seconds longer.

'I wouldn't dream of allowing you to go on your own,' James drawled, turning towards his car and expecting her to follow him.

'Don't be ridiculous!' She hesitated in front of the door, which he was holding open for her. 'I'm perfectly capable of getting myself to the town and finding where I should be going!'

'Nonsense.' He smiled implacably and, while she felt inclined to stand her ground and argue the matter till the cows came home, Simon removed the decision from her hands by opening the back car door and clambering into the seat.

The smile James gave her made her scowl.

'Do you *always* get your own way?' she snapped, sliding past him into the passenger seat and pressing her legs together.

'Always,' he assured her, half turning to look at her. 'You look stunning, by the way.' His mouth curved into a smile that sent a little thrill racing down her spine. 'But don't feel obliged to thank me for the compliment.'

'I won't,' Sara returned, instantly regretting her reply because it was unnecessary. 'But thank you anyway,' she added, turning to stare straight ahead.

'I brought my teddy,' Simon piped up from behind. 'Will Mrs...Mrs Babysitter mind?'

'I think she would love to see your teddy.' James started the engine and allowed Sara to stare frozenly ahead at the scenery while he chatted with her son. All that ice, but he had tasted those lips, had felt a surge of heat come from her straight into him and he knew that under the ice lay a hot pool of fire just waiting for him to ignite.

As they turned left and began the drive up to the manor,

Sara couldn't hold on to her pointed silence any longer. Her mouth dropped open as she took in the length, breadth and width of the rolling estate.

'This isn't all *yours*, is it?' she gasped, turning to stare at his averted profile.

'All of it,' he confirmed, a little nettled by the fact that his property impressed her, even if he didn't. 'Over there, to the right, there's a rose garden and even a miniature maze.'

Sara stared at the gracious manor rising up with effortless grace, dominating the courtyard which sprawled around a magnificent circular flower bed that was bursting with colour. A silver Rolls-Royce was parked neatly in front of the house.

'Is it a castle?' Simon breathed, awestruck, standing up so that he was peering between them with his teddy clutched in his arms.

'Not quite,' James said, laughing. 'Not uncomfortable enough.'

'And your mother lives here *on her own*?' Sara asked. The pale gold frontage seemed to stretch on forever, rising in places to turrets that belonged to something from a fairy tale.

'She has staff, naturally.'

'Oh, naturally,' Sara said, missing the amused look he threw at her. 'It must be awfully lonely for her.' They got out of the car and Sara stared upwards at the imposing façade. 'Rattling around here on her own, even if there *are* staff.'

'I come up and see her at least once a month,' James grated, not caring for the description of his mother *rattling around* in the house and caring even less for the assumption that she must be lonely.

'And then there are two of you rattling around.' Simon

tugged at her hand and she let herself be pulled towards the heavy oak door. 'Didn't you ever think of selling? Maybe buying something smaller for your mother? I would, if it were me.'

In that split instant he knew how she would react if he admitted that he had indeed thought of buying somewhere smaller and that the place he had in mind was only a stone's throw away, was in fact the Rectory which she had only just occupied.

She was wary enough of him already. In fact, she positively bristled with uneasy suspicion whenever he was within striking distance of her. Hearing that he wanted her house was not exactly going to fill her with trusting warmth, was it? Lust or cold-headed practicality? he wondered.

His eyes slid across to the long column of her neck as she gazed upwards, pale and beckoning in the mellow light of the evening sun.

Cold-headed practicality, he thought, would be dealt with later. It wouldn't be a problem. But it was not in his nature to issue an outright lie and so he cleverly evaded the question.

'This is our heritage,' he told her truthfully enough. 'And I would never sell it. It belongs to the Dalgleish family as it always will.' No lie there. His intentions weren't to sell the family home, merely convert it into something else, something that would do justice to its grandeur. 'Now, let's go inside.' He lightly placed his hand on her elbow and so engrossed was she in her surroundings that she barely noticed.

'Can I see the trains as soon as we get inside?' Simon asked hopefully.

'I hope he'll be OK—he's pretty much better now—but

he has been so ill with that chest infection—' Sara looked worriedly at James.

'I have my mobile phone. You can be contacted and be back here within half an hour. Surely this is what happened when you went out in London?'

'It was different there,' Sara said quickly. 'Lizzie knew him from birth, knew what to do if he got sick.' She had had to, Sara thought regretfully. Working long hours had necessitated that and long hours were what she had had to do to pay for the mortgage because Phillip's idea of maintenance had only ever been the very occasional flamboyant present for his son. And in the past two years, not even that.

As far as Phillip had been concerned, she had chosen to have the baby and so she could damn well take care of him financially herself. He was over-committed as it was with his apartment in London and a house in Portugal. When he had had the nerve to imply that she might have got herself pregnant as a passport to a wedding ring, Sara had ceased to talk about maintenance and done everything within her power to make sure that she took care of herself and her son to the best of her ability.

'Lizzie?'

'His nanny.'

'You had a nanny?'

'I had to work. There are such things as a mortgage, bills, food, clothes. Little things that usually have price tags attached to them.' She knew that she was being ridiculously defensive as all her old guilt rose to the surface and not for the first time. Guilt at having got pregnant in the first place, guilt at having to work, guilt at the hours she worked because being a top commodities trader had never been a nine-to-five job. So much guilt that she could drown under it if she let herself.

She was relieved when they were inside the house and Maria was with them, clucking over Simon, warmly asking Sara questions about what she thought of their town and tartly telling her son that his choice of colours did nothing for him, that he should have worn something a little less severe, considering they would be going to a casual little barbecue, some nice little checked shirt that didn't make him look as if he was taking a few hours' break from work.

'I don't *have* any checked shirts.'

Sara slid a sidelong glance at him and her mouth twitched at the cornered expression on his face.

'I look fine,' he muttered, looking pointedly at his watch.

'And do *you* agree?'

Sara found two pairs of eyes focused on her, one dark, the other navy blue and a lot more disconcerting. She chose to meet the dark pair.

'He looks all right,' she conceded.

'*All right?*' He couldn't help it. He did not consider himself by any means vain, but he was used to being seen as somewhat more than *all right*. *All right* was a pedestrian description to be applied to a pedestrian man and he struggled to contain a ludicrous feeling of pique in the face of those green eyes which were now doing a more detailed inventory of him.

'The shirt *is* a little on the sombre side, colour-wise,' Sara elaborated, unable to resist having a go, even if it was a very small one. It was just so satisfying to dent that massive ego of his. 'Not very summery, if you know what I mean, but I guess not bad.'

'Well,' he smiled slumberously, his blue eyes roving over her in a mimicry of her own physical appraisal of him except taking far, far longer, lingering over the pert swell of her breasts, the slenderness of her waist and the length of her naked legs, 'then I should be thankful that you will relieve the dullness of my clothing, shouldn't I?' He did another leisurely appraisal of her, this time starting with her feet and working upwards until he was looking at her flushed face with lazy amusement.

'Now off you go, children.' Maria positively hustled them to the front door. 'Simon and I want to play with a certain set of trains before he gets too sleepy!'

'I won't be long and I'll take him home as soon as we get back.'

'He will be sleeping!'

'He won't wake up. He sleeps like a log.'

'He can sleep the night here,' Maria said, frowning. 'There are more than enough bedrooms to accommodate one small boy.' She smiled. 'And you as well, if you don't want to spend the night away from him. Now, you run along the both of you.'

Sara hovered uncertainly then bent to give Simon a hug. When she stooped, her dress rode even higher up her thighs. The statement outfit was proving to be a liability.

'There's no need to worry about him,' James soothed as soon as they were in the car with the manor house diminishing behind them. 'My *mama* loves children, like all Italians. Left to her, I would have a dozen children so that she could spend her time bustling around them.'

Sara slid a glance at him and couldn't imagine a less likely candidate for a dozen children.

'Then why don't you oblige her?'

'I will...when the time is right.'

'And if it hasn't been right so far, then haven't you asked yourself whether it ever will? Maybe there's a pattern there. Never the right time in the right place for the right woman.'

'The right woman...hm...interesting concept... You

mean I should stop dating blonde bimbos and look for another kind of woman to warm my bed?' His attempt to lighten the conversation went down like a lead balloon.

'Oh, no,' Sara said coolly, 'you just need to find the right blonde bimbo. She's out there somewhere!' She couldn't help it. She gave a bitter, sarcastic laugh and felt the sting of tears press against her eyelids.

'Tell me about your job.' The road straight ahead led almost directly to the village hall. James took the first left so that he could get there by the most circuitous route. 'What did you do in London?'

'I...I was a commodities trader.' Sara could almost hear the silence of surprised disapproval ricocheting around the car. 'And before you tell me that that was no kind of job for a woman, I might as well let you know that I was very good at it. More than that, it paid very well, which happens to be extremely handy when you're bringing up a child.'

'I can see why you needed a nanny,' was all he said. 'Commodity trading is an exhausting job. I don't suppose you got to see your son as much as you would have liked.'

The gentle sympathy in his voice caught her unawares and she found herself floundering between resentment at his observations and an overpowering urge to pour out her feelings. She had become so accustomed to carrying the weight of single motherhood on her shoulders, to pushing on however tired or depressed or just plain fed up she might be, that confiding in other people was a talent she had lost a long time ago. Even her girlfriends had not been privy to her innermost thoughts. She'd met them whenever they could arrange to, which was infrequently because most of them worked in the same high-octane field as she had, and they chatted about bonuses, holidays, frustrations at work but seldom about how they really felt. They were all young, in enviably well-paid jobs, they had no time to be depressed. They laughed, ate at expensive restaurants and veered away from anything that might imply that their lifestyles were not all that they were cracked up to be.

'I suppose you think that I was an irresponsible mother, bringing a child into the world and then not even spending any quality time with him, but I had no choice. Trading was the only thing I was good at. I didn't go to university, I was a hopeless secretary. I would have been fired sooner or later if my boss didn't happen to notice that I had an ability to predict market trends. And trading is a game you can't slow down without getting left behind.' She could hear the pitch of her voice rising in defensiveness and took a few deep, steadying breaths. 'Are we nearly there?'

'Nearly.'

She waited for him to continue trying to drag information out of her and was half hoping that he would because in the darkness of the car it felt good to talk, like being in a confessional, but he didn't. He just pointed out one or two landmarks to her and then prosaically began to talk about places she could visit, things Simon might like to see when they got a chance.

Why wasn't he talking about *her*? she wondered feverishly. For a minute there she had actually thought that he was genuinely interested, genuinely sympathetic to what she had gone through for the past five years, and there was a dam inside her waiting to burst. But suddenly he had stopped asking questions, lost all interest.

As soon as he had heard what she had done for a living, Sara thought slowly. She had been so right to bracket James Dalgleish and Phillip in the same category. Neither of them had really liked a woman who possessed an intellect that could threaten them. Phillip had slept with her because she had been a novelty for him and because he had liked the way she looked, but where was he now?

Getting married and moving to Sydney. Getting married to a woman who was blonde, helpless and had never done a day's hard work in her life. Getting married to a woman who was seven months pregnant. She herself had not seen her ex for nearly nine months and her friends had been all too willing to explain why. She suspected even he might have felt some twinge of feeling for her and the son he had never really acknowledged. In due course, a letter would arrive and there would be one line of regret for the way things turned out but rather more than one somehow laying the blame for everything at her door, and a good deal more devoted to how he had finally found what he had been looking for all his life. The letter would arrive to a flat occupied by tenants and she sincerely hoped that they would drop it in the nearest bin. She detested Phillip, but rejection still hurt and what hurt even more was knowing that her son had been rejected as well.

By the time they reached the village hall, her mood had sunk to rock-bottom. She could barely look at the man walking in with her, and when he brushed against her arm as they entered she visibly flinched.

Thankfully there was no need to stay glued to his side. Fiona had turned up and was waving at her from across the room, and the sea of hostility and suspicion she thought she would find was absent. Everyone was too busy having a good time. The music was loud and operated by an enthusiastic youth with shoulder-length hair and there was a long buffet table extending across one side of the hall, on which she assumed food would be laid out in due course.

It was as far removed from a fashionable London nightclub as it was possible to get.

'I'll get you a drink,' James said into her ear. 'Stay here.' He moved away into the crowd, stopping every two

feet to have a few words with someone, and Sara immediately headed towards Fiona.

Stay here? Did he imagine that he could issue impera-
tives and she would mindlessly obey? Out of the corner
of her eye, she could see him still trying to get to the bar,
where three middle-aged gentlemen were trying to keep up
with the crowd of people putting in their orders, and she
smirked with satisfaction at the thought of him returning
to that spot by the door to find that she had disappeared
into the crowd. Of course, it wouldn't be long before he
zeroed in on her, but by then she would have proved her
point.

If this had been London, she thought with another of
those pangs of regret, she could well and truly have lost
herself. The crowds and the darkness of a nightclub would
have easily swallowed her up. Not so here. They had
dimmed the lights but dark it certainly was not and the
crowds couldn't hide a fly for more than twenty minutes.

And if she had been with her friends…but she wouldn't
have been with her friends at a nightclub. They would have
been at a smart wine bar or an expensive restaurant, swap-
ping anecdotes about who was doing what at work, and at
the back of her mind guilt would have been nagging away
that she had left Simon at night when she had been out all
day. At least here she didn't feel guilty about leaving him
with Maria for a couple of hours. They had had a good
day together, doing some weeding, baking some bread,
taking time out to just sit in the garden where she had
sleepily watched him play with his Lego on a rug while
she read a magazine. Little, simple things that her friends
would never have understood because they belonged to a
fervently child-free culture and talk of children bored
them.

Fiona and her three friends all had children and it was

weird to discuss Simon openly without seeing only polite interest on their faces. It was even interesting to discuss schooling in the area when she knew full well that the chances of their staying put was only fifty-fifty, if that.

She felt his approach before she saw him. Even in a crowded room, with disco music rattling out in the background, she still felt his approach. It made the hairs on the back of her neck stand on end and she steeled herself for his inevitable remark about walking off when he had pointedly told her to stay put.

She was aggrieved to find that he was glaringly indifferent to whether she had walked off, stayed put or even headed back in the direction of home.

He handed her a glass of wine, which she drank with record speed, and then ignored her while he chatted amicably with her companions. Fiona tried to include her in the conversation while her bright eyes darted between the two of them, taking in their body language. But their histories went back a long way. Mutual friends were mentioned, incidents referred to, and after a while Sara excused herself to get some more wine. Two glasses and she was feeling much better.

'Not running away from me by any chance?' His velvety voice washed over her and she turned to him with a radiant smile.

'Don't look now but your ego's showing,' Sara said smugly, happily accepting her third glass of wine. A pleasant contentment washed over her. 'Not surprising, though, considering that all the lassies are fluttering their eyelashes at you.'

'So you've been watching me, have you?' His gaze swept over her with lazy speculation. It gave him a kick of satisfaction to think that she had been following his progress through the room, looking at every woman he had stopped to talk to. Her green eyes were glittering up at him, amazing eyes, like green glass. He raised his glass to his lips and continued to stare at her upturned face until she reddened, although, he noticed, she didn't tear her gaze away as she normally would, so that she could rush behind her defences. She met his stare and matched it.

'Of course I haven't been *watching you*.'

'Well, I've been watching you,' he said softly, 'along with most of the other unattached males in this place. Would you like to dance?'

Before she could formulate an answer, he had circled her waist with his hands and was pulling her in the direction of the makeshift dance floor.

Her soft compliance as she leant into him made him tighten the muscles around his loins and a hot wave of unexpectedly primitive emotion flooded through him. He tightened his hold on her, pulling her closer into him so that he could feel the crush of her soft breasts against his chest and so that she could feel the hardness between his legs that would be telling her exactly what he wanted to do with her.

'People will talk,' Sara murmured, allowing her head to rest lightly on his shoulder.

'Because we're dancing?' He knew exactly what she meant. It wasn't that they were dancing, but how they were dancing. There was not a millimetre of space between them and she was gyrating slowly against his body, in time to the slow, steady beat of the love song.

Lord, but was this how she danced with other men? The thought sent a shard of searing jealousy straight through him and he curled his fingers into her long hair, tilting her face to his.

'Do you go to a lot of nightclubs in London, Sara?' he

asked huskily and she gave a low-throated gurgle of laughter and shook her head.

'I try and not go out at all. Or, at least, not very often. Sometimes on a Saturday evening, although Sundays were always the worst for me. Don't you find Sundays the loneliest day of the week?' She trailed her fingers from his shoulders to the back of his neck and he audibly caught his breath.

'How much have you had to drink?' he queried unsteadily.

'Three glasses. And counting.'

'Three glasses and full stop.'

'I hope you're not telling me how much I can drink, Mr Dalgleish, because if you are then I'm afraid you don't know me at all.'

'Because you don't take orders from a man?'

'That's right.' God, it had been a long time since she had danced like this with a man. Thinking about it, she didn't remember ever dancing like this with a man, not even Phillip, who had hated dancing anyway and was scathing of anywhere that loud music was played and he might be obliged to get up and dance.

'Now, that's something that might come between us,' he murmured lazily.

'Because you like ordering people about?'

'Because when I sleep with a woman I like to be in charge.'

His words floated over her and into her and then crashed through her consciousness, leaving behind a surge of excitement that made her nipples harden against the lacy covering of her bra.

'Are you hungry?'

'Wh…what?'

'Because I see they're beginning to put out the food over

there.' The music came to an abrupt halt, someone announced that food was served and that everyone had to form an orderly queue, and he pulled away from her.

Something in her stomach. She needed something in her stomach. She could feel the alcohol, precious little but more than she was used to drinking, swishing around inside her. The barbecue smelled delicious.

'It will sober you up,' James said in an undertone and when she was beginning to wonder whether the postscript to that remark was that, sober, she wouldn't carry on making a fool of herself, he continued with a lazy half-smile, 'so that I cannot later be accused of having had my wicked way with someone under the influence of drink.' His eyes tangled with hers.

'You won't be having your wicked way with me,' Sara protested weakly.

'Shall we join some of the others outside?' He had to stop looking at those drowsy, beckoning eyes or he would have no choice but to abandon eating and drag her somewhere private, to hell with what the entire town had to say on the subject. Corporate businesswoman she might well have been, but when it came to emotions she was the most intriguing woman he had ever met and the complex combination of vulnerability and gutsy intelligence was driving him crazy.

Sara was barely aware of the conversation swirling around her as she munched her way through chicken, a sausage and some bits of salad and bread. The only thing she was aware of was the energy emanating from the man sitting alongside her on the bench, his thigh grazing hers every so often.

When the music started back, drifting through the open windows to where outside lights had been switched on to accommodate the gathering darkness, James stood up and announced that it was time for them to leave.

'Sara wants to be back early as it's the first time my mother is babysitting her son.'

Her chance was now, to agree with him and leave, but to go where and do what, or to disagree, stand her ground and put her provocative behaviour down to a little too much wine on an empty stomach. Right now, she felt as sober as a judge.

Wrong time, wrong place and definitely, she thought, wrong man. She was behaving like a teenager instead of the responsible mother that she was, flopping all over him like a wet rag and acting as though that husky voice of his and his body pressing against hers so that she could feel his arousal was because of *her*. When instead he was only a red-blooded male responding in typical fashion to a reasonably attractive woman who had too much wine inside her for her own good.

But she had been in a deep freeze for five years. Somewhere along the line she had forgotten that she was only twenty-six, hardly over the hill.

'He can be a bit nervous with strangers, to start with,' Sara said, clearing her throat and standing up. 'I promised him that I wouldn't be back late. Where shall I put my plate and glass?'

'Leave it here,' Fiona said, catching her eye and grinning broadly. 'I'll take it in. Some of us poor, hapless souls have been roped into doing all the clearing away, so we'll be here until the break of dawn. Or at least until eleven-thirty when our resident DJ packs up and leaves.'

'That would be my brother,' Helen explained, smiling, 'and he'll pack up exactly when I tell him to.'

It was only when they were outside in the clear, cool air that a sickening rush of nerves washed over her, and when she stepped gingerly into his car it intensified to the point where she had to rest her head back and close her eyes.

He didn't start the engine immediately. Instead, he turned in his seat and looked at her. 'If you want to back out, tell me now.'

Sara slowly inclined her head so that she was looking straight into his glittering eyes. 'I don't know what to do,' she answered truthfully.

'I know what you *want* to do,' he murmured, reaching out to slide his fingers along her cheek and into her hair, and Sara's breath caught painfully in her throat.

'Where will we go?'

'To the Rectory.' He gave her a killing smile that made her shiver with fear and searing anticipation. 'And don't worry,' he dipped his fingers to her half-parted mouth and gently traced its outline, 'I'm not a beast. If you change your mind along the way, I won't take advantage of you.' But she wouldn't, he thought with a flare of triumph that made his loins physically ache. She wanted him as badly as he wanted her. He could feel it in the loaded atmosphere between them. The air was thick with unexpressed needs. He was not surprised when she gave him an imperceptible nod and only then did he turn away and fire the engine into life.

CHAPTER FIVE

EVEN to Sara's racing mind, the drive back seemed a lot shorter and was accomplished in silence. A silence pregnant with slick excitement.

'Changed your mind yet?' James asked softly, when they reached the Rectory and he had killed the engine.

'Changed yours?' She laughed a little wryly. 'We're behaving like teenagers. At least I am. It's just that...'

'Just that what...?'

'Oh, I don't know.' She shrugged and stared out of the window. Yes, she wanted to sleep with him. Badly. Too badly, and that was the problem, but how could she explain that to him? How could she tell him that she was frankly terrified of opening herself up to another man when her experiences with the last one had left her mortally wounded? He would roar with laughter. This wasn't about having a relationship as far as James Dalgleish was concerned, it was about having sex, and having sex was not something he would associate with agonising.

'Look, why don't we go inside and we can...talk?'

'Are you interested in talking?' She looked at him and he felt a sharp tug somewhere inside at the worried expression on her face. 'No, of course you're not,' she said on a little sigh. 'Why should you be? What does sex have to do with talking?'

'Come on.' He slung open his car door and strode round so that he could pull hers open for her. 'If you need to talk until this time next week, then I'm going to listen, so out you come and we'll go inside and get ourselves some good, strong coffee.'

'You don't have to...I know the last thing you want to do is drink coffee at a kitchen table and chat, especially when...especially since...'

He didn't answer. Instead he took her limp hand in his and gently pulled her out of the car.

'Where are your keys?'

'I can open the door.' She detached her hand from his so that she could rummage around in her bag, and as soon as she had found the keys and opened the side-door immediately wanted to slip her hand back into his.

No wonder I'm in a state, she thought jerkily. When was the last time she had wanted physical contact with a man? But what the hell must he be thinking of her? She certainly wasn't living up to her image of a savvy London girl who had moved in the fast lane and knew how to behave accordingly. She was acting like an adolescent suffering an extreme case of first-date nerves.

'There's no need...'

'If you say that once more, I'll throttle you. Now step aside, and go into the kitchen. I'll make us some coffee and we can take it into the sitting room. Then we'll...talk.' He leaned against the frame of the door, towering over her, and she stood back to let him brush past.

'Perhaps we should go back to your house. I need to check and make sure that Simon's OK.'

'He'll be fine.' He stuck the kettle on, fetched mugs, spooned coffee into them and resisted the temptation to turn around and drink in the figure on the chair. Having given him the green light, she was now applying the brakes as if her life depended on it, and to his amazement he wasn't in the slightest bit annoyed. Frustrated yes, but annoyed no. And he still wanted her. Instead of dampening his enthusiasm, her hesitant retreat seemed to have fuelled him even more. He must be mellowing with age, he thought with wry bemusement.

'Now, you go into the sitting room. You can call my mother and find out whether everything's all right, but she would have called me if there had been a problem. I took my mobile phone with me. Still, if it puts your mind at rest…'

'Why are you being so understanding?' Sara asked warily. 'And don't tell me that you're an understanding man by nature.'

'Well,' James shot her a slow, amused smile that made her stomach curl like a fist inside her, 'I must say I've never known any woman who's used aggression as part of her courtship routine.'

'We're not courting one another, though,' Sara returned quickly, 'so I'm allowed.' Courtship? James Dalgleish? Had he ever courted a woman in his life? She very much doubted it, and then hard on the heels of that thought came another—what would it be like? What would it be like to have this big, powerful, self-confident, sexy man go weak at the knees at the thought of a woman? To find himself unable to function unless she was around? The thought of it made her blush and she hustled towards the sitting room, acutely conscious of him following closely behind her.

'You can't hide away forever.' Those were his first words the minute she had sat down and he had moved across to the bay window so that he could perch against the ledge and stare down at her.

'Because I didn't jump into the sack with you doesn't mean that I'm hiding away from anything!' Sara lied, but there was no vigour in her voice. He was staring at her in the same probing way that she would have shied away from a day ago, but which now made her want to just…just let him in. She had no idea where the urge was coming from but her helplessness to fight it off frightened her.

'Of course you are.' James sauntered towards the sofa and sat down next to her, depressing it with his weight. It was small enough for his thigh to rest lightly against hers and all those crazy, racing pulses leapt into life as he turned to look at her, stretching out his arm along the back of the sofa so that it was resting loosely behind her shoulders. 'Why else would you have run out here, to the back of beyond?'

'You know why. Simon…Simon has had these recurrent chest infections for years; he needed to get out of London. This house, coming when it did, just seemed like the hand of fate.'

'You could have moved to the country and still been within commuting distance of your job in London.'

'Why are you pinning me against the wall with your questions?'

'Because you said you wanted to talk and talk you will. What's the relationship with Simon's father?'

'What's that got to do with anything?' She began to look away and he caught her chin in one hand and forced her to look at him instead.

'Just about everything,' he grated. 'I want to sleep with you, but I have no intention of sleeping with a woman who's still involved with her ex.' It shocked him just how much he hated the thought of someone else having a claim to her body, to her mind.

'And here I was, thinking that you were one of those typical, unscrupulous high-fliers,' Sara mocked in an attempt to lighten the atmosphere. It didn't work. He continued to look at her with such unsmiling concentration that she felt giddy and the curling feeling in her stomach began to spread to other places in her body.

'You still haven't answered my question.'

'I don't *have* any kind of relationship with Phillip,' Sara said in a rush. Her cheeks were pink with colour. 'No, I'm lying. I have got a relationship with Phillip, but it's more along the lines of loathing.' She gave a bitter laugh. 'You could say we didn't part on the best of terms.'

'You mean before you came up here?'

'I mean when he discovered I was pregnant. There. Satisfied?'

'I'll tell you when I'm satisfied,' James murmured. 'And I'm not. I take it he didn't like the thought of becoming a daddy?'

'What's the point in talking about this?' Sara squirmed.

'The point is that you can't live your life if you're still attached to your past.'

'That's psychobabble.'

'Is it? I bet you haven't had a relationship with any man since Simon's been on the scene,' he said astutely. 'Have all the men in your life over the past five years just been good friends, Sara?'

Pride struggled with weary helplessness and she shrugged. 'You don't understand. You go out to work because you want to not because you have to. I've worked so that I could pay off the mortgage and raise a child. I haven't had a choice and there's no room to clock-watch when you're a commodity trader. It's not a nine-to-five job and just the smallest hint of weakness would have cost me my job. I haven't had…had time to devote to cultivating a relationship.' She found that she was wringing her hands together and she made an effort to still them.

'So you worked from dawn till dusk and spent your leisure time feeling guilty because you had to leave your son in the care of a stranger.'

'She wasn't a stranger,' Sara said, hearing the misery in her voice with distaste. Self-pity was an indulgence which she had always viewed with contempt, except in the very early hours of the morning, when the rest of the world was asleep and she could allow her mind to drift over its past and build castles that were never going to be.

'You could have got another job, something less demanding. Moved out of London, worked somewhere in one of the counties.'

'You don't understand,' Sara muttered, tugging her face out of his controlling grip so that she didn't have to look into those disturbing, piercing navy blue eyes.

She knew why he was doing this, sitting on this sofa, encouraging her to spill out her life history. He wanted to sleep with her and was prepared to help her over this little stumbling block simply as a means to an end. What confused her was her own temptation to yield. She had spent too long on her own, she thought feverishly, too long warding off the rest of the world. She had confided in Phillip and look where that had got her.

'So you keep telling me. Well, then, why don't you enlighten me?'

He watched the fractional tilt of her head and the stubborn compression of her mouth and thought that if he had any sense at all he would leave her to her zealously protected thoughts and walk right out of the kitchen door. He wasn't interested in playing lengthy games with the opposite sex.

'Scared, Sara?' he murmured softly. She didn't answer, just continued to stare unblinkingly in front of her. 'What did that bastard do to you?' he enquired and it was the gentleness in his voice that did it for her.

She felt the prick of tears behind her lids and was mortified when one oozed out of the corner of her eye.

'Sorry,' she mumbled, rubbing her fist against her eye and taking several deep breaths. He silently handed her a crisp white handkerchief and she dabbed her eyes without looking at him and then clenched the handkerchief in her hand. 'I bet you hate women who cry.'

He flushed darkly when she slid her eyes sideways to catch the expression of discomfort on his face.

'Thought so.'

'I don't hate women who cry, *per se*,' James said, wondering how he had suddenly happened to find himself on the back legs.

'You just hate it when they cry because they want more from you than you're prepared to give.'

'We weren't talking about *me*,' he rasped uncomfortably and Sara impulsively reached out and stroked the side of his cheek. It was the first time she had glimpsed any loss of that phenomenal self-control and he suddenly looked like a boy, caught having to confess to something he didn't want to.

James caught her hand in his and nipped her soft palm, looking into her face as he did so. 'Witch,' he murmured, 'don't think you can change the subject whenever you want to. I'm not through talking to you quite yet.' He trailed his tongue lightly against the soft underside of her wrist and she gasped at the burst of pleasure that the simple touch invoked.

Phillip had been her first and only lover but his lovemaking had been targeted towards his own satisfaction, something she had only seen in retrospect and with the advantage of hindsight when the limitations of his personality had become stunningly obvious. She had had no points of comparison but instinctively she knew that James was not cut from the same cloth. At least not as far as the sexual game was concerned.

She was breathing quickly as he trailed a leisurely path with his mouth along her arm, finally pulling her towards him so that he could assault her mouth in a kiss that was lingering and coaxing but ultimately promised total possession. Every pore in her body was screaming out for satisfaction.

'I...I thought you wanted...to talk.'

'Later. Now...shall we go somewhere more comfortable?' He paused to murmur against her mouth and Sara nodded drowsily at him.

'Upstairs. My bedroom. It's the first door on the left.' She found that she could barely utter the words coherently.

Before she could put her trembling legs to the test, he had reached out and scooped her up, carrying her through the sitting room as though she weighed less than a feather, then up the stairs and along the landing until he could nudge open the door to her bedroom with his foot.

'Please, no lights,' Sara begged, when he made to turn on the overhead light.

'I'll compromise,' he drawled by way of response, and promptly switched on the little lamp on the table by the side of the king-sized bed, so that the room was bathed in a very soft glow. 'I want to see you, my darling. I want to see your face when I touch you and I want you to see me.'

He watched her cheeks turn pink and marvelled how a

woman who had obviously held her own in the demanding, cut-throat world of trading could be rendered as shy as a kitten when it came to her own sexuality.

He had laid her on the bed and he looked at her as she stared at him with fascination, her red hair dramatic against the pale cream bed linen.

Deliberately he removed his clothes, item by item. First his shirt, then his shoes, his socks and his trousers, never letting his eyes leave her face. Her breath was coming in short little gasps. Did she know how much of a turn-on it was for him to be watched the way she was watching him now? he wondered. What was going on in her head? She didn't want to be attracted to him, had fought against it tooth and nail, but she was. So how valuable was his conquest? One part of her was his, but he was slowly discovering that capturing that one part was not going to be enough. It helped that she wasn't harbouring any nostalgic feelings about her ex, but he still wanted more than her physical capitulation.

He was thickly and impressively aroused when he stripped off his boxer shorts and he smiled with indolent amusement as her mouth parted at the sight of him.

She couldn't help it. She dazedly thought that his body was as much a work of art as it was possible for any human body to be. Broad-shouldered, with his powerful chest narrowing to a slim waist and hips and legs that no one in their right mind would ever have associated with a businessman. She could discern the flex of his muscles and sinews beneath the olive-toned skin, and when her eyes alighted on his proudly erect manhood she found that she couldn't tear them away.

He walked towards the side of the bed and extended his

hands, reaching out for her to take them so that he could draw her to her feet.

The thought of her naked body was something to be savoured. He wanted to be the one who removed her clothes, so that he could see her nudity inch by inch, appreciate every tiny bit of it in slow degrees.

He unzipped the dress from the back and she arched as he kissed the slender column of her neck, then her shoulders as the dress was tugged down to her waist, exposing her breasts straining through the lacy bra.

Later. He would savour them later, feast on them, but for now he was content to span her waist with his big hands and draw her close so that he could take her mouth in a lingering kiss.

She was tall and slender, just the opposite of the small, voluptuous women he had always favoured, but there was something unbearably erotic about the sensuous length of her, the perfect flawlessness of her pale skin.

He brought his hands up to cup her breasts and she sighed with pleasure, automatically pushing them towards him, conducting her own inventory of his body with her hands. She ran them along his shoulders, then circled his tight brown nipples with her thumbs, then moved to caress the hard, flat planes of his stomach.

She was wearing too many clothes. She wanted to feel him, flesh against flesh, and as if the need was as strong in him as it was in her he dragged down her dress, which fell to her ankles, allowing her to step out of it.

'Now, bed…'

'What about the rest of my clothes?' Sara asked, dipping her eyes at the naked yearning in his expression.

'Oh, don't worry, I shall get to that…'

There was something shamelessly wanton about lying

semi-clothed on a vast bed, with a big man towering possessively over you. Sara smiled with half-closed eyes, inviting his ravishing appraisal of her, which was no less searing than the one she was affording him.

There was no yesterday and no tomorrow, only this moment, right here and now, timeless.

Sara pushed herself up against the pillows and reached behind with trembling fingers to unclasp the bra. Sensation was racing through her, betraying every line of defence she had ever adopted when it came to the opposite sex. She just knew that she wanted this man's eyes on her and his hands on her and his body to possess hers utterly.

James moved towards the side of the bed and lowered himself alongside her, watching her quivering body and relishing the thought of tasting every last inch of it. As her bra was undone and before she could pull it off, he straddled her so that his length covered hers and he supported himself on his elbow as he slipped his free hand under the bra to cup the soft mound of her breast.

He felt her low moan as he began teasing one nipple, rolling it gently between his thumb and forefinger. He nudged up the bra and feasted on the sight of her bare breasts. Lord, but he would have to control his urge to take her immediately, right now, and release the pounding, physical ache of his desire in his loins.

He lay over her and caught his hands in her hair. Her head was flung back and another moan escaped her as he traced her lower lip with his tongue, then tasted the sweetness of her mouth in a slow, sensual kiss that had her writhing like a cat beneath him.

It had been a long time, and even when she had made love all that time ago it had never been like this. Through her hazy mind, she knew that she was being touched by a man who had complete mastery in the art of making love. His mouth was demanding and hungry yet delicately lingering and she was so absorbed with the pleasure of it that she was hardly aware that he had nudged apart her thighs, the better for her to feel his rampant maleness pressed against her. He moved slowly over her, his hard shaft pressing against her moist cleft with an evocative rhythm that made her gasp.

'Enjoying yourself, *cara*?'

'You…you know I am.'

'Then why don't you tell me?'

'Don't stop. Please.'

Her words sent fierce adrenaline rushing through him. He slid off the bra and eased himself lower so that he could trace the tight bud of her swollen nipple with the tip of his tongue, and when she could bear it no longer she tangled her fingers into his hair and pushed him down so that he could suckle on her nipple and draw it shamelessly into his mouth.

A groan escaped her and her voice, so husky that she barely recognised it as her own, pleaded with him to take her. Her briefs were wet with her unbidden arousal, she could feel it, and when he eased them off she quivered with relief and instinctively parted her legs, inviting his entrance.

But he wasn't ready. He shifted his attention from one breast to the other, teasing the full pink disc with his mouth while his hand trailed down to her stomach and navel, then with inexorable slowness to the slippery crease between her thighs.

Sara tensed as he probed and then rubbed the sensitive clitoris that had her releasing her breath in shaky gasps as if she was fighting for air.

She was perched on the edge of orgasm, then she was free falling, unable to resist the powerful shudders of soaring pleasure as he continued to rub her before easing his finger deep into her moistness. Her body literally shook and trembled under the assault of sensation, and when she finally stilled she could barely open her eyes to look at him.

He would be disappointed but she had been powerless to resist his stimulation. She groaned with frustration and looked at him.

'I'm sorry,' Sara whispered and he smiled at her.

'What for?' He lay next to her on his side and turned her to face him.

'For...for...you know why...' As if to demonstrate what she found difficult to say, she touched him and his hardness pulsed in response.

'You don't think that we've finished already, do you?' Green eyes widened.

'I've only explored a part of your body,' he informed her with a low, sexy laugh.

As if to prove his point, he raised her arm and proceeded to trace a path with his lips along her side, reawakening ripples of sensation in her. Then he moved his attention to her stomach, to the soft indentation of her navel, then down to the most intimate place of all, where his skilful fingers had just finished their masterful assault.

'No!' Sara tried to clamp shut her legs, but without success.

'No?' He looked up at her, then, to further addle her, he blew gently against the still swollen nub of her femininity. 'Why not?'

'You can't...I've never...'

'Never had a man's mouth down there?' The shockingly

forthright question had her blushing furiously and she would have bucked against him but it would have been useless. His weight was rendering her immobile. 'There's a first time for everything, though, isn't there?'

Without allowing the chance for debate, he lowered his head and with almost unbearable delicacy touched the tip of her clitoris with his tongue.

From feeling spent only minutes previously, Sara's body charged into life as if a jolt of electricity had run through it. Where she would have writhed, he held her still with his hands firmly placed on her hips. Then he was licking with a rhythmic pressure that had her groaning with undisguised rapture.

She had never reached these heights before and her whole body was trembling with a rippling onslaught of sensations that had her crying out.

Then when she thought, anguished, that she would again no longer be able to restrain herself from capitulating to what he was doing to her body, he was breaking away from the honeyed moistness and moving to cover her body with his in one fluid movement.

'Contraception,' he murmured and her eyes flickered open at the prosaic nature of the remark.

'Wh...what?'

'Are you using any?' he questioned softly, 'because if you aren't, then there are other ways of...reaching a climax without penetration...'

He was responsible, her brain registered dimly, responsible enough to think about the consequences of what they were about to do. She half smiled. 'There's no need to worry,' she said, stretching up, feline-like, to coil her arms around his shoulders. 'And no need to talk either,' she whispered.

In actual fact, she was on the Pill, not because her sex life required it, but because the Pill regulated her periods and helped to lighten the flow. The explanation was there if he wanted it, but right now she wasn't intending to launch into it. Her body was screaming for fulfilment and she could tell from the glitter in his eyes that he was as well.

Sara felt him enter her and her body tensed as every muscle stretched to accommodate his size. He eased himself in slowly, withdrew slightly, eased himself further in and then he was moving inside her, deep thrusts that had her spiralling towards the most powerful climax she had ever experienced.

And she witnessed his own soaring passion as his powerful body arched back on one long, final thrust and he shuddered to complete fulfilment.

He could have made love to her again. He wanted nothing more than to lose himself once more in her exquisite body and let her lose herself in his, but there was a thread of uncertainty running through him that made him wonder whether she would just pull back, retreat again to a place where he might not be able to reach her.

He had wanted her and now he felt himself consumed by the possibility of having her again. His vague plan to somehow get to know her so that he could manoeuvre his way into buying the Rectory lay in splinters at his feet, but he didn't care. At least not at this moment in time. At this moment in time the only thing he cared about was repeating the mind-blowing experience they had shared.

'We…we have to go and collect Simon,' was the first coherent thing that came to her mind as he lay on his side and tugged her so that she was facing him.

'It's…' he glanced at the clock on the mantelpiece over

the fireplace '…eleven-fifteen. He'll be asleep already…'
He didn't want to scare her off but just lying here next to
her was making his body stir into life once again. 'So he
won't notice whether you're there now or…in an hour's
time…and I can think of other things we can do to fill the
time…' He stroked the side of her breast then rolled one
nipple between his fingers, feeling a flare of triumph as it
hardened at his touch.

Sex. It was all about sex, and she honestly couldn't
blame him. They had made love like people who had spent
years starved of physical contact. Right in her case, but in
his case? He was just a highly skilled lover who knew how
to press the right buttons to get the right responses.

'No,' she said weakly, disturbed by the thought that
there should be something more than just the act of making
love, however glorious that was in itself.

'Why not?' He removed his hand and she felt the loss
of contact with a shiver of dismay.

'Because…because we just can't.'

'Can't…?'

Sara twisted her head so that she didn't have to look
into his eyes. Those eyes made her doubt everything she
had ever believed, made her wonder whether shying away
from men so that she could never be hurt had actually been
such a good idea after all. She didn't want to doubt herself.
She had Simon to consider. There was no way that she
would expose him to having a man around, only for the
man to disappear just as his own father had. And James
Dalgleish was a disappearing kind of man. You didn't need
a degree in rocket science to spot that a mile off.

'I need to get dressed.'

'Oh, no, you don't.' He gripped her arm firmly enough
to anchor her to the spot but not so hard that he was phys-

ically hurting her, although she knew that the slightest attempt by her to get off the bed would result in enough pressure for him to ensure that she went nowhere.

'How long do you plan on running away, Sara? Another year? Two years? The rest of your life?'

'You're hurting my arm.'

'*Por Dios,* woman! We all screw up once in a while! The trick is not to end up haunted by it!' He could feel her withdrawing with every passing second and his powerlessness to do anything about it made him want to break things. But aggression would get him nowhere. He forced himself to calm down, released her arm and gave her a long, measured look.

'*You've* screwed up? *Ever?*'

'Yes, if you must know.' He felt as if he was stepping off the edge of something, but *what*...? 'When I was young, I had a fling with a woman ten years older than me. I thought it was love until I surprised her at her flat one afternoon with another man. Turned out I was a little plaything being cultivated by the pair of them as an easy route to some quick cash. Marry me, divorce me, end up rich. Nice, quick, foolproof.' There was no reason why he should have kept this untold story to himself, but it still confused the hell out of him as to why he had felt so damned compelled to tell it in the first place.

'What did you do?'

'I learnt my lesson,' he said abruptly.

'But you didn't have a child.'

'No.'

'And children get hurt.'

'And adults can use that to hide behind!'

'I want to get my son back now.' Her heart was beating like a drum and something inside her head was screaming out to her that one wrong move now would land her waist-deep in quicksand.

'Feel free.' He lay back with his hands behind his head.

'What do you mean, *feel free*?'

'I mean feel free to go and get him. I'll be waiting right here till you get back.'

'Why is it so hard for you to take no for an answer?' Sara flared in sudden anger. She swept her legs off the bed and stormed towards the bathroom, clutching her bundle of clothes in one hand.

OK, so maybe she shouldn't have slept with him, but she had and she didn't regret one minute of it. She just didn't want it to go any further. Why couldn't he accept that?

She had a very quick shower, changed and half expected that he would have left but when she returned to the bedroom it was to find that he was still there, although thankfully back in his clothes and lounging against the bay window.

'I'll be waiting right here for you,' he informed her steadily.

'Why?' The question was torn from her.

'Because we want one another and it's no good pretending otherwise. You're not some virginal maiden in terror of a rampant male, you're just someone who's ready to close the whole world out as a self-inflicted punishment because you made a mistake a long time ago.'

'And having hundreds of relationships is as bad as having none! The truth is that you enjoyed a romp in the hay and now you'd quite like to enjoy a couple more, hence your apparent need to climb into my mind and point out all the things you think I'm doing wrong!' She burned at the memory of how good sex with him had been and how easy it would be to carry on hopping into bed for just as long as he wanted her, just to repeat the glorious feelings he had aroused in her. How easy it would be to let him into her life and into Simon's. 'You're not exactly trying to understand me from a purely unbiased point of view, are you?'

His eyes narrowed at her. 'Do you know what you need?' he asked, moving so slowly towards her that she could easily have yanked open the bedroom door and fled down the stairs. However, her legs appeared to have turned to lead and she stood just where she was, only managing to shuffle a few steps backwards until her back was pressed against the door. He stopped inches away from her and then proceeded to place the flat of his palms on either side of her. 'You need to be shaken into seeing sense.'

The thudding of her heart became a steady, painful drum roll.

'Why don't you stop hiding away and face facts? We're both adults who happen to be attracted to one another. Overwhelmingly attracted,' he added as an afterthought. He traced her bare arm with his finger and she shivered convulsively. 'See? Your mouth might be saying one thing but your body is telling a completely different story. Like me to prove it?'

'No!' Sara squeaked, mesmerised by his eyes.

In some obscure part of his brain, he realised that this was his only trump card. For a while, she had abandoned the hold her past had on her, but all the old defences were back, except one. She couldn't defend herself against his touch. He had never chased a woman in his life before, but, dammit, he was prepared to do anything to chase this one. He didn't know why. He just knew that there was a raw, primitive urge in him that wanted her...badly.

'You're scared of a relationship and I'm not interested in one, and maybe you're right, maybe we both have our reasons, so you could say that our needs meet neatly in the centre.' He lowered his head and outlined her mouth with his tongue. She didn't respond but neither did she draw back. 'Let go, Sara. We make good sex—no, we make magnificent sex. Why not?' He pushed himself away and she realised that she had been holding her breath. 'Think about it. I'll be gone by the time you get back with Simon.' He paused at the door to give her a brief nod. 'I'll be in touch.'

The barracuda circling its prey. Sara closed her eyes briefly and, once she had heard the slam of the kitchen door, wearily headed down the stairs.

CHAPTER SIX

IT WAS raining outside. Nothing spectacular, just an incessant fine drizzle that turned the London streets into slippery grey grime. James pushed himself away from his desk and swivelled his chair round so that he was staring out into the darkening skies. An uninspiring view, but even if he went to the massive glass windows and looked down the view would be equally uninspiring. By now, most of the nine-to-fivers would have already left work and the pavements would be relatively deserted. The City, with its monuments to financial success, thronged with people during the day but by night it was comparatively quiet. Only the diehards would be still at work at a little after nine at night.

Diehard workaholics, he thought grimly, and me. Two weeks ago he would have classified himself as one of those workaholics, but in the space of a fortnight his ability to function seemed to have taken a knocking. Several times he had found himself staring at the rows of figures on his computer only to realise after a few minutes that he had actually not been taking anything in at all.

Like tonight. Friday night. He would normally have reviewed all the details of this latest merger by now and would be getting geared up to go out, maybe to a restaurant or one of the more low-key, members-only jazz clubs that he favoured, with something delectable, nubile and willing.

But he was only halfway through his review and had already lost interest. As for the delectable, nubile, willing companion…

He clicked his tongue in irritation and began prowling through his spacious office.

The last woman he had taken out four days ago had been an unmitigated disaster. She had seemed quite sexy and vivacious the last time he had met her three months ago at a stunningly dull cocktail party hosted by one of his friends for a foreign ambassador with extensive, useful connections. She had flirted outrageously with him and had been suitably peeved when he had told her that he would, regrettably, not be around to continue their flirting because he was due to fly to New York the following day, and then on to the Far East. He had taken her number and promptly forgotten all about her. Until four days ago, when taking her out had seemed an inspired idea. Delectable, nubile and willing had been just what he needed to combat the daily intrusive images of a tall, slender red-haired witch who had sent him packing and in the process left him nursing emotions that were driving him crazy.

Unfortunately, Annabel had failed to achieve what he had hoped she would. Her short, tight, sequinned dress had screamed garishness, her all-over tan had added to the impression and her conversation had left him bored out of his skull.

Back to the proverbial drawing board, he thought grimly. But he wasn't going to get in touch with Sara. In the cold light of day, his words, casually spoken before he had headed out of the Rectory, had been exposed for what they were. A pathetic play for a woman who had made it clear in no uncertain terms that she might have slept with him once, but beyond that she was going nowhere. At least she had been honest enough not to fall back on the tired excuse about having had too much to drink, but he couldn't stop the nagging, unpleasant suspicion that several glasses of wine had played a bigger part than he cared to admit.

He was so absorbed in frowning contemplation that it took a few seconds for the sound of the telephone to connect with his brain, then for his hand to connect with the receiver.

The minute he heard her voice, he froze before slowly turning around so that he could perch on the edge of his desk and look outside at the darkening sky.

'And to what do I owe the pleasure of this call?' His voice was cold, uninviting.

Hundreds of miles away, Sara heard it without the slightest tremor of apprehension.

'I'm so glad I got through. I thought perhaps you might have gone out as it's Friday night.'

Which only reminded him why precisely he hadn't gone out. His lips thinned with angry self-disgust.

'Cut the pleasantries, Sara, and get to the point. Why have you called and what do you want?'

Get to the point? Sara nearly laughed. Oh, yes, she'd get to the point, all right, in her own sweet time.

'And thank you so much for asking how I am, James. As well as can be expected, now that you don't mention it.'

'How did you get hold of my mobile number?'

'Oh, I asked your mother. I told her that Simon wanted something from Harrods and I wanted you to see whether you could bring it up for him the next time you came.'

'And I am supposed to what…? In response to that? Feel a sudden surge of curiosity? Admire you for your inventiveness? Just say what you have to say and get off this line. I'm on my way out and I don't have time to stand here having a conversation with you.' In which case, he thought cynically, why do I not simply hang up? Rage and frustration washed over him and he found that he was still gripping the receiver.

'I don't expect admiration for my inventiveness, but the surge of curiosity might be nice. I phoned because I wanted to hear your voice, because I want to see you, James.'

'You want to see me. Would that be so that we can have a re-run of our last conversation? You *do* remember our last conversation, don't you? The one when you told me to leave?' He found that he was prowling the office with the phone, like an animal in a cage. He even felt like an animal, awash with primitive feelings that he couldn't seem to decipher.

'I remember it. I've thought about it. I've done nothing *but* think about it...' Not quite true. She had had one or two other things on her mind very well. Just as well he couldn't see into her mind, just as well he couldn't see what was really going on inside her, underneath the controlled, smoky voice with just the right mixture of apology, seriousness and invitation.

But God, it hurt to hear him. Hurt in every pore of her body, in places she never even knew existed. And to think she had once considered Phillip the only man capable of delivering pain! What he had delivered had been a bouquet of flowers in comparison.

'I've spent hours just remembering, James. The way we laughed together, the way you made me feel...' The way you used me.

The bitter memory of her conversation with Lucy Campbell rose up inside her mind like a monster.

'So,' the small blonde had drawled with a malicious little smile playing on her lovely mouth, 'I hear you and James Dalgleish can't keep your hands off one another...'

Sara had bumped into her purely by accident the day

before and, from the position of not knowing her from Adam, was rapidly made aware of precisely who she was, how long she had known the Dalgleish family, and where her ambitions lay. Very definitely in the direction of sex, marriage and babies.

'Then your source of information needs to brush up on her spying skills.' But Sara flushed guiltily at the memory of them in bed together, making love with fierce, explosive urgency. She had done what she had needed to do, but all she could do was remember. He was still with her.

'Really?' Lucy's mouth curved into a well-bred smile of amusement. 'I shouldn't bother getting my hopes up if I were you,' she mused thoughtfully. 'James is not open to being caught, especially by *you*.'

'I'm not trying to catch anyone…'

'I don't suppose he told you…' One fine eyebrow was arched speculatively. 'No…of course he wouldn't have. No one can say that he isn't clever…'

'Told me what?'

'Why he's taking such an interest in you. Good heavens, James could have his pick of any woman, anywhere. So…why you?'

'I don't have to listen to this.'

'No, you don't, but…' Lucy shrugged with just the right amount of insolent indifference to forestall Sara's decision to walk away. 'I would if I were you. In fact, you'll probably thank me afterwards…'

'I doubt that.' But still she wavered.

'Oh, I wouldn't bank on it. For someone who's supposed to be smart, and believe me I've already heard all about your big, powerful job in London, you're incredibly trusting. I mean, do you really imagine that James Dalgleish, a man who could have literally *anyone*, would be interested in *you* if there wasn't a motive?'

'Motive? What are you talking about?'

'The Rectory, of course. Hasn't he mentioned it to you? That he wants to get his hands on your house? Has wanted that place for years? I must say, darling, that I have to take my hat off to him. What better way to get what he wants than to sleep with the woman who owns it? So much easier to persuade someone to do what you want them to do when you're lovers, wouldn't you say?' She looked at Sara with a smirk. 'See? Now, haven't I done you a favour?'

Sara dragged herself back to the present and the task that lay before her.

Revenge.

And why not? Why the hell not? She had been used and she wasn't going to slink away and lick her wounds in private. Phillip had been a disaster, but James…

Her stomach clenched at the devastation he had managed to wreak. And he had managed it because she had been a fool, simple as that. She had allowed herself to trust, to feel, to open up to him and he had played on her trust to get a little closer to what he had wanted. And it had not been her.

She found that her fingers were white, clenched around the telephone cord, her nails biting into the soft flesh of her palm. She forced herself to relax. But it was so hard, because even now, knowing it all, knowing him for the kind of man he was, that deep, sexy voice was still managing to pierce through her like a knife.

'Haven't *you* thought about us at all?'

'A trip down memory lane, Sara?' But dammit, yes, he remembered. All too clearly.

'I haven't slept since you left, James…' And she hadn't. She hadn't slept, functioned, barely eaten. She had been in pain. And then when she had met Lucy, had realised what was going on, she still hadn't slept, and the pain was still there, the pain of knowing that she had been manipulated by a man she had finally seen as a far cry from Phillip.

'This is a pointless conversation.' But still he couldn't replace the receiver and he could hear a husky shakiness in his voice that made him want to hurl something very heavy straight through the window.

'Remember how good we were in bed? You said so yourself and you were right. We made love and it was never like that for me. Never.' The truth of that acknowledgment made her eyes hurt with unshed tears. She drew in her breath and continued speaking but her voice was wobbly. 'The way you touched me…the places that you touched…I felt alive. When you kissed me, I felt as though I was on fire…and then when you kissed other parts of me, James…my breasts, my nipples, my stomach…'

'Just good sex. I believe that was the conclusion you arrived at.' He was having difficulty thinking clearly. Her words were evocative and her voice filled his head like incense.

'And I thought that good sex was not a reason for carrying on with a relationship…' Images of him assaulted every corner of her mind.

Good sex. A meeting of two bodies, but lord, so much more than that. For her.

She had sent him on his way, yes, and he had supposedly walked out of her life two weeks ago, but she could see now, through her anguish and disillusionment, that he would have re-entered it soon enough. He was a clever and experienced man and one with a mission. He would simply have banked on her attraction to him to railroad through her defences. And then when the time was right, he would have begun talking to her about the Rectory, allowing his ability to make love to overcome her questions.

Just you remember that, Sara told herself bitterly.

'I'm here in London for a couple of days,' she said, scenting her words with promise. 'I have to sort out arrangements with my flat. Routine stuff. I really would love to meet up with you. I'm staying in a hotel in Kensington, actually, so I'm quite central…and we could talk…'

'And you think I should make time for you?'

'Yes, yes, I do. I dented your ego the last time we met and I would like to make up for that…' She very nearly said that she had hurt him, but of course he wouldn't have been hurt by her rejection. Just temporarily frustrated until he felt the time was right to pounce again.

'Oh, really? And how do you intend to *make up for that*?' A dented ego was something he could deal with. He mentally began a process of damage limitation by telling himself that that was really all there was to it. That the hurt and anger he had felt was just a reflection of a man accustomed to having everything being denied something.

'I would very much like to buy you dinner. You name the restaurant. I'm here on my own, so there'll be no need for me to rush back to my room…' She purposefully dropped her voice a couple of notches lower. 'Not that it's that much of a room, to be honest. Just a dressing table and a chest of drawers and a bathroom and, of course, a bed…'

Was she doing this on purpose? James thought, stifling his sudden urge to groan. He had not seen her as an out-and-out flirt before but either she was genuinely naïve in not knowing that a few choice words could send a man's pulses rocketing, or else she was blatantly offering him…herself…and the thought of that turned him on as nothing on this green planet ever had in his life before.

'I was going to bring Simon with me,' she was saying, although he was only dimly aware of her voice because his mind had taken off on a tangent and he seemed incapable of reining it back in, 'but your mum said that she would love nothing better than to have him stay with her. I don't know if she told you, but he's been over there a couple of times…to play with the train set. He's never had a train set of his own; it just wasn't possible in the flat in London. Anyway, I would like to see you, James. Of course, if you don't have time…'

He would have time though. She was sure of it. With a cynicism she had not thought herself capable of, she reflected that he still wanted the Rectory. The bait was dangling very close to him. She was sure he would grab it, but just in case…

'I think it makes sense, though, don't you, James? We should be on speaking terms, considering we'll probably bump into one another whenever you happen to be in Scotland. It's a small place and if tongues wagged when we had that one silly kiss…' she laughed throatily '…well, they'll be wagging even more if you show up and insist on walking past me on the street without saying a word…'

The lifeline of cold rationality rescued him from his warring pride.

He relaxed fractionally and moved to sit back down in his swivel chair.

'So we meet up and discuss…what? Politics? The weather? World poverty?'

'We meet up and discuss what a fool I was…' Sara allowed herself to pause while her mind raced ahead to her own conclusions, that she had indeed been a fool—to have involved herself with him in the first place '…to think that I could say goodbye to you and walk away unscathed…' Truth was cleverly intermingled with lies. She would never have imagined in a thousand years that she would be capable of a cold-blooded game of revenge, but there was a knife twisting in her gut that made it much easier than she might have thought possible.

He still wanted her house. He would come. And she would sleep with him because she enjoyed it. She would take what he had to offer her instead of squeezing shut her legs and talking about principles, and when she was finished she would dump him, but not until she had informed him in no uncertain terms that she had known from the word go what game he had been playing and thanks for the good time but the house was staying in her possession.

'Also,' Sara murmured convincingly, 'Simon is fond of your mother. If you decide that you want to have nothing to do with me, then it might be awkward for them both...'

'Well, why not?' James drawled. He had a dinner engagement the following night with a client, but it wouldn't be a problem to either defer that or else let Ray Cooper cover for him. 'If keeping up appearances means that much to you.' His voice was lazy, bored, indifferent, but he couldn't help himself from feeling a certain brooding excitement at the thought of seeing her again. An irresistible weakness.

'Where would you like to go?'

'I can't say that I really care one way or the other and I haven't got time now to debate such an irrelevance. As I said, I'm on my way out.'

'In which case, I know an excellent Italian restaurant. La Taverna...' Overplaying her case at this point wouldn't be a good idea. He was a man of formidable pride and she had dented it. She didn't need him to walk away from her invitation.

'Right.'

'It's in Chelsea. Just off the King's Road as a matter of fact. Quite informal.'

'Right. I'll be there at seven-thirty, even though this charade leaves me cold.'

'Seven-thirty.' Sara filled her voice with bubbling pleasure. 'Can't wait, James…'

She spent the following day in a state of barely suppressed excitement underlined with grim determination to see this plan through.

She had arranged to meet three of her friends for lunch, had envisaged a fun, gossipy and bonding couple of hours with them but was bitterly disappointed. Her mind was too full of what lay ahead in a few hours' time and she had moved away from ribald tales of office politics, promotions in the offing and prospective bonuses.

Had this been what it had been all about for her as well? The feverish plans to make even more money? The restricted lunch breaks and long working hours so that she could afford the nanny and the mortgage and the lifestyle that she had usually been too exhausted to appreciate?

It niggled at the back of her mind and she realised, with another familiar spurt of pain, that these were the very things she would have wanted to talk to James about. She would have enjoyed nothing more than to sound him out about what she was feeling.

And she would have done—a lifetime ago.

Now, though…

She got dressed very slowly for an evening seducing the enemy.

She was wearing a short cream silk skirt that floated sexily around her thighs and exposed her long legs to the absolute maximum. A figure-hugging cream top with sleeves to the elbows that just hit her waistline, leaving a tantalising glimpse of skin whenever she moved. High shoes that emphasised her height. Hair loosely curling down her back.

Half of her hoped that he would already be at the restaurant, waiting for her, so that he could be afforded the full impact of her walking slowly towards him. The other half hoped that she would be the first to arrive so that she could have a little time to get her thoughts together before she laid eyes on him.

Plan or no plan, she wasn't a complete idiot.

She knew that just seeing him for the first time in two weeks was going to have an effect on her. She might be bitterly hurt at his treatment, and that alone would be enough to give her the courage she needed to do what she wanted to do. But she would also have his disturbing sexuality to contend with as well. She would have to withstand those amazing eyes on her face, hear that voice that could send electric currents racing along her spine, watch the sensuous curve of his mouth.

He was there by the time she arrived, waiting for her.

Sara saw him as soon as she walked into the restaurant. Indolently lounging on his chair right at the back, cradling a drink in his hand.

God, but he looked right at home here. Swarthy, black-haired, so ferociously good-looking that she gave a small gasp. She couldn't help it.

She wanted his eyes to travel the length of her, but as she walked towards him she still felt horribly and acutely self-conscious.

Fortunately it didn't show in her voice when she finally made it to the table and was standing looking down at him.

'Haven't been waiting long, have you?' She smiled. Panic, misery and a certain amount of treacherous elation rushed through her. She took her time to sit down. 'I would have got here a little sooner, but the traffic was absolutely foul. It's so easy to forget how mad things are down here compared to Scotland, isn't it?'

'What are you drinking?'

If he was trying to imply uninterest, then he was succeeding. Sara leaned forward, elbows on the table, and smiled at him. No response.

'Wine, I think. What have you got there?'

'Whisky.' He swallowed a mouthful and continued to look at her coldly.

'Shall we share a bottle of white wine? I need something cold. It's so warm out there. I can't remember a summer like this in years.'

'Ah, the weather.' His mouth curled into a humourless smile. 'Favourite standby of people struggling for conversation.' He leaned forward and Sara felt the full force of his masculinity like a physical blow.

'I'm not struggling for conversation, James, I'm attempting to make some.' The waiter came and there was temporary relief from the effect he was having on her as he scanned the wine list and ordered a bottle of Chablis.

'And who am I to thwart your efforts? So, the weather. Is it still sunny in Scotland? Or have there been a few showers?'

'Don't.'

'Don't what?'

'Be facetious.'

'You forget, this was your splendid idea. To meet up so that we could chat like two sensible adults and smooth the path for a workable relationship should we ever happen to meet when I'm next up there.'

'What have you been doing since we last…saw one another?'

'Have we finished with the weather?'

The wine arrived, was poured, and Sara drank most of her glass in the space of a few seconds.

Where was all the charm? she thought acidly. Now that his plans had been scuppered, did he not see any further point in trying to expend any on her?

'I've finally been meeting a few people.' She twirled the wine glass in one hand and propped her chin in the palm of the other. 'Fiona has been wonderful. Asking us over for tea, introducing Simon to some of the other children, introducing me to some of her friends. I just wish I could have been able to get into it a little bit more...'

'At which point,' he leaned forward as well so that the distance between them was narrowed to the point where giddiness took over, 'I expect I am to ask you what you mean by that remark...'

'What's the point making things difficult between us?'

'You need to ask that question?'

This was how he had done it, of course. That way he had of focusing absolutely and entirely on her. Even now, when every pore of him breathed hostility, he could still make her feel sick with self-awareness. He had a male aggression that made Phillip seem like a boy in comparison.

'We're adults. Adults make mistakes. I've already confessed to making one, to turning you away...'

'Something no woman has ever done.' He knew how he sounded. Bloody petulant. He could have kicked himself but the words were out before he could retract them.

'And I've never had a one-night stand in my life.' She watched, gratefully, as the waiter poured her another glass of wine and was aware of them ordering food, but only just. 'Have you missed me?'

James felt himself flush darkly. 'I think I prefer conversing about the weather,' he drawled, noticing the delicate flush that invaded her cheeks at his response. 'As to what I have been doing...' He sat back, giving himself some breathing space. The directness of her question had rattled him. If he had tried to answer that one, he was certain that she would have been able to glean the truth from his expression. 'Working.'

'All work and no play...'

'Makes James a dull boy?' They were making short work of this wine, he thought and he was nettled by the admission to himself that he felt as if he needed it. What the hell was he doing here?

'Hardly dull, from what I remember...'

'How is my mother?' he asked heavily. He had ordered some kind of fish, which appeared to have now been placed in front of him and looked delicious, although the consumption of food was the last thing on his mind.

'Fine. Enjoying the weather and the gardens, you know...'

'And Simon?' It was a struggle to keep the conversation low-key and normal but he had to. He had to stay in control because, against every sensible bone in his body, he was responding to her, to whatever dance she was leading him, and it enraged him.

'Simon is fine. He...he really enjoys living up there. Of course, I've told him that the weather helps and that it's completely different in winter, with the cold and the snow, but that just seems to get him more excited. Would you believe he's never seen snow?' Sara began eating. Instead of being coolly in control, she felt flustered and vulnerable. She had to remind herself why she was here, why she was having dinner with this man...

'No, London never gets snow, does it?' He gave a short, derisive laugh. 'And now we are back to the weather.'

No, we're not, Sara thought fiercely. We are *not* going

to run around in circles, getting nowhere. I am *not* going to abort my plan and let you get away with using me. I won't be hurt by you and allow myself to run away.'

It was so tempting to ask him *why*, to ask him whether he had felt anything for her at all, that she had to lower her eyes and take a few deep, steadying breaths.

'So we are. Silly, isn't it? When there's so much else to talk about.'

'For instance?'

'For instance I could tell you that you look good, that I'd forgotten just how good you look.' She quietly closed her knife and fork, leaving her food unfinished, and met his eyes steadily.

'What are you playing at?' He pushed his plate away, deposited his napkin on it and sat back, staring at her, willing himself to get a grip, knowing that nothing was showing on his face but that his bloody nervous system was in a state of chaos.

'I'm talking.'

'Talking.'

'That's right. That's why I got in touch with you. So that we could have a conversation, although…'

'Although what…?' he asked, his words dropping softly into the silence between them.

'Although I can think of much more interesting things to do…'

CHAPTER SEVEN

'OH, REALLY?'

'Really. To be perfectly honest, I could have handled everything with my banker and the estate agents by phone or e-mail. There was no real need to travel down here to London, but…' Those intent blue eyes could make a girl think she was drowning, Sara thought.

'But you just couldn't resist the desire to feast your eyes on my magnificent self.'

'No, that isn't all there is to it. And it's rude to draw attention to yourself like that. Makes you sound egotistic. Which, of course, you are.'

James glanced away but she could see that he wanted to smile and that little glimpse of humour made her heart contract.

'So I am rude, egotistic…I cannot imagine why you would make a trip to London to communicate with someone with those personality traits.'

'I really did want to talk to you, James. I really did think that it would have been crazy to just cease communication completely when we're going to inevitably keep bumping into one another. And you may be rude and egotistic but you're also interesting and fairly amusing.'

'Fairly amusing. Well, we're stepping up the ladder of compliments. Now that you've had your way telling me what you think of me, I feel it's only right that I tell you what I think of you…'

A little shiver of apprehension raced down her spine. She didn't want him to tell her anything of the sort. She just didn't need any more of his lies, any more pretence that he was interested enough in her to have formed opinions of her at all.

'You look alarmed,' he murmured, letting his eyes wander away from hers, to her mouth, to her breasts. 'I think you're immensely complex and a complete mystery. One minute you're lecturing to me like a minister on a pulpit, the next minute you're flirting with me and inviting me back into your bed. Now, that makes no sense, does it?'

'Does it have to?' Sara laughed and tossed her head. She had never tossed her head in her life before and was surprised that the gesture seemed to come so naturally. 'Women are allowed to be unpredictable, aren't they?' She rested her head on her hand and gazed at him with a half-smile.

Unbelievably, she was enjoying this.

'I thought men loved unpredictability in women. Besides, if I'm mysterious and complex, then I must also be unpredictable. They go hand in hand.'

'Not all men love unpredictability.' He didn't. It appeared, though, that she was the exception because the way she was looking at him now was making his senses reel and it was all he could do to keep his hands in check.

'You mean *you* don't?'

'I mean I should get the bill and...'

'And...?'

She could sense the wary restlessness in him and on the spur of the moment she reached out her hand and covered his, very, very lightly and very, very briefly, just long enough to stroke the side of his thumb with her finger. Then her hand was back in place and burning. His power over her could threaten everything, but she wouldn't let it.

'You're skating on thin ice, Sara.' He raked his fingers

through his hair, but his eyes never left her face, not for one single second.

'Care to explain?'

'What if I decide to take you up on your very generous offer? Are you really going to feel any differently about me if we sleep together again? And again after that? Am I not still going to be the big, bad wolf who should keep away from your door?'

'It's all a question of choices, isn't it?'

'Choices?'

'I can choose to foresee the difficulties and walk away before they arise, or I can choose to run headlong into whatever lies ahead and realise that experience, whatever the outcome, counts for a lot.' Too much talk and too much truth. She smiled seductively. Another little talent she didn't know she possessed. Whatever this man brought out in her, he was unique. 'I choose the latter.'

Who the hell was he to talk about skating on thin ice when he could barely think straight with those feline eyes looking at him?

The circular table separating them was small bordering on tiny and he had to fight the temptation to slouch slightly further down into his chair, just far enough so that he could insert his thigh underneath that very short, very sexy skirt of hers. Feel the softness of her crotch against the hardness of his knee. God, he wanted her.

'I don't think this is the place to have a prolonged conversation, though…' She was unaware that the lowering of her eyelids and the flick of her tongue over her lips was as erotic as a striptease.

'Where,' he heard himself saying, 'do you have in mind, in that case…?'

Sara shrugged and looked down as she casually traced the rim of her glass with one finger. 'Any suggestions?'

Several, he knew he should say, *and all involve two minutes on the end of a phone while you're heading back up to Scotland and I'm here, working, going out with women I can predict and getting on with life before you came along and managed to clutter it up.* He was as cynical as they came! Jaded from experience and permanently watchful of the dangers of losing his massive self-control.

He signalled to a waiter for the bill.

Sara could see the questions racing through that clever brain of his. But his questions didn't matter. He was going to pay the bill, no dessert, no coffees, no chatting over liqueurs, and that could only mean one thing. He was going to come with her. She felt a kick of satisfaction and, hard on the heels of that, a rush of undiluted, naked longing.

This was going to be a learning curve for her, she thought a little wildly. She couldn't go through life choosing men who thought nothing of pulling the rug out from under her feet. She would toughen up and if it was at his expense then that was just too bad. He deserved everything he got.

Knowing what she now knew, she should have been left cold by him, but the minute she had laid eyes on him she had felt her body begin to react, and as he paid the bill, ignoring her insistence on paying half, she felt the lick of excitement steadily getting stronger.

The silence between them was electric. As was the fact that he didn't touch her. Once outside the restaurant, he shoved his hands in his pockets, only withdrawing one to hail a black cab. He leaned down, gave the driver an address in Chelsea, and once they were both inside he sprawled against his side of the car so that he could look at her.

'So, are you going to tell me what brought about this change of heart?'

'I already told you,' Sara said, taking quick breaths, 'I thought things over and, well…you were right. It's crazy to go through life being affected by what Phillip did. We're adults and we were…' She sighed with remembered pleasure and that sigh had nothing to do with revenge or bitterness.

'Good together in bed? Fantastic, in fact?'

Sara raised her eyebrows in unexpected amusement. 'I think I can hear your ego again.'

'Tut, tut. Now, that's not very nice considering you're the seductress trying to woo me back between the sheets, is it?' His deep, velvety voice caught her amusement and shared it. It gave her an uneasy premonition of how simple it would be to fall right back into the trap of opening up to him, because on a very basic level she just seemed to click with him.

'I've never been called a seductress before.' Uneasy premonitions didn't have a part to play.

'Mm. I can understand why. Brutal honesty isn't usually the mark of the seductress.'

His voice was wickedly smooth and she dared to extend her hand so that it was resting lightly on his thigh.

'Blame my job,' Sara murmured, her pulses leaping at the casual physical contact. 'Being brutally honest becomes a habit after a while. Does it scare you?' She moved her hand fractionally higher and was almost disappointed when he covered it firmly with his own before she could take her explorations further.

'Oh, I don't scare easily. Not,' he added in a drawl, 'that you won't have to use other feminine wiles to tempt me…'

'Other feminine wiles such as what…?' Was this really

her talking? Flirting outrageously and loving every minute of it? Good lord.

His response to that was to remove his hand from where it had been covering hers. Sara thought that if she listened hard enough she might just be able to hear the wild beat of her heart and the leap of her pulses as she edged her hand higher until it lay over the hard rod of his erection, which she could feel throbbing beneath the fabric of his trousers.

He shifted slightly. 'Now, if I'd had my driver I might just have asked you to take your technique a little further.' He could almost smell the musky aroma of her excitement, filling his nostrils and making him want to unzip his trousers and push her hand harder against him.

'But regrettably,' he said roughly, 'no driver and we're just about here at my apartment.' On cue, the taxi slowed down and Sara's pulse rate returned to something approaching normality as she slipped out of the cab and watched with her arms folded across her as he paid the fare and then turned to look at her.

'This time,' he murmured, walking up to her and positioning himself directly in front of her with his legs slightly parted, 'no turning back. If you think you're going to suffer with agonies of conscience afterwards, or even before for that matter, then you can leave in the next cab. This isn't going to be a one-night stand.'

'You mean you want an affair.'

'If you want to call it that.'

'What else can we call it?'

'We can call it whatever we want to,' he informed her silkily, 'after all, it's just a matter of vocabulary. But we both know what we're talking about.'

'What about a relationship, then?' Sara threw at him. She knew that he wouldn't like the idea of that, for all his talk about it just being *a matter of vocabulary*. An affair was something frothy and light that dissolved in a puff of wind, but a relationship was something more than that and, considering that he had his own hidden agenda for sleeping with her, then going beyond a bit of froth would not be something he would even contemplate for a minute. Oh, no, that would be just a little too much like hard work for him.

'I don't have a problem with that,' he surprised her by saying. In the dim pool of light reflected from the nearest street lamp, he could see her startled expression. She wasn't interested in a relationship, he thought. Never mind what she said about moving away from her past, she was still as trapped in it as she ever was. He felt a sudden, searing determination to snap her out of it, focus her entirely on him, as a lover and as a man as well.

'Feeling a little scared at the thought of getting to know me, Sara?' he murmured mockingly and she tilted her chin up defensively.

'Not at all,' she lied.

'Good, so shall we go up to my apartment? I don't know about you, but it's a little too chilly to stand out here debating points of detail.'

The building was severe and imposing from the outside. The white façade was broken by intricate black wrought-iron railings around the long windows, and apart from a few window-boxes there was a total absence of green. It was as different from his mansion in Scotland as it was possible to get. Somehow it summarised the life in London that had woven such a magical spell over her when she had left it behind, but which, now that she was in it once more even if only for a couple of days, was already beginning to impinge uncomfortably on her.

Two of the four-storeyed buildings had obviously been

cleverly knocked into one so that the reception area was not a small hallway, leading up to a single staircase, but a large central area, impeccably tiled, and at one end there was a small walnut desk manned by a uniformed middle-aged man who half stood when James walked in.

'I thought you'd given up the night shift,' James said, grinning as he collected his mail.

'I had, sir.' The weathered face returned the grin. 'But then I discovered that it beats being at home with the wife, the mother-in-law, the daughter and the little nipper. Soon as the mother-in-law goes back to Oz and Gary finishes the house repairs so that Ellie and little Tommy can move in, then I'll take back up my day post. Be able to watch a little night-time telly in peace and quiet.'

'And I guess you spend all day sleeping?' James raised his eyebrows and tapped the wad of post against the open palm of one hand.

'Not *all*, sir. There's a limit to what the wife will tolerate.'

James was still grinning as the elevator door purred shut on them. 'He's an institution here,' he explained with a devastating smile. 'Been here as long as I have.'

'Which is how long, exactly?' Sara asked curiously.

'Almost six years. Before that I had a mews house in Richmond but this is a helluva lot more convenient for central London.'

'And no troublesome garden to take care of.'

'And no troublesome garden to take care of,' he agreed, standing back to allow her to exit first. 'I presume that was your reason for an apartment as well?'

'Yes,' she admitted, 'although with a child, a garden would have been ideal. But I just would never have had the time to look after it and it would have been too small in central London, anyway, to employ the use of a gardener.'

'So you went from one extreme to the other.'

'Simon adores it.' She shrugged, watching him as he smoothly unlocked his door and pushed it open, automatically turning to deactivate his alarm.

'And you?'

Sara pretended to ignore the question. It wasn't difficult. He had switched on the light and she was quite literally speechless at what she saw. Acres of space. Acres of space for a London apartment at any rate. Shallow stairs led away from the door and down to a superb sunken sitting area which rose on one side to give an open view of yet another sitting area, less formal, with a television set at one end and alongside that a desk with a complex array of office equipment. On the other side, the sunken area led up to a spacious dining area and beyond that the kitchen, which was, unheard of in a London flat, large enough to house a kitchen table as well as all the usual culinary paraphernalia. A long counter, topped with black granite, separated the kitchen from the dining area, but aside from that one division the eye could travel the width of the room without being obstructed by any doors. And the gleaming wooden flooring emphasised the illusion of vast space.

Stretching behind were the doors that led to the bedrooms and bathrooms. It was elegant but understated, as only truly very expensive places were. The paintings on the walls were small, discreet and vaguely familiar.

'And I thought that my apartment was luxurious,' she commented drily, stepping tentatively down the stairs to the sitting area and looking around her slowly.

'Something to drink?' Which reminded her of the reason she was here in the first place, and an unexpected flutter of nerves rippled up to the surface.

'Please.'

'Coffee? Tea?'

'A glass of wine, if you have it.' She followed him up to the kitchen and perched awkwardly on one of the softly padded chairs by the table. 'It's an amazing place,' she said, watching as he poured her a glass of wine and one for himself, before sitting opposite her at the table. Her eyes skittered away from the aggressive planes of his face and the only thing running through her head was the fact that she needed to keep talking. She was no longer the seductress out to even scores. She just felt like a nervous, timid young girl out on her first date with a man who was light-years ahead of her in the sophistication stakes.

'How on earth did you find it? A place like this is like gold dust in London. You must have spent months, years searching.'

'I own the building, actually.' James watched the changing expressions on her face with amusement. 'Or, rather, it's been in the family for as long as I can remember. We used to own quite a bit more as a matter of fact but a lot's been sold along the way to help cover the costs of running the estate in Scotland.'

'Oh, indeed. Don't we *all* have to flog a few of our London assets so that we can keep our country estates running?'

He grinned at the sarcasm, which Sara half wished he hadn't done because she then became all too uncomfortably aware that, manipulator or not, the man had bags of charm, too much for his own good.

'Where were you before you lived in London?' she asked hurriedly.

'Oh, a bit of here and a bit of there.' Those amazing eyes! They would have held her captive if she wasn't so intent on avoiding them. 'Building up my businesses, handling my father's investments. I liked the idea of being fairly rootless.'

'I thought you still were…fairly rootless.'

'I have this place,' he made an expansive gesture to encompass the apartment, 'and Scotland. I'm as rooted as it's possible for any man to be.'

'Not many men own properties all over the globe,' Sara pointed out.

'I consider myself very fortunate in that respect.'

Sara toyed with the stem of her wine glass.

'I'm surprised you haven't been snapped up by now.' She wanted desperately to remember how she was going into this, with her eyes wide open and cold-bloodedly aware that hers was a game without emotion. She didn't want to succumb to any phoney charm. She'd already gone down that road. 'Eligible playboys are always the first to go.'

'That's been your experience, has it?' The lazy smile dropped from his face. 'And I'm not a playboy. In fact, the very description is an insult. Playboys travel from party to party, spending Daddy's money and chasing pretty young things.'

'And you don't chase pretty young things?' She gestured around her. 'This isn't *Daddy's*? You don't party with the best of them?' She dared him to contradict her, to put her back in the angry frame of mind she needed to keep her perspectives within sight.

He looked at her carefully, as if he was making up his mind about something, then he smiled.

'Actually the building belongs jointly to my mother and me now, not that she ever gets the chance to come down to London except for Ascot and Christmas shopping. Sometimes it's odd to think that she was once a model jet setting all over the world.'

Sara was well and truly deflected. 'Didn't she miss…all of this?'

'Oh, she took a little while to settle, she once told me. She missed the shops and the hectic travel and the buzz, but then after a few months she found herself being drawn in to village life. And, of course, she adored the old man. Apparently, she returned to London a few months after she had moved up and found that a lot of her friends were not quite the exciting young things she thought they were.'

A bit like me, Sara thought bitterly, except the only male who stood any chance of holding back her return was five years old. The friends aspect she could understand. *They* hadn't changed, it was *her* lifestyle that had altered. But as for being drawn into village life, she couldn't see it happening. She still had one foot up north, one down south and no one to help her make her mind up.

'How are you finding life in the Highlands?' he asked curiously and immediately her antennae were up. This would be his first step, she thought. He would never come right out with his plan to buy the house from under her feet. He would gently but relentlessly move in and use whatever was necessary to get what he wanted.

'Different.' Sara stood up and stretched. 'Do you mind if I remove my jacket?' Without giving him time to answer, she pulled off the short cream jacket, which left her only in her tight top that fell neatly to the waistband of the skirt.

'Not going to carry on? Shame.' His hooded blue eyes lingered on her. 'I like the thought of my woman doing a striptease in my kitchen.'

His woman. Sara felt a shiver of pleasure at the possessive terminology. Possessive but frankly meaningless. The only thing that really got to this man when it came to women was sex. And she wanted to get to him, didn't she?

She pulled the top over her head and dropped it on the table between them. Her fingers had been trembling when she did that, but as his eyes drifted over her breasts pushing against the lacy bra she felt the same rush of power that had surged through her earlier. The silence between them was erotically charged, only broken when he pushed back his chair and hooked one ankle around another so that he could pull it towards him, enabling him to stretch out his legs and continue his lazy, broodingly sexy appraisal of what she was doing.

In that instant it occurred to her that she would never have been able to do what she was doing if she hadn't been genuinely and intensely attracted to him. She wanted to touch him and have him touch her and she would, but in due course, when the build-up had left them both weak with need.

He had tipped his head back so that his eyes appeared drowsily half-closed as he watched her.

Sara unhooked the bra and slowly pulled each strap down, then the lacy piece of not much was off and joining the discarded top on the table.

Her breasts pointed proudly out for his inspection. She heard his swift intake of breath and half smiled.

She shimmied towards him until she was standing right in front of him, then, very slowly and not taking her eyes away from his darkly flushed face, she rid herself of her skirt. She almost wanted to scream out loud with her desperate craving to be touched. When her body did finally make contact with his, she was sure that she would explode into a thousand fragments.

It almost did. It felt as if it would anyway as he dropped his legs from the chair so that he was holding her between them and then flicked aside the crotch of her panties so that he could lean forward and deeply inhale the scent of her dusky womanliness. He filled his nostrils with it and she allowed herself to drown under the weight of mindless sensation as he ruffled the fine hair between her legs, blowing against it, preparing her for the delicate probing of his tongue on the tip of her swollen, sensitised clitoris.

With a muffled groan, Sara clasped the back of his dark head with her hands and arched back, shifting her stance slightly so that she could more easily open herself up to accommodate the dark head there between her legs.

At one point she heard herself pleading with him to stop in a voice that she barely recognised, and when he did draw back she was still shuddering from the impact of his ravaging, intimate kiss.

'Sit on my lap,' he commanded shakily and she obeyed. He tilted her back and then subjected her throbbing breasts to the same oral exploration that he had afforded her most private parts.

He sucked on each nipple, drawing the roused bud into his mouth so that he could tease it with his teeth and his tongue. His moist mouth was connecting to invisible sensory lines within her body, shooting pleasure straight from the tips of her nipples to those parts of her body which could only be appeased when she rubbed them against the rough fabric of his trousers.

If she carried on doing this she knew that she would not be able to stop bringing herself to an uncontrollable climax, and as if sensing this he pulled back from her throbbing breasts and roughly told her that he needed to get out of his clothes *now*.

What he didn't tell her was that he had never felt so wildly, devastatingly out of control before. He could feel himself bulging against his trousers and it physically *hurt*.

It didn't take him long to divest himself of his clothes, practically ripping his shirt off his back, popping a couple of buttons in the process which bounced across the kitchen floor.

This time when their bodies met, flesh against flesh, there was no room for seductive foreplay.

Their bodies were hot and slick and ripe to be melded together as one. He pulled her back onto him, letting her have just the merest build-up as he clasped his big hands on her waist and encouraged her to feel that intensely arousing friction once again as she rubbed herself wantonly and rhythmically against his hardened shaft. This time there were no knickers and no trousers to impede the heated satisfaction of feeling him massive between her thighs, each thrusting movement bringing an incoherent moan from her parted mouth.

Then with an unsteady groan he inserted himself into her, his powerful body shuddering with satisfaction as she began to undulate on top of him, steadily up and down, increasing her tempo so that her beautiful, bountiful breasts bounced just there by his mouth, just there where he could almost catch them. And God, he wanted to taste them again.

As she moved, his hands swept upwards to capture one jiggling breast and he sucked fiercely on the engorged pink nipple.

It was too much. Did she cry out? She didn't know. Her eyes were closed, her head thrown back, the upper part of her torso pushed forward to accommodate his devastating mouth on her breasts, and then she was free falling through space and time, tumbling over the edge and feeling him taking the same electrifying ride that she was on.

Their bodies were locked into one another and Sara felt that first burst of shattering sensation give way to climactic ripples that took her to a series of peaks that had her sagging when she finally came back down to earth.

It felt somehow *right* when he drew her to him and wrapped his arms around her, slowly tracing the line of her spine with his fingers. She was so peaceful that she could very easily have nodded off.

'I hope you're not too tired...' His voice was a low, husky murmur in her ear and she opened her eyes drowsily to find herself staring at his firm jawline and a glimpse of his mouth that told her he was smiling. Her fingers itched to stroke the edge of his mouth and she resolutely kept them still.

'You couldn't...' Her voice was as husky as his and she didn't recognise the sexy laugh as belonging to her when he informed her that she really shouldn't say things that could possibly constitute a challenge to a man like him.

'But this time I think we'll be a bit more conventional and avail ourselves of my king-sized bed.' He kissed the tip of her nose and she straightened to stare down at him, unbothered by her nudity. They walked with their fingers linked out of the fabulous open area towards one of the doors, which opened into an equally impressive master bedroom.

This section of the house was carpeted and plushly so. Her toes squirmed delightedly into the thick pile and he tugged her towards the bed.

This was a big bed for a big man and the linen was uncompromisingly masculine, a mixture of dark greens and vibrant burgundies that would have left a perfect stranger in no doubt as to the sensual nature of their occupant.

And, just in case she was in any doubt herself, he spent the next hour and a half showing her just how sensual he could be. The frantic urgency of their first bout of love-making, when they had been devoured by a consuming need to get to one another, driven by a primitive sexual craving that had left them spent and breathless, was replaced by a lingering, almost tender and equally fulfilling exploration of each other's bodies. It was a slow, melodic dance that took them both to the same dramatic heights, but via a different route.

Afterwards, with her brain in neutral and her senses swimming pleasurably in the aftermath of their lovemaking, Sara coiled herself on her side so that they were facing one another with their bodies lightly touching.

'I should be going back to my hotel,' she murmured half-heartedly and he stroked some hair away from her face.

'I can't think why.'

Sara's brain struggled to get a grip of something very important that was edging there just out of reach.

'I can't stand the thought of your hanging on to your past, you know.' James's voice was deadly serious and he found that he was staring down at her with such ferocious intensity that he forced himself to dilute it with something like a low laugh.

'I'm not. Not any more.'

'Tell me about him. Tell me what went wrong.'

'Everything went wrong and it's too long a story to tell, anyway. Long and tedious and unnecessary.'

'We have time.' He found himself driven to glimpse that part of her life that was capable of making his teeth snap together in frustrated anger.

'You mean you're not going to suggest that we... indulge again?' Sara enquired lightly to break the sudden tension, and the ploy worked. He smiled. Did he know how much younger he looked when he smiled?

'I'm no longer a teenager,' James said drily, because he wanted her to talk and sex would wait. He smiled again and that smile did it. What harm was there in spilling out a bit of her personal history to him? It wasn't a state secret, for heaven's sake!

So she found herself telling him about her background, about growing up in the East End of London, helping her father with his market stall, a very thriving market stall, but a market stall nevertheless. She was an only child with a quick brain and her parents had lovingly fostered her talent for schoolwork. By the time she was nine she could run the market stall as efficiently as the best of them and she had enjoyed it. She'd learnt to barter, begun to predict trends in what sold and when it sold and why it sold.

'I never realised it was a talent that would get me where I eventually got, but I was good at…well, trading, I suppose…' She sighed and stared mistily into the distance. Once started, she was discovering that the torrent was un-stoppable. Phillip had met her at a social occasion when her star was beginning to shine. He had zeroed in on her and, fool that she had been, she had taken him at face value, she was clever but not clever enough to spot the snob behind the charming veneer.

'So I never thought twice about telling him all about my parents, where I had grown up. He was appalled. Not,' she added truthfully, 'that I think that that was the reason it all went pear-shaped. But it certainly didn't help matters. He had no need for bright stars with dubious backgrounds. In fact, as it turned out, he had no need for bright stars at all. He's marrying someone with no pretensions to a career but presumably good breeding stock. Unlike me. The preg-nancy was the last straw. He felt guilty to start with, he wasn't a complete monster, but soon he began implying that, since it was my fault, he had no duties to deal with it, with his own son. Every so often he would come around unannounced, I suppose when one of his twinges of guilt got a little hard to handle, but all that stopped after a while.

He hadn't wanted a child and he especially couldn't deal with a son who wasn't the picture of robust health.' Sara sighed and managed a weak smile. 'So there you go.'

'Market trader,' James murmured softly, reaching to place a kiss on her mouth, 'I like it.' And he did. Although if anyone was to ask him precisely why, he would not have been able to provide an adequate answer.

CHAPTER EIGHT

BY THE middle of August, Sara realised that her initial decision to leave Scotland in time to get Simon back to London for school at the beginning of September was no longer on the cards. She had done nothing about arranging somewhere to live, had checked out no schools either in or around London, and whenever she thought about it her mind went unhelpfully blank.

She blamed James. For someone who worked and lived in London, he had certainly found it inside himself to break with his routine so that he could see her, sometimes two or three times during the week, always in the evening when Simon was not around. When he came up on the weekends, all three of them, she insisted that they meet only at night. She said that her days were just too full trying to get the house together and seeing about the million and one things that still needed doing. In fact, she made sure not to be around on the Saturdays she knew he would be travelling up to his estate.

She arranged to explore anywhere and everywhere. She took her shopping trips as far away from home base as she could. She even made a mammoth effort to take Simon across to Edinburgh, giving themselves a little stay-over treat, although all she could think about was the prospect of seeing James when she got back on the Sunday evening.

She adored the way he waited impatiently for her. She could imagine him striding through the millions of rooms in his mansion, frowning with his hands shoved into his pockets, waiting for her phone call informing him that Simon was settled.

'It's ridiculous,' he had ground out the weekend before, when she had calmly informed him that no, she couldn't possibly go out with him during the day. ' I need to be in your company and yet when I come up here you do nothing but insist I keep away.'

Her laughter had managed to coax a reluctant smile from him, but pretty soon she knew that she wouldn't be able to hold him at bay by telling him that those were her rules and she wanted them respected. He had held off so far but he was like a caged tiger, biding his time until he could push further forward.

She also knew that pretty soon she would have to do what she had set out to do—confront him with his own unpleasant little scheme to buy her house and declare herself the winner, show him that she was nobody's fool and that she could play the sex game as competently as he thought he could.

She was sitting in the garden, half reading a book and half keeping an eye on Simon, who was busily digging up some weeds for her in the hope of finding either worms or buried treasure. She rested her head back, closed her eyes for a few seconds, and when she opened them again it was to see James standing in front of the French doors, watching her.

Sara sat up and blinked but the vision refused to disappear. In fact, the vision strode towards her, long, lean and unfairly sexy in his lightweight trousers and short-sleeved shirt that hung over his trousers.

'I thought you had a thousand things to do and weren't going to be around,' he said, finally standing in front of her and staring down at her flushed face.

Simon had stopped his energetic exploration of the flower bed so that he could look at James.

'What are you doing here?'

'You know, you're doing very little for my concentration, lying there in next to nothing.' He smiled very slowly. 'Now, what if some passing stranger had called round and found you dressed like that?'

'Dressed like what?' Sara peered anxiously over to Simon and smiled reassuringly at him. James followed the direction of her gaze to smile at the boy, who grinned back and looked prepared to launch into conversation. Sara thought she'd better nip that in the bud so she told him cheerfully that if he dug a bit deeper she was sure he would find what he was looking for.

'Which is what?' Blue eyes that had the power to scorch refocused on Sara's flushed face.

'Buried treasure or worms. Either is equally acceptable. And you still haven't told me what you're doing here, not,' she added as a postscript, 'that it isn't very nice to see you.' Except not here and not now. She had managed to make very sure that contact with her son was minimal and things weren't going to change there.

Settling scores, which was the object of the exercise or so she kept telling herself, was one thing. She could handle the consequences, but Simon had to be protected from involvement with James.

'I...I thought we had arranged to meet up a bit later...'

'We had but...' James looked up into the cloudless blue sky and squinted. The hot summer agreed with him. Naturally inclined to swarthiness, he had been given by the sun a deep, bronzed colour that made most other people look anaemic in comparison. Especially her, with her ultra-fair skin that needed protecting. Not that he seemed to mind. In fact, she blushed as she remembered some of his more potent adulations of her body.

He glanced back down at her and grinned. 'It was so bloody hot that I couldn't resist driving over to see if I could catch you before you went out. Somehow,' he leaned over, trapping her in her sun lounger, 'Mama, wonderful company though she is, was not quite the woman I fancied spending my Saturday with.'

Sara licked her lips. 'Actually, I was on my way out...'

'In a pair of shorts and a cropped top that barely covers your breasts? Not if I have any say in that.'

'I was going to change first!'

'Out where?'

'Out to the market, actually. I need to buy some vegetables, food for me to cook for us tonight.'

He hadn't straightened up and the warm suggestiveness of his eyes as they roamed over her face and the upper part of her body made her nipples ache.

'Good,' he murmured, 'I fancy a trip to the market. Always such an adventure, that market of ours. I can drive us there. We can have lunch somewhere.'

'No!'

James frowned and pushed himself up. 'No? Why not?' He narrowed his eyes suspiciously on her face. Sometimes, not very often, he had the disconcerting feeling that the earth, on which his feet were very firmly planted, was shifting ever so slightly under him. This was one of those times. Shouldn't matter a bean, of course, since sex was all there was between them, hot, vibrant, compulsive sex, but he didn't like her immediate rejection of his company.

'Because...then you'd see what I'm buying and the meal tonight wouldn't be a surprise.'

'Let me take you out. You know how much Mama enjoys coming here now to babysit Simon...'

Which was something else, Sara thought guiltily. She hadn't planned it that way, but Simon and Maria seemed to have developed a natural bond and it had been easier to see him away from her own house. More often than not, they went back to his estate and he cooked for her, tempted her palate with delicacies he carried up with him in his helicopter, little morsels of paradise from Fortnum and Mason or Harrods.

Sometimes he would feed her some of the delicious treats, making her recline on one of the sofas in one of the sitting rooms, door firmly closed so that she could stretch out in naked abandonment and nibble what he presented to her. He would kneel by her side, every bit the adoring slave, and then his adoration would become physical, from her toes to the top of her head.

'No, really, James, I'd rather I just went down to the market and got what I need to get.' She reluctantly swung her legs over the side of the sun lounger so that she could make the point. 'And I'll get through it a lot quicker if it's just me and Simon.'

'I have two perfectly functioning legs,' he said tautly, 'I don't think I'll hold you up. If anything, I can help, take Simon for a milkshake, leave you to shop in peace for a couple of hours.'

'No!' Sara said sharply. Her eyes slid across to where her son was busily making an unholy mess of the flowers she had planted only days earlier. Obviously his designated spot had failed to yield the expected treasure. She would have to sort that out later.

'What's the problem, Sara?' OK, so he was being high-handed and obstinate, but he didn't like to think that his company was surplus to requirements, that she didn't want him around whenever and wherever she could have him, because as far as he was concerned that was how it stood with him at this moment in time. He couldn't stop thinking about her. It was the most severe case of lust he had ever experienced. And when they were together she was as fired-up as he was, so he couldn't understand how she could draw lines around them the way that she did, the way she was doing now.

'There *is* no problem.' Their eyes met and she was the first to look away. 'Come on, Simes, upstairs. You've got to change. We're going into town to do some shopping.'

'But I haven't found any treasure,' Simon wailed, not budging.

'What you need is a metal detector,' James said, strolling across and, to Sara's dismay, reaching out one hand to take his. 'Now, a metal detector will tell you where to find your buried treasure. It beeps whenever it senses something interesting in the ground.'

Simon was looking a little too enthralled by that for Sara's comfort, and it was even more alarming when they both followed her inside the house with Simon willingly complying with James's brisk assertion that he would change him so that his mother could get dressed.

'There's no need,' she protested feebly, only to find herself staring into two pairs of implacable eyes.

Of course, James got his way, accompanying them to the market. This was just what she didn't need, and as soon as she could she made her feelings absolutely clear.

'This wasn't part of the deal,' she hissed as they ventured into the open-air food market and she could be assured that Simon was distracted enough not to overhear a word they were saying.

'What *deal*?'

'Me. You. Us. *That* deal.'

Since that was precisely the arrangement he had always enjoyed with every woman he had ever dated, he was surprised to find himself seething with anger at being informed that he was merely part of a deal.

'I don't know that I care for that expression.'

'Why? It's only a *matter of vocabulary*.'

'Ha, ha. What was the real reason for not wanting me tagging along, Sara? Were you planning on meeting someone in town? A man?' He struggled to hide the primitive stab of jealousy underneath a tone of amused cynicism.

Sara stopped to stare at him. 'Don't be ridiculous.'

'Is that what I'm being? You seemed pretty determined not to have me around and don't think I haven't noticed that it's the same on all the weekends I've come up here. You're free for the evening, but inexplicably occupied during the day. Wouldn't you say that that was a little strange? A little *revealing*?'

Sara turned away and gave all her attention to the boy behind the stall and then surprised him by handing over the correct amount of money before he had time to consult his piece of paper, do his sums and tell her how much she owed.

'Well?' James pressed. 'What do you do with yourself during the daylight hours? If there's some man here you've been seeing, I'll...'

'What? Hound him out of town? String him up from the nearest lamppost?'

'Both,' he muttered, scowling, not that he believed that for a minute. He would have heard long before now.

'There's no man. How could I have the energy for anyone else?' she asked truthfully, which went a little way to putting the shadow of a smile back on his face. He took the bags of fruit and vegetables from her.

'We will have lunch together, the three of us,' he stated flatly, and Sara raised her eyebrows at his peremptory tone of voice. 'I know a very pleasant pub about twenty miles away.'

'Twenty miles?'

'No distance at all.' He shrugged and gave her one of those familiar looks that never failed to make her go warm all over. Wicked, arrogant and searingly sexy all wrapped up in one. 'And then I will deliver you and Simon back to the Rectory in one piece and leave you to get on with the absorbing task of cooking for your man.'

'Cooking for my man. Hm. Aren't you just the sort of sensitive, twenty-first-century guy that every liberated woman dreams of finding?' It was so easy to drift into this kind of teasing banter with him and his sense of humour never let her down. He could make her giggle like a teenager. She was practically giggling now as he visibly puffed himself up and looked every inch the sexy caveman, even though he could cook like a dream when he put his mind to it.

'Yes,' he grinned back at her, 'that would be me. The cap certainly fits so, if you don't mind, I think I will wear it. Now, in a *very sensitive* manner, I will take these bags to the car and expect to see you what time...? In about half an hour?'

Sara sighed and gave up. 'OK. A quick lunch and then *you go home* or I shall have your mother swearing at me for hogging you to myself whenever you come up.'

It was only hours later, after an extraordinarily good lunch at a pub in a small village that made their own town seem like a cosmopolitan city in comparison, that Sara took time out to sit down and think. She didn't like where her thoughts went. Somewhere along the line, in that murky place between theory and practice, it had become just too damned comfortable being with James. If he had railed against her for shunning his company during the day, she could have told him that she yearned for him when he wasn't with her. She had managed to hang on to that little piece of maternal protectiveness that made her shy away from encouraging contact between him and her son, but for how much longer?

Today had been something of a revelation. She had watched helplessly as James had bonded with Simon. She was his mum, who made sure that he washed his hands, brushed his teeth, didn't eat too much of the wrong foods, read books with him and did puzzles, but James had talked to him in an amusing man-to-man way that had had Simon's eyes dancing with delight. He had carried him from pub to car on his shoulders, bouncing him up and down until her son had laughed till tears had gathered in his eyes. He had seriously discussed the possibility of doing a spot of manly metal detecting together.

Now, as she prepared vegetables, she knew that she would have to do something about the situation.

She would have to break it off, show her hand, but when she thought of doing that, which was frankly what she had set out to do in the first place, her mind baulked.

Realising that she had peeled far too many carrots for two people, she switched to chopping onions, and when her eyes began to water firmly told herself that the onions were to blame.

Cool it down first. That was what she would do. Take her steps carefully because…because…

Because her heart had disobeyed every instruction her

head had given it, she realised with panic. Her heart had boldly opened up and been swept away while all the time she had been kidding herself that she was pulling the strings and being the hard woman she never had been and certainly wasn't now.

The Rectory was a place of seeming orderly control by the time seven-thirty rolled around.

Simon was comfortably tucked up in bed, fast asleep after being read his favourite book for five minutes. The kitchen smelled of garlic and herbs and the fragrant lamb she had spent the afternoon making, even though her mind had been miles away.

She was wearing a straight sleeveless dress, slightly fitted to the waist and then falling softly to mid-calf. Very old-fashioned, especially with her long hair falling in ripples down her back, very Victorian. Very un-sexy. Not an inch of unnecessary leg visible and no part of her body outlined. If she was going to stick to her guns and begin the painful process of phasing him out of her life, then she needed all the help she could get.

Nevertheless, she still felt her resolve wobble by the time the doorbell went and she pulled open the door to find him standing there, with an enormous bouquet of flowers in one hand.

It was the first time he had made any gesture like that and it took her aback. Flowers seemed to imply romance and romance wasn't what he was about.

'From the gardens,' he said roughly, noting her reaction and registering grimly that flowers probably weren't part of the 'deal' either. He thrust them at her and followed her into the kitchen, watching while she floated around, finding a vase, filling it with water, deftly arranging the flowers with an expertise that only his mother seemed to share.

What was she wearing? He hadn't seen her in anything like that dress before, was surprised that she even possessed something as dreamily feminine as that, considering her wardrobe must still bear the imprint of her power outfits. It left an awful lot to the imagination and, on cue, his imagination began to run riot until he had firmly poured cold water over it.

'Hand-picked?'

'What?'

'The flowers. Hand-picked, I presume?'

James shrugged carelessly. 'Not too difficult, considering the profusion of them in the gardens. Smells good in here. Is Simon asleep?'

Sara didn't want to discuss Simon, but mention of his name did remind her that her mission was to bring closure to this peculiar little relationship she and James were having, one which meant relatively little to him she was sure, but which meant far too much to her.

She would never tell him that she had found out about his little plan to use her to get the Rectory. It was humiliating enough now to think about that without bringing it out into the open and besides...she had played a tit-for-tat game that had massively backfired on her. The games were over, the only truth was that she had to get him out of her life because she was so hopelessly embroiled with him now.

'Tell me what's happening in London,' she invited, steering the conversation into neutral waters. 'What's playing at the theatre? Are there any open-air proms happening? I used to go to the open-air proms every year when I was in London. There's nothing quite like listening to good music outside, surrounded by people, with a picnic hamper by your side and friends around you.'

'Any friends in particular?' James took the proffered glass of wine and swallowed a mouthful.

Recently he seemed to have unearthed a distastefully possessive streak that he was finding difficult to control. What friends had she gone there with? He had gone to one open-air prom, last year in fact. He hadn't seen her there then. Who had she been with? Her ex-boyfriend? Some other man? A whole tribe of them?

'Friends from work.' Sara went across to the Aga, opened the door and released a wonderful smell of cooking.

'Do you keep in touch with them still?'

'Of course I do!' She had conversations down the end of the phone with some of them. They considered her something of a curiosity now that she had left the bright lights behind, and she considered them a little dysfunctional to be so wrapped up in making money, even though she could wryly admit that she had numbered one of them only a matter of a couple of months ago.

'And these friends...are they male or female?'

'Both,' Sara said lightly. 'A bit like yours, I expect.'

'I don't encourage female friendships.' James rested the wine glass on the kitchen table so that he could link his fingers behind his head. From this angle, he could inspect her every movement with lazy, leisurely concentration. 'I find even the most dispassionate female friend usually ends up wanting more than I can give.'

'You're not as irresistible as you think you are,' Sara informed him. She hadn't done a starter, favouring a pudding instead, and now she began bringing dishes to the table and telling him what he would be eating.

James listened politely, sat squarely in front of his plate, allowed her to dish out a little of everything for him.

'Are you telling me that *you* don't find me irresistible?'

'I think we understand one another,' Sara told him lightly. 'We both know what we want out of this relationship.' In his case, sex and her house, in her case love, marriage, babies, the whole fairy tale that experience should have warned her didn't exist. Fortunately, he wasn't going to find that out.

'Which is?'

'You know what. Fun.'

'And your need to exorcise your demons.'

'Meaning?'

'Your ex-lover.' It shouldn't have bothered him. After all, wasn't he getting what he wanted? To bed the woman sitting opposite him and eating with the composed air of a saint? It bothered him like hell.

Sara shrugged and let him assume.

'Simon enjoyed today,' she said, into the tense little silence that had greeted her non-answer.

'So did I.' He paused. 'Do I hear a *but* coming…?'

'But,' Sara said obligingly, 'I really don't want a repeat performance.'

'Meaning what exactly?'

'Meaning that, while I appreciate your efforts, I don't want you to get involved with my son.'

'Why is that?'

'Do you have to keep asking questions? Can't you just accept what I tell you at face value?' She closed her knife and fork. She had been able to eat only a fraction of what was on her plate. Her appetite seemed to have done a runner.

'I've never been a great believer in accepting things at face value. There's always a deeper agenda.'

Something, she thought, he would know a lot about, considering his agenda.

'OK. The deeper agenda is that I don't want Simon getting attached to someone who isn't going to be around for very long.'

James wasn't about to let that one go. 'The dinner was delicious,' he said carefully, sitting back and folding his arms with an expression that could stop a leopard at twelve paces. 'I take it from your remark that you've already assigned a time limit to us?'

'No, of course not…'

'Simon benefits from having a man around occasionally. I'm not about to try and step into his father's footsteps, although from what you tell me that wouldn't be very difficult considering the kitchen table we're sitting at is capable of more paternal feelings. But…'

'There are no buts, James,' Sara said sharply. 'If you don't like the situation then you can clear off.' Every word was like having a knife dragged through her heart. She could feel her eyes beginning to water and hastily stood up so that she could focus on something other than his gimlet-like, narrowed stare.

'This isn't getting us anywhere.' The low murmur came from closer to her than she had expected. With her back to him, belligerently attacking the plates into a state of cleanliness, she had been unaware of his approach.

Frankly, his response alarmed her. Hadn't she just given him the perfect opportunity for a fight? She knew him well enough by now to know that he wasn't the sort of man who tolerated female attacks with equanimity, so why was he not ramming home his point?

Sara felt his arms slide around her waist and she stiffened, then began to melt.

One touch. That was all it took. When he bent to rest his mouth against the nape of her neck, she felt the bones in her body soften.

'If you feel that strongly, then of course I won't try and barge in on your little nuclear family.' Somehow he made that sound as though it was a criticism of her but she was losing the will to fight because his teeth were now gently nipping the side of her neck and making her legs feel very shaky in the process.

'Is that why you've been dodging me during the day whenever I've been down?' he murmured, reaching forward to switch off the tap and then replacing his hand a little further up her torso, beneath her left breast, in fact. 'It's perfectly understandable.'

Sara made a concerted effort to shift herself around, which she managed to do successfully, only to find that his long, lean body had no intention of moving. He kissed the tip of her nose. Then very gently kissed her mouth.

Why, why, why? Why couldn't he help her along and be as predictable as every other man on the face of the earth? *Because if he was,* she thought to herself, *then you wouldn't have fallen head over heels in love with him.* Nor would she still be falling, even though she knew full well what he was about.

She heaved a small sigh of resignation and coiled her arms around his neck, drawing him down so that his gentle kiss could be replaced by her more urgent one.

Wrong response. Definitely not in accordance with her well-thought-out plans. Definitely not a sensible manoeuvre when it came to protecting her vulnerable heart.

'I've made pudding,' she managed to protest.

'It. Can. Wait.' He punctuated the three words with hungry kisses. When he strode towards the kitchen door and slipped the latch down, all Sara could do was wait in the familiar nervous excitement for him to be back close to her.

'Now,' he murmured, pulling her to him and winding his fingers into her hair, 'I can think of a hundred more pleasurable things we can do than argue.' He smiled slowly. 'Well, only one, as a matter of fact, but that can be done in a hundred different ways, mm?'

Not a hundred, as it turned out. In fact, the kitchen proved the venue for the appetiser only and Sara had never before imagined that a kitchen table could be that satisfying an instrument in lovemaking.

Her floaty dress, which she had worn as an armour against his advances, didn't stand a chance. Not that he removed it. Just pushed it up to her waist, where it bunched around her, leaving him free to tug down her underwear so that he could explore the honeyed moisture between her legs. If the floaty dress didn't stand a chance, then neither did she, when it came to his ability to arouse her. All she could do was lie back, her head flung over the back of the chair, and enjoy his full attention.

She didn't want to come, fought against it, but the insistent flicking of his tongue against her sensitised bud proved too great a stimulation to resist and the waves of pleasure rushing through her in rapid succession left her moaning and writhing until she shuddered to her explosive orgasm.

Afterwards, face flushed, she lay limply with her dress still inelegantly at her waist, breathing heavily.

'Delicious dessert,' James murmured with a wicked smile and Sara looked at him drowsily.

'That's the corniest line I've ever heard.' She smiled back and ran her fingers lightly through his hair. He was

still squatting in front of her parted legs and he placed a
very tender kiss right there.

'Now, shall we go backwards?'

'Go backwards?'

'Enjoy some main course...'

For which the sitting room, with its big, soft sofa,
proved just the right place. The curtains were open and the
light was fading but there was still enough to bathe the
room in a dusky, mellow hue. Through the French doors,
the rolling scenery made her feel as though they were making love out in the open.

'Simon's upstairs, sleeping,' Sara said feebly.

'And we're downstairs, pleasuring one another. I've
locked the door, so there's no need to worry, and we'll
hear him anyway if he wakes up.'

This time, there were no clothes to stand between their
bodies. Sara looked at him as he stood in front of her,
disposing of his, and idly thought that he had a magnificent
body, lean, strong, powerful and utterly lacking in self-
consciousness.

And when he looked at her, he made her feel the same
way. Her nudity was something she basked in and his keen
eyes flicking appreciatively over her unclothed body was
a massive turn-on. The fact that she had already been plea-
sured did not mean that he couldn't arouse her again. And
again and again.

Afterwards, while Sara lay supine on the sofa, James
strolled across to the French doors and closed the curtains,
then he switched on one of the table lamps.

'What about the pudding I've slaved over?' she teased
contentedly, looking up at him as he stood over her. She
yawned and stretched and he smiled at her. A vision of
absolute satisfied fulfilment. He could stay there forever

feasting his eyes on her smooth, pale body, watching the way her breasts moved when she raised her arms above her head so that the pink nipples were large circles beckoning him.

'You stay right where you are.' He began shoving on some clothes, just boxer shorts and trousers and, as an afterthought, his shirt, which he didn't bother to button.

'Don't be silly, you're the guest.' But she just stretched again, languidly, and raised her heavy eyes to his.

'Which, of course, means,' he drawled with lazy intent, 'that you have to make sure that I'm one hundred per cent satisfied, and you can stay right there and think of all the ways you can do that. In the meantime, I shall fetch us both our dessert, *mademoiselle,* just so long as you tell me where to find it.'

'Larder. Just some iced brownies, I'm afraid. I'm lousy at desserts.' But what joy having him fetch them for her. There was a throw on one of the chairs, and she really should cover herself with it, but the effort involved seemed a little bit too much. Besides, and she revelled in this thought, wouldn't he just tear it off her the minute he returned?

She was aware of him returning even before he re-entered the room with the plate of brownies in one hand and two glasses of wine precariously in the other.

Sara propped herself up on her elbow and surveyed him as he deposited the wine on the table in front of them, then sat on the sofa by her, depressing it with his weight.

He dipped his finger into some icing and held the finger out to her lips, which she proceeded to suck with her eyes tantalisingly fastened on his.

'Good?'

Sara nodded.

'Well, I'd better try some for myself, in that case.' At which he repeated the exercise, but instead of proferring his finger to his own mouth he spread a sample on one of her nipples and then...oh...she could only moan as he licked it off very thoroughly before doing the same with the other aching nipple.

She was like a cat being stroked and stretching itself to its fullest so that the stroking could last forever.

Forever.

James didn't pause in his ministrations of her eager body. The realisation crept over him and it was something that he had known for a while.

Forever.

It was a good place to be.

CHAPTER NINE

JAMES sat at his desk, his long legs stretched out in front of him, planted solidly on the shiny, polished surface. At least he knew that there would be no interruptions of any kind. Everyone had gone home. He had all the time in the world to reflect. Shame that the reflections were of such a sordid nature, but then he had had ample time to consider that it served him right.

From the minute he had laid eyes on Sara King, he had stupidly thrown all his natural caution to the winds. Even when she had spun him her pathetic little story about not wanting him around because she wasn't prepared to have an affair, he had gone, only to return the minute she had crooked her finger. And how his stupidity had returned to bite him.

He looked coldly at the small black and gold bag burning a hole on the desk. Thinking about the ring inside only made him more enraged, but, like Sisyphus toiling up the mountain, it seemed that he had no choice but to stare at it and grimly acknowledge his misplaced trust.

Of course, he would have to deal with it. He had been played for a fool and he had no intention of allowing her the luxury of thinking that she had got away with it.

He swung his long legs from the desk and within minutes he was on the phone, making arrangements with his pilot for his flight up to Scotland. Then he slipped the bag into his jacket pocket. Touching it made him grimace with distaste but he almost enjoyed the feeling of repulsion because it was a strong and necessary reminder of the fact that he had been taken for a fool.

The helicopter would leave in an hour and a half. By the time he made it up to the Highlands, it would be after ten. His mother would probably be asleep. He hadn't told her that he would be arriving a day ahead of schedule. He hadn't known it himself, not until this afternoon.

If he had any sense, he would leave the inevitable meeting with Sara until the morning, but he wasn't feeling sensible. Besides, he told himself, she would have Simon around in the morning. The minute she realised that he was on to her she would hide behind her son, knowing full well that a full-blown argument would then be out of the question. And James felt ripe for a full-blown argument.

Far from calming him, the flight up gave him a little more time for his rage to intensify.

His mind wandered back to the conversation he had had with Lucy Campbell, who had called him at work simply on the spur of the moment because she happened to be in London. They had had lunch at one of the trendier places that Lucy adored because they gave her the opportunity to look at people and know that they were looking at her.

Lord knew, he would never have found out about the conversation she had had with Sara but a couple of glasses of wine had put her in a mellow mood, and, from teasing him about the fact that the Rectory had passed him by, she had confided that she had explained his desire to get his hands on it to the current owner, just, she had admitted sheepishly, to see her reaction. Jealousy pure and simple, she had admitted airily. After all, hadn't *she* been after the biggest fish in town for most of her years? But, now she had got herself a boyfriend with whom she was head over heels, she could be open and honest.

It had taken him only a matter of seconds to work out why Sara had suddenly decided, out of the blue, to get in touch with him, to throw herself at him. Revenge through seduction. He didn't care what her reasons had been. All he could feel was his own raw pain and all he could think was that he had been on the brink of proposing marriage, of becoming the vulnerable idiot once again.

Vulnerable. Idiot. Two words that had never before entered his vocabulary, or anyone else's for that matter, when it came to describing him.

As predicted, it was almost a quarter past ten by the time the helicopter touched down on the estate and getting on for ten-thirty when his car pulled up outside the Rectory.

He hadn't even bothered to go into the manor. Instead he had gone straight from helicopter to car, with his briefcase slung into the back seat.

As he had half expected, the lights were out at the Rectory. If she was up in bed she probably wouldn't hear him banging on the kitchen door, so he went to the front door instead and kept his fingers depressed on the bell until he heard the shuffle of footsteps. There was no peephole in the door. The Rectory had never been updated to include such modern conveniences. There was, however, a key chain and she opened the door just enough for him to see her peering out at him with a frown. The frown turned to delighted surprise.

Tousled red hair streaming down her back, eyes still drowsy but sexily so, mouth curving into a smile of greeting as she unlatched the door. It all added up to a woman eagerly pleased to see her man unexpectedly.

The woman should go into acting. She would be a natural candidate for an Oscar.

He wondered whether she had simulated pleasure when

they had made love as well or had she ground her teeth together and stuck it out because, at the end of the day, all she wanted was a chance to pay him back?

It galled him to think that, as he followed her into the kitchen, he was still half hoping that his conclusions had all been wildly off course.

'What on earth are you doing here, James?' she tossed over her shoulder. 'I thought you were supposed to be flying in tomorrow.'

'My business dinner was cancelled so I thought I might as well come a few hours earlier than planned. Pleased to see me?' He revelled masochistically in the need to hear her beautiful lips formulate their ready lies. She didn't let him down. In fact, she swung around and wound her arms around his neck so that she could draw him towards her, and instead of pulling back he attacked her mouth with an aggression that startled her. Though not for long. If she could fake passion then she did it very well, he thought, because her mouth almost immediately responded to his urgent plunder and her body curved against his. He could feel himself get hard in response and he roughly pushed her away.

Oh, no. Not tonight. Sex was definitely not on the menu tonight.

'Were you sleeping?' he asked, leading the way to the kitchen so that she was obliged to fall in step with him.

'What's wrong?'

James turned around to find her staring at him from the door, a small frown replacing her earlier expression of delight.

'Wrong?'

'You seem a little…strange.'

'Must be the stress of work,' he lied smoothly, watching her watching him. She was just a little too observant for his liking and it irked him to realise that she possessed, unusually for a woman or at least any of the women he had ever slept with, a talent for reading his moods.

She seemed to accept the explanation, at least for the moment, and filled the gap by chatting about what she had been up to. Buying school uniforms for Simon, getting to meet a few more of the local women her own age at an informal coffee morning for some of the mums at the school, trying to bake a cake and oh, she had bought six chickens and intended to have farm-fresh eggs every day.

James listened to this saga of rural contentment without saying anything. Eventually, Sara's voice dwindled away and the silence was not the kind she had become used to with him. It wasn't the companionable silence they always shared. This quiet had an edge to it and it frightened her.

'Why is work so stressful at the moment?' she asked, searching for the most obvious explanation for his peculiar behaviour. She must be imagining it, of course, because why else would he have come to see her at this time of the night if not to be relaxed in her company?

'Work is always stressful.' He had made a pot of coffee and he handed her a cup, removing himself to the opposite end of the kitchen table, from which he could inspect her from a relative distance. 'Didn't you find that when you worked in London?'

'Well, yes.' She tried a bright smile but it felt worn at the edges. It was late, even though she no longer felt tired, and the expression on his face was disturbing her at some indefinable level. 'But then with a child in tow, life tends to be stressful at the best of times.' More silence in need of filling. And not a move to touch her. By now they would normally be all over one another, unable to stop themselves from touching, like teenagers exploring one another for the first time instead of two adults who had already made love more times than she could remember.

'So, living here must be a dream come true.' He shot her a cool smile and noted with satisfaction the dampening effect it had. The lovely mouth began to droop and her eyes took on a guarded wariness that still had some power, infuriatingly, to pierce the part of him that he had galvanised into self-mending.

'I'm not sure about a dream come true,' Sara said with a hesitant smile. 'But yes, there's a certain magic that I would never have believed to exist when we first arrived.'

'No?'

For some reason she had never confessed the immediate dislike she had felt for the place when she had first arrived. Hiding away in the Rectory rather than going into the town now seemed like a distant dream. Perhaps she had shied away from that little admission because to insult the Highlands would have been to insult him. And then later, she found that she couldn't.

But now she felt uncomfortably goaded into rambling on.

'I guess it was such an enormous change from London. Well, you of all people must know what I mean, but then it's always been different for you because you've always lived here.' Now she could hardly believe she had stuck it out in London for so long, and with Simon as well. Mad. 'When I first came up, well, I was convinced that I'd done the wrong thing. It had seemed like fate when I found out that I'd been gifted this place and I grabbed hold of the opportunity with both hands, but leaving London was a wrench. I'd become accustomed to the noises and the chaos and the way that everything was lived in the fast lane. Always. A bit like your mum must have felt when she moved up here.'

Mention of his mother made his lips thin. His dear *mama* was not going to like this turn of events. She had developed a great deal of affection for Simon and for Sara too, come to that. Her pointedly tactful silence on the subject of her son finally finding the woman of his dreams was proof galore that that very prospect had been running through her head.

'Course, Simon adores it up here.' She was wittering. She nervously gulped some of her coffee and wondered whether he would take up the conversation if she remained silent or whether he would just sit there, with that disconcerting, forbidding expression on his face, until she began wittering again.

'So you've said before.'

'I'm sorry. Repeating myself. Must be getting old.'

Silence.

'I wish you'd tell me what's wrong.' The plea was wrenched out of her and she laughed to conceal the fear that was beginning to consume her. Fear of what, though?

'Guess who I saw today.'

'I don't know. Tell me.'

'Lucy Campbell. You remember her, don't you? It would appear that the two of you have met. Small, attractive blonde given to gossip.' He sipped some coffee and watched her face as she digested this piece of information.

'Small, attractive blonde.' So this was where it was leading. His unexpected appearance at her house, his brooding expression, the way he was making very sure not to come too close to her. He was ending their affair, if that was what it was. The fact that she had intended to be the one doing the ending never occurred to her. She had lost sight of her original plan to use him the way he had used her. All she could think of now was the prospect of never seeing him again. No more shared laughter, no more of his dry teasing, no more of that wonderful feeling of waiting for him to knock on her door, no more losing herself in their lovemaking, thinking everything was all right in the world.

He had found someone else just as Phillip had found someone else, though strangely losing Phillip had been nothing compared to what she felt now, even though he had fathered their son in the course of their brief, doomed relationship.

'Yes, I believe I do remember her, now that you mention it.' The clever girl had spilled the beans about his plans to buy the Rectory from under her feet, and look at that, she had got her man in the end.

'I thought you might.'

'Well,' Sara stood up and carried her cup to the sink then she remained there, with her back pressed against the counter and her hands splayed out on either side of her, 'you really needn't have rushed over here to tell me, James. Couldn't it have waited until morning? These things happen, after all, don't they?' She shrugged and lowered her eyes for a second.

'What things?'

'I suppose you two were destined for a life together from an early age. Isn't that how it works in this part of the world?'

'Arranged marriages?' His lip curled in cold distaste.

'Well, maybe not arranged but *expected*.' No room for serious interlopers to come along, although she had never been a serious interloper, had she? They had never talked about commitment or a future together, and he had certainly never mentioned the love word.

'Two mothers making plans for their little toddlers crawling around on the ground together? The perfect match of children with similar backgrounds, used to similar lifestyles…' She felt tears of self-pity pricking the backs of her eyelids. Different place, same old story. The daughter of a market trader should never dare hope for the impossible with a man like James Dalgleish. Ditched by two men for basically the same reason. Must be some sort of record.

'You insult my mother,' he said coldly. 'You also seem to forget that she came here as an outsider so the thought of marrying me off at the age of four to a suitable local girl would never have occurred to her. Nor am I the sort of man,' he laughed shortly, 'to meekly marry a woman because she fulfils the right criteria, even though there's a lot to be said for an arrangement of that nature.'

His words should have filled her with relief but they didn't because his expression hadn't softened.

'Besides,' he added silkily, 'Lucy has found herself a man and from all accounts she's madly in love.'

'Oh. That's nice…' Now she was confused.

'Isn't it?' He pushed his chair back so that he could stretch out his legs in front of him and afford himself a wonderful view of the apprehensive woman still glued to the kitchen sink counter. 'Although, of course, she *was* carrying a torch for me when you last spoke to her…now, what *was* it you talked about?'

'I…I don't remember.'

'That I find hard to believe.' He raised his eyebrows in a mimicry of incredulous disbelief and Sara suddenly felt like a rabbit trapped in the headlights of an oncoming car. An oncoming car that was fully aware of its existence but determined not to stop. 'You must have a memory like a knife. Part and parcel of the training you would have gone through for that job of yours.'

'I wish you'd stop playing games. Just tell me what's going on. Why did you come here so late? To tell me that a woman I met once has got a boyfriend? I can't think that sharing that piece of information really necessitated a drive here at ten-thirty in the evening!'

Her cheeks were flushed and he could see the confusion in her eyes.

Maybe, he caught himself thinking, he had been wrong about her. Maybe he had added two and two together and arrived at five.

'She told you that I had wanted the Rectory for years.' He saw the confusion in her glorious eyes cloud over with sudden guilt and the response was damning. 'Didn't she?' He smiled coldly when she didn't answer so he continued with his inexorable monologue. 'And naturally you assumed that the reason I had shown interest in you was that I wanted something from you. Please, feel free to contradict me at any point.'

'Why didn't you tell me from the beginning that you were interested in buying my house?' Her heart was hammering. Let him shower her with accusations. She wasn't going to sit down and play the easy victim.

He flushed darkly, grudgingly admiring her ability to toss his argument right back in his face. Which didn't excuse her behaviour, he reminded himself. She'd used him and what really filled him with self-disgust was the fact that he allowed himself to be used because he couldn't keep his hands off her, because he enjoyed her company, because he became addicted to it until all that rubbish about marital bliss and happy-ever-after stories ended up scrambling his very sharp brain.

'Maybe I met you and decided that the owner was more important than the bricks and mortar.'

Sara laughed a little hysterically.

How had all this gone so disastrously wrong? Three hours ago she was dishing out fish fingers for her son and happily contemplating seeing the man who was now shooting her down in flames.

'Or maybe you just decided that it would be easier to get what you wanted if you strung me along!'

'Is that when you decided that two could play at that game? So after your high-principled exit from our relationship you telephoned me out of the blue so that you could restart things between us but on your agenda?' His guilt that she might have had a point in being furious with him if she had truly believed that he had sought her company for no other reason than to soft-soap her into getting what he wanted was immediately banished by her failure to deny his accusation.

He thought of the ring resting in his jacket pocket and any inclination to see her point of view was stillborn.

She had used him and he wasn't a man to be used. Not under any circumstances.

'I suppose that was my initial reason for calling you,' Sara confessed in a low voice, 'and I'm not proud of myself.' She took a deep breath and forced herself to continue. 'I don't think there's anything to be gained from revenge but you have to understand—'

'Oh, I do, do I?' James interrupted harshly. 'I think you're confusing me with someone else.'

'Could you just listen to me? For a minute?' The pleading was back in her voice but she just couldn't help it and she was desperate to clear the air, to get across her point of view.

'I need a drink and something a little stronger than a cup of bloody coffee.' He pushed himself off the chair, knowing full well that he really should cease this pointless debate because it wasn't going to lead anywhere. But not yet, he told himself. He just couldn't let go of it yet. It was a form of weakness and, dammit, he knew that, could have kicked himself for it, but he couldn't help himself. One stiff drink and he would clear off, shake this woman off him for good and get back to normality.

'There's some whisky in th—'

'I *know* where the whisky is. You forget what a good job you did of making me feel right at home in your house.'

He vanished towards the small utility, where she was temporarily storing her meagre supply of alcohol, and when he returned he was carrying a stubby glass containing a generous supply of the brown liquid.

He resumed his position on the chair. Inquisitor with his suspect trapped in front of him. Or at least that was how it felt to Sara.

'I know you're angry. Furious even. And I don't blame you, but *I* was pretty angry myself when I found out that you had plans for my house. I imagined that the only minor obstacle was taking care of me and, instead of being up-front and honest, you decided to take care of me in your own way.' They both had a point of view so why was it that she felt like the one who was floundering? 'I'd been through Phillip—'

'Oh, stop hiding behind your ex, using one bad relationship as an excuse to justify your behaviour.' He pelted a mouthful of drink down his throat and shot her a steely, grim look.

'I'm not hiding behind anyone! I'm just trying to explain how I felt when I decided to...to...'

'Reverse the tables? Take care of me in *your* own way?'

'I was angry and hurt.' She looked away and bit her lip to control the flood of emotion inside her.

'And put those two together and what else do you get but a little dollop of cold-blooded revenge?'

'It wasn't like that,' Sara muttered. She took a couple

of shaky steps forward to try and close the yawning chasm between them, but the expression of icy dislike stamped on his face was enough to make her swerve away until she too was back in her original position, elbows resting on the kitchen table, body urgently leaning forward.

'And what was it like?' The remainder of his drink went down his throat and he had to say that it hadn't done the trick. He didn't feel any calmer. He just felt like another one. Which he wasn't going to have because once she'd finished her pretty little speech he was out of there.

'It was...it should have been...well...I wanted to be cool and calculating and in control of the situation but...'

Against every ounce of better judgement, he found that he was waiting for her reply.

'I guess I just wasn't the kind of person who could... deal with what I had started. I...it was fun between us. I...enjoyed your company...'

'And yet you still made sure that I was kept away from Simon. Never mind all the fun and enjoyment you were having with me.'

'Stop twisting everything I say!'

'But how can I not? In the space of a couple of hours, as I sat in a wine bar in Kensington, you changed into someone else.' He gave her a look of killing contempt. 'A truly remarkable metamorphosis. However, you will excuse me if I fail to stand back in admiration.'

'I can't stop you from believing the worst of me, but you were no angel,' Sara muttered defensively under her breath. But he had said that the bricks and mortar had mattered less than the woman who lived within them. Had he meant that or had it just been his own way of making sure that he didn't put himself on a par with her? She was racked by doubt and sickened by the motives that had propelled her into the situation she now found herself in, even though those motives had been lost very early down the line.

James ignored her barely audible protest.

'And tell me, how far did the pretence go, Sara? What were you thinking when we made love? That it was all part and parcel of your plan to reel me in and then…what…confront me with my evil, wicked plan?'

'Oh, what's the use in talking about any of this?' she said wearily.

'You still haven't answered my question.'

'I don't have to answer any of your questions.'

'But you are going to.'

'Am I? Why? Because I love hearing the way you sneer at everything I have to say?'

'Because you are a woman and women have a peculiar tendency not to want anyone to leave them with a low opinion.'

'And you should know, being the master connoisseur of them.'

But not of the one that mattered. The thought left him temporarily winded, but then the formidable self-control took over once again, and he was back with the reins firmly grasped in his hands.

'I told you…when we made love…it was…' The words were coming out piecemeal and it was galling to realise that he was absolutely right about the nature of the opposite sex. Either that or he knew her well enough to predict her thoughts and impulses.

'I didn't lie in bed with you thinking nasty, vengeful thoughts.' She tilted her chin up defiantly. 'And I know you won't believe this, but my intentions in getting in touch with you might not have been…noble…but they fizzled away.'

He shrugged as though her explanation was something

he could leave or take and that stung. He wasn't even going to try and understand. He had come to confront her and then he would leave without a backward glance.

What had she been for him except a bit of fun? It was all well and good for him to adopt his high-handed attitude, but he didn't love her and never had. His pride might be temporarily dented, but he would recover within hours, while she…

James stood up and thrust his hands into his jacket pockets. Instantly he felt the bag with the little box containing the ring inside.

Sara scrambled to her feet. It was all over and it seemed as if it had only just begun and she didn't want him to leave. But she wasn't going to wring her hands and beg and not in a million years was she going to tell him that revenge had mattered not one jot because she had fallen in love with him.

'And how far, just out of curiosity, was this little plot supposed to go?' He spoke with casual indifference and mild interest.

'I told you, it wasn't a plot. I didn't spend all that time scheming. I made a mistake, I acted the way I did because I was angry and hurt, I thought you had used me, but…'

She might well not have spoken. His long fingers curled around the small square object in his pocket and his face hardened into a cynical sneer.

'Did you perhaps envisage that I *would fall in love with you*?' He managed to make that sound as implausible as a day return trip to the moon and Sara visibly winced. He gave a bark of dangerous, unpleasant laughter. 'Was that the aim of the game, Sara? Did you think that you had what it took to weave a magic spell over me with a little sexual expertise and some fluttering eyelashes?' He watched the painful blush colour her cheeks and felt like a swine, but the box was still sitting hot in his hand and all the anger was still there, waiting to be fanned.

'No, of course not. It...it was nothing like that...' Sara stammered but she could feel a guilty flush sting her cheeks. Guilty because her dreams had been the impossible. Yes, she *had* wanted him to propose. Now that he had voiced it, she could see with dismay right into the depths of herself and she knew that she had wanted that slice of perfection, marriage to the man she had foolishly fallen in love with. Not so she could throw it back in his face with triumph, but because she wanted to spend the rest of her life with him.

'Your face is giving you away. Shame. After your sterling performance over the past few weeks.' He began strolling towards the door and she followed him in silence.

When he reached the kitchen door, he paused to look round at her. She was white-faced. Good, he thought, but there was no thrill of victory. In fact, he felt bloody lousy considering he had vented all his anger and, he told himself, had a lucky escape.

'Unfortunately, we are certain to run into one another occasionally,' he drawled, 'unless, of course, you decide to move back to London, which is probably where you belong anyway.'

'I won't be returning to London.' Her voice was hollow with the effort of not crying. 'Simon is settled here. He's looking forward to going to school in September. And I don't belong in London any more.' Which left her with the unanswerable question of where exactly *did* she belong? She had let herself forget the mistakes of the past and at some dangerous inner level had conceived the notion that she belonged wherever James belonged.

James shrugged, one of those elegant gestures that seemed uniquely his. 'Your choice. But I'm warning you that when we do run into one another, I really would rather not have any scenes. We're just two adults who had a bit of fun and called it a day when the fun began to get a little thin on the ground.'

'And, of course, no one will think twice, will they,' Sara said quietly, 'because the fun always gets a little thin on the ground when it comes to you?'

'That's right.' He pulled open the kitchen door and noted that she had stopped a few feet away from him. She looked thoroughly battered and he hardened his jaw against the weakness of compassion. She had already given him all the answers he needed and now was the time to get out. The next time he came up to see his mother, he would make damn sure that there was a beautiful woman on his arm. Let her be under no illusion that what they had was special. That would be his little private torment and he would soon put that to bed.

'Oh,' he said casually, 'and I would rather you ceased having anything to do with my mother.'

'You can't dictate who I see and who I don't.'

'Oh, but I can and I do.' His smile was cold enough to cut through steel. 'I do not see the point of any cosy relationships between my mother and either you or your son. And I suggest you pay very close heed to my warning because if I ever come up to the Highlands and walk into my house to find you there...' he left a telling pause '...let's just say you would not like my reaction...'

Well, things couldn't get much worse, could they? He had paid his surprise visit and done what she assumed he had come to do. Namely, reduce her. He had twisted her stammered attempts at explanation, walked over her need to talk, sneered at her heartfelt apologies. Now he was telling her to keep away from his mother, with whom she had developed a warm relationship and whose fondness for Simon had been instrumental in getting him to make friends.

Without making a point or exerting any pressure, she had arranged a couple of little tea parties for some of the grandmothers of children of similar age. She was a charming, delightful woman and Sara would miss her, because she knew that she would do as James had asked.

But she wouldn't stop communications without some word of explanation and that she would do in the morning. By phone. Maria always woke up before seven, a habit that seemed to creep up with old age, she had once laughed, and James rarely wandered down before nine. He liked to read the newspapers in bed because, he had once told her, it was a luxury he could never afford when he was in London.

She tilted her chin up now and folded her arms across her chest. She might as well go out with some semblance of dignity even though she felt mortally wounded.

'Goodbye, James.'

For the briefest of seconds he hesitated, struck by the realisation that this time the goodbye was final. The hesitation was swiftly replaced by his conviction that he had done the right and only possible thing. He didn't answer. Instead he gave her a brief, mocking nod of the head and closed the door behind him.

Yes, it had all gone according to plan. He had had his full-blown argument but he was still angry. He made it to his house in five minutes flat, a record he was sure, considering the darkness of the small road and the unpredictability of the turns. He had driven like a bat out of hell.

He let himself in, relieved that the house was in silence and his mother had not been on one of her jaunts down to the kitchen to fetch herself something warm to drink, a habit which she still maintained even though there was everything in her massive bedroom to make whatever she needed without having to traverse the house in darkness.

He walked through the various rooms, discarding his jacket in the vast kitchen on a chair along the way, and headed straight for the drinks cabinet in one of the smaller of the sitting rooms.

No lover tonight, he thought cynically, but who said there wasn't peace to be found in a few glasses of very fine malt whisky?

CHAPTER TEN

WHERE was he?

Where was he?

One minute on the phone. Wasn't that what they always said? One minute on the phone, one moment of distraction and a toddler could be lying face down in a pond or climbing out of a window in an attempt to net a passing butterfly or...or...

Sara felt panic ram into her like a fist and she hurled herself up the stairs, shouting out his name, pushing open doors, racing to all his favourite places to see where he might have gone.

God, but it was only seven-thirty in the morning! He was still in his pyjamas! She herself had only slung on a pair of jeans and a T-shirt so that she could drag herself down to the kitchen after a night of absolutely no sleep whatsoever, so that she could fix him a bowl of cereal!

Nausea rose up to her throat as she checked each room, frantically looking under beds, inside cupboards, realising that there was no boy hiding underneath or within.

Then the garden.

Lord, but she cursed its hidden corners as she ran like a maniac, panting now so that when she yelled his name it was more subdued and somehow more desperate.

Think.

She forced herself to try and imagine what could have compelled him to run and where.

She had been on the phone. To Maria. Half sobbing.

173

Explaining everything. Wondering aloud, anguished, whether she shouldn't just return to London...

Whether she should leave Scotland behind...

Then it clicked. It was like having a charge of electricity run through her body, and in response she began to run. Out of the house and across the fields that separated the sprawling Dalgleish Manor from the Rectory.

It would be a route her son would know well. He had walked it often enough with Maria, taking the short cut that bypassed the small road. The scenic route, Maria had used to tell her, so that they could look at the flowers and the birds and a bit of wildlife before the manor house rose up before them like an impregnable fortress.

It was the only way he knew how to get there.

And as she raced across the fields, she knew that that was where he was.

He had taken himself off because the conversation she had had with Maria, one which she had conducted in front of her son, not aware that his childish brain was taking in every word, every shaky sentence, had galvanised him into flight.

She dreaded to think what the outcome would be if he *wasn't* there. If there was some part of the house or the garden which she had left unchecked, some ominous part that could house a thousand dangers to a child.

The manor was within sight before she spotted him. His bright fire-engine-red pyjamas, the fluffy bedroom slippers he had remembered to put on for once. He was carrying his teddy bear under his arm and Maria was with him, stooping down, listening to whatever he was saying.

She could barely breathe by the time she made it to where they were. Then she was sweeping him up in her arms, smothering him while he waited patiently, bemused, for her to put him back down.

Maria straightened and looked at her. 'Silly boy.' She ruffled his hair affectionately. 'Seemed to think he would be leaving today, going away from us forever, before he could find any worms or finish planting those little seeds you bought for him last week. He was worried about the chickens.' She clicked her tongue and Sara met her eyes with grateful relief.

'You're a noodle, aren't you?' Could he feel the desperation seeping out of her like sweat when she held his hand?

'You said we were going to…leave. *I heard you on the phone, Mum.*'

'I was…' Sara looked sheepishly at Maria, who obligingly took up the thread as they made their way into the house.

'Just in a foolish mood,' she murmured placatingly. 'Mummies sometimes get like that.'

Simon nodded. 'I know.'

'Shall we go home now?' Sara asked.

'Can I have a look at the trains first?'

'You're still in your pyjamas.'

'But, Mum, Teddy hasn't seen the trains. Not really. He was tired the last time I came over. He fell asleep. *Please?*'

'You can help yourself to some coffee,' Maria mouthed quietly over his head. 'Give yourself time to calm down. I know how you must be feeling,' she murmured. 'When James was young, he gave me something of a fright myself. Boys. So very different from girls, I believe.'

Sara didn't want to hear about James. Just the mention of his name made something deep inside her contract in untold pain.

Surely Maria must be aware of this? After all, Sara had confessed everything to her. Had told her how she felt, poured it all out, and it had been like a swell of water bursting through a dam.

Yet…she found herself clinging on like a fool to whatever his mother had to say, anything that might break through the barrier of nothingness that had gripped her since James had stalked out the night before.

'He ran away, you know,' she was saying, bustling in the kitchen now and pouring Simon a glass of squash. It was a drink that she had never kept in the house before and it touched Sara to realise that she now stocked it, in preparation for whenever her little part-time charge might come around.

'He could only have been six or so at the time. His father had been telling him all about the salmon fishing. Had told him that he could go too when he got a little older. Of course,' Maria smiled in fond memory, 'James thought that there was no time like the present. It took us an hour and a half before we found him and I was never so frantic in my life before.' She crossed herself and shook her head. 'Now, I will take Simon and Teddy to see the trains, and you can make some coffee for yourself. James,' she lowered her voice, 'is still sound asleep.'

Lucky old him, Sara thought miserably. How nice to be able to climb into bed and know that you were going to sink into blissful, forgetful sleep. She wondered whether she would ever be able to achieve that again.

Never, she thought hollowly. Never. Not if being here, under the same roof as him, could make her feel so acutely aware, so horribly, and against all odds, happy. Just knowing that somewhere in this vast house he was in a bed, sleeping.

The silence in the kitchen wrapped itself around her as she filled the kettle, listened to it boil, spooned coffee into a mug.

Then she sat at the kitchen table and sipped her drink and stared out at the never-ending fields in front of her.

It was almost a shame when she heard the sound of footsteps heading into the kitchen. She very nearly wished that she could have just a few more minutes on her own, to wallow in her thoughts, before Simon and the inevitable daily routine swept her up again, leaving her no time to savour her misery.

She was half standing when the abruptness of the silence broke through her thoughts and she looked up.

It was neither Maria nor Simon at the kitchen door.

'What the hell are *you* doing here!'

He looked dreadful. Sara had a fleeting moment of satisfaction to see just how awful he looked. His hair was everywhere, sticking out as though he had spent hours raking his fingers through it, and his chin was dark with stubble. More disconcertingly, he was in a dressing gown, which was loosely tied at the waist.

Then the moment was gone as she took in the hostile antagonism in his blue eyes and the cold twist of his mouth.

'I...I came over because Simon—'

'Oh, spare me.' He strode into the kitchen and poured himself a glass of water straight from the tap, which he swallowed in one long gulp.

'What do you mean, *oh, spare me!*' She shot up from the chair and faced him angrily, hands on her hips, her green eyes blazing.

'I mean, if you think that you can swan up here in an attempt to make some peace, then you're—'

'*Make some peace?* Believe me, I wouldn't be such a...such a *bloody idiot!*'

'Then what the hell are you doing here? I told you I don't want you to come near this house. How many times would you like me to repeat it?' He had felt like a zombie when he had rolled himself out of his bed in search of something to quench this horrendous thirst of his. The whisky consumption had ended up being rather more enthusiastic than he had intended. He had slung on a dressing gown as an afterthought on his way out of the room. His legs had felt like jelly and his head...God, his head had been thumping.

All gone. One look at her and it was as if every muscle and nerve and pore in his body had been activated into alertness.

'If you would just stop for a minute and listen to me—'

'Listen to you? Why should I listen to you?'

'I came here because Simon is here...' Not quite the way it happened, but, dammit, the sight of him had thrown her into a state of utter confusion. She could barely get her words out, never mind put them in order so that they made sense.

'You mean you had the nerve to *bring your son up here*?' He slammed the empty glass onto the kitchen counter and Sara was surprised that it didn't shatter into a thousand pieces under the ferocity of the gesture. 'I suppose you thought that you could wheedle your way into my mother's good books? You disgust me.'

'Don't be such an egotistic idiot!' She pushed her hair away from her face and glared at him. Loving him and hating him and hating herself for feeling so invigorated even after everything that had been said and all the accusations hurled at her. Even when he was staring at her as though she was something vile that had crawled out from under a rock.

'I didn't bring Simon up here so that I might bump into you and start grovelling for forgiveness! And I didn't bring him up here to try and wheedle my way into anyone's good books! I wouldn't be here *at all* if he hadn't run away!'

'Run away!' The rampant disbelief in his voice made that sound as though, as far as excuses went, she had come up with something that hovered very near the bottom of the pile.

'That's right! I was on the phone...and when I turned around and looked for him, he was gone! I was out of my mind with worry! I only realised where he might have come when I'd searched the house from top to bottom...!'

'And why would you realise that he might have come here?'

The robe was altogether too distracting, Sara thought feverishly. She could see too much of that hard, bronzed torso and to see was to imagine a thousand things.

'Because...' She faltered, and when her eyes met his she could see the cold glitter of triumph in his blue ones.

'Because...?' He turned, poured himself another glass of water, which he downed in another long gulp, and then looked at her. 'Your little piece of fiction getting a little too involved?'

'Oh, stop it.'

She sank her head in her hands and, fool that he was, he actually wanted to go across to her, close the distance between them. His mouth tightened in self-disgust and he wondered, not for the first time, how he could have been through one catastrophic love affair all those years ago, only to repeat the experience like a child sticking his fingers into an open fire twice in succession.

Not that he had known anything about love as a young man. No, he had waited till now to fall head over heels with someone who had pulled his strings as if he had been nothing but a puppet.

'I realised he must have come here,' Sara said quietly,

raising her eyes to his, 'because I was on the phone to your mother at the time. You forget how much children take in. Simon was sitting at the kitchen table, eating his breakfast, not making a sound. I almost forgot he was there at all.'

'And what were you talking to my mother about?' He shoved himself away from the counter and moved towards her before sitting down heavily on the chair facing hers at the opposite end of the table. 'I suppose making up some lie about my role in all this? You seem particularly good at dissembling.'

'I wasn't making up any lies about anything and I'm no good at dissembling.'

'Really? I beg to differ.'

'Stop behaving as though I'm the only demon in all of this! As though you're entitled to wear a halo! You cultivated me because of what you thought you could get from me. You seduced me to—'

'To *get nothing*!' He banged his fist hard on the table and then clenched and unclenched his hands as though barely controlling an overwhelming urge to do violence. 'I might have thought at the beginning that it would be helpful to get to know you, to find out whether you intended to remain in the place...but at no point would I have gone down the road of climbing into your bed so that I could gain unfair possession to the key to your house!'

'You can't blame me for thinking that you would!'

'Because you consider me such a low form of life?'

'Because I'd been hurt once and I...' Sara drew in a deep breath and looked at him steadily. When it came to the crunch, there had been too many misunderstandings. This would be the last time she would ever have her chance to speak the utter, unadorned truth and she was going to grasp it.

'...I was foolish enough to think that I had been used again, hurt twice. Except...' He was still looking at her but there was a deathly stillness in his eyes that was draining all her courage away. 'Except what Phillip did to me didn't seem so important, not next to what you had accomplished. Because what I felt for him...look, Simon ran over here because of something I said. I told your mother that I was thinking of leaving, going back to London...he got worried.'

'You were saying about your ex-lover. I do not believe you finished your sentence.'

'You're making me nervous. I wish you wouldn't stare at me like that.'

'Where would you like me to look? At the walls? The ceiling?' His voice was scathing but his face was a study in attentiveness. It would be the last time she would command quite so much attention from him. You could hear a pin drop.

'What I felt for him was nothing like what I felt for you. Correction, *feel* for you. I was young and innocent when I got involved with Phillip and when it all went wrong, well, I thought I would never recover. When I look back on it now, I see that I recovered very quickly. I was bitter, of course, on Simon's behalf, and angry as well that he had rejected his own son, but I got on with living, working, being a mother. But with you...' She looked at him helplessly, knowing that one harsh word would release her from her need to pour everything out before they walked away from one another one last time.

But no harsh word was forthcoming and his expression revealed nothing.

'I was so utterly devastated, James, that yes, I wanted to retaliate, wanted to seduce you to teach us both a lesson. Me a lesson in not trusting and you a lesson in taking advantage of me…I didn't stop to wonder how it was that seduction should have been so easy, so pleasurable. I should have hated you, should have hated you touching me, shouldn't I? But I didn't and the reason I didn't was that I had fallen in love with you. There. Now, you can throw that back in my face, but—'

'You're in love with me.' Pure, undiluted happiness stole into his heart like a thief in the night, not that she was looking at him with the wondering eyes of a woman in love. More glaring at him, and he couldn't help himself. He smiled. A long, slow, utterly satisfied smile.

'Yes, it's funny, isn't it?' Sara snapped, springing to her feet and striding across to him, hands furiously on her hips and her hair tousled across her face. 'Positively hilarious when you think about it. So much for evening the stakes! You'll be thrilled to know that I didn't manage to achieve anything at all except to dig myself deeper into the hole I was hoping to jump out of. Hysterical. I can see you think that from the grin on your face.'

She turned to walk away, to go and get her son so that she could leave this place without completely breaking apart.

The hand that snaked out as she was swinging around, therefore, caught her unawares and this time Sara found herself falling. Again. This time literally—into his lap.

'Not so fast,' he purred and the colour rose up into her cheeks in a wash of pink.

'I've said what I wanted to say, now let me go! And you can wipe that insufferable grin off your face!'

'No, I can't. Now, tell me again. Tell me that you love me…'

'I don't intend to repeat anything for your benefit. Now *let me go!*'

'No.'

'What?' Sara struggled but it was impossible to make any headway. His arm was draped securely across her waist, just below her breasts.

And, feeble-minded idiot that she was, she couldn't help her body responding, growing hot, her nipples hardening just because she was so close to him, touching.

'I said no. I won't let you go. I want to savour this moment.' He inched his arm a bit higher so that he could stroke some hair from her face.

'It's horrible and *rude* to gloat,' she hissed.

'This is the second time you have called me rude. You will have to work on my training.'

Her response was lost as his mouth met hers, crushing every word she could utter, devouring her until she could barely remember what he had said, never mind what she had intended to ask. He kissed her ruthlessly and she weakly gave up and allowed herself to return the lethal kiss.

'Now, any more struggles and I shall have to do that again. Again and again and again. Until you hear what I have to say.'

'Which is?' She was shocked by how breathless she sounded.

'Which is that my story is very much like yours. Now, sh. Just listen, my darling.'

My darling?

'Have you been drinking?'

'Of course I have.'

'Oh.' Disappointment trickled into her, lifted when he gently kissed the corner of her drooping mouth.

'Last night. Quite a bit, in actual fact. Anything to help me get through the pain.'

Her eyes rose tentatively to meet his and what she saw there sent a flare of hope racing through her, stretching its tentacles into every bone in her body before wrapping around her rapidly beating heart.

'I told you that I had once been duped. And after that, I learnt self-control. When it came to women, they were my playthings, but I made sure never to get involved. I told myself that I was simply playing the game of relationships according to my rules. The truth was that I never met a woman who made me want to break them. Until you came along.'

Sara looked at him, mesmerised. If this was a dream, may she never wake up.

'Yes, I wanted the Rectory. And if you had been anyone but you, I would have barged in and offered to cut you a deal. A very generous deal. But you...your smile, your voice, that hesitant little way you have of looking every so often...I couldn't cut any deals. All I could do was give in to the desire to be in your company. When you made a move on me in London, everything inside was telling me to run a mile and get back to the life I used to know, where everything was under control, but I couldn't.'

'No?' Sara said stupidly, and he shook his head ruefully and smiled.

'No. You had got under my skin, lodged somewhere deep inside me, and all I wanted to do was be with you. When I realised that—'

'No, please don't say it. Please don't. I have never been sorrier or more stupid about anything in my life before.'

'I was like a wounded animal. I came back here and drank as much as I could before I lost interest in drinking and just wanted to sleep it off.'

'James.'

'Will you stay right here? Don't move. Not an inch. I'll be back in one minute. There's something I want to show you.'

He was gone literally the minute, so short a length of time that she could hardly think of what it was he wanted to show her. She was too busy basking in the euphoria of every word he had just said. She wanted to commit each syllable to heart and hold them close to her so that she could fetch them out whenever she needed to.

'This is for you.' He flicked open the lid of the black and gold box and she could only gape at the exquisite ring inside.

'But it's a ring,' she said foolishly.

'Correction. It's a ring for you, my darling. Have I rendered you speechless? Try it on. See if it fits. No, let me put it on your finger. I want to remember this moment for the rest of my life.'

'This moment...' And it did fit. Perfectly. The solitary diamond was dazzling.

'I'd intended to ask the question when I came up this weekend. I...' A dark flush spread across his cheeks and he looked like a boy, grappling to find the right words.

So beautiful. She placed her hand on the side of his face and he immediately turned it over so that he could press his lips against the palm of her hand.

'I haven't had much practice at this sort of thing...'

'Much?' Sara laughed shakily.

'Any. I just want to say that I waited all my life for you. I wish I'd known that you were right there all along, in London, with your son... My darling, will you marry me?'

'Absolutely. Yes, yes, yes. Marry you, be with you forever, live wherever you want us to live...'

'Which is right here, of course, unless...'

'Right here.' She sighed with exquisite happiness. 'Who would have thought it? Right here is where I feel I belong, next to you. Just as your mother felt being here with your dad.'

The thought was like dawn breaking over the deep blue sea. Right here. Now and forever.

Their lips met and their kiss was a seal of all eternity.

HIS CONVENIENT FIANCÉE

by

Barbara McMahon

Barbara McMahon was born and raised in the south but settled in California after spending a year flying around the world for an international airline. Settling down to raise a family and work for a computer firm, she began writing when her children started school. Now, feeling fortunate in being able to realise a long-held dream of quitting her 'day job' and writing full-time, she and her husband recently moved to the Sierra Nevada mountains of California, where she finds her desire to write is stronger than ever. With the beauty of the mountains visible from her windows, and the pace of life slower than the hectic San Francisco Bay Area where they previously resided, she finds more time than ever to think up stories and characters and share them with others through writing. Barbara loves to hear from readers. You can reach her at PO Box 977, Pioneer, CA 95666-0977, USA.

Don't miss Barbara McMahon's exciting new novel, *The Forbidden Brother*, out in July 2007 from Mills & Boon® Romance.

CHAPTER ONE

MOLLY knew she was stalling. As she paced the crowded sidewalk in front of the Magellan Hotel on trendy Union Square, her thoughts flew in a thousand different directions. She did not want to go up to the reception. Yet to avoid it would be cowardly. And give rise to even more talk. She'd been the victim of enough gossip for the last three months. She really, really didn't want to add to it today!

Another cab swerved to a stop before the hotel's main entrance and when the uniformed doorman stepped to the curb to open the door, Molly recognized Harold Satten and his wife. He was one of Justin's cohorts—a fellow account executive at the firm they all worked for, Zentech. Just her luck they spotted her at almost the same time she saw them. Another couple on their way to the Zentech event. The same event she should have arrived at some ten minutes ago.

"Hello, Molly. This is the place, isn't it?" Harold asked, joining her on the sidewalk.

"On the twenty-fifth floor," she confirmed, smiling a polite acknowledgment to Harold's wife.

"Shall we go?" he asked.

"I'm waiting for someone," Molly replied, the lie rolling off her lips with unaccustomed ease.

"Oh, I thought you were alone."

Sheesh, she thought, refraining from making a face

with effort. Did the entire world know about the big breakup? Well, of course they did. Brittany made sure of that. Poor Molly. Brittany hadn't *meant* to come between Molly and Justin, but when they fell in love, what were they to do, she asked anyone within earshot—usually when Molly could also overhear.

"No, I'm waiting for someone," she repeated, glancing up the busy street as if seeking a familiar face.

"We'll see you up there, then," Harold said.

Holding her fake, polite smile until they were out of sight, Molly sighed. Yes, they would see her. It was a command appearance. And ordinarily she would have been thrilled. It was her design concept, after all, and her innovative ideas for the account that had been the pivotal point in signing one of Japan's huge conglomerates, Hamakomoto Industries, to the lucrative contract. Steve Powers was the account executive, but it was her artwork that had clinched the deal.

And hadn't that made Brittany furious? The two women were both with the art department of Zentech, a high-tech, full service company that led the way in innovative concepts for businesses. And from the first day Molly had started, Brittany Taylor had had it in for her.

After almost seven years, Molly would have thought she'd have grown immune. But Brittany's deliberately luring Justin had been the final straw. Molly would not give in to the pitying glances and murmured condolences on her breakup with Justin. No more miss nice girl, she was fighting back!

The celebratory reception had started ten minutes

ago. The press, media and important and influential movers and shakers of San Francisco were on the impressive guest list. Everyone who was anyone would be there.

Including Justin Morris—and Brittany.

Molly walked a few feet along the sidewalk, ideas spinning. Maybe she could disappear for a couple of weeks, and then tell them at work she'd been kidnapped by aliens. Or maybe she could fake a fall and sprained ankle. She eyed the dirty cement with distaste. Not such a good idea.

Or maybe she could pull off the idea her neighbor Shelly had come up with—pretend she was engaged and her fiancé hadn't been able to make the event. Harold could attest to her pacing the sidewalk as if she were impatiently awaiting someone.

It was pathetic. She was probably the only woman in San Francisco who couldn't come up with a date for a business reception. But most of the people she knew well enough to ask, also worked at Zentech. The last thing she wanted to do was have anyone there know she was thinking of subterfuge to minimize damage from Brittany's latest attack.

Ordinarily going alone to a company event wouldn't matter a bit. But that was before last week's conference where Brittany had cast aspersions on Molly's ability to stick to a long-term project—as witnessed by her flighty behavior with relationships. As if Molly had been the one to dump Justin.

Molly ground her teeth just thinking about Brittany's smarmy sweetness and the others around the table, glancing between them. She knew, of course, it was professional jealousy. Brittany's last several design concepts had not been accepted, where Molly's had. But knowing didn't help.

Four months ago Molly had been thinking wedding bells. Justin had been dating Brittany on the sly. Molly's fantasies had fizzled instantly when she learned the truth. If he wanted Brittany Taylor, he was welcome to her! They deserved each other.

The worst of it, however, was the fact she, Justin and Brittany all worked for the same company. Everyone had seen Molly and Justin as a couple at the Christmas party. And everyone knew, thanks to Brittany, that she and Justin were now the romance of the century.

Molly frowned. She hated feeling like the dumped also-ran while Justin paraded around with super sweet Brittany.

"Stupid, stupid, stupid," she muttered. She should have known better than to even think about dating a coworker. Every time she saw him in the halls of Zentech, she was reminded again of the way he played around and that she'd only been one of many. Brittany would most likely be on the receiving end one day, but not today.

Now Molly was expected to show up at the reception and act as if life was great. Of course no one else had to face Justin and the oh-so-stunning Brittany and pretend it didn't matter. Taking a deep breath, Molly faced the hotel. She'd give it her best shot.

Glancing around one last time as if expecting a miracle, she realized unless she dragged a perfect stranger up to the reception, she was going to show up alone. Time to put on the ring she'd brought and brazen it out.

Except she suspected Brittany would see right through the scheme. The woman was not one to sit around silently and let others get on with their lives. She liked to gloat.

Anger touched her. If Justin had been any kind of friend, he would have stayed away from today's event. It should have been her shining moment. Instead, she had an ex-boyfriend everyone knew about and his new smug girlfriend hogging the spotlight.

She'd heard the rumors flying around the office over the last few weeks. Seen the sly speculative looks from coworkers. Felt the sympathetic glances. She'd been caught up in the art layout and design for Hamakomoto, but not to the exclusion of coming up for air and noticing what was going on from time to time.

Hoping she could pull it off, she needed to save face in front of all of the influential businessmen. She raised her chin and marched directly into the lavish lobby of the hotel. A discreet sign to the left caught her eye. *Magellan's Pub.* Ah, maybe a bit of Dutch courage would help.

She entered the dimly lit space and gazed around. Except for a couple looking like honeymooners sitting at a table against the wall, and a man leaning against the far end of the bar talking with the bartender, the place was empty. Obviously too early for most serious drinkers.

She walked to the gleaming mahogany bar and perched gingerly on a high stool. The bartender left his conversation and headed her way.

"What can I get you?" His smile was friendly.

Probably because he doesn't know about Brittany, Molly thought glumly. She could just imagine it turning sympathetic if he knew her situation.

"I'll have a gin and tonic. No, wait, I hate gin. Give me bourbon straight up. No, wait, I don't like that, either. Maybe a nice glass of Chardonnay. No, wait, would that be enough? How about a rum and Coke? No, wait, I always had that with Justin, bad association. Damn!"

"So what do you really want?" the bartender asked.

"What I really, really want is something tall, dark and dangerous," Molly said morosely, wishing she could order up a temporary fiancé as easily as she could a drink. She glanced at her watch. It was almost four-thirty. If she didn't get up there soon, her tardiness would have an even greater impact. She could imagine the gossip running rampant.

"How about blond and friendly?" he countered.

"What?" She looked up into bright blue eyes beneath a blond mop. The man looked as cute as could be. But not the stuff of romance.

"Nope, tall dark and dangerous or none at all. I'll have a rum and Coke." She couldn't avoid the only drink she really liked the rest of her life because of Justin.

The bartender began to prepare the beverage, eyeing her as he did so. "Trouble?"

"Does everyone who comes in here have troubles?"

"Only those who come in at four in the afternoon." He set her glass on a coaster in front of her.

"And I'm part psychologist you know, comes with the trade."

"Umm." She took a sip. Never much of a drinker, she wondered how much this would help. It wouldn't do to show up at her company's celebratory event fiancé-less and inebriated!

She glanced at her watch again. It was getting later by the minute. Was there already talk—instigated by Brittany, of course. She could just hear her sly innuendoes and see her wide-eyed innocent, sympathetic act. Molly wondered if she was up to facing another bout.

"Waiting for a date?" the bartender asked.

"I wish. I'm supposed to be upstairs at the Zentech reception on the 25th floor."

"I imagine drinks up there are free."

She sipped again, then opened her clutch purse. Taking out her grandmother's engagement ring she looked at it. Glancing at the bartender, she held it up. "If I wore this, would you think I was engaged?"

"Are you?"

"That's not the point. What would you think?"

"I'd think a pretty woman like you would be taken, engagement ring or not."

She blinked, smiled. "Wow, maybe blond and cute would work after all."

He winked at her and glanced at the other end of the bar. Molly looked down there and met a dark scowl. The man couldn't possibly hear them, he was too far away and the soft strains of background music muted other sounds. She studied him for a moment.

Now he would fit the bill. Tall, dark and decidedly dangerous. He looked like a pirate who had been poured into a business suit. He wasn't handsome exactly, his face was too rough-hewn for that. But there was a decidedly arrogant air about the man that would set Brittany back on her heels. Who was he? And why was he in a bar at four o'clock?

She looked back at her friendly bartender.

"He would work," she said whimsically.

"You think?"

"If he'd stop frowning long enough to look like a devoted fiancé. But I think I'll go with the ring and excuse."

"What excuse?"

"That something came up at the last minute and my darling fiancé couldn't make it after all."

"Why the need for a darling fiancé?" he asked leaning on the bar with one arm, apparently ready to listen for as long as it took.

She stared at her drink for a long moment, feeling once again the embarrassment Justin's deflection had caused. Odd, that was the only emotion she felt. Hadn't she loved him after all? She'd enjoyed being with him. They'd even talked of plans for marriage. Shouldn't she be brokenhearted?

Instead, she was embarrassed.

"To save face. Did you know the Japanese feel strongly about saving face?"

"How did we get to the Japanese?"

"There will be a number of Japanese people at the celebration. I know Mr. Yamamoto and Mr. Harishni. They liked my designs, you see. I have to attend. It just would be so much easier to face everyone with a fiancé in tow."

"Because?"

"Okay, Mr. Psychologist Bartender, it would be easier because the man I thought I was going to marry will be there today with his new girlfriend. I have done my best to avoid both of them for weeks, but it doesn't always work that way. I would so love to waltz in without a care in the world with someone extra special with me. Justin and Brittany work where I do, so everyone knows the situation and feels sorry for me." She frowned. "I hate that part."

"And the tall, dark and dangerous fiancé in tow would give you that extra cachet you'd need to pull off carefree?"

"Got it in one!"

The bartender laughed. "I have just the man for you. And maybe we can kill two birds with one stone. Hold on." He moved down to the other end of the bar.

Molly watched, fascinated. He wasn't really going to ask that tall, dark stranger to pose as her fiancé, was he? And even if he did, the man would never agree. He didn't look the type to agree to anything that didn't further his own enlightened self-interests.

She'd had it with corporate types who moved to their own agenda. Hadn't that been Justin to a T? At least in retrospect, she thought so. At the time, she'd been flattered by his attention. Now he treated her like a poor besotted fool who had misinterpreted his overtures of friendship. Ha! He'd been clear, but changed his tune when Brittany made her play—including pushing his projects through faster.

If she got involved anytime soon with someone else, she'd make sure he was friendly and nice and didn't have some secret desire to move ahead no matter who he stepped on.

And never again would she get involved with corporate types!

She watched as the bartender spoke to the other man, glancing back at her. Proposing her idea?

Mr. Tall Dark and Dangerous shook his head. No surprise there, though her heart dropped. Had she really held a glimmer of hope he'd agree?

She couldn't hear the words, but could see the bartender arguing the point. Something he said must have made an impression. The stranger studied her for a long moment, flicked a quick glance at his watch and then the door to the pub. He nodded once at the other man, stepped around the end of the bar and headed her way.

Molly's heart fluttered. Ohmygosh, was the man coming to talk with her? She clenched the ring tightly in her hand, her gaze fixed on him as he walked the length of the bar. She couldn't impose on a total stranger. She'd been joking when she said that to the bartender.

"I'm Nick Bailey. Donny said you needed an escort for the Zentech reception," he said, nodding toward the bartender.

She swallowed hard, was she really going to get tall, dark and dangerous? "Yes. No. Actually, I, uh, need, uh, *wanted* I mean, something more than just an escort. I need a temporary fiancé—just for tonight," she said all in a rush.

"All night?" He raised an eyebrow.

"Ohmygosh, no! Just for the reception upstairs, actually. It'll be over by eight at the latest."

He studied her a moment as if weighing her words. "What exactly do you expect from a temporary fiancé?"

"Not much." She let her gaze run over him, her heart still acting weird. He was tall and immaculately dressed. The suit looked custom-made and expensive. His dark hair was well cut, his eyes steady and dark as they assessed her in return. She shivered at the reaction. He still looked like a pirate.

For a foolish moment, Molly was glad she looked her best. The new dress Shelly had talked her into was fashionable and fun—within acceptable business bounds. It was hard to know what to wear to business functions when she was used to paint-splattered jeans and tunics or shirts with chalk and charcoal dusting them.

But she had to hold her end up against Brittany!

She smiled up at him, feeling wildly reckless. "Mostly you'd just have to stand around and look good. I think you'd do that perfectly. There'll be food and drinks on the house. I'd introduce you to various people, but you don't have to do anything really or say much. I could buy you dinner afterward if you like. As a thank-you."

"So all I have to do is just be there?"

She nodded. He would be so perfect. He was taller than Justin, and ten times more masculine. His voice was deep and sexy, and he already had her fantasizing things a real fiancée would fantasize.

Oh, oh, maybe this wasn't such a great idea after all.

He glanced at the bartender in exasperation, then nodded at Molly. "All right, I'll go with you. If you can wait a few more minutes.'' He glanced at his watch. ''I'm expecting someone.''

''You will?'' She, too, glanced at the bartender. He had the most peculiar smile on his face. ''Uh, why?'' Molly asked, afraid to believe her good fortune.

''Why not?''

''Well, you don't know me.''

''I hardly think you could do much in a room full of businessmen and women. You don't know me, either.''

''You don't look the type to do favors for strangers,'' she said bluntly.

''Not as a rule.'' He glanced at the bartender. ''But in this case, it'll help me out, as well.''

''Oh.'' She glanced at the ring, then slipped it on her finger. She was right, he was a man with his own agenda. Fortunately, it coincided with hers tonight. ''Okay then, it's only for a few hours. I appreciate it. I'm Molly McGuire.''

''Molly McGuire.''

''Don't even think it. I've heard every joke ever invented.''

Amusement showed in his eyes. ''I'm sure you have. I'm Nick Bailey.''

Before Molly could shake his offered hand, a sultry, female voice projected through the pub.

''Nicky, darling, I've been looking all over for you. One of the bellmen said he saw you come in here.''

Molly swung around and saw a voluptuous dark-haired woman saunter across the room. For a moment Molly almost wished her own short light brown hair was long and dark as the newcomer's, that she could fill out her clothes as this woman did and that she could perfect such sensuous moves by merely walking.

Most of the time she pulled her hair back so it would not get into her eyes when she painted. And she forgot to eat a lot of the time if she were involved in a project, so voluptuous curves were out.

Her musings were interrupted when she became aware the man beside her had stiffened. He stepped closer to her before greeting the newcomer.

"Carmen. When did you get back in town?" he said evenly. There was a thread of tension in his tone.

Molly didn't understand what was happening, but she could recognize things were growing tense.

"I told you I would be back, darling. And I don't have any plans to leave again for weeks." Carmen walked closer than necessary and reached up to kiss him, but he sidestepped, placing his arm across Molly's shoulders.

"Molly, I'd like to introduce Carmen Hernandez, an old friend. Carmen, I don't believe you've met Molly—my fiancée."

"Fiancée?" Carmen's sultry Latin looks flared into anger. "What the hell do you mean?" She gave Molly a disbelieving look and swung her attention back to Nick. "If anyone is getting married, it'll be you and me! What kind of game are you playing, Nicky? I don't believe this! You can't brush me off so easily. You're mine and no one else's!" Carmen's temper rose, bringing flushed color to her dusky cheeks. Her dark eyes glared at Molly. "I don't know who you think you are, but he's mine!" Contemptuously she ran her gaze over Molly. "You don't have what it takes to hold a man like Nick." Dismissing her, she turned to Nick.

"Nick—"

"Maybe you two would like to discuss this in private," Molly said, stung by yet another woman. Did she have a sign hanging around her neck saying *Insult me, I don't mind*?

Nick's hold tightened on her shoulders as if the two of them faced the world together. Nice staging, she thought, even as she wondered what she'd gotten herself into. She thought she was the one needing help. Obviously she was not the only one.

Was Nick Bailey in a similar situation as she was? How ironic, yet it would explain why he so quickly agreed to her outrageous suggestion. Molly felt she'd been thrust on stage of a play in progress—without a script.

"We broke off things weeks ago," Nick said. His reasonable tone contrasted nicely with Carmen's passionate anger, yet Molly heard the underlying steel. Molly liked a man who could be cool under fire.

"*You* said we should end things, but I'm not ready to give up on us!" Carmen said dramatically, her hand reaching out to grip his arm. "I love you. You know that. You've been cruel ignoring me, playing hard to get. I won't be pushed aside."

"Carmen, we're through. And all the drama in the world isn't going to change that. Besides, I'm engaged to another woman." He lifted Molly's left hand and let what little light came from over the bar sparkle on the diamond.

Carmen scarcely glanced at the ring. She glared instead directly at Molly. "You probably think you pulled off some kind of coup snaring Nicholas Bailey. But let me tell you, things don't end here.'' Raising her eyes to Nick, she narrowed them in anger. ''You can't get rid of me so easily, lover!''

Spinning around, she stalked from the bar, in stark contrast to her earlier sensuous entry. Molly felt as if a whirlwind had just blown through.

''That went well,'' the bartender said.

''Shut up,'' Nick responded. He released Molly and raised an eyebrow. ''Shall we head for the Zentech Reception? After Carmen's act, it should be a piece of cake.''

''At least that answers my question about why you'd agree to this cockamamie scheme. You needed me as much as I need you. More, I think. I doubt Justin's going to get so emotional when he hears we're engaged.'' Though she hoped Brittany would be put in her place! Let her believe Molly was no longer interested in rekindling the relationship with Justin because she was involved with someone even more exciting.

Nick frowned. ''She'll cool down.''

''But I doubt that's the last we'll see of her. I'd expect her at the wedding if I were you,'' Donny said. ''Her way of making sure.''

Molly looked between the two men. ''What wedding?''

''Ours, of course,'' Nick said. ''Come on, let's go see who we can shock at Zentech's party.''

CHAPTER TWO

MOLLY and Nick were alone in the elevator as it whisked them to the upper floor of the lavish hotel. Her thoughts were spinning. She would walk in with the most dynamic man there. One she was supposed to be engaged to. Would they be able to carry it off? Obviously Carmen had bought into the concept. But that had been brief, and surprising. The woman's temper had ruled. Upon closer reflection, would she realize how impossible the entire scenario was?

She glanced at Nick. He stared straight back at her, his look intimidating.

"So I have this straight—some guy dumped you for a new girlfriend and you want to appear engaged so he won't know you're upset," he said bluntly.

"I see sensitivity training plays a big part in your life," Molly murmured, annoyed at the way he put it.

"What?"

"Never mind. I guess you've nailed it. Thanks for feeding my ego. If you don't mind a suggestion or two, no one will believe we're engaged if you continue to look like you're perpetually angry. Can you smile or something? And while you're at it, could you pretend you find me captivating?"

"Captivating?"

She nodded. "I've always wanted to captivate someone. Don't you think a new fiancé would be captivated?"

"Absolutely."

She could tell by the gleam in his eye that he was mocking her. So be it, as long as he did as she asked. She only had to get through this evening. Then she could make up something to cause a breakup in a few weeks. By then she'd be hip deep in work for the new account and would ignore Justin and Brittany. And once her coworkers caught a look at Nick, any pity for poor dumped Molly would vanish in an instant.

Amazement that Molly McGuire from the art department could attract anyone like him would more likely be in the forefront of any new gossip and speculation.

The celebration was in full swing when they reached the huge ballroom. Banners hung from the ceiling, announcing the new consortium. The mammoth floor to ceiling windows comprising two walls gave a splendid view of San Francisco, from Union Square far below, to the blue expanse of the bay, glimpsed in the distance, to the sweeping towers of the Bay Bridge.

"There you are, Molly. I wondered where you were." John Billings, the president of the firm greeted her. He looked at Nick with curiosity in his gaze.

"Hi John. Sorry we're late, we got held up. I'd like you to meet my fiancé, Nick Bailey."

The die was cast. She hoped she wasn't making a huge mistake.

"Nick, good to meet you. I heard rumors our Molly was seeing someone special. You must know how proud we are of Molly and her work. She was the key component in the presentation. We wouldn't be here today without her."

Molly flushed with surprised delight. She hadn't expected the accolade. That surprise was expanded when Nick rested his hand on the small of her back and said, "Molly is very determined—she goes after what she wants."

Molly felt a leap of sensation explode at his touch. She lost the trend of the conversation for a moment. She'd never felt so charged up from a mere touch before. What was going on? Maybe she should not have had that rum and Coke.

John moved on and others spoke to her as they moved through the room. Congratulations on her design work were called. Greetings were exchanged, questions fielded about Nick as she introduced him to everyone.

Suddenly a pathway cleared and Justin and Brittany appeared. The group around Molly quieted, eagerly watching.

"Molly, good to see you. We were wondering where you were," Justin said. "Get tied up with last minute work?"

"Why, hello, Molly. We were beginning to wonder if you were going to show up or not," Brittany said, clinging to Justin as if he were a life preserver and she in danger of drowning. The tall blonde was model slim and flawless. The ice blue dress clung to a thin figure that showed it to perfection.

She dressed up well, Molly had to give her that. Normally she wore jeans and work shirts like the rest of the art department.

But for once, Molly didn't care about Brittany. Or Justin. She was savoring her moment of triumph.

Nick stepped forward and offered his hand.

"Blame me for keeping Molly. Nick Bailey. Are you someone who works for Molly?"

Justin's startled look was priceless. He frowned, shook Nick's hand and shook his head. "I don't work for Molly. We work together sometimes on projects. I'm Justin Morris, an account executive for Zentech." He looked at Molly. "I didn't know you'd be coming with anyone."

"Really?" Molly said, smiling up at Nick, startled to see the warmth in his own gaze as he met her eyes, his arm coming around her shoulders again. "Now why would you think that?" she asked, refraining from looking at Brittany.

"It's hard to share Molly," Nick said. "But this event is important to her, so we came. Better late than never." He glanced at Brittany, dismissing her with carelessness, returning his attention to Molly.

Molly almost laughed aloud at Brittany's stunned expression. With her good looks, she rarely had men pass her over with hardly a glance.

Molly looked at Justin and felt a sudden pang. She'd wasted several weeks of her life mourning the end of their dating. And now, nothing. Was she so fickle? Or had she only been in love with the notion of being a part of a couple? Had the glamour of being sought after, wined and dined in fashionable restaurants gone to her head?

Whatever, she was relieved to no longer be under his spell. She felt gloriously free. She no longer had anything to prove to Justin Morris or Brittany Taylor!

"We have to move on, Nick already met John. Now I want him to meet some of our new Japanese partners," Molly said.

"Is that your engagement ring?" Brittany asked, staring at Molly's hand. Her tone implied she could hardly believe Molly could ever get engaged.

Molly showed off her grandmother's ring. It was lovely, if set in an old-fashioned style.

Just then a photographer snapped a couple of pictures, the sudden flash startling.

Brittany preened, leaning forward a bit, smiling at the man.

Molly stepped back, pushing against Nick. She looked up at him and smiled. "Shall we mingle some more?"

He leaned forward until he was just a whisper away.

"Is this captivating enough for you?"

"You're doing great. I really appreciate it," she said in a low voice for his ears alone.

Another flash exploded.

Looking around, Molly frowned. "You'd think in this day and age they could take photos without being so intrusive."

"It's an important event for the company," Justin said. "I'm sure they want to record it for the annual report." He, too, had turned toward the photographer, smiling genially.

Molly was content to let Justin and Brittany claim the limelight. She was ready to leave. Mission accomplished.

"If you'll excuse us," Molly said, stepping away.

Nick left his hand on her shoulder as they walked through the crowd.

"That's all I could have asked," she said with satisfaction. "Thanks."

"The encounter with Justin and Brittany—is that the sole reason for the big deception?"

"Brittany, mostly. I can't stand her. We've both worked at Zentech for almost seven years, and it doesn't get easier."

"She's a self-centered woman on the make."

Molly glanced up. "Most men find her fascinating."

"Most men find her body fascinating, there's a difference," he said firmly.

"I'm not sure I see the difference."

"Maybe you have to be a guy. So tell me Molly McGuire, what do you do for Zentech? Your president thinks highly of you."

"I've worked there since I graduated from the art school. I'm one of the art directors now. Recently I got lucky in getting assigned on the project for the Hamakomoto account."

"Lucky? Or talented?"

She grinned. "I like your thinking. Mostly I direct layouts, or full spectrum designs for our clients, such as corporate literature, stationery, ad designs, Web sites, you name it, if it's art involved, my team can do it!"

"And how does Justin play into all this?"

"He's a guy I dated for a while. If Brittany wasn't so awful, our breaking up wouldn't have been such a big deal. But she's a real witch. And I'm tired of her patronizing attitude." She glanced over her shoulder and saw the woman in conversation with the photographer—probably arranging another picture that would show Brittany to best advantage. "Justin is one of the account executives at Zentech, so we're always thrown together. Mostly I wanted to save face before the rest of the crew. It's hard not to feel like I'm constantly the object of pity when walking through the offices.''

"So mission accomplished. Then we're finished here?"

She nodded. "As soon as we speak to our clients. Are you in a hurry to leave?"

He shook his head. "Your encounter was milder than ours with Carmen."

Molly smiled, nodding to another guest. "If Justin had been Latin, do you think he'd have thrown a scene?"

Nick looked over the crowd and spotted Justin. "Not unless it served his needs."

"He is focused on the main chance—for his advancement. But aren't all corporate types?"

"Are we?" Nick asked.

"You tell me."

"Maybe you're right."

Despite her earlier misgivings, Molly realized she was enjoying the reception. She felt a twinge of guilt every time she introduced Nick as her fiancé, but squelched it knowing most of the people she talked to didn't know her except as a business contact. She'd arrange to have the breakup known in a couple of weeks and move on.

It was close to eight when the event wound down.

Molly and Nick began to move toward the elevator. She couldn't complain about his attention, it had been focused on her the entire time. Actually, it was quite heady. If she ever captivated anyone, she hoped he'd act as Nick had all evening.

The elevator was crowded on the ride down, so conversation was limited. Walking through the lobby a short time later, Molly felt a hint of regret that the evening was coming to an end.

"Thanks again, Nick. I appreciate all you've done."

"The help was mutual. Donny knew Carmen would prove troublesome."

"And you didn't suspect?"

"We were through a couple of months ago. And she knows it. But I heard she was coming in today. I thought having the confrontation in the bar at that time of day would make it easier than somewhere more public. I was not about to meet with her in private. Never trust a woman scorned."

"Succinct advice. I'll remember that. She seems like the type who loves creating a scene."

"She is dramatic. Like your Brittany."

"Please, Brittany isn't mine. And if I never see her again, it would be too soon!" But she would be at Zentech the next morning, as she had for the entire time Molly had worked there. Oh well, some things must be endured. At least Molly had lost the pity of her fellow workers. Most had been delighted to meet Nick, and seemed happy for her. She'd intercepted more than one interested gaze directed at her escort. Her stock had shot up.

He escorted her out to the sidewalk. The fog was drifting in, dropping the temperature rapidly. Tourists still wandered along the sidewalk. The clang of the cable cars could be heard as they lumbered up Powell Street.

"Do you have a car?" Nick asked. "Or need a ride home?"

"No, I came in a cab. I'll get one and be home in no time."

He nodded to the doorman and in seconds a cab slid to the curb.

"Thanks again, Nick, for helping me out." She held out her hand.

"I'm sure a fiancé gets some perks," he said, ignoring her hand and sweeping her into his arms to give her a quick kiss.

Another flash—from a camera, or from the excitement of his kiss? Molly wasn't sure. Several hours of chitchat and she knew little about the man. She had not expected a kiss—nor to feel like she did receiving it.

Then she was bundled into the cab. "Goodbye, Molly McGuire."

"Wow," she said softly, looking over her shoulder out the back window as the cab pulled away. Justin wasn't the one she should lament losing. But Nick Bailey might be.

CHAPTER THREE

NICK BAILEY stared at the lifestyle section of the paper his PA placed on his desk the next morning with frustrated anger. Damn, he should have suspected last night. Why hadn't he? Just because he'd been playing a role didn't mean others didn't take it seriously. Or that he should have let his defenses down. Now he needed to do damage control before things got out of hand.

"Something you wanted to share, boss?" Helen asked. The fifty-five year old woman had been with Nick since he'd taken over the reins of Magellan's Hotels ten years earlier. The chain of luxury hotels covered the west coast, from San Diego to Seattle. The flagship hotel was the first, San Francisco's gem. He made it his headquarters as his father had prior to his death a decade ago.

The black and white newspaper photos he stared at were a surprise. Why hadn't he considered the newspapers when cameras were flashing last night? Molly had mentioned recording the event for posterity—he knew the company had had a number of roaming photographers. But so, apparently, had the local newspaper.

Eyeing the photos, a feeling of disquiet pervaded. Had it been a setup—some sort of con? Play up the engaged feature, then hold him up for some kind of extortion? Or had she been merely trying to align herself with him, hoping for some kind of gain? A lot of advancement came from connections. And Nick had had women after him since he'd started in the business world—wanting a share of the money or glamour running the hotels brought.

But he had not expected this.

He and Molly were headline news on the lifestyle section. *Notorious Marriage—Shy Hotel Guru Nick Bailey Landed at Last?*

He was sure Donny had never anticipated such a turn when he suggested Nick play fiancé to a stranger.

The idea had held merit when he'd considered Carmen and her increasing demands. He'd tried to break things off gently. Then not so gently. But she didn't seem to get that they were through.

Would the confrontation last night confirm it for her?

How ironic if the newspaper article sealed their ending, yet opened a can of worms with Molly McGuire. He felt a twinge of disappointment at the thought Molly would be contacting him soon with some suggestion or demand.

Helen stood by the desk, studying the splashy pictures, leaning closer to scan the article.

"I haven't sent her flowers or arranged a reservation at any of your usual restaurants," she murmured.

"It's not what you think," he replied, folding the paper and tossing it to the corner of the desk. He'd get Donny to check it out. Find out just who Molly McGuire was, what she was after, and nip anything she had in mind in the bud. He hadn't reached the success he enjoyed by being passive!

"I think an engagement means you are planning to

marry the woman. What's not to think?'' Helen asked.

"The reporter got it wrong. We're not engaged.''

"One picture has a ring flashing.''

"Do you have the figures from the Portland site?''

"Changing the subject, boss?'' Helen walked back to her office and began to look through the folders and reports that were stacked on her desk.

When the phone rang, she grabbed it without breaking stride.

Glancing up, she smiled. "Donny's on line one,'' she called.

Nick snatched the phone. "You and your dumb ideas.''

"Seen the paper, huh?''

"I never considered the media would be there. Maybe Molly arranged it. Ever consider a breach-of-promise suit? What with palimony awards going like gangbusters, maybe she thought to cash in on something like it. How much do we know about her?''

"Hey, she seemed nice enough. Want me to run a check on her?''

"Yes. Let me know once you find out something.''

"You're lucky you didn't land on a spot on Channel 8 news. The kiss was a nice touch.''

"What kiss?'' Nick knew full well what kiss. How had Donny known?

"Didn't you see page two?''

Nick reached for the paper, flipped it open to page two, where the article continued. There was a photo of his goodbye kiss. One impulse after months of grinding work, and it's captured for the world. Damn.

"So are you going to see her again?" Donny asked.

"No. It was for one night only, remember? Hell, you arranged it. But I don't like loose ends, and this article doesn't ring true. Find out why it's in the paper and see what we can do for damage control. And find out what Molly's game is."

"Hey, cuz, I live to serve. But don't you have a publicity department that could put a better spin on it?"

"And have anyone else know the full situation? Not damn likely. You're it."

"And Carmen?"

"She got the message yesterday."

"Until the first time she sees you someplace without fiancée in tow. If she suspects trouble in paradise, she'll move back in for the kill."

"Charming. I'll worry about that when it comes. Have you turned up anything yet on that other matter?"

"Give me a break, Nick, I just started a couple of days ago. These things take time. I have to make friends before anyone confides in me. If I push, they'll clam up forever."

Donny Morgan had opened a private investigative agency several years back, after ten years with the Los Angeles Police Department.

Nick had hired his cousin in an attempt to discover if there was embezzlement from the bar. Sales figures had fallen recently, yet any time Nick glanced in, the place seemed to be doing great. He had suspicions but needed proof before proceeding. Donny had agreed to go undercover to find the proof.

"How's Aunt Ellen?" Donny asked.

"About the same." Another worry. His mother's failing health had caused concern for several weeks. The nurse who watched her full time was always optimistic, but the doctor seemed more reserved.

Nick hated the helpless feeling he had around his mother. He wanted her to get well, resume her normal activities. Return to the vibrant woman she'd once been.

"Give her my love the next time you see her. Gotta go."

Helen dropped off the folder he wanted, and took the newspaper, studying the new photo as she walked back to her desk.

Nick focused his attention on the report, doing his best to push Miss Molly McGuire from his mind. If she thought to make anything of last night, she'd soon know better. They had an agreement for one night. That was all. End of story.

But he wondered what she was doing at that moment—plotting and planning?

Molly worked straight through lunch. She'd arrived early at the office to catch up on several projects pushed to a back burner when working on the Hamakomoto account. Now that the Hamakomoto deal was signed and sealed, she had other assignments that needed her attention. The bulk of her duties over the foreseeable future would be overseeing the Hamakomoto line, but she still had a couple of accounts that were favorites. She'd delegate others when the workload grew to be too much.

But that would be in the future. More immediately,

she planned to treat herself to a pampered weekend at a spa in the wine country—starting tomorrow. The long hours leading up to the final agreement with the Japanese firm had put a dent in her leisure time. She was taking off early Friday afternoon and wouldn't return to the city until Monday morning. She could hardly wait!

She reached for another portfolio, enjoying the sense of accomplishment that accompanied clearing up loose ends. She spread the sketches on the wide drawing table, hitched her chair closer and reached for her charcoal. She wanted to finish the last drawing before taking a break.

The murmur through the wide-open space the artists use stopped. Molly glanced up—right into the dark eyes of Nick Bailey.

She stared at him, surprised to see him. Hadn't they said goodbye forever?

Instantly she remembered flirting and playing the role of devoted fiancée last night. He didn't look like he was ready to flirt today.

The dark suit and pristine white shirt he wore emphasized his rugged masculine looks. He carried himself with a confidence that insured he would never go unnoticed. Just standing there, he seemed to fill the space. Funny, she'd never thought the large open room particularly small before.

He glanced at the other artists, who all quickly became involved with their work, except for Brittany. She was across the floor, separated from them by a dozen workstations, but she stared across the room at Nick and Molly.

If Nick noticed, he ignored it. He looked directly

at Molly. "We need to talk." That steel beneath his easygoing tone surfaced. Just as it had with Carmen.

"About what?" She regarded him warily. What was he doing here? How had he tracked her down? Of course, he'd known she worked for Zentech. How hard was it to show up at the front desk and ask for her?

But why had the receptionist let him come back unescorted? That was not standard operating procedure.

"Have you seen today's paper?" he asked.

She shook her head. "I don't read the local newspaper that often. Why?"

He paced behind her desk to the bank of windows. She had a prime workstation—right next to the wall of windows which provided a lot of natural light. One day Molly wanted to have a corner office with windows on two walls, but for now this was all she could get. At Zentech, offices were for account executives, not art directors.

He turned and slid his hands into the trouser pockets, studying her with that familiar frown.

Molly refrained from fidgeting, but it took a lot of willpower. She glanced around the room quickly, noting how everyone appeared to be working. But she knew they were listening avidly. At least Brittany was too far away to hear anything. Molly refused to give more fodder to the gossip mill.

"Come with me," she said, hopping down from her high stool and heading for the exit sign. The only place to have privacy would be the stairwell. Pushing open the fire door, she checked to make sure they were alone before turning to face Nick.

"What is it you want? I must say I didn't expect to see you again."

"Didn't you? I find that hard to believe. Especially after the press coverage at last night's event."

"The press? I knew they would be there. Our new account is big news. The plans we have impact several San Francisco firms as well as satellite locations around the globe. Did someone try to interview you?" Not possible, Nick had been by her side all evening. Unless it had been after she left.

"There are photos of us in today's paper—complete with story about our whirlwind romance and engagement."

Molly stared dumbfounded. "What? I didn't give them any story. I didn't even talk to a reporter. You were with me the entire time, you know I didn't." How had the paper picked up on the engagement story and why? The coverage should have focused on the new contract. "Though I guess we weren't exactly making a secret of our supposed engagement. I mean, that was the whole reason we went there together, remember?"

"It doesn't matter much who gave it to the reporter. The fact is it's in today's paper and has probably been read by everyone."

"So it'll blow over in a day or two. I mean, who cares if an art director from Zentech gets engaged?"

"The entire social and financial sector of San Francisco does when her fiancé is Nicholas Bailey of Magellan Hotels."

Molly's knees went weak. She plopped down on a step staring at Nick. Running her suddenly damp palms against her jeans, she shook her head. "Impossible. You can't be the head of Magellan Hotels. They've been around for decades and are family owned.''

"Founded by my grandfather right after the war. Taken over by me when my father died ten years ago.''

"What were you doing hanging around a bar in the middle of the afternoon?'' she asked. "I thought you—'' She stopped abruptly.

Resting a foot on the step beside her, he leaned closer, resting his forearm on his raised knee. "You thought what?''

"Never mind. Sheesh, I never made the connection. And when people asked you what you did last night, you never said you owned the hotel! You just said you were in the service industry.''

"Which hotels are. But Zentech wasn't my company, I wasn't going to take away the limelight from your special evening.''

"So what do you want—for me to send a retraction to the paper?'' Molly couldn't believe it. The head of Magellan Hotels had agreed to act as a temporary fiancé? It didn't make sense.

"Did you give them the story?'' he asked.

Molly shook her head.

"Then it's unlikely they'd take a retraction from you. And after the photographs they published, I doubt anyone would believe it anyway. Besides, it's gone beyond that. My mother saw the article, and the pictures, thanks to her busybody nurse.''

"And she doesn't approve?'' Molly could understand that. She'd want to meet a proposed fiancée of any son she'd ever have before he popped the question. "Tell her the truth. I'm sure she doesn't move in the same circles Brittany and Justin do, so her knowing won't blow my cover. Anyway, I plan for us to break up soon."

"How?"

She shrugged. "I'll go to a few events alone and if anyone asks, I'll just say it didn't work."

Nick hesitated. "Not yet."

"What do you mean, not yet. Of course I wouldn't do it the very next day after telling everyone. But soon. Before it goes on too long."

"You'll have to hold off."

"What? Why?"

"My mother's been in failing health for some time. This article has changed her attitude completely. Her nurse and doctor think it's just the thing to get her back on her feet. She's shown more improvement since reading the article than she has in weeks."

"What's wrong with her?"

"She had pneumonia last winter, and never completely shook its effects. She's lost weight, lost interest in everything."

Molly drummed her fingers on her thigh. "Okay, then we don't do a retraction."

"There's more. She wants to meet my fiancée."

"Tell her we broke up."

"I just told you, she's changed completely because she thinks I'm getting married. She wants to meet my future bride. She wants input into the wedding. She's showing an interest in something for the first time in months. If you think I'm going to kill that, you're crazy."

"But we aren't engaged," Molly protested.

"You know that and I know that. And Donny knows. But to the rest of the world we are. Didn't you introduce me as your fiancé to everyone at the Zentech affair last night? I bet I could call a dozen in this morning to confirm it."

"It was just for the night." She was beginning to suspect where he was going with this.

"I helped you out, now it's your turn to help me out."

"I did, with Carmen."

"I did with Justin *and* Brittany. That's two to your one. You still owe me."

Outraged, Molly jumped to her feet. "I do not owe you anything." He rose and they stood staring at each other, on the same level since Molly was standing a step above the landing. She noticed the hard look around his eyes, the determination in every nuance. The slight hint of aggression.

"Then you won't mind if I stop by Justin's office on my way out and let him know the whole thing was a sham? Or maybe let Brittany know we were just fooling?"

"You wouldn't."

"Try me," he urged softly.

"Why would you want people you know to believe you're engaged to me? I'm a daydreaming artist who wears jeans and cross-trainers. If you are who you say you are, you're rich. You probably have dozens of women falling at your feet. Who would believe we are engaged?"

"Interesting slant, don't you think? But the fact is the newspaper reported it, complete with captivating photographs. Anyone who sees them will believe it."

"I think you're nuts. How do I know any of this is even true?"

"Do you think I'd make it up?" His eyes gleamed dangerously. "Get a newspaper."

Molly tried to think of options. How could a silly, harmless deception turn out to become such a big deal? Which would become even more compounded if she perpetuated it.

"What do you want me to do?" she asked suspiciously.

"Come tonight to meet my mother. We'll have dinner at her home. I can't guarantee she'll join us for the meal, but she'll at least get to meet you. Pretend we are engaged. Once she's better, we can tell her we didn't suit and break it off. But not until she is well again! This is the first encouraging sign we've had. I'm not going to jeopardize it!"

"How do I know you are really the head of Magellan Hotels?" Did he think she just waltzed off with complete strangers?

"Come back to the hotel if you like. I'll show you my office, let you meet my secretary who will vouch for me. She worked for my father before me—has known me since I was a kid," he said. He stepped closer, crowding Molly's space. She took a step backward until she was up against the wall.

"There are a dozen people the other side of that door," she warned. It was a foolish bluff. He wasn't really threatening her. But he was taking up all the air. She gazed at him, reminded again of pirates plundering and taking what they wanted.

"I'll have Donny join us tonight, if you'll feel more comfortable."

"Donny?" She needed more room. Slowly she eased to her right, away from Nick. He didn't push the issue. His intimidation technique worked great. She wondered if she could try it sometime.

"My cousin, the bartender."

"Your cousin tends bar? And you expect me to believe you're the head of Magellan Hotels?"

"He's a private investigator working on a case. Don't tell anyone. And since he got me into this mess, I figure he can be there to help us out of it."

"You could have said no."

"And had no defense against Carmen?"

Molly shook her head. "Don't try that on me. You don't need any help against Carmen or any other woman."

"But I do need your help with my mother. We've tried every treatment the doctor suggested. This is the first thing that has given me hope."

She stared at him, hearing the sincerity in his tone. He had helped her out last night. How hard would it be to pretend for another evening? She sighed.

"Okay, give me the address and I'll show up at seven. One night only. Then we're even."

"Not acceptable. I need you to play along until she is better. Then we can stage a fight, break up and go our separate ways."

"And just how long to you expect that to be?" Molly asked wondering if she'd taken a fall down the White Rabbit's burrow?

"As long as it takes. A few weeks, a month or two at the most."

"A month or two? I can't put my life on hold for

a month or two! You're asking me to disrupt my entire life for you. And I don't even know you."

"I figured we'd come down to this. How much?"

She stared at him. Then glanced down at her chest. She didn't see the sign but she knew it was there.

"Do you lie in bed nights thinking up ways to be insulting?" she asked, moving to the door, throbbing with the unfairness of it all. She'd never asked for any of this.

"I have better things to do in bed."

Immediately images of him and Carmen sprang to mind. She didn't want to think about that.

"Well then your talents must come naturally. I'm not asking for a thing from you! And I'm backing out of tonight." She threw open the door. "Find a way to tell your mother the truth."

"The truth?" Justin asked, standing near the door in the open work area. "What truth?"

Molly wanted to jump back into the stairwell and slam the door. Was she living under bad karma or something? What was Justin doing here? She was caught.

Nick stepped into the breach. "My mother wants us to have a huge, lavish wedding. Molly wants something quiet and intimate, but she hates to hurt my mother's feelings," he said smoothly.

"Was there something you wanted?" Molly asked Justin. Of course no one asked her what she wanted— which was to be left alone and not have ex-boyfriends and current fiancés glaring at each other with that macho display men had when fighting over a woman. Puh-lease, it was too much! Especially since Justin didn't care a fig about her, and Nick only wanted a pretend arrangement.

"I need Nathan to mock up a layout for me, but he said he's working on something else for you and you'd have to okay being bumped. It won't take him long. You're always ahead of schedule, it won't delay your deadline. Help me out here, Molly," Justin said.

Molly glared at him, knowing she was taking out her frustration on the man, but it was so like him. Suddenly she realized how often he had charmed things from her when they'd been dating. Had that been the reason he'd been so attentive?

"Go ask Brittany. See if she has someone who can help you out."

"She doesn't."

"Then wait your turn. Next time schedule better." She turned back to Nick. He was leaning casually against the doorjamb, as if he didn't have a care in the world. Only the tightness around his eyes belied his pose.

"I have things to do, even if you don't," she snapped.

"I'll pick you up after work. We aren't finished our discussion."

Conscious of the eyes and ears of the others, Molly knew she was trapped. She nodded, but she wasn't happy about the situation. "I get off at five. But I'll have to change clothes. I can meet you there." Then it struck her—she didn't know where he lived. And a fiancée should know that, shouldn't she? But she couldn't ask with Justin hovering over her.

As if he could read minds, Nick shook his head. "You know I don't mind taking you home and wait-

ing while you change. See you at five, darling."
Leaning over, he kissed her again, drawing it out beyond a mere brush of lips.

Molly almost exploded. She didn't want a kiss. She
didn't want anything from the man. But, conscious of
Justin, of Brittany and half a floor of coworkers, she
made no fuss. Her blood was pounding when Nick
pulled back and winked, which drove her crazy! She
watched him leave then glanced at Justin who still
stood smoldering next to her.

"When did you meet him?" he asked.

"After we stopped dating. I've got work to do."
She stalked to her drafting table and hitched herself
up on the high stool. Picking up the charcoal, she
couldn't believe all that had happened in the few moments since she'd first picked up the pencil.

"I need Nathan," Justin said. He'd followed her to
her drafting table and acted as if he was planted there
until he got the response he wanted.

"What part of no do you not understand?" she
said. Her temper was growing shorter by the second.
If he had a lick of sense, he'd detect it and leave her
alone.

"Hey, what's got you upset? It's an easy favor.
You always helped me in the past. We're still friends,
Molly, right?" He moved closer, as if to charm her
into getting his way.

Molly could just imagine the gossip that would run
rampant that afternoon. She kept her head down, eyes
on her paper.

"No, we are not friends. No, I will not bump
Nathan's current workload. Go charm Brittany.

Surely she'd give you what you want, you two being so tight and all.''

"Jealous?" he asked softly.

"Hardly," she scoffed. "Our breaking up was the best thing to happen to me. I met Nick and look where I am now."

Right between a rock and a hard place, but Justin didn't know that.

Finally realizing she meant what she said, he left, grumbling the entire time. Molly tried to pick up where she'd left off. But images of Nick danced in her mind. He would drive her totally insane if she continued to have anything to do with him. He had no business kissing her in full sight of the entire art staff. Heat washed through her as she remembered her reaction. He was certainly an expert. But if they were even going to discuss a pretend engagement certain rules had to be established. She'd make that perfectly clear to him tonight when he picked her up.

Before or after dinner with his mother?

Was that for real? Was his mother suffering ill health? Could the news of a possible wedding have made her feel better?

Molly stared at the layout, all thoughts of work fleeing. She didn't wish anyone ill. It wasn't such a hardship to her personal life to pretend to be engaged. She hadn't exactly been burning the midnight oil with dates recently.

And much as she might like to snap her fingers at Nick Bailey and his arrogant demand, she couldn't turn her back on a sick woman.

Or was Nick Bailey playing some kind of mind game with her? He'd seemed genuinely annoyed with the newspaper spread. Which reminded her. She rang the receptionist and asked if she had a copy of the daily paper.

When a newspaper was delivered, Molly turned to the lifestyle section, reading every word of the article, studying each photograph. The poses the photographer had captured were convincing. Even she would have thought it true if she hadn't known better. And the sidebar article told her a bit about the marriage-shy hotel magnate. She quickly scanned a short list of names he'd been associated with, suspecting those women hated having their names listed as former girlfriends. Except maybe Carmen, who could be the type to like any kind of fame she could get.

Not so Molly. Yet she had no one to blame but herself for the article and the predicament she was in. If only she and Shelly hadn't concocted such a dumb idea. If only she had marched in to last night's reception alone and unentangled, and faced Justin, Brittany and the pity of her coworkers.

She reached for a telephone book and looked up the number for the Magellan Hotel on Union Square and dialed it. After a surprisingly easy screening, she was connected with Nicholas Bailey.

"Bailey."

She'd recognize that voice anywhere.

"Just checking to make sure you are who you say you are," she said, and hung up.

Okay, so he probably was the head honcho of a hugely successful hotel chain. She could deal with that. What she wasn't sure about was pulling off the charade he asked. One night to save face among casually acquainted businessmen and women was quite different from days or weeks of fooling family.

How ironic. The last man she'd want to get entangled with was another corporate executive with his own agenda.

What if his mother really started planning a wedding? How cruel to snatch it away once her health improved. Wouldn't it be better to tell the truth now and give her hope he would find someone soon to fall in love with and marry?

She wondered if Nick's mother knew about Carmen. There's someone who would relish a temporary engagement. Hoping, of course, to turn it into reality. Somehow, Molly didn't see her as someone Nick or anyone else would take home to meet mother.

Promptly at five, Molly stepped outside the highrise office building. Despite the heavy traffic and parking premiums, Nick had parked directly in front of the building.

No matter the true situation, Molly couldn't help feel a small thrill when she saw him. For a moment—just an instant—she wished they were just two people going out together with all the exploring of likes and dislikes that came with meeting a new man for the first time.

"Satisfied?" he asked, opening the door for her.

"About?"

"Who I am."

She ignored the comment and slid into the car. The leather seats felt wonderful, soft and conforming. She would love to have a car like this one. And it probably cost a mint. Welcome to the world of the rich, Molly, she thought whimsically.

"Hi there Molly McGuire," Donny said from the back seat.

She half turned to see him. The bartender/private investigator's grin was infectious as ever.

"Hi yourself. I think you should have just filled my drink order yesterday and ignored the other request."

"Ah, what a tangled web we weave... But you and Nick are naturals. He helped you out, you helped him out. Works for me."

Nick slid in behind the wheel and started the engine.

"I spoke with Mrs. Braum before I left work. She's my mother's nurse. Mother is looking forward to meeting you. We'll stop by your place so you can change and then head for home."

Molly became immediately defensive. Her job didn't exactly go with designer suits and pristine white shirts. She had charcoal smudged on one thigh. A dusting of chalk along the left leg and on the arm of her shirt.

She didn't work in some pristine office setting, but with materials that spilled, smeared, and crumbled. She hadn't wanted to meet his mother dressed this way, thus her earlier request to change clothes. He could at least give her credit for that.

Nick pulled into traffic and soon made the turn onto the Embarcadero.

"Don't you need directions?" Molly asked. He was heading for her apartment building, but how had he known?

"I know the way."

"How do you know where I live?"

"Donny told me."

She looked over her shoulder into the back seat. "And how do you know?"

He grinned unrepentantly. "I know all. You two had better spend the next few minutes or so going over your backgrounds, so you don't mess up when you meet Aunt Ellen," Donny suggested. "I've given Nick the high points about you, and drew up a quick page about him," he continued, sliding a sheet of paper over the seat back.

Molly took it and began to read. Vital statistics, age, birth date, where he attended school.

"What do you mean, you gave the high points of my life to Nick? Did you investigate me?" She turned and glared at Donny.

"Hey, I thought we were keeping me undercover," Donny said to Nick.

"Like we could do that with you saying you'd given me the high points in her life. Anyway, she knows about your assignment."

"It's supposed to be a secret," Donny complained. "Need to know, and all that."

"Except for family," Molly murmured. "How close can a fiancée get? Just think of me as your new cousin-to-be. So I'm to memorize all this before dinner? Did Nick get a crash course, too?"

"You're an only child, though your mother is one of five siblings, who all had children, so you have lots of cousins," he began to recite. "Your parents live in Fremont, where you grew up. Currently they are on a once-in-a-lifetime cruise, courtesy of your father's company for a banner year in sales. Your mother teaches at the School for the Deaf. You excelled in high school, and were an honors student at the School for the Arts. You've lived for six years in a renovated loft flat near China Basin. You appear to have lots of friends, but,'' he flicked her another look, ''few serious boyfriends.''

''You could have asked me, I would have told you what you need to know.'' Molly was ruffled he'd had Donny investigate her. Maybe she should hire someone to investigate him, see how he liked it.

''I still need to know your favorite colors, foods, kind of movies you like, and books, that kind of thing,'' Nick said.

''Couldn't get all that in the few hours I had to work,'' Donny apologized.

''I need to know that about you, too.'' Was she going along with this? What happened to putting her foot down and insisting on ground rules? Granted he helped her out of a sticky situation yesterday and today with Justin. But he couldn't call all the shots. She was putting herself out for him and wasn't even sure she liked him.

Nick smoothly maneuvered the car through the traffic, even as he began to respond, ''My favorite color is blue, favorite food southern fried chicken— even though I know it's supposed to be bad to eat fried foods. I like action adventure movies, when I get a chance to rent them. I rarely see them at the theater. I have season tickets for the 49ers and the symphony. I like Mozart. Don't read much, but when I do it's mysteries. What about you?''

Okay, so maybe he wasn't just a man with an agenda. ''I like blue, too. My favorite food is chocolate. I think it should be listed as one of the basic food groups. Comedies are my thing—books and movies. And sometimes a really good romance. I do not care a thing about football. I do like music of all kinds, however.''

"I now pronounce you man and fiancée," Donny said from the back.

"Shut up," Nick and Molly said in unison.

"Have you thought of a reason your mother hasn't heard of me before seeing the newspaper this morning?" Molly asked. "I mean, isn't that odd? Or are the two of you not close?"

"We are as close as most, I suppose. And the reason I kept you away was because of her poor health, of course. I sheltered her from a lot, I don't think she'll suspect anything is wrong."

"And, it's been such a whirlwind affair anyway, right?" Molly said.

"What do you mean?"

"Didn't you read the article in the paper? Did you only look at the pictures? According to a reliable source, whom I suspect was that witch Brittany, it was a whirlwind romance. It would have to be, since I was seeing Justin until recently. And we all know about Carmen."

"I sure hope Aunt Ellen doesn't know about Carmen," Donny said. "Or you're toast, my friend."

Nick stopped before an older, six storied apartment building. He double parked, then looked at her. "We'll wait here."

"Fine. I'll make it quick." Molly opened the door and hurried inside, grateful for a few minutes to herself. Maybe she should just lock her door and never leave again.

Yet, while she wasn't sure it was wise to get involved in the scheme, she was curious about Nick. Where he had grown up. What his mother was like. Chances were good that none of them had anything in common and after tonight, no one would suspect a thing wrong when they broke off the engagement.

Once again in the luxurious car twenty minutes later, Molly watched as Nick drove competently in the rush-hour traffic, up California Street's steep hill and into Pacific Heights. In only seconds, he turned on a cross street and before long pulled into a driveway on Washington Street and stopped by a lovely old home. The Tudor architecture was softened by the bougainvillea that grew along the corners of the house and the lovely mock orange shrubs with their fragrant blossoms.

"Is this where you live?" Molly asked. Some of the homes were close to a hundred years old, built shortly after the great earthquake and fire. They were large, beautifully constructed, and costly.

"My mother does. I live in an apartment on Nob Hill. A word of warning, Molly. I do not want my mother upset. She's in frail health and I will do anything I need to for her to get better. Are we agreed on this? No discussion about anything controversial, got it?"

"Gee, this is a match made in heaven. Threats, insults, investigations and more threats. What more could a woman ask?" she said.

Donny got out and opened the door for Molly. "Show time. Did you memorize the facts I gave you?"

"I haven't even finished reading them. I know—

I'll slip into the bathroom, commit everything to memory then tear the paper into tiny bits and flush away the evidence.''

''It could be worse, she could be without a sense of humor,'' he said over the top of the car to his cousin.

Nick scowled and held out his hand. Reluctantly, Molly walked around and put hers into his, feeling his fingers close over hers. Someone should curb his autocratic tendencies, she thought. Turning to face the house, she hoped they could pull off their crazy charade for the sake of a sick woman. But she had a bad feeling about it.

CHAPTER FOUR

NICK led Molly into a formal living room before excusing himself to check on his mother. Molly suddenly wished she'd had a bit of time with Nick to fine tune their story. It was one thing to bluff their way through a casual business reception—but something else again to converse with a family member at great length.

Molly gazed around the room, fascinated despite her worry. It was elegant, fashionably furnished with a blend of antiques and modern pieces. A little cool and sterile, to her mind. She liked more color, some clutter.

"Nick was raised here?" she asked Donny.

Donny nodded looking around as if following her thoughts. "And scared his mother half to death all the time he was growing up that he'd destroy something valuable. It was bad enough for the rest of us when we came to visit, don't touch this, don't sit on that. I don't know how he stood living here. There is a family room in the back, where the TV is and all. He spent most of his time there. Aunt Ellen was too worried about her Ming vase, or the brocade on that old chair to give either of us free rein in this part of the house."

Since the old chair looked as if it belonged to a museum, Molly understood Ellen Bailey's concern.

She wondered if Nick had been a rough and tumble

little boy. Had he run through the house yelling and playing, or saved his roughhousing for outside? Had he played football in high school? He had the build for it. She began to read the paper Donny had prepared, maybe she'd find the answer there.

Nick entered a few minutes later. She looked up, could quote facts and figures, but she didn't know the man at all.

"I don't think this is such a good idea," she said.

"If it was a good idea last night, it's a good idea tonight."

"Last night was different."

"How?"

"It wasn't family I was trying to fool." She waved the paper Donny had given her. "Am I really supposed to memorize all this stuff?"

"It's not like it's a lot. I'm only thirty-six."

"You went to college at Stanford, have a masters degree in business. You like to travel—you've been to a couple of places I haven't even heard of."

"And your point is?"

"We don't suit at all. Your mother will spot that in a New York minute."

"We'll soon find out. If you do your part well, she won't. She already believes the story, she's not looking to analyze anything." He took Molly's arm gently. "Come on, she's awake and anxious to meet you." Looking at his cousin, he said, "We'll be down soon."

"Don't hurry on my account. I think I'll check in the kitchen and see what's cooking."

"When Mom called to invite us, she said Shu-Wen would have dinner at seven. It'll be ready soon."

"You are not listening to me," Molly complained as they climbed the wide stairs. "We don't know enough about each other to fool anyone."

When they reached the top, Nick caught her in his arms. "I'm listening. I'm ignoring what you have to say. We will make this work. Too much depends on it."

"But—" She'd scarcely opened her mouth to protest when Nick covered her lips with his, successfully stopping any argument Molly might have voiced.

She stood in his embrace, quickly feeling her defenses melt as his kiss went on and on. His lips were warm and firm, and expert at drawing a response. His scent filled her senses and the heat they generated would have warmed a small house! He was a master and she felt like a novice. She'd had boyfriends before, but none who kissed like this. No wonder Carmen hadn't wanted to give him up.

Endless time later he pulled back and looked at her, satisfaction reflected in his gaze.

"Now you looked kissed."

"And the point is?" she asked, gazing into those dark eyes that seemed to hide so much. Her heart tripped at double time, her breathing didn't approach normal and her body heat had to register in the triple digits. How was she supposed to think coherently?

"I want my mother to believe this engagement. I'll act captivated, as long as you act adoring."

"Umm, adoring, huh? Okay, I'll give it my best shot." Bemused, Molly would have promised almost anything.

When they stepped into the large bedroom the first thing to catch Molly's eye was the hospital bed jutting from the far wall. It seemed to dominate the room. A nurse rose and smiled, walking toward them.

"I'll leave you with Mrs. Bailey. Call when you wish me to return," she said, passing to leave the room.

"Mother, I'd like you to meet Molly. Molly, my mother, Ellen Bailey," Nick said as they crossed to the bed.

The woman lying there looked almost too frail to sit up. The bed had been raised to a semi sitting position and she was propped against pillows. Painfully thin, her skin had the look of old parchment.

Her eyes held curiosity, but her smile was welcoming.

"It's nice to meet you, Molly McGuire. I wish I could say I've heard about you, but Nick kept me in the dark."

"I'm delighted to meet you, Mrs. Bailey."

"Call me Ellen, my dear. As for you, young man," she said to Nick, "We will have a talk later about keeping something this momentous a secret."

Nick walked quickly to her side and kissed her cheek. "Nothing to tell until recently. Now you know. You'll tire yourself out getting upset about it. Molly's here now and you two will have plenty of time to get to know each other once you're feeling better."

She patted the edge of the bed. "Come sit beside me, Molly and tell me all about yourself."

Molly sat gingerly on the edge, half turned toward Ellen Bailey. "There's not much to tell, I live here in the city, work at Zentech in the art department. Born and raised in California."

"As was Nick. I'm from Boston, originally. Never thought I'd want to leave when I was a girl, but Thomas Bailey swept me off my feet. Tell me how you met Nick."

Molly stared at her, while her mind spun a thousand miles an hour. Would she want to hear that they'd met at a bar? In fact, one could say Molly picked him up. The idea struck her as funny. Nick Bailey didn't seem the type to be picked up by anyone.

"I met her at a function her company held at the hotel," Nick interposed smoothly. "Was captivated from the first."

"So that's why you announced your engagement at last night's Zentech function. Full circle." Ellen nodded as if it made sense.

Molly gave a weak smile and looked at Nick. Let him field all questions, it would save wear and tear on her nerves!

"Sit down, Nick. You'll give me a crick in my neck towering over us that way," Ellen said with a frown.

Pulling a chair close, Nick sat down, close enough to Molly his leg bumped hers. She was suddenly shockingly aware of his presence and had to concentrate hard to hear what his mother was saying. If she moved her foot just a bit, she could touch him again she thought wildly. It caused her insides to quiver and she lost her train of thought. She'd been touched by men before, why did Nick's presence wreak such havoc to her nervous system?

"This is the first time you've had company in a

couple of months, I don't want you to overdo,'' he cautioned.

"Don't ever get sick, Molly, he'll worry you to death with trying to get you well instantly. I'm not going to have a setback. On the contrary, I'm feeling stronger right now than I have in a long time.'' She patted Molly's hand. "All because I got to meet the woman Nick's planning to marry. I must confess I never thought I'd see the day. His dad and I had been married more than five years when we were his age. And Nick was already toddling around.''

Nick's narrowed gaze warned Molly to be careful, as if she needed any warning. She felt she was walking through a field of land mines.

"I bet he was a handful.'' She slanted him a glance. "He still is.''

Ellen laughed. "You will be good for him. Tell me about your wedding plans. You aren't going to let me read about that in the newspaper, now are you?''

Molly shook her head, her mind going blank. She was hardly used to being a fake fiancée, she had never thought about a wedding.

"Will you be married here in San Francisco or at your home church? Where are you from originally?'' Ellen asked.

Molly felt Nick's foot brush against hers in warning. Honestly, if he couldn't trust her to perpetuate the charade, why bother?

"We haven't discussed any details yet,'' she said. "I'm from Fremont originally, so probably would want to go home to get married. Since it's only about 40 minutes away, it wouldn't be too far for friends to drive.''

"And have you set a date?"

"Not for a while," Nick said. "We want to explore being engaged first."

"We should get started on preliminary plans at least," Ellen said. "Churches and reception halls are booked months or even years in advance. In addition, Molly will need time to acquire a trousseau. And you will wish to plan a fantastic honeymoon. Will you be living in Nick's apartment, or getting something larger?"

A tiny Chinese woman appeared in the doorway, carrying a tray. "Dinner ready, Mrs. Bailey," she said as she entered. She greeted Nick, was introduced to Molly as Shu-Wen Li, the housekeeper. Mrs. Braum followed her into the bedroom.

"Need any help, Mrs. Bailey?" the nurse asked.

"In a minute. I'm still visiting," Ellen said fretfully.

"We'll let you eat, now, mother. I'm sure Shu-Wen has dinner ready for us downstairs. I'll bring Molly back to say goodnight before we leave," Nick said as he rose and held his hand out for Molly's.

She slipped it in and smiled up at him in what she hoped was an adoring pose. She was shocked by the thrill of sensation that shot through her. His hand was warm and firm. When his fingers laced through hers, her heart stuttered. This had to stop! She could scarcely think or breathe or do anything but feel the sweeping delight that pulsed through from his touch. The man was practically a stranger! Get a grip, she admonished.

Hands linked, Nick led the way downstairs. From the satisfied glimpse on his mother's face before they left, Molly knew the woman was reassured by his actions. From a distance it probably looked full of love. Ha! If she only knew.

"Shu-Wen popped in a minute ago and said dinner was ready, she just had to take your mother's tray up first," Donny said when they entered the living room. "How did things go?" He was sitting on the sofa, a drink in hand.

"Fine." Nick dropped her hand and headed for the small bar in the far corner. "Want anything?"

"Don't ask that," Donny said. "Look where that question got us yesterday."

"I'm fine," Molly said, feeling oddly bereft with the loss of Nick's touch. "Your mother is very ill, isn't she?" Nick had told her, but seeing her had reinforced his words.

"She's been sick for months," Donny said.

"She's looking better today," Nick said, turning with a small drink in hand. He sipped the amber liquid and looked at Molly. "She has some color in her cheeks and her eyes were as lively as ever. I wouldn't have thought my getting engaged would be a miracle cure for anything. But if it is, so be it." He raised his glass. "To Molly."

"Fiancée extraordinaire," Donny said, raising his glass, as well.

Molly understood Nick's worry. If his mother's thinking they were engaged would aid her recovery, Molly knew she had to keep going. She wanted the woman to recover as quickly as possible.

They could pull it off. If she deferred to him when his mother asked personal questions, it would work. All she had to do was speak as little as possible and gaze adoringly at Nick. Maybe she should try out for little theater productions when all this was over, she thought. She was getting a lot of practice in acting.

She was still bothered by the nature of their deception. Ellen Bailey seemed genuinely happy to think her son was getting married. She would feel disappointed when she discovered the truth. Molly hoped she wouldn't have a relapse.

When they moved to the dining room for dinner, Molly was pleased when the two cousins began to discuss business as they ate. She didn't mind. She could tune them out and take time to think. She glanced around the formal room. The antique furniture and heavy brocade draperies made it more elegant than anything in her parents' house. Which emphasized once again the differences in their backgrounds. She was surprised Ellen didn't think she was after Nick for his money.

"You're quiet, Molly," Nick said at one point.

She looked at him. "Nothing to say."

"A woman who doesn't speak if she has nothing to say? Snap her up, Nick!" Donny teased.

"She's already snapped up," Nick said shortly.

Donny looked at him with an odd expression. "So she is. Tell me, Molly, how did the deception go with your Zentech friends last night?"

"They seemed to believe it."

"Amazing, maybe you have a talent for acting, cuz," Donny said to Nick.

"Did you suspect I wouldn't be able to pull it off?"

Donny shrugged, his eyes alight with amusement. "And Carmen, what are you going to do with her?"

"Not a thing. She also got the message."

"Maybe." Donny winked at Molly. "Time will tell."

When dessert had been served and coffee poured, conversation waned. A little later Nick glanced at Molly's empty cup.

"Are you finished? We can say goodbye to mother and I'll take you home."

"I could call a cab."

"I'll take you," Nick said impatiently. "What kind of man would send his fiancée home when he could take her home himself—if only for the walk to the door?"

Molly nodded, feeling silly. Of course they had to play out the charade. Truly engaged people would love arriving at the door at the end of a date—and the kisses that would follow. She hoped he was teasing. She didn't think they needed to share any more kisses!

Ellen was dozing when they peeped in. The nurse motioned them closer. "She made me promise to wake her. But she'll be groggy. She ate most of her dinner. It's the first time she almost completed a meal since I arrived."

Gently she patted Ellen's shoulder. Her eyes flew open. Spying Nick and Molly, she smiled broadly. "Did you two enjoy dinner?" she asked struggling to sit up.

Molly could see the fatigue smudging the woman's face. "It was delicious. I hope you feel better soon."

"I will. I was thinking we should have an engagement party—to introduce you to all the family and friends. What do you think, Nick?"

The nurse placed several plump pillows behind her.

"It's a great idea, Mom, but we will wait until you're completely well before embarking on a party."

"Very well. But you two be thinking about it. In the meantime, I'll do my part by getting better faster than you'd ever suspect. Then we'll see about asking a few friends in so they can meet Molly!"

"Good night, Ellen," Molly said, leaning over to kiss her cheek.

"Good night, my dear. Next time you and I will spend more time together."

Once in Nick's car, Molly turned to him. "We need some guidelines for this."

"What do you mean?" he asked. Donny had elected to call a cab, so Nick and Molly were alone in the car.

"You know, what we tell people, what we do as a couple. I don't think I should get to know your mom too well, she could be upset when we part ways."

"We can hammer out the deal tomorrow evening. You'll have to stop by from time to time to see her or she'll suspect something's wrong and that would cause her undue worry which I do not want to see."

"Tomorrow evening? I won't be here, I have plans. I'm going off for the weekend."

"With a man?" The words were snapped out.

"Not that it's any of your business, but no, not with a man." Interesting reaction, she mused as he drove down one of San Francisco's steep hills. If she were involved enough with a man to go off for the weekend, she certainly wouldn't have had to ask a stranger to step in at the Zentech reception.

''Where were you going?'' he asked.

''I *am* going to a spa in Napa.''

He frowned. ''A spa? Where you wallow around in mud and drink celery juice?'' His tone was just short of horrified.

''I worked hard on the Hamakomoto account. This is my reward to myself.''

''Postpone it. Donny made a good point. I can't be seen places alone now that I'm engaged or it will start rumors which could get back to my mother. I have a charity event I'm attending on Saturday, you'll have to go with me.''

''I do not have to do anything! I've had this weekend planned for ages!''

''Postpone it, I'll pay for a full week there when this is over.''

Molly fisted her hands and pounded her knee. ''Stop trying to fix everything with money. Is that the only thing you can think of? Didn't it occur to you to just ask as a favor?''

Nick shook his head slowly. ''I figured I'm asking you to postpone your weekend, the least I can do is make it up.''

''Try asking and see what happens.''

''Will you come with me to the fund-raiser Saturday night?'' He said it through clenched teeth.

''Gee, you asked so nicely, how can I refuse?''

By the time noon rolled around on Friday, Molly had second thoughts. And thirds. Reluctant to give up on her special weekend away, she wondered what she was doing going to some charity event where she'd feel totally out of place. The chances were good

Nick's mother would never hear she hadn't gone. And she didn't figure he'd be so newsworthy there'd be more pictures in the newspaper so soon after the last spread.

Molly got a quick bite of lunch and debated taking the rest of the afternoon off. She'd asked for the time and it had been approved.

Deciding she'd rather have it later when she could go away, she set to work once she'd finished eating. Wistfully she glanced out of the windows. It was a lovely day in San Francisco. She should have gone for a walk at lunch, or eaten in the small nearby park. Maybe she'd walk home after work.

She had just sketched a preliminary mockup for a new ad program when there was a stir through the open office. She glanced up.

"Oh, oh," Molly said softly, mesmerized by the sight of Carmen Hernandez sauntering her way through the desks and drawing tables like she was on the promenade of some fashionable resort. Every man in the room had his eye on her. And quite a few of the women, but for different reasons. Once again Molly wondered what was going on at the front desk. Didn't that scatty receptionist know better than to let people wander through the offices at will?

When Carmen reached Molly's work area, she glanced around frowning. "This is where you work?" she asked. The gleam in her eye did not forebode well.

"Yes." So much for any show of civility, Molly thought, unexpectedly amused. What had Carmen expected? And how had she found her? She'd probably seen the write-up on Zentech's reception and the photographs. The whole city now knew where she could be found.

The woman shrugged in a very sexy manner, glancing around the room as if to gauge the reaction of every red-blooded male there.

Satisfied she had their attention, she looked back at Molly. ''Where is your ring?'' she asked, pouncing on the lack.

Molly glanced at her hand. She'd removed her grandmother's ring once the reception the other evening had ended. Scrambling for an excuse, she waved her hand around her drawing table. ''It gets messy and I have to wash my hands a dozen times a day. I'm afraid I might lose it.''

''If Nick gave me a diamond, I'd never take it off,'' Carmen declared dramatically.

''But he didn't, did he?'' Molly asked cheerfully, wishing Carmen would get to the point of her visit—if there was one.

Carmen's eyes narrowed. ''Not yet he hasn't. But you two aren't married, either. Where did you meet him? Does he know you work here? That you work at all? Or does he think you are as wealthy as he is? A man of his position has to worry about gold diggers.''

You ought to know, Molly thought.

''Nick knows all he needs to about me.'' Molly rose, aware of the heightened interest of everyone within hearing distance. She glanced across the bull pen, grateful to see Brittany was not at her workstation. One blessing, but from the avid gazes of her coworkers, she knew more gossip was coming.

She'd give anything to return to her nice, quiet, placid pre-Justin life of a few months ago.

"I do not see what he finds of interest in you. We were lovers for a long time," Carmen said insolently studying Molly.

"How nice for you both."

"You aren't jealous?" Carmen asked in surprise.

"Should I be? Whatever was between you and Nick ended before I met him."

"Such passion between two people doesn't end. He's upset about something, trying to show me he is no longer interested by asking some little nobody to marry him. I can give him fire and passion. What can you give him? You're thin, small and washed out. He needs a real woman! Before long, he'll break it off with you and come crawling back to me. You mark my words!"

Molly was growing irritated with the dramatics. And, she suspected, if she had truly cared about Nick, she might have been upset to learn of a passionate affair. She'd never been involved in one herself and often envied other women when they gossiped about making mad, passionate love to their men.

"Well, if he does, more power to you. But I hardly think it's going to happen," Molly said, wondering how she could get rid of her unwanted guest. Was this part of being engaged to a hotel magnate? She wasn't impressed. Her first instinct had been the best—avoid the man at all costs. Why hadn't she listened?

"You will see!" With another dismissing glance around the art department, Carmen turned and walked away, but not before getting in the last word, ''You have nothing. I can give him all he wants.''

The silence was almost deafening as every eye watched her depart.

Two women near Molly laughed softly and applauded. ''If the hunk who was in yesterday is the man you two are fighting over, good going, Mol,'' one said. ''Who is she?''

''No one important,'' Molly sat back down, and stared at the layout. She was amazed at her calm reaction to Carmen's blatant attempts to cause a scene. She didn't do confrontations that well. Was this going to be something she had to expect while temporarily engaged to Nick Bailey?

Slipping away a few moments later, she called him.

She was put through immediately. His secretary was obviously another who thought the engagement was for real.

''Bailey.''

''Hello, darling,'' she cooed. ''I just couldn't wait until I saw you next to hear your voice. Is your day going as well as mine?''

''Molly?''

''Do you have other fiancées lurking around? Someone else Carmen can go harass?''

''Carmen? What's going on?''

''She wanted to make sure I knew what a passionate affair the two of you had. And how you'll be resuming it in the not too distant future once you dump me. Let's get one thing clear on this situation— when we end this farce, I get to dump you. I'm tired of being the dumpee.''

''She came to your office?''

"Yes, but don't worry. I doubt she'll be back. She was not impressed."

"I didn't expect her to do anything like that. I hope you played your part."

"Hey, I live to please. But I would appreciate her not coming around again."

"I have no influence over her. If she'd accept our engagement is real, she'll turn her sights elsewhere."

"My guess is she'll hold out—hoping once the engagement ends she can step back in," Molly said thoughtfully.

"Carmen's not that patient."

"How patient does she need to be? We're not going to be engaged that long. Your mother will be well in no time."

"Don't keep talking about ending the engagement, someone will overhear you."

"No one can overhear. I wouldn't be holding this conversation with an audience!"

"Not now, but if you stay in that mind set, you'll let it slip when someone is around," he warned.

"Oh, gee, that would be too bad."

"I can make sure it is." That hint of steel came across loud and clear.

"Another threat. Honestly, Nick, is that how you go through life? I'm your fiancée, show some adoration." She almost laughed, imagining his face on the other end.

"You're right. I'll pick you up for dinner tonight. We'll practice being adoring and captivated. Your performance last night left something to be desired."

"What? I did great. Your mom is convinced I adore you." Molly was startled at the extent his comment bothered her. What kind of performance had he expected?

"You tighten up every time I touch you. People truly in love would be more comfortable around each other."

"You'd probably know more about that than I do, having had such a passionate affair with Carmen."

"Forget Carmen. You need practice."

"And you don't?"

"So we'll both practice. Seven o'clock okay?"

Molly agreed to the time and hung up. Her heart skipped a beat in anticipation. Just what kind of practice did Nick have in mind? Something that would make them more comfortable around each other—like more kisses? Sheesh, his kisses had done everything but make her *comfortable!*

Nick couldn't believe he was having dinner with Molly again. Or that he'd insisted. He'd seen her Wednesday night at the reception, last night at his mother's place, and had plans to see her tomorrow night at the charity ball. Tonight was overkill.

But Molly McGuire frankly intrigued him. She was unlike anyone he'd met in years. Feisty and focused, she had a balance that was missing from women like Carmen. The last thing he thought of when thinking of Molly was mercenary.

In fact, when thinking of Molly, it was hard to remember anything except her bright eyes, her irreverent attitude, her smart mouth.

A mouth he couldn't wait to kiss again.

Rising, he paced to the window, looking out across the expanse of Union Square to the glimpse of the bay. He couldn't see her apartment in China Basin, but he knew the general area. Not that she was home.

He shifted to look toward the financial district and the high-rises that held Zentech's offices. Tall buildings filled his view. Which one was Molly's? Thoughtfully he studied the buildings. Was she playing a deep game? Or was she as open as she seemed.

He didn't see how she could have set up their first encounter, yet stranger things had happened. Maybe she'd heard rumors and set out to see what would happen.

He shook his head. There was no way she could have known about Carmen.

Yet—he couldn't help think how their pictures had been in the paper. How much a splash the news had made of his supposed engagement. Molly McGuire would bear watching.

But as long as she didn't cause a problem, he'd continue the charade. His mother's recovery was of primary importance. If having her believe he was engaged to Molly speeded that recovery, he'd keep the engagement going indefinitely.

And, if last night was any indication, his mother would surprise them all with a miraculous convalescence and be back to her normal self in a short while. Time enough then to end his involvement with Molly.

In the meantime, they would be forced together by the nature of their deception. Donny was looking into her background. Nick wasn't one to take things on surface value. He liked full facts and figures. Still, there was no sense wasting an opportunity. He hadn't gotten where he was in business by ignoring opportunities when they unexpectedly appeared, but ruthlessly exploited them when they suited his ends.

Promptly at seven, Molly heard the knock on her door. She opened it, not surprised to find Nick on the other side. What did surprise her, however, was the flutter in her stomach when she saw him.

He seemed taller than she'd remembered. More formidable in the dark charcoal business suit and gray shirt. The subdued tie completed the understated but powerful look.

No smile lit his face. No sign of welcome.

"Ready?" he asked.

Molly nodded, wondering if she were a total idiot to spend the evening with him. If he was going to frown throughout dinner, she'd rather have take-out and eat alone!

"Is this okay?" she asked, motioning to the bright peacock blue dress. She had no idea where he planned to take her. Compared to his somber attire, she felt like a neon sign. But she liked bright colors.

His gaze drifted from her face down the length of her body. Molly felt the flutter kick into high gear.

"A simple yes or no would suffice," she snapped, afraid he'd see how his look affected her. The last thing she wanted to portray was her reluctant interest in the man. He was out of her realm, she knew that. Tonight should prove interesting.

"Yes."

She glared at him, miffed he hadn't said something more, like the color brought out the blue in her eyes, or he liked the way it brightened things up.

Not that this was a real date, she needed to remember that.

On the other hand, he had been the one to say they needed practice. Maybe he should start with compliments!

"You didn't say where we were going. Am I overdressed?" she asked as she stepped aside to allow him to enter. That would give him an opening.

"Depends on what your plans are." He reached out to cup her chin, tilting her face slightly and brushing a light kiss on her lips. "If you're going to bed, you're definitely overdressed."

"Dinner?" she said, annoyed to find her heart racing and her breathing labored from a slight kiss—and the image his words evoked. She had no business thinking of dark bedrooms, satin sheets. She'd never slept on satin sheets in her life! Darn, he was right, they needed practice to become comfortable together. "But kissing isn't the way to start."

"Start dinner?"

She frowned, realizing she'd said that last thought aloud. "No, start being comfortable," she stepped back, putting several feet between them. "I thought you said we needed practice to become comfortable each other."

He nodded, watching her from narrowed eyes. "Touching, kissing, affectionate gestures in public. Practice."

"Right, but we're not in public now."

He shrugged, glancing around the open loft apartment. The ceiling rose twenty feet from the living area. The loft bedroom was built over the kitchen area where the ceiling was only ten feet high. The spaciousness was unexpected.

As were the colorful paintings on the wall, the eclectic mix of comfortable furniture. The floors were wooden, with rugs scattered here and there. It suited her, he thought, eyeing the circular stairs to the loft. What was her bedroom like?

The comment he'd made earlier had been designed to throw her. She fired up when teased. He was starting to look for the signs.

The dress she'd donned was perfect for an elegant dinner à deux. He noticed the way it fit snugly at the breasts, clung the length of her slender body. She wasn't as endowed as Carmen, but there was something femininely sexy about Molly that was missing from Carmen's flamboyant style. And at the moment, Nick found he preferred quiet elegance to flash.

Molly picked up a warm coat, the summer fog cooled the temperatures quickly after dark. Nick reached for it, his good manners showing.

He piqued her curiosity.

Despite being coerced into their engagement-of-convenience—and mostly Nick's convenience—she was fascinated by the man. Once they got to know each other a bit better, maybe some of that fascination would fade. But until then, she'd enjoy the mystery.

The biggest mystery being why he needed her to pretend to be a fiancée when he could probably have any woman in San Francisco jump at the chance.

CHAPTER FIVE

NICK was silent as they rode through the streets. Molly vowed she would not be the one to initiate conversation, and gazed around as if she'd never seen the city before. People were on their way home from work. A few stopped into the stores that were still open. As Nick drew closer to Little Italy, the stores and high-rises gave way to restaurants and nightclubs which would soon be bursting with customers. Friday nights were a time to cut loose.

He parked on Washington Square and looked at her.

"Italian suit you?"

"Fine."

She almost laughed at the wary look that came into his eye. She could be as succinct as he.

"What's the joke?" he asked.

"None. Just wondered if this was all part of your plan?"

"Plan?"

"You know, the practice makes perfect plan. 'Cause if it is, I have to tell you, you have a long way to go?"

"Indeed?"

"If this were a real date, don't you think you'd act differently?"

"This is a date. One where we can hammer out some rules for our engagement."

''Oh, gee, there you go again, sweeping a gal off her feet with romance.''

He leaned toward her, his eyes gleaming. ''Are you looking for romance?''

Molly was captivated by his gaze, her eyes locked with his. Once again she experienced that breathlessness, that flutter in her midsection. His dark eyes gleamed in sensuous awareness. What would it be like to have him romance her?

''No.'' Was she denying herself? Or him? She moved back, closer to the door, trying to break the spell that enveloped her. ''No, I'm not looking for romance. But you said we needed to practice. I would have expected more—finesse, I guess.''

''Finesse?'' He seemed startled. Then he laughed.

Molly blinked, caught by the change in his expression. Her heart skipped a beat. Heat flooded through her as she watched, mesmerized by the awareness that caught her by surprise. She could be attracted to this man. More than attracted.

She had better watch herself around Nick Bailey.

''My turn to ask what's funny.''

''I see I need to polish up my act,'' he said, reaching for the door handle. In a moment he was opening her door, ushering her from the car.

''Something tells me you wouldn't need much practice.''

''And what is that something?'' he asked, motioning to a small Italian restaurant across the street.

''I'm sure you have loads of experience.''

''You are giving me more credit than I deserve.''

''I don't know. I met Carmen, remember?

Definitely high maintenance. And I suspect she's not your first."

"I'm thirty-six years old, would you expect a man my age not to have dated?

"Dated? Ah, so that's what you call it. Carmen might be upset at so bland a description."

His jaw tightened. "I really don't want to spend our evening discussing Carmen. I'd rather spend it discussing you."

"Me?" Molly said in surprise.

They reached the double doors to the restaurant. Entering, they were immediately in the thick of a small crowd.

"Damn, I forgot it was Friday night," Nick murmured. Moving to the maître d's station, he glanced at the list the man was reviewing.

"It'll be a wait," he warned.

Molly shrugged. "I don't mind."

When he gave his name to the maître d', however, the man beamed at him. "Mr. Bailey, this is indeed a pleasure. I'm pleased to see you and your fiancée. Come this way, I have the perfect table for you."

Dumbfounded, Molly followed, ignoring the mumbles of disgruntled people behind her.

In seconds they were seated in a small table for two, in a secluded alcove. It was quiet, elegant and obviously one of the best tables in the house.

Presented with a menu, Molly hid behind it until the man left.

She peeped over it at Nick.

"Must be nice to have a friend in the right place."

"Never saw the man before that I remember. But I have eaten here a time or two."

Molly dropped her gaze to the menu. Had the man seen the paper and remembered? Even if he had, why seat them immediately?

"Does this happen often?" she asked, laying the menu aside. She knew she'd have the veal, she always did when eating Italian—it was her favorite.

"What?"

"Going to the head of the pack."

Nick shrugged and placed his menu on top of hers. "Sometimes, if they know who I am and think it'll get them something."

"A big tip?"

"A recommendation from our hotel when out of town visitors ask for a good place to eat."

"Ummm, that could be fun. Maybe we should eat out often while this engagement lasts. I bet I'll see some places I've never seen before."

Nick stiffened almost imperceptibly, but Molly noticed.

"What?"

"What do you mean?"

Her eyes narrowed as she studied him across the table. "You didn't like that comment. What set your back up?"

"Let's just say I have certain reservations."

"About?"

"About the whole setup."

She blinked and leaned back in her chair. "What setup? Our fake engagement?"

"Two days ago I didn't know you. Now the entire city of San Francisco believes we are engaged. I'm still waiting to find out what you expect from this?"

She rolled her eyes and frowned at Nick. "You

drive me crazy! I needed someone for the Zentech reception—one night only! You're the one perpetuating this engagement. Why do you persist in thinking I'm trying to get something from you? Are you always this suspicious and cynical?''

"Always, it keeps trouble at bay."

Molly ignored him, rummaging around in her small purse. She withdrew an index card, and a pen, and began scribbling on it.

"What are you doing?" Nick asked.

"I don't know if this is legal, but it should be. I'm disavowing any claim on anything of yours." She signed it with a flourish and tossed it across the table.

"If that doesn't suit you," she said tightly, "then consider our engagement off, and figure out how to tell your mother!"

He looked at the note.

The waiter arrived. Nick slipped the card into his jacket pocket while the man placed the water glasses on the table.

"Ready to order?" the waiter asked.

Once their selections had been given, Nick looked at Molly. Color remained high in her cheeks. Her eyes held an angry sparkle. He shouldn't bait her, but he continued to be intrigued by her reactions. The limited time they would spend together for this engagement should prove interesting.

"Nick Bailey, I thought it was you." A tall man dressed in business attire came to the table. "Congratulations, I read about your engagement in the paper. This is your fiancée?"

Nick rose and shook hands with the man and nodded. "Molly, I'd like you to meet Jason Holton. Jason, Molly."

Jason smiled at her. "Nice to meet the woman who finally captured our friend. None of us thought we'd ever see the day. When's the wedding?" He looked at Nick, "I expect it'll be the biggest one San Francisco has ever seen, think of all who will crash the event just to see the impossible happen."

"Nick has proved elusive in the matrimonial stakes, has he?" Molly asked, amused by the embarrassment Jason heaped on his friend.

"He plays the field like—" Jason suddenly realized to whom he was talking. "Uh, you know how it is until a man finds the right woman."

"Maybe you should return to Celeste and let Molly bask in her ignorance of my past," Nick suggested dryly.

"We're just starting dinner, maybe we can get together for a drink when we are all finished," Jason suggested.

"We have plans," Nick said firmly.

Jason glanced to Molly, back to Nick. "Sure, sure, I understand. Another time." He slapped Nick on the back and nodded to Molly. "You can meet Celeste next time. Congratulations, you two."

Molly waited until he was out of earshot, then leaned forward to speak quietly.

"Just how is it until a man finds the right woman?"

Nick raised one eyebrow. "I believe that's the kind of thing he'd never bring up once he has found the right woman."

"And here you were trying to tell me you didn't have that much experience."

"Jason exaggerates. He and Celeste married right out of college, and he still feels he's missing something by not playing the field."

"And is he?"

Nick shook his head. "I think they have a happy marriage, there's never been a hint of rumor about them. Still, there is the grass is greener feeling. I'm one of his last friends to still be single."

"And why is that?" Suddenly Molly realized she truly wanted to know about the man. Not for answering questions that might come up, but to satisfy her own curiosity. She knew what color he liked, what his favorite food was, but there was so much she didn't have a clue about.

Not that she needed to get too involved. This temporary engagement was likely to end as suddenly as it started. But until then, she'd satisfy that curiosity and find out as much about Nick Bailey as she could.

He shrugged. "At the age most men start looking for a mate, I was struggling to take control of Magellan Hotels. My father died suddenly of a heart attack. I had barely started work for the chain. I thought I had decades to learn the ropes, ease my way up the chain of command until I took over for my father. Instead, at age twenty-five, I was the majority stockholder and successor to my father."

"You're trying to tell me you haven't dated for the past ten years?"

"Of course not. But the kind of dates I had weren't the kind leading to marriage. A date for a business event, or charity affair."

"Or just for fun?" she asked.

He nodded. "Or for fun."

"But not the kind of women you take home to mother."

"The minute a man takes a woman home to meet his mother, he never hears the end of it."

Molly smiled, trying to envision Nick as a browbeaten man, plagued by his mother's prodding if he ever brought a woman home. Somehow the picture didn't gel. Nick had never been browbeaten in his life!

"Something tells me you could have stood up to your mother."

"Not lately." He leaned forward. "I still don't know what you want out of all this, but I'll do almost anything to get my mother well again."

Molly looked at him, wondering who had taken so much, he couldn't understand that some people would help out just as a kindness. He was convinced she was a mercenary. Would he ever see her differently?

"Guess you'll have to wait and see, won't you?" she asked, knowing it would drive him crazy—waiting, wondering. The thought boosted her morale like nothing else could have.

"A word of warning. I'm not a pushover. Be careful or you could be the one ending up hurt."

Molly almost wished she had just gone to the reception alone and faced Brittany and Justin without the elaborate scheme that seemed to have backfired. Almost, but her interest in Nick was growing as she learned tidbits about him. For now, he needed her.

After a delicious meal, and excellent service, they left. Waving to Jason and Celeste, on their way out, Molly was glad they were not going to have drinks with friends of Nick's. It was one thing to pretend to his mother while she was bedridden, something else again to keep up the facade with friends who knew the man well, and would know instantly she wasn't his type. Friends were more likely to be analytical than his mother.

As Molly slipped into the front seat of the car a few moments later, she was struck by the lack of practice. Hadn't that been his reason for taking her to dinner? Instead, they had chatted almost amicably over dinner, their talk innocuous at best. He had not held her hand. Had not kissed her. Had not called her sweetheart or darling or anything romantic even when the waiter served as audience.

When Nick slid in behind the wheel, she half turned to look at him.

"So what about this practice you talked about?"

"Anything special in mind?" he asked lazily. He looked at her. It was dark, the only illumination from the streetlights and neon signs on the nightclubs and restaurants along the perimeter of the Square.

If anything, the shadows and dim illumination made him seem even more the pirate. Molly shivered in delightful anticipation. Could she hold her own?

"You brought it up."

"What did you have in mind?"

"Primarily getting to know each other a bit better—so you aren't so jumpy when around me," he said lazily.

"I am not jumpy!"

He leaned closer, sliding his hand behind her neck. Molly's heart sped up, beating in double time. Mesmerized by the dark eyes that held hers, she tried for a deep breath. Her skin tingled where his warm palm touched. All coherent thought fled, her senses went on full alert.

"So if I kiss you, you'll be fine with it?" he asked.

Fine was hardly the word to use, she thought. Ecstatic, wild, excited, thrilled might come close. Not that she'd share that with the arrogant man. Time he was taken down a peg or two.

"I'll be fine with it," she said, leaning closer herself. "The question is will you?"

She closed the scant inches between them and placed her lips against his. Almost smiling at the start of surprise she detected, she gave her best shot.

In a flash, Nick took control of the kiss, drawing her close, opening his mouth and feeding the growing passion with his expertise. Deepening the kiss, he encircled Molly with his arms. She clutched his shoulders, holding on for dear life lest she spin away.

A kaleidoscope of colors exploded behind her closed eyelids, her senses floated, expanded. She was aware of his scent, his touch, his heat. His tongue danced with hers, drawing a deeper response. Her heart beat heavy, she could feel his pounding. The temperature rose dramatically until Molly wished she could open a window and let in the night fog to cool down.

But not if it meant moving away from the kiss.

If only it would continue forever. What magic had he wrought that she forgot good sense and longed for what couldn't be?

Endless moments later, Molly eased back and looked up at Nick. She cleared her throat, wishing she felt sophisticated and urbane and had a clever repartee. But mostly she wanted to throw herself against him again and kiss him until morning.

"Maybe this isn't such a great idea," she said. "I know you want practice and all, but I think that's all I need for tonight."

Nick rubbed her damp lips with one thumb, leaned back, and glanced around.

"Dammit, I can't believe I forgot where we are. Parked right on Washington Square in the middle of a Friday evening. Half of San Francisco could have driven by."

"It's dark. No one could see in the tinted windows," she said practically, leaning back, feeling suddenly cold. He could have said something to lighten the mood. Instead, he was back to frowning again.

He started the car and smoothly moved into the street, heading back to China Basin and her apartment. Molly didn't initiate any conversation, and Nick was decidedly quiet.

She gazed at the lights, trying not to dwell on the blood still rushing through her, or the tingling awareness that seemed to fill every cell. They had shared a kiss. Big deal.

But it was, she thought, still feeling the excitement. She had never felt quite like this before. Was it from kissing a man she scarcely knew? Forbidden fruit, so to speak? Or was there something special about Nick Bailey?

She didn't feel he was an easy man to know. He ruthlessly commandeered her cooperation in the charade, yet for loving reasons that seemed at such odds with his reputation. After *he* suggested the scheme, he doubted her enough to have her investigated. Yet his manners tonight had been attentive and interested.

Molly's street was empty of traffic when Nick turned on it. Parking, however, was a different matter. There was not a vacant space for two blocks. When they reached Molly's apartment building, Nick double parked and looked at her.

"I won't come up, if that's all right."

Molly stifled a short laugh. The last thing she wanted was anything more of Nick tonight. Tomorrow evening was time enough to deal with her raging hormones and gain a modicum of control. She wouldn't be responsible for the consequences if he kissed her again tonight.

"That's fine. I'll see you tomorrow, then."

"The cocktail hour starts at seven, I'll swing by about fifteen minutes before that. It won't take long to get to the hotel where they're holding it," he said, watching her with hooded eyes. "It's formal."

She nodded and opened her door. "I expected as much. Thanks for dinner. It was—interesting." She slid out before he could say anything and hurried to the front door.

"Molly?"

She turned. He'd gotten out of the car and looked at her over the top. "That kiss earlier—it wasn't just about practice."

She stood in amazement as he slid back behind the wheel, gave a casual wave, and drove off.

Early Saturday morning, Nick took a deep breath of cool air. The scent of eucalyptus and the sea mingled, filling his lungs with energy. He leaned over, stretching. Pushing against his car, he warmed muscles he'd need for his run.

Running in Golden Gate Park was something he didn't do as often as he'd like anymore. There was a five kilometer course he enjoyed that took him through some of the quietest parts of the park, and even had a stretch along the beach.

A dark Jeep pulled in behind him and Donny climbed out.

"Couldn't you find another time and place," he grumbled, walking over to Nick, sipping coffee from a take-out place.

"Nope." Nick looked him over, faded shorts, scuffed running shoes, and baggy T-shirt. Donny and he dressed alike.

"Ready to go?"

"No, I have to finish my coffee." Donny leaned against the car and closed his eyes. "Unlike you, I was up until three this morning." He opened one eye and looked at Nick. "I assume unlike you. What time did you take Molly home?"

"Long before three." Nick reached out and snagged the cup, flipping off the top and taking a long drink.

"Hey, that's mine."

"Sooner finished, sooner we can start," Nick said, handing it back. "Learn anything?"

"About Molly or the bar?"

"Either, both." Nick tried to keep his tone neutral, but he was curious about anything Donny might have found out about Molly. Curious and wary.

"Nada. She's clean."

"I don't need cop talk. I didn't think she was involved in some crime. Do you think she's got a plan in mind by going along with this scheme?''

''The only thing I can come up with is she's never been involved long term with anyone. I don't think she's trying to rip you off. There's no pattern to show that. And women in their late twenties don't just turn to conning people. She'd have to have experience before now if that was her goal.''

Nick nodded, turning and looking down the path. He had known Molly wasn't a con, but it was good to have it verified.

''Let's go,'' he said, starting to run.

Donny caught up in a second and the two men began to pace themselves, falling into the familiar routine with ease.

''And the bar?'' Nick asked.

''Something definitely going down there, cuz, and I think it's Harry Coker.''

''Harry? He's been there for two years. We only noticed the shortages about eight months ago,'' Nick said.

''So you said. However, things change. I'm running a background check. Maybe something came up eight months ago to turn him.''

''Do you know for sure it's Harry?''

''I'm getting proof.'' They ran in silence for a short while. ''You going to prosecute when I get it?''

''Damn straight I am.''

''Figured you would. What if it's a kid who needs an operation or something?''

''Find out what's going on and leave the consequences to me,'' Nick ordered.

''Aye, Boss. Besides I'm not nearly as interested

in that as I am in what you're going to do about Molly.''

"I'm not doing anything with her."

"Dates four nights this week sounds like something."

"How did you know about last night?"

"Hey, I'm the hot-shot investigator, remember."

They broke from the canopy of trees into the segment that ran parallel to the beach. The breeze was strong, keeping them cool even as they racked up another kilometer.

Nick thought about Donny's question as they pounded on the packed dirt path. What was he going to do about her?

That kiss last night had nothing to do with practice, and all to do with desire.

He hadn't felt like that around a woman since he'd been a randy teenager. Even when entangled in some affair, he was known to keep his cool.

But kissing Molly had blown that out the window. One of the hardest things he'd done recently was to leave her at her apartment and not go up with her.

"Want to share the joke?"

"What?" He looked at Donny.

"You're smiling. Some joke?"

"No." He was just wondering what she'd thought about his parting comment.

Saturdays were Molly's favorite day. She rose early, had a quick breakfast and then began to paint. Sometimes beside the floor to ceiling windows catching the north light. Sometimes on location, especially when the weather was good.

But it was always her day—a treat to herself for putting up with clients and account executives and bosses who sometimes expected miracles, and who all thought of art as a commodity rather than a creative process.

She liked working for Zentech, but she loved painting. Her dream was to one day be able to support herself solely by her art. But that day hadn't arrived.

She had several pictures currently hanging in two galleries in town, one near the wharf, one near Union Square. Both small establishments, both still growing in reputation. The paintings she'd already sold helped augment her salary, enabling her to buy her flat when the building had changed from rentals to purchases. Her hobby, as her parents called it, enabled her to vacation in exotic locales—which she of course immediately set about to capture in oil.

Today she wanted to put the finishing touches on a painting she'd been doing in Golden Gate Park for several weekends—of a section of the Japanese Tea Garden. The weeping willow tree's airy branches drifted toward the water, a small stone bridge arched over the stream. Done primarily in shades of green and brown, she was pleased with the way it was coming.

She wore comfortable jeans, a soft cotton top covered by her paint-splattered smock. It was warm enough she didn't need shoes. Her ablutions this morning had consisted of a quick shower and brushing her teeth. Her hair had dried wavy after a quick combing and she pulled it into a ponytail to keep it out of the way.

She studied the canvas, head tilted slightly to the

right, as she decided just where a bit more work was needed. A couple of hours and she'd be done. She reached for the oils.

Normally as soon as she touched brush to paint she was lost in a world of color and texture and shape. But today the comfort zone didn't appear. She dabbed a leaf, and thought about Nick and his kiss. She studied the water, but saw instead the two of them at dinner last night. Despite her best efforts, she had not learned as much about him as she wanted. He was either a champion at dissembling, or more reserved than she'd suspected.

Once again, she dragged her attention to the canvas. She did not want to keep thinking about Nick. Today was her only day to devote fully to painting. She had chores to do around the place tomorrow and then the workweek started.

What was Nick doing today? Did he spend it in the office? At a golf course? Sailing? Shouldn't she know the very basics of a supposed-fiancé's hobbies? Stopping in the midst of painting when she didn't have to was almost unheard of, but she put down the palette and brush and went to rummage through her purse.

She pulled out the paper Donny had prepared. She'd glanced through it when going to Nick's mother's house the other day, but not absorbed everything. She reread it quickly. Just as she thought— Donny hadn't listed leisure activities.

Fat lot of good that report was, she fumed, returning to the easel. She resumed touching up the painting, her mind half focused on the work, half on wondering about Nick Bailey.

CHAPTER SIX

SOMETIME later the phone startled her. She rarely got calls on Saturday—most of her friends knew her only-day-to-really-paint. If it were a telemarketer, she'd really be annoyed, she thought as she put down the brush and went to answer.

"Hello?"

"Molly, Ellen Bailey. I hope I'm not calling at a bad time." The voice sounded stronger through the phone than it had the other evening.

"Now is fine. How are you?"

"Much better, thank you. I know it's short notice, but I am feeling strong enough to have company for lunch. Would you join me? It will give us a chance to get to know each other—without worrying about Nick."

"Worrying about Nick?"

Ellen laughed softly. "Well, we can't really talk about everything we want if he's sitting here with us, now can we?"

Molly became intrigued. "And what would we be wanting to talk about without him?"

"How he was as a little boy, for one. I have some albums if you are interested in seeing some old family photographs."

Molly glanced at the painting. It was finished, she was merely holding on to it because she always hated to finish a project. Until she was consumed by a new project, she felt let down, at loose ends.

"If you have other plans, I'd understand," Ellen said with dignity.

Molly didn't have other plans, or any real reason to refuse, except she didn't wish to become more involved. But the loneliness in the woman's tone touched her. How much would it take to spend a couple of hours with Ellen Bailey?

"No, I have no other plans. What time shall I come?"

"Twelve-thirty would be fine." She gave Molly directions, then hung up.

Molly hesitated a moment, then tried to call Nick at the hotel. She was mildly surprised to discover he didn't work on Saturdays. And there was no one there to tell her where he might be.

"The least he could have done was given me his cell phone number, or even his home number," she grumbled, as she tried in vain to find a listing in the phone book. Another thing to discuss. This being engaged was growing more complex.

She worried about how Nick would react when he discovered Molly and his mother had shared a meal without him.

"Probably suspect me of trying to con her out of his inheritance," she thought, picturing his annoyance.

"Oh well, that'll teach him to keep his fiancée in the dark!"

Molly was shown into Ellen's bedroom upon arrival. The older woman was wearing a lacy champagne colored peignoir and propped up on a dozen pillows. She beamed a warm welcoming smile when Molly entered. Even in such a short time, Molly could see improvement.

"I'm so glad you came, Molly. Forgive me for not getting up. I tried it, and it was so much of a strain, I decided it would be better to rest and devote my energy to our visit, rather than sitting in a chair, or taking the stairs."

"This is fine. If my being here tires you out, let me know and I'll leave." Molly glanced at Mrs. Braum, the nurse. The woman smiled her greeting and retired to sit near the windows.

"Having you here is like a tonic. Would you like something to drink?"

"I'll wait for lunch. How are you feeling?" Molly sat in the straight chair near the bed. Ellen still looked almost as frail as she had the other night. Molly suspected she'd lost a lot of weight while sick, and that part of her recovery delay was due to lack of energy. She needed to rebuild her reserves.

"Much better, thank you. Oh dear, I noticed the other night you weren't wearing an engagement ring. I was hoping you'd just left it home or something. Didn't I see one in the newspaper photographs?"

"Uh," Molly tried to think. She hoped her expression didn't give her away. She was not good at subterfuge. "Actually I have a lovely ring, but I don't wear it when painting, I don't want to get oils on it. I was painting when you called. I forgot to put it back on when I cleaned up."

She was going to have to remember to wear her grandmother's ring!

"I can't wait to see it. Tell me again how you and Nick met and when he proposed. Was it a total surprise? Was he romantic?" Ellen asked wistfully.

"Donny introduced us," Molly said, hoping she wasn't going to be questioned to death. What had he told his mother? How awful if they got their stories mixed up. "Not too long ago, actually. It's been a whirlwind romance." To say the least.

"I would love to hear about Nick as a boy," Molly said. The key to getting through lunch was to have Ellen talk about Nick, freeing Molly to just listen. No way to make a faux pas doing that!

"Mrs. Braum, would you bring me that first album," Ellen said.

The nurse rose and brought the album. "I'll run downstairs and see how Shu-Wen is doing with lunch. I believe it'll be ready shortly."

"We'll be here," Ellen said dryly. When the nurse left, Ellen smiled at Molly. "She's a dear, but I think it's time she moved on. As soon as I can, I'll be back on my feet and ready to help with the wedding. I'm looking forward to meeting your parents, too. Were they thrilled their daughter is getting married?"

"They, um, don't know about the engagement."

"Why not?"

"They're on a cruise right now. It's sort of hard to reach them." Of course Molly had their itinerary and contact information, but she would not be telling them about this engagement. With any luck, it would all be over before they returned home.

"I'm sure they'd love to hear from you," Ellen said slowly, studying Molly thoughtfully.

Molly nodded and smiled brightly, pointedly looking at the album. "Do you have baby pictures of Nick?"

When the door flung open a few moments later, Molly, Ellen and Mrs. Braum all looked up in surprise. The three women had been examining the photographs in the album. Molly had been absorbed by the glimpses of Nick as a child. He'd looked like a mischievous kid. When had he acquired that serious air?

Nick stood in the doorway, surveying them all with disbelief.

"Molly, what are you doing here?" he asked.

"Visiting your mother," she replied, her gaze taking him in. Gone was the immaculately attired business mogul. Gone the Armani suits and wing tip shoes. Instead, he looked even more like her disreputable pirate. Running shorts displayed his muscular legs, his hair was mussed as if he'd been in a wind tunnel, and the way his T-shirt stretched across an impressive chest almost had her salivating.

He'd obviously been doing something physical and on him it looked great.

Her eyes met his and saw the suspicion.

Here we go again, she thought, glancing at Mrs. Braum and his mother. Had they noticed?

"We're looking at the family album," she said to fill the silence.

"What are you doing here, Nicholas?" his mother asked.

"I got a call from Shu-Wen. She said I was to come right away. I thought something had happened."

Ellen made a tsking sound. "I asked her to call you

to let you know Molly was here. I invited her for
lunch. I thought you might wish to drive her home
later. But it wasn't an emergency.''

''Molly's staying for lunch?''

''Yes.''

From the glare Molly received from Nick, it didn't
take a rocket scientist to figure out he did not want
her to stay. She was trying her best to think as a
fiancée would think. What did Nick expect her to do
when his mother invited her?

''Then I'll change and join you both. Maybe I
could see Molly for a minute.''

Ellen relaxed and smiled broadly. ''Of course.''

Molly wished she could smile. She knew Ellen was
imagining a passionate greeting between lovers.
Instead, as she followed Nick into the hall, she feared
retribution. He closed the bedroom door, isolating
them in the hall.

''What game are you playing now?'' he asked in
a hard tone.

''Umm, that would be the one you started, I believe—fool your mother for as long as it suits you?''

''I mean here. Why did you come here this morning? Did you honestly think I wouldn't find out?''

She was getting a bit annoyed by his constant sus-
picions. ''She invited me. I demurred. She insisted.
Weren't you the one trying to get her better ASAP?
I think she's lonely. And bored. I'm a diversion.''

''Bored? She has tons of friends. She could call
one of them.''

''How about her doting son?''

''I don't ignore her. We're not talking about me. I

don't want you with my mother when I'm not around, is that clear?''

''Why not?''

He ran his hand through his hair in pure frustration. ''Just leave it at that. I'll go change and join you shortly.''

Daringly Molly danced her fingertips up one muscular arm. ''Don't change on my account,'' she said teasingly. She almost laughed at the startled look on Nick's face. It was priceless. Maybe she should start playing the role of fiancée and see if that was what he really wanted.

He caught her fingers in his hand, squeezing gently, holding on.

''Now what?'' he almost growled.

''The angle? Aren't you always looking for an angle? Why not try trusting sometime,'' Molly asked.

''I learned fast that trusting in life can get you kicked in the teeth.''

''Gee,'' she leaned closer, ''we wouldn't want that to happen, you have such nice teeth.''

''All the better to bite with,'' he replied, drawing her closer until he pulled her into his arms.

''And do you bite?'' she asked, daring him with her smile, her pulse racing in anticipation.

''Sometimes.'' He watched her every second it took for him to slowly lower his head until his lips touched hers.

He tasted warm and male and slightly salty. She wrapped her arms around his neck and held on as he deepened the kiss. He was strong, solid, muscular and hot. She caught the heat from him, almost bursting into flames.

Nick knew he should stop. He didn't want any more involvement with Molly McGuire than necessary. But she was so soft in his arms. Her mouth so sweet, the way she kissed inflamed him. He wanted to sweep her away, take her to his room and keep them occupied for a week.

The thought shocked him. Slowly he eased back, resting his forehead on hers, watching her eyes flutter and then open.

"Done?" she asked.

She had a sassy mouth. He wanted to kiss it again.

"I'll join you two as soon as I change."

"Do you have to go home to change?" Her voice was low, husky. Nick didn't want to move an inch.

"No, I have some things here. I won't be long."

"Then I'll try to contain myself until you join us." Molly stepped back, brushed down the front of her shirt and reached to open the door.

"Careful what you say to my mother," he warned.

"We're just looking at baby pictures. You were a cute little boy, were you also as suspicious then of everything?"

"Life teaches some hard lessons."

"I can't imagine anyone teaching you anything." Molly replied with a saucy grin. "But you'll be happy to know I'm getting good at this pretending. It's the practice, you know." She opened the door and stepped in as if she belonged.

He wanted to follow her immediately, watch everything she did, make sure she wasn't trying to worm her way into his mother's graces enough to wreak havoc. Molly knew his mother was fragile, was she somehow planning to take advantage of that?

Nick showered and changed in record time. He didn't trust Molly. He'd been out in the real world long enough to know women wanted him for the money he had to spend, the good time he could show them. Loyalty and love had little to do with anything these days.

As he walked along the hall toward his mother's room, he tried to remember just when he had become so distrustful around women. When Gillian Prentice had jilted him his senior year in college? Or after the play Marissa Bellingham had made shortly following his takeover of Magellan Hotels? He still owed his friend Hamilton for arranging for him to hear her admit she only wanted to marry him for the potential earnings he had. That had been a blow. Since then, cynicism had served him well. Each woman whom he dated knew right up front he was not interested in marriage. Even Carmen, much as she would like to change the rules.

There was no reason to suspect Molly was any different. To the contrary, there was a wider gap between the two of them than the women he usually dated. She lived in a small apartment in China Basin. He lived on Nob Hill. She painted to supplement her income. He had the family fortune at his back.

Donny may think she was on the up and up, but Nick suspected she'd seen a ripe opportunity fall into her lap and was taking every advantage.

He'd put up with it to help his mother—but watch her like a hawk.

Opening the door, he was surprised to see his mother laughing. She had color in her cheeks. Her eyes sparkled when she looked at Nick with delight. The change was almost miraculous.

"There you are. Come in and listen to Molly tell about painting her apartment."

He pulled a chair over and sat close enough to Molly his knee touched hers. When she shifted slightly to end the contact, he leaned over and put his hand on the back of her chair.

Just like he's staking a claim for all to see, Molly thought wishing Nick wouldn't crowd her space. She had been doing her best to entertain Ellen, but now she felt tongue-tied as awareness of Nick threatened to swamp her.

"I thought you painted pictures," he murmured.

She gave him a look and shifted a bit to the left. "I do paint pictures, but I wanted to brighten up my flat from the first moment I moved in. The walls were some dreary green. I wanted them bright and cheery."

"Tell him about your makeshift scaffolding," Ellen urged.

Molly looked uncertainly at Nick. Not for him some makeshift arrangement, she suspected. Heck, he'd hire a battery of painters if he wanted any color changes.

"Well, you know my place has a loft, so the walls on three sides go up almost twenty feet."

He nodded. He had only been inside that one time, but he remembered the layout.

"I borrowed my neighbor, Shelly's, table and put hers and mine side by side, then put up a couple of chairs and had a board running between them. It worked great."

He stared at her. "You could have fallen and broken your neck."

"It was a pain to move it every time I needed to change places, but it worked perfectly. And saved a ton of money. I had a painter give me an estimate, and it was lots more than I wanted to pay."

Nick could picture her on the makeshift scaffolding, and envision her setup collapsing, tumbling her to the floor with chairs and board crashing down on top of her.

"Don't do it again," he said sharply.

Molly looked at him. "What?"

"It's too dangerous. Don't do it again."

"I was very careful," she said.

"And it was before she met you, Nick," Ellen said. "I'm sure the need won't arise again, will it? After all, Molly won't be living there much longer. We haven't discussed your wedding at all, but don't hold off because of me. I'm feeling stronger every moment. And to have a definite date will spur me on to recover even faster."

Molly looked at Nick, her eyes wide. Now what? They dare not set a date, no telling what Ellen would do. But how did they stall without giving away their charade?

"We want to wait for Molly's parents to return. Once they do, we can all get together and discuss things. They don't even know we're engaged," Nick said easily.

Grateful for the reprieve, Molly smiled at him. "Clever," she mouthed in approval. Turning back to Ellen, she nodded. "I'm sure you understand I want to talk to them before Nick and I move forward. This has been a whirlwind romance, you know.''

"But one that was meant to be. You two are perfect together.''

Once lunch was finished, Nick urged his mother to rest telling her he'd take Molly home.

When they reached the lower level in the house, Molly stopped him. "You don't have to you know, I can call a cab.''

"I want to talk to you.''

"Oh-oh, another lecture?''

He frowned. "I do not give lectures.''

She laughed and patted his arm, aware of the strength of his muscles, the heat emanating from him. Then she turned, almost sighing for what couldn't be. For a split second Molly again wished things were different between her and this dynamic man. Wished she herself was more trusting, could believe men and women from such diverse backgrounds could meet and find common ground. But she'd been burnt trying that. She was on her guard.

And this wasn't even an attempt to find common ground. They'd entered into a pact to aid the recovery of an ill woman.

As they sped toward the wharf, she leaned back in the luxurious car and gazed idly out the window. She had enjoyed her visit, learned a lot about Nick. And connected with Ellen Bailey in a curious way. The woman seemed to be a mix of haughty grandeur and loneliness.

"What did you and my mother talk about?'' Nick asked.

"This and that. Mostly about you as a boy. She thought I'd want to know all about you. She doesn't seem to think she was a great mother—more concerned about her antiques than letting a little boy run wild in the house."

"She was a fine mother."

"And she wishes she had more children. A little girl, definitely."

He flicked a glance her way. "I never knew that. I thought one was all she wanted."

"She said she and your father both hoped for more, but it wasn't to be. She also misses your father a great deal. He died ten years ago, and she's still lonely for him. That's sweet in a sad way."

"She has friends. Charity work."

"Nick, they were married twenty-seven years. He was the love of her life. Of course she'd miss him. She'll probably always miss him."

"She could get married again."

"Only if she found someone she loved as much as your father. What do you think?"

"That all that love stuff is overrated and a bunch of hype. Men and women marry for various reasons. If their hormones are raging and they want to call it love, let them."

"Okay, you get the cynical man of the year award. But just because you don't believe in love, doesn't mean your mother doesn't. And she won't settle for less."

"And you, do you believe in love?"

Molly was silent for a long moment. "I want to," she said sadly. But truth to tell, she wondered if she'd ever find it. Infatuation was hard enough. Would she recognize life-time love if she ever stumbled upon it?

Maybe she just hadn't found the right mate for her. Her parents were happy. Ellen had been happy with her husband. Molly was twenty-eight years old and had thought a couple of times she'd found a man she could share her life with. With each disappointment disillusionment set in. Maybe she was expecting too much.

When Nick pulled to a space near her flat, she reached for the door handle. His hand on her left arm stopped her.

"I'll pick you up tonight around six forty-five."

"I'll be ready."

"I'll get the door," he said, opening his own and sliding from beneath the wheel.

He opened hers moments later.

"Until later," she said.

"Molly," he said as she started to walk toward her building.

"What?"

"There are going to be a lot of people there tonight watching to make sure this is for real. Including Carmen."

She grinned. "Don't worry, I'll wear the sexiest dress I have and be all over you like mustard on a hotdog."

He groaned slightly and shook his head. "Charming analogy."

She waved and walked away.

He stood watching her. She was sexy in jeans. What would she be like in a sexy dress? He was almost afraid to find out.

*   *   *

"So tell me again about this guy," Shelly said sometime later as she sprayed the hair style she'd just completed on Molly. She looked at her friend in the mirror.

"The last thing I remember, you were going to pretend to be engaged, flaunt your grandmother's ring in Justin's face and waltz through the reception. Next, I see your face in all the newspapers, complete with fiancé. Now you're going someplace where everyone who is anybody in San Francisco will see you, and you tell me it's all a scam?"

"Not a scam," Molly protested, touching one curl lightly. "This looks great! Thanks, Shelly." She crossed to her bed and took the dress, holding it up to her. "It's basic black, but it'll work, won't it?" she asked her neighbor.

"I remember when you bought it. You trying to put the make on this guy? He'll be drooling."

Molly laughed. "I don't think so. Stay around awhile and meet him. Mr. Business-is-Everything."

"That's why he's a gazillionaire."

Molly looked at Shelly. "He's rich, I know, but a gazillionaire?"

"Hey, he owns Magellan Hotels. That isn't chump-change. So maybe he's not Bill Gates, but he's still got to be rolling in dough. My mother always said it was as easy to fall in love with a rich man as a poor man."

"I'm not falling in love with anyone," Molly protested, slipping into the dress. It was a snug fit. She'd loved it the first time she'd seen it. With silver threads shimmering throughout, the dress drew attention like flames drew a moth. It was short, with thin straps baring her shoulders. The snug bodice faithfully outlined every inch of her body. She was glad she walked to work most days, to keep off the pounds. This dress would show even an extra ounce.

She slid her feet into the scarcely-there high-heeled sandals. Nick would still top her by a good six or eight inches, but she felt taller wearing them.

Shelly rummaged around her dresser top, and came up with crimson lipstick.

"This!" she announced. "That dress and your attitude cries out for red."

"My attitude?"

"The one you're adopting for your performance tonight. You've got to compete with Carmen, and who knows who else at this event."

"I'm not competing with anyone. This is a fake engagement. If Nick wants to move on to someone else, fine by me." But as she leaned closer to the mirror, applying the crimson red lipstick, she felt a twinge of jealousy. It shouldn't, but it did bother her to think he might be attracted to someone else.

Which was foolishness to the extreme. They had entered an engagement-of-convenience. It would not last. And she'd be an idiot to think for one second that Nick Bailey could be attracted to someone like her.

CHAPTER SEVEN

PROMPTLY at six forty-five, the doorbell rang.

"Businessmen obsess about time like they do everything else," Molly muttered as she crossed to open the door. She caught her breath when she saw Nick. He wore a tux. She'd thought he looked yummy enough to eat earlier that day in running attire, now she knew why women wanted men to wear tuxedos. Wow!

"Ready?" he asked, his gaze running down the length of her.

She wasn't sure, but she thought she saw a flare of heat in his eyes.

"Just about. Come in and meet my next door neighbor, Shelly." Molly quickly made introductions, amused by Nick's wariness and Shelly's open suspicion.

"It was your idea about the false engagement, wasn't it?" Nick asked.

Shelly nodded. "But you added a twist. In my scenario, there was no guy."

"It wouldn't have worked," he said.

"And this will? What happens when someone catches you two?"

"As long as it's after my mother recovers, no harm done," he shrugged.

"Don't mind me," Molly said, reaching for a light coat. "I do have some say in this."

109

Nick looked at her, his expression impassive. "Shall we go?"

"Have fun, and don't forget what my mother said!" Shelly said, heading out of the flat before them. She waved and entered a door down the hall.

As Molly checked to make sure her own door was locked, Nick asked about Shelly's last comment.

Molly could imagine his expression if she told him.

"Nothing, just some motherly advice. Is there anything I should know before we get there, or am I to just wing it all night?"

"We'll be sitting with some friends. The Petersons and the Harrells. I've known both men for years. Tim Peterson's wife is his second, and they've only been married a few months. Betsy and Baxter Harrell have been married since college days."

"Is that where you know them from? College?"

They reached the car and Nick opened the passenger's door for Molly. She shivered slightly in the cool night air. The fog had blanketed San Francisco bringing a damp chill. It also gave a luminescence to the city lights, diffusing them and mingling to provide an eerie overcast that glowed.

Nick joined her and soon had the car heading for a rival hotel where the charity ball was being held.

"Your friends?" she reminded him. "From college?"

"No." He flicked her a glance. "From when we were boys."

"They lived near you?"

"We saw each other at Mrs. Porters's Dance Academy, if you must know. My mother insisted I attend, as did the others."

"Dance Academy?" Molly murmured.

"And if you breathe a word of that to anyone, heads will roll."

She laughed softly. "I'll keep that in mind. So both your long-time friends are married, but you're not."

"No."

"Ever been?"

"No."

"Ever going to be?"

He was silent for a moment. "I expect so, one day. Don't you?"

"Eventually, if I find the right man for me."

"And how will you know?"

"I'm hoping I'll recognize my soul mate when he shows up. Marriage is for so long, I sure don't want to make a mistake."

"Divorce is easy enough."

"Not for me. I'm getting married and planning to stay that way until we die. Like my folks. Like your parents. Your mother still loves your father, you know."

Nick didn't respond. Molly knew it wasn't because of traffic, it was light for a Saturday night in the city. Soon they were driving into the valet parking lane of the hotel.

She stepped out and waited for Nick, tucking her hand into his arm as they entered the hotel. From now on she had to remember she was the darling fiancée of a powerful man. She just hoped she could act convincingly enough to fool the world. Or at least Carmen Hernandez.

They found their table easily enough and Molly soon met Nick's long-time friends. She liked them both and was equally taken with their wives. Tim's second wife, Annessa, was years younger than the rest of them, even younger than Molly. She was friendly and pretty, and, Molly guessed, around twenty-three. Had Tim already gone through a midlife crisis and obtained a trophy bride? Molly glanced at Nick. Maybe waiting for the right mate made more sense. Molly didn't want to ever experience the heartbreak of divorce.

"It's not often Nick can surprise us, but he did with you," Tim said once introductions had been made. "Last I knew he was seeing—" He stopped suddenly and looked at Nick almost in panic.

"Carmen," Nick said easily. "Don't worry, Molly knows all about Carmen."

She leaned closer and flirtatiously smiled up at him. "All about her?" she said in a husky whisper meant to carry.

The others laughed. Nick's gaze locked with hers and for a moment, Molly felt as if there was only the two of them. His hand came up, as if he couldn't resist, and brushed against her cheek. "All the important stuff," he replied.

"Oh, oh she has him wrapped around her little finger already," Baxter said.

"Captivated," Nick said, his gaze never leaving hers.

Molly almost believed him. When he did fall for someone, that woman would know his devotion all her life. Lucky woman!

The music started. "Shall we?" Nick said rising.

The others protested they wanted to get to know

Molly better, but he merely smiled and took her hand, leading her to the dance floor.

"Next time tell them everything in advance. I feel like I'm constantly explaining the story of my life," Molly said as he swung her into his arms. They moved perfectly together.

"The academy paid off," she said as he expertly led them around the floor, moving in time to the rhythm, never bumping into others.

"This'll be a nine-day wonder, then everyone will forget. If I hadn't already agreed to come to this, we could have stayed away. But coming without you would have been impossible without giving rise to gossip in the local column that my mother would have picked up at once."

"She seemed better today."

"I agree. Which is why we continue a bit longer."

"I still think the letdown when we tell her will be a shock."

The song ended and they headed for their table. When they drew near, Molly saw Carmen sitting in the chair she'd had. She took a deep breath. Great, another confrontation from the Spanish Bombshell. Just what she wanted—not.

"Your friend is tenacious, I'll give her that," Molly said.

She felt Nick pause a moment, anger almost radiating. "It's going beyond tenacious."

"Hello, lover," Carmen said smiling smugly. She glanced around the table at the others, almost preening with every eye on her.

"I don't believe this is your table," Nick said.

"I don't believe you are engaged. We meant too

much to each other for you to fall madly in love with someone else in the few weeks we've been apart. If you are trying to make me jealous, I will confess you have succeeded. Now, get rid of her.''

"Oh, boy," Tim said softly.

"Oh, Nicky, don't listen to her," Molly said, holding his arm, pressing against him with her breasts. "I love you. We were meant to be, don't let her get her clutches into you, darling. I couldn't bear it without you!"

He looked at her as if she'd lost her mind, then something clicked. Amusement danced in his gaze. Sweeping her into an embrace, he kissed her. His arms held her firmly. He leaned over slightly, tipping Molly back until she was totally relying on him for support. The music faded as blood began pounding through her veins. She forgot about their charade, could only feel the power of the man, the magnetism, the sexy attraction that she could never deny.

The kiss went on and on and on. Finally the rest of the world began to penetrate and Molly gave a soft moan of protest.

Nick stood, releasing her slowly, his eyes on her. "Does that convince you I'm totally captivated?" he asked.

For a second, Molly felt she was in two dimensions, one where Nick did care for her, and had shown the world. The other the narrow walk of deception, where they needed to fool everyone by whatever means necessary.

"I'm convinced," Betsy said.

"Me, too," Annessa said. "Tim, you never kiss me like that."

"Honey, I don't think anyone in the world was kissed like that before."

Carmen glared at them, pushing back and rising. She did not speak as she stormed away.

A lone clapping sounded and Molly looked at Baxter. "Good job, some people have to be hit on the head to get the message. But, Nick, you set a hard standard for the rest of us!"

Molly sat down in her chair and tried to join in the conversation that bantered about. But her mind was focused on the kiss. How long before her pulse returned to normal, she wondered. Unable to resist, she peeped at Nick from beneath her lashes. He was studying her. Maybe the others believed theirs was a love match. She smiled, hoping she looked like the adoring fiancée he wanted her to portray.

What she wanted was the safety of her own flat. Away from curious glances and conversational land mines. And away from the lure of Nick Bailey. She was getting the lines blurred between reality and fantasy. She knew she'd been the one to ask him to act captivated, but did he have to do such a good job? He couldn't distance himself a tad now that they'd convinced everyone they were in love. If she didn't keep a tight rein on herself, she was in danger of losing her head—and her heart.

"What is it you do for a living, Molly?" Annessa asked.

"I work as a graphic designer for Zentech," Molly replied, glad to focus on something beside Nick.

"Zentech, isn't that one of the leading high-tech firms in the Bay Area?" Baxter asked.

Molly nodded.

"So how did you and Nick meet?"

"Donny introduced us," Nick said easily, his hand on the back of Molly's chair, his fingertip gently tracing patterns on her shoulder.

Molly could hardly concentrate on the conversation. She was exquisitely aware of Nick touching her, and the shimmering sensations that danced on every nerve ending as a result. Did he have any idea what he was doing?

"So when's the big day?" Tim asked.

"We haven't decided yet," Molly said quickly. "My parents are on a cruise and we want to wait until they return before making any plans."

"How is your mother," Baxter asked Nick.

"Recovering, thanks."

"And is she happy her only son is getting married?" Betsy asked, smiling broadly. "I bet she can't wait to become a grandmother. At least that's what we hear from our parents all the time!"

Molly glanced at Nick and almost laughed at his stunned expression. Most people did expect to have children once they were married. He looked as if the idea had never crossed his mind.

"She hasn't said," he replied.

Waiters began weaving their way through the tables, beginning to serve the meal. Before long, the music changed, became softer, more conducive to conversation. At the end of the meal, brief speeches were made, and the total amount garnered for the Foundation was announced. Once the applause died down, the dance music began again and Nick took Molly's hand and led her to the dance floor.

"It's going well, don't you think?" she asked as

they began to move to the sensuous music. "They all think I adore you," she said smugly. "I'm a great actress. Maybe I missed my calling."

He looked down at her and tightened his arms slightly. "Don't get too complacent, I've known these people a long time."

"And your point is?"

"I'm not sure they are convinced."

She glanced at the table, but it was empty, the others dancing, as well. "How can you say that? They think it was a whirlwind romance!"

"Maybe they bought into it tonight, but your not knowing about my apartment when they mentioned the view had Tim, at least, looking thoughtful."

"So, if they learn the truth, they won't tell your mother, will they?"

"It's not that anyone would go up and ring the doorbell to tell her I'm not engaged, but word has a way of spreading. Look at the situation we're in."

"Well I had no idea newspaper photographers would be at the reception, or have any interest in my phony engagement. Your cousin should have told me who you were instead of setting up the whole thing."

"Maybe he thought you already knew."

"Back to that again? Honestly Nick, I don't know how you make it through the day with all the suspicions you harbor." The joy of the dancing vanished. Molly tugged on his hand. "I want to go home. We came, were seen, and insulted by your ex-lover. Your friends have been given a display of our deep and abiding love. So what's keeping us here?"

He pulled her closer. "What's the rush? Don't you like dancing?"

"With someone I like."

He spun them around. "And I'm not in that category?"

She shrugged. Suddenly she smiled right into his eyes and murmured for his ears alone, "Carmen on my left."

A moment later, Molly spoke louder. "We could go back to my place, darling."

Nick knew it was for show, Carmen must be closer. But he was startled with the realization he wanted to go back to Molly's. That he was tired of the night, of dealing with image and power and manipulations. Molly's flat was quiet and unpretentious.

"Then let's say our goodbyes."

In only minutes, they were in Nick's car, heading toward China Basin. Molly relaxed against the seat-back, still humming the last song. "All in all, I had a good time."

"You sound surprised, didn't you expect to?" Nick asked.

"No. This really isn't my kind of thing. I was worried I'd do something terrible and all your friends would pity you for getting engaged to me."

"Really?" That intrigued him. He couldn't imagine any other women he knew thinking that, or admitting it aloud. They'd have all been so excited to be seen with him, the last thing they would have cared about was his friends' reaction.

As she remained quiet, he was struck about how much Molly intrigued him in other ways. He still wasn't sure their meeting had been totally accidental, but she hadn't pushed to capture his interest like he expected. She was quietly confident in her own way.

She seemed content with her life the way it was going and hadn't once suggested they change their status from pretend to real.

In fact, she had not asked for a single thing from him.

Nick frowned. That couldn't be right. Everyone wanted something from him. But even offering to compensate her for her postponed weekend at some spa had been refused.

For the first time, Nick began to wonder if Molly was for real. If it wasn't some act she was playing, but the genuine article. Were there women who weren't out for the main chance?

It was still early for a Saturday evening, and parking was easy in front of Molly's building.

''I guess you're in a hurry to get home,'' she said when he stopped the car.

''Invite me in for coffee,'' he countered.

She looked at him in surprise, her gaze drifting to his mouth. ''Just coffee?'' she asked.

Nick opened the door and went to open hers. He was making no promises tonight. Molly looked like every man's fantasy in that dress with her hair up, begging to be undone and allowed to fall to her shoulders. Those same shoulders now covered by her coat, but which had been tempting him all evening.

When they entered the flat, she shrugged off her coat and draped it across a chair. She walked to the open kitchen and Nick watched her hips sway beneath the dress. He loosened his tie, and removed his jacket. It was suddenly too warm.

He followed her and leaned his hip against the counter, crossing his arms over his chest as she prepared the coffee. She glanced at him from time to time. Did she feel the same draw of attraction? Or was she merely wondering how soon she could get rid of him?

"You can wait in the living room," she said.

"Trying to get rid of me?"

She faced him and nodded emphatically. "Yes, you make me nervous."

Nick moved closer, crowding her until she was back against the sink. He placed a hand on either side of her and leaned closer.

"How nervous?"

"Very nervous," she said, her eyes challenging him, her whole body challenging him. He wanted Molly McGuire.

Her palm came to rest against his chest. He waited. Was she going to push him away? She didn't. The warmth of her hand seemed to burn through his shirt.

Slowly he leaned closer to kiss her. He hadn't tasted those lips since the kiss earlier at the ball. It had been hours. He wanted another taste.

"This isn't a good idea," she said in a throaty low voice even as her face tilted up to meet his.

With a soft sigh, Molly closed her eyes, and met his lips with hers.

It was a gentle kiss, sweet and tender. He held himself in check, letting her call the shots. She moved against him and he wrapped her in his arms, relishing the feel of her feminine body against his, the flowery scent of her that seemed to surround them. Her honey-eyed taste remembered.

The shrill whistle from the teakettle interrupted. Slowly he released her, already wanting more.

"Go on in the living room, I'll bring the coffee in a moment," she said.

Nick nodded and left the tiny kitchen. When he entered the high-ceilinged room, he remembered her telling his mother about her painting foray. He looked up. The walls were high. If she ever did it again, he hoped she'd hire a painter.

The bedroom loft had a half wall that gave privacy from the living room, but would enable Molly to look over if she chose. He wanted to climb the spiral stairs and see her bedroom. Did she have a large bed, or a single?

Turning away from the disturbing image of Molly in bed with someone else, he looked at the painting on the easel near the window. He crossed the room to study it. He didn't know the exact spot but he'd bet it was from the Japanese Tea Garden. She had captured it in early morning, with fog still drifting overhead, the serenity and peaceful setting reflected perfectly. He could almost feel the cool air, see the ripples in the water. He hadn't realized she was so talented.

"Do you take anything in your coffee?" she asked.

He turned but didn't move away from the painting. "Black. Do you have a buyer for this painting?"

She walked over and handed him a mug. She shook her head.

"Who handles your work?"

"I have some in a couple of galleries. Buchards on Market and Samuel's at the wharf."

He looked at the painting again. "I'll buy this one."

Molly sipped her tea and studied the painting. She looked at Nick with curiosity. "Why?"

"What do you mean, why? It's a sale, isn't it?"

"I guess. I'm just surprised, that's all."

He looked at the paintings that were hanging on the walls. Stepping around Molly, he went to study each of the three. One was a seascape, bold and daring. He could almost taste the salty air. The one near the chair and lamp was of an English country garden, lots of flowers, and so romance-y he knew it would appeal to women everywhere. The third one, near the bookcase was another of Golden Gate Park—of the grassy areas where families picnicked and children played.

"Why are you working at Zentech when you could make a fortune with the painting?" he asked, turning to look at her.

"Zentech is bread and butter, the rest is jam," she said.

"So will you sell me the painting?"

"Sure. Do you want me to have it framed first?"

"Yes."

She named a figure Nick thought ridiculously low, but he wasn't going to bargain up. If that was the price she set, so be it.

She went to the sofa and sat down, tucking her legs beneath her. Placing her cup on the coffee table, she looked at him.

"I read the fact sheet Donny prepared, before I went to see your mother, just in case. He didn't list any hobbies. Do you work all the time?"

He came to sit beside her, close enough to touch, but with space between them. Placing his cup beside hers, he leaned back against the cushions. "I don't have time for hobbies. Unless you count running. I try to get in a few hours a week. But Magellan's takes most of my time. Not just the one here, but all up and down the coast. Some weeks I feel I'm living in an airplane."

"Do you read when on the plane?"

"Sure, reports, spreadsheets, market analyses. Why the interest?"

"Just in case."

"In case?"

"I'm questioned about it around your mother. She'd think it odd if I didn't know more about you. She told me about your growing up, though come to think about it she didn't mention Mrs. Porter's Academy."

"That's classified information, don't you be spreading it around, either."

She laughed and Nick was lost.

He reached for her, gratified when she came willingly. A few kisses and he'd either take them up those spiral stairs, or leave before he got further involved.

But one kiss was all she gave. Then she pushed back, touched his cheek lightly and rose. "You need to go."

He stood beside her. "Or I could stay." His hand encircled her neck, urging her closer. But Molly stood firm.

"No, you can't stay. Nick, this is a pretend engagement, entered into solely to help your mother. And I'm not the type to sleep around."

"But you think I am?"

"Carmen could answer that for us."

He shook her gently, then released her. "I may have had an affair or two in the past. At my age, did you expect me to be a monk?

"I don't expect anything from you—except for you to leave now."

"What are you doing tomorrow?" he asked as he went to pick up his jacket.

"Errands, and chores, why?"

"Chores?"

"Vacuum this place, do laundry, I don't know, whatever needs to be done."

"Spend the day with me," he said. "When my mother asks, you don't want me to lie, do you?"

Molly laughed. "This whole charade is a lie. What's one more."

"Spend the day with me."

"Doing what?" Molly knew she shouldn't but temptation was strong. She would like to see more of him before they called a halt to their engagement. And if his mother continued to recover as fast as she seemed to be, the need for their engagement would end soon. Long before her own parents returned.

"Whatever you want."

"Oh wow, that's tempting."

"Within reason," he added hastily.

"How long since you've ridden a cable car?"

"What?"

She smiled. "Okay, here's the deal, we meet at the top of Lombard Street and walk down the crooked part then head for the wharf. We can ramble around there for a while, even check out Pier 39. Then take a cable car to Chinatown and have dim sum for lunch. Are the Giants playing? We could go to the stadium and watch a ball game. I'm not crazy about football, but don't mind baseball. It's going to be gorgeous tomorrow.''

''Sounds like a tourist outing, hit all the high spots of the city.''

''So why should tourists have all the fun. We live here, we should enjoy the high spots ourselves!''

''Ten o'clock?''

''At the top of Lombard.''

He nodded and left.

Molly stared at the door for a long moment, bemused by his agreeing. She hadn't expected that. Would he enjoy the day?

She hoped so. If nothing else, it could provide a shared memory she could take out and enjoy in the years ahead.

CHAPTER EIGHT

PROMPTLY at ten, Molly reached the top of the hill where Lombard began its crooked descent. The hydrangea hugging each curve were in full bloom, their pink and blue snowball blossoms adding color to the already picturesque block.

She'd worn her hair tied back, to keep it out of her face in the ocean breeze. The jeans and a shirt covered with a sweater were casual. She wondered what Nick would wear. Maybe those running shorts.

She grinned at the thought and watched as people began the descent by car, slowly maneuvering the tight hairpin turns.

Tourists walked down the steps, some stopping to take a photograph of the many blossoms.

She glanced at her watch. She'd thought Nick was always punctual. It was two minutes after ten—

"Parking is a bear around here," he said behind her.

When Molly turned, Nick leaned over and kissed her as if it was the most natural thing in the world.

"I took the cable car, didn't have to worry about parking."

"Do you even own a car?"

She shook her head. "Why bother when public transportation is so easy. Ready?"

"Lead on, McDuff." He threaded his fingers through hers and they began their Sunday together.

Molly held his hand, loving the feel of his warm palm against hers. Loving the pretense of being a couple, out to make happy memories and enjoy the time they spent together.

Justin had never made the effort, and they'd been dating. But except when Molly really put her foot down, all their time together had been about Justin. How had she convinced herself she cared anything about the man?

Nick and she were practically strangers, knew they had nothing in common and a limited time together. Yet he was a lot more open about doing things than Justin. Was it because they weren't really a couple? Or was Nick just a different kind of man?

"You didn't object when I suggested dim sum for lunch, you like Chinese food?"

"With Shu-Wen as our cook, what do you think? She's been with mother for years and often prepared Chinese. As a kid there was a time when I loved to spend afternoons in the kitchen, watching her prepare sui mai or potstickers. She'd always have to test one or two—so I'd get an early start on dinner."

"I love it myself. I'd eat dim sum for lunch every day if I could. But most of my friends at work don't care that much for it. So once or twice a month is our limit."

"Do you also like Japanese?"

They discussed food likes and dislikes as they walked along. Soon Lombard Street was behind them and they were heading for Fisherman's Wharf. As they descended the steep hills, the blue bay lay before them. Whitecaps dusted the water from the brisk ocean breeze. Molly felt warm as toast in her sweater, with her hand held in Nick's. She had no trouble keeping up with him, but he wasn't strolling.

From food they moved on to discussing architecture, using examples of the places they passed as to what was appealing and what was functional.

Mingling with the crowd later on the wharf, Molly was charmed by the way Nick protected her, drawing her out of the way of a bunch of rowdy teenagers, sheltering her from being jostled at a crosswalk. And keeping the street vendors from becoming a nuisance with one look.

She wished she could capture that look.

In fact, she wished she could capture the entire day! She was enjoying herself far more than she'd expected. And all because Nick was so much fun to be with.

Gone was the suspicious hotel mogul. Instead, he was just a man, and she was just a woman, both bent on having a great day together.

But it's still make-believe, she reminded herself. They would never have met had she not wandered into the bar at the Magellan Hotel and poured her woes on the bartender.

When they passed Samuel's Galleries, Nick stopped and went back, pulling Molly with him.

"Isn't this one of the galleries that carry your work?" he asked.

"Yes." She was surprised he remembered. Before she could say anything else, he led them inside.

"Show me," he said.

Molly pointed to the left where several of her paintings were displayed. They wandered over and she watched Nick as he studied each one. His impassive expression gave nothing away and she was on tenter-hooks wondering if he liked the work or was trying to find a way to be polite.

He looked at her. "They're good."

"Thank you."

"I especially like the sailboats."

She smiled. "I do, too, actually. It took a lot of tries to get the sea just right."

A discreet salesman hovered nearby. Nick caught his eye and the man came promptly over.

"May I assist in any way?" he asked.

Nick withdrew his wallet and pulled out a business card, handing it to the salesman. "I'm interested in purchasing these paintings," he said, gesturing to the wall which held Molly's pictures.

The man blinked, read the card and then looked at Nick. "All of them?"

"All the ones by Molly McGuire."

"What? Nick are you crazy? You can't buy all the paintings," Molly protested, astonished he'd even suggest the idea.

"I have eight luxury hotels. We decorate with top quality artwork, why can't I add these paintings to our collection?"

Molly didn't know what to say. There were seven paintings. It had taken her more than two years to paint them. Was he serious about buying them all for his hotels?

She tried to see the angle, wasn't he always doing that? Why he would spend so much money on paint-ings just because he knew the artist? There had to be a hidden agenda she was unaware of.

The salesman looked from one to the other, obviously unsure how to proceed. Molly almost smiled at his confusion. She could certainly empathize. He probably had never had anyone buy seven paintings at one time—especially with the prices Samuel's had given them.

"I'll have the addresses sent tomorrow for you to ship. I don't want them all at one hotel. Will your firm send an invoice?"

The man cleared his throat. "Would you excuse me for a moment. I'm not sure how we'll handle this." He quickly headed for the back of the gallery.

Nick studied the paintings again.

"You don't have to do this," she said.

"Of course I don't," he said arrogantly. "But I'd be a fool to pass up good work when I see it. Besides, I expect the investment will grow in value."

Molly felt a warm glow spread through her. This tough businessman was buying her work because he thought it would increase in value. It was the nicest compliment she'd ever received!

"Ah, Molly, my dear," Harold Samuel came from the back, trailed by the salesman. "How nice to see you again. And Mr. Bailey, I'm honored to have you visit our gallery." He beamed at them both, turning his gaze to Molly. "And congratulations are in order, I believe. I saw the article in the newspaper about your engagement."

She smiled and stifled a groan. Had the entire world seen that newspaper article?

"We are happy to crate and ship the paintings wherever you wish, Mr. Bailey," he said to Nick. "If it is convenient, just have the addresses faxed to us tomorrow. We'll have them shipped by Wednesday."

He motioned the salesman forward. "Molly is the artist. And this is her fiancé. A romantic gesture of the highest order—buying her collection to place in your hotels. You won't regret it. Molly does marvelous work."

"I think so," Nick said.

"But you have taken my entire inventory of her work." He shook his head and looked at Molly. "When may I expect more?"

"Soon. The piece I just finished has already been sold," she said, flicking Nick another glance.

"That one is for my personal collection," Nick said.

"I understand. I do hope we may represent more of your work in the future," Harold said genially.

They spoke a few moments longer then Nick and Molly left, Molly still reeling from the transaction.

"I don't know what to say," she murmured as they continued walking along the wharf, dodging tourists, watching kites in the distance dancing on the breeze. The total amount for seven paintings was staggering. She'd thought the gallery had overpriced them when they were first hung. Nick hadn't even haggled. Maybe Harold knew what he was doing!

"Want to go with me to select the right spot in each hotel where they can hang?" Nick asked.

She eyed him uncertainly. Was he joking? Most likely. The head of the corporation didn't place paintings. He had dozens of minions for those kinds of tasks.

Molly shrugged and didn't respond. No sense letting him know how much she'd love to see her paintings in the lobbies of Magellan's Hotels. Maybe she'd check out the one on Union Square in a week or so, to see if there was truly one of her painting on display.

"Getting hungry?" Nick asked.

"Yes." The fresh air and sunshine had sparked her appetite. It seemed like forever since she'd had breakfast.

They decided to walk to Chinatown, noticing how the buildings changed from the newer ones near the wharf to older buildings as they approached Little Italy at Washington Square. Molly glanced at the restaurant they'd eaten in a few nights ago as they walked past. She already had memories shared with Nick.

Soon they turned onto Grant Avenue where Molly always felt as if she'd taken a side trip to Taiwan. The aromas emanating from the restaurants were heavenly. And the old women carrying shopping bags, walking bent over with the weight of small grandbabies tied on their backs emphasizing a culture so different from her own which flourished in San Francisco.

He led the way to a restaurant known for its excellence. Entering, Molly was bemused to notice they were the only non-Asian customers in the place.

"It's wonderful in here," she said as the hostess promptly seated them.

"Best dim sum in town."

As the carts rumbled by and Nick selected for them, Molly was content to watch. He'd ask if she wanted a dish and she was willing to try them all—even the ones she didn't recognize. He ordered in

Chinese, not just pointing to the plates on the tray. Shu-Wen's influence, she knew.

"Delicious," she pronounced taking her first bite. "Does Shu-Wen ever make dim sum?"

"Occasionally. Mom would have a luncheon for her Garden Club and as a special treat Shu-Wen would prepare dim sum, but it's a lot of work to have this variety for a small group."

Just then Nick's cell phone rang. He excused himself and flipped it open.

"Bailey."

Molly took another bite and gazed around, trying not to eavesdrop on his conversation, which was impossible since he was so close.

"Yes, as a matter of fact, she's right here."

She looked over at that.

He held out the phone. "It's for you."

"Me?" She took it and said hello.

"Molly, dear, I suspected you two would be together. It's good to know Nick is taking some time off from work to spend with you. I enjoyed our lunch yesterday," Ellen Bailey said warmly.

"I did, too."

"What's that noise in the background?"

"We're at a restaurant having lunch," Molly replied.

"Oh dear, bad timing. I won't keep you, dear. I just wanted to see if you are free on next Saturday evening. I thought I'd have a small group of family friends in to meet you. It wouldn't be a formal engagement party, I know you'll want to wait for your parents to return for that. But I'm dying to show you off to my friends."

Molly looked at Nick. Some of her consternation must have shown, because he took the phone from her.

"What's going on, Mom?"

Molly watched as his expression darkened. "No, don't do that. You need to rest up and get better before entertaining."

He was quiet a moment, then took a deep breath. "Mom, can we discuss this later? … No." He flicked Molly a glance. "Actually, we had made plans to visit some of the other hotels. We'll be gone all weekend."

Molly felt her breath catch. The two of them going off for a weekend? She didn't think so. He was using it only as an excuse to fob off his mother. While planning for a future event seemed to be acting as a tonic, a party seemed excessive right now. But so did Nick's excuse!

He flipped the cell phone closed a moment later and slipped it back into his pocket.

"This is getting out of hand," he said.

"Maybe, but it also seems to be working. She's feeling lots better, isn't she?" Molly asked.

"She would be overdoing it if she hosted a party this weekend, no matter how few and close the friends. Anyway, I told her we wouldn't be in town."

"I heard." Molly cleared her throat. "As an excuse, it sounds good."

He raised an eyebrow. "Sounds good?"

"I mean, if she thinks we're out of town, that's as good as being out of town, right?"

"I meant it. We'll fly down to L.A. or San Diego and stay at the hotel there."

Molly opened her mouth to protest, "You may be

used to ordering your employees around, but I don't take orders from you.''

''What?''

''Maybe I have plans next weekend.''

''Do you?''

Her mind went blank. Surely there was something she could claim. ''I'd have to check my calendar.''

''Come on, Molly. There's nothing that can't wait. You already canceled your visit to the spa. Let me make that up to you with a trip to our San Diego hotel. It's really special—right on Mission Bay, with catamarans and paddle wheel boats, miles of sugar beaches and dining to delight all the senses.''

She grinned. ''You sound like a commercial.''

''Hey, I'm proud of our hotels. Especially that one.''

''Why that one?''

''It's mine from start to finish. I acquired it after my father died, built its reputation by some innovative ideas. It's one of the most popular in the chain.''

He stopped a cart to order har gow and shu mai. Molly was beginning to feel full, but the food was so delicious she didn't want to stop.

She ate thoughtfully, still hearing the ring of pride when Nick spoke of the San Diego hotel.

''Did good business dictate you buy the hotel in San Diego?'' she asked.

He shook his head. ''It was a gamble. The hotels my dad had managed were doing well, but not spectacularly so. Money was a little tight and I went out on a limb to finance the acquisition. But I wanted a hotel in that market and when one became available, I snapped it up.''

"Risky."

"Of course, but if you want something enough, it's worth any risk."

"And why did you—want it I mean? Wasn't what you had enough?"

"It would have been, but it was my dad's and grandfather's before him. I wanted something to prove I could make a difference. And I needed something to show the staffing at all the hotels I knew what I was doing when I proposed change. That I could lead the company in a new direction and have it flourish."

"You succeeded." Magellan Hotels were world famous.

He nodded calmly and placed another dumpling on his plate.

"Was it scary?" she asked.

"Challenging," he replied.

Men looked at things differently, she knew. But it took guts and determination and a lot of confidence to put an existing company in jeopardy to go forth with a new and risky venture. She was glad it had turned out well for him.

"So are you coming to see my baby?" he asked.

"We could just pretend we went away. If neither of us answers our phones all weekend, your mother would never know we were in town. It's not as if she's likely to go out and spy on us."

"I'd like you to come."

She hadn't expected that. "Why?"

"To see it. You missed your spa trip, let me make it up to you for helping me out."

"You did that by buying seven paintings." She

shook her head, still astonished he'd have done such a thing.

"The sailing one will be perfect in the lobby in San Diego. Come with me Molly and see it there."

His phone rang again.

"Dammit, can't a man have a day off?" he grumbled as he flipped it open again.

"Bailey."

Molly was glad for the interruption. She couldn't imagine herself taking off for a weekend with Nick. Would he expect more than studying how the picture looked in the lobby? She almost laughed, of course he would, he was a man, wasn't he?

Even if their relationship had been different, Molly wasn't the type to go off on weekends with men. And their relationship was not as they were pretending.

But if she could establish some guidelines, dare she take the opportunity? She hadn't ever stayed in a Magellan Hotel, probably wouldn't in the future, they were too expensive. Why not indulge herself—as long as they both knew going in it would be strictly platonic.

"I'll be right there."

Nick's words penetrated her thoughts. She watched as he flipped the phone closed.

"I have to go." He raised his hand, quickly summoning the waitress for the tally and bill.

Molly gulped down the rest of her tea and wrapped the custard desserts in a napkin. "What's up? Is it your mother?" Had something happened to her in the interval between the first and second call?

"No, Donny's holding someone he thinks is the

one skimming money from the bar. Before we call the cops, I want to talk to him.''

It was only a few blocks from the restaurant to Union Square, and Nick set a fast pace.

"Shouldn't you let the cops interrogate him?" she said breathlessly, trying to keep up.

"They will, I want first crack. It's my hotel he's ripping off." The implacable tone made Molly glad he was not angry with her!

When they reached the hotel, Nick went straight to the elevators. When one arrived, it was empty. They stepped in and Nick pushed button thirteen.

"The hotel's offices are on the thirteenth floor?" Molly asked. If she'd been asked, she would have thought they would take the top floor—for the view.

"Some guests are superstitious. This way, no one has to stay on the thirteenth floor. And the view is almost as good as at the top," Nick explained, but from the leashed energy she knew the answer was absently given, his focus was on what Donny had told him.

The offices were beautifully decorated, pale gray walls with original artwork displayed tastefully. The deep burgundy carpet was thick beneath her feet. At Zentech plush offices were only for the most senior staff members. Even entry-level clerks enjoyed Magellan's plush design.

Nick headed away from the elevators, a moment later pushed open a door and entered the office.

Molly paused at the doorway and studied the lay-out. Donny stood near the window. Gone was the genial bartender. Instead, he looked as dangerous as Nick. They both glared at the man in the chair in front of the desk. He was squirming in the seat, obviously nervous and trying to put on a brave face, but intimidated by the two men towering over him.

"I'll just wait out here," Molly murmured. Stepping back, she pulled the door closed. Sitting near the secretary's desk, she opened the napkin she'd carefully carried and began to nibble on a custard tart.

Being with Nick was certainly never boring. He intrigued her more and more each time they were together. He could be fun and act carefree, but she knew it was an act. Always beneath the surface he was focused on his priorities. And his business was at the top of the list.

On the other hand, she mused, listening for any sounds from the office, one always knew exactly where he or she stood with Nick. So far she had not seen any signs of manipulation or currying favors like Justin had displayed.

She frowned, wishing she had not thought about Justin. Her own judgment was at fault there. How could she have thought he cared for her—or that she loved him?

She knew—Molly's brain almost stopped functioning.

No. She was not going to say she knew the difference. She didn't know anything. She was *not* going there. She did not, could not, would not love Nick Bailey!

They had nothing in common. Except for the man in the office who had stolen from the bar, they would never even have met.

So they entered a temporary arrangement to hasten

Ellen's recovery. Didn't mean they even had to be friends.

She was not falling in love with Nick!

Molly rose, glanced at the door, and made her decision. He would never miss her. And she had to get a life. Something away from the disturbing influence of Nick. And away from the thoughts that plagued.

She pulled a sheet of paper from the nearby printer and scribbled a hasty note. Leaving it where Nick would be sure to see it, she took off like a shot. She was playing with fire to stay around Nick. Once she'd served her purpose, she'd be out of his life so fast her head would spin. It would be totally crazy to develop any feelings for the man.

But even as she descended in the elevator, she feared it was too late.

Molly stepped out into the sunshine. But the joy in the day had faded with the worry she had done something so stupid as to fall for the man.

Turning right, she began to walk. Maybe the fresh air would clear her head of foolishness.

But as the blocks fell behind her, her mind didn't clear, but constantly remembered every moment she'd spent with Nick, from dancing in his arms last night, to the first time she'd met him, to the kisses they'd shared.

Molly was startled when she looked up and realized she was home. She lived miles from Union Square. She stormed inside and went to Shelly's door, ringing the bell impatiently.

Shelly opened, looking at her in surprise.

"Hi, Molly, thought you were going out with the hunk today."

Molly walked past her friend and paced into the middle of her living room. "I am so mad I could spit!" she said.

"Whoa, date not go well?" Shelly closed the door and watched Molly pace in agitation.

Molly waved her hand. "It went fine, until the thief was caught and I think I'm falling for the blasted man!"

"You're falling for a thief?"

"No—Nick Bailey."

Shelly smiled. "So what's the problem. I told you it was as easy to fall for a rich man as a poor one. Think what fun you can have spending the night in a different hotel whenever you want!"

"I don't care a bit about staying in hotels. I have a perfectly wonderful flat right in this building."

"Which you won't stay in if you marry Nick. I suspect he wouldn't want to live down here."

"Marriage? There is nothing like marriage between us. You know his agenda in this whole pretense. Once his mother is fully recovered, it's sayonara Molly."

"Maybe not, he seemed to like you when he picked you up. Has he ever kissed you?"

Molly shrugged. "Maybe once or twice. But it meant nothing. I kissed Justin, and that went exactly nowhere, too."

"I wouldn't put Nick and Justin in the same sentence," Shelly commented dryly. "They are nothing alike."

"They are, too," Molly stated firmly, trying to convince herself. "They are both men with their own agendas."

"No. Justin set out to feather his own nest. Nick

was coerced into the situation, and only asked you to continue when he saw the benefit to someone else—his mother.''

Molly stopped pacing and looked at her friend. ''What am I going to do?''

''Enjoy?''

''It hurt my feelings when Justin dumped me so unceremoniously. But this is much bigger, Shelly. We're talking about my heart here.''

Shelly went to give Molly a quick hug. She gestured to the sofa, ''Sit down and let's talk about it. Maybe you can make him fall in love with you.''

''Oh, yeah, I have a life-size picture of that ever happening. You haven't seen Carmen—the kind of woman he usually dates. Trust me, falling in love with me is not an option. I have to stop seeing him now. I could be imagining all this, don't you think? It could just be wishful thinking as a reaction to Justin's dumping me and all.''

''Sure. Out of sight, out of mind. You can stay away from him all week with work and all. Then next weekend take that time off for the spa like you planned before. By then his mother will be fully recovered and you're off the hook!''

Molly nodded, trying to garner enthusiasm for Shelly's suggestions. She could take her postponed trip, but she couldn't help thinking about a weekend in a Magellan Hotel in San Diego.

''He bought all my paintings,'' she said slowly.

''What?''

''We went to the wharf, and he remembered Samuel's Gallery had some of my paintings on display. We went in to see them and he bought them all.''

Shelly stared at her. ''You're kidding?''

''No. He never even haggled. He told me he wanted the one I just finished, as well.''

''Oh, wow.'' Shelly's eyes were wide as she considered this bit of news.

Molly nodded. ''Oh, wow, is right.''

''It's such a romantic gesture.''

''No, just business. They have lovely paintings in the hotels, original art. He's planning to add my work to the hotels' collection. Except the one I just finished, which he said was for his personal collection.''

''Maybe you should give him the benefit of the doubt,'' Shelly suggested slowly. ''Maybe we're calling this wrong. I never heard of anyone buying a collection of work from a relatively unknown artist like that.''

''I don't think there is any doubt. I saw how ruthless he's been with Carmen. And you should have seen him when he walked in on the thief—no mercy at all. I don't want to be at the receiving end of that. If I cut loose now, I can get over him quickly—maybe I'm just romanticizing the entire thing. We did have fun this morning, so I could be fantasizing more about what might have been instead of reality.''

''I'm not following you,'' Shelly said, perplexed.

Molly jumped up. ''I'm not, either. I think I'll go home and have some chocolate and figure out how to stop thinking about Nick Bailey.''

Shelly rose as well and followed Molly to the door. ''Or give yourselves a chance. You're a terrific person, Molly, I don't see why he wouldn't fall head over heels for you.''

Molly hugged her. ''You're a true friend. Want to go to a movie one night this week? I'll have a lot of free time.''

''So you really aren't going to see him anymore?''

''I don't think it's very smart if I do. What's the point? He can tell his mother we are seeing each other. Make up something about my being too busy to visit. She'll get better in a short while, and he can tell her we drifted apart.'' She smiled, hoping the bleakness that enveloped her heart wasn't showing. With a half wave, she headed for her own flat.

But despite her brave words, tears trembled in her eyes. Her heart ached like it had been punched. She was falling for the man. What a mess. Trying to get out of one situation plunged her into a worse one. One, moreover, she suspected it would take her a long time to recover from.

Alone in her flat, she walked to the picture, dashing away the tears. He liked her work. He wanted this picture for his personal collection.

When he looked at it, would he think of the artist who had painted it? Or only see the cool morning in Golden Gate Park?

The phone rang. Molly ignored it. She listened to the answering machine when it clicked on.

''Molly? It's Nick, are you home?'' The silence ticked by. ''Call me when you get home,'' he said before hanging up.

She walked over and replayed the message, listening to his voice. Then she deliberately erased it. She was not going to moon over the man like some teenager with a crush.

Turning, she took the picture off the easel. Tomorrow, she'd take it to have it framed and then crated for shipment. And that would be that.

CHAPTER NINE

By WEDNESDAY, Molly began to think she should have confronted Nick and explained she wanted out of their agreement. He'd helped her out for one evening. Surely all the pretending she had done squared the account.

By Tuesday, she unplugged her answering machine—there were too many messages from Nick to keep it plugged in. Seeing the flashing light when she'd walked in, she hadn't listened to him, but erased them all.

Maybe she'd send him a note. That way she wouldn't have to see him again, but would make it clear they were through and it was up to him to concoct some story for Ellen as to why they were no longer engaged.

And the sooner the better. She spent more time thinking about him than attending to work. She'd been studying this layout for ten minutes and couldn't even remember what it was for.

Suddenly a feeling of disquiet came over her. She looked up. Nick was crossing through the open area as if he owned Zentech. No, come to think of it, the owners didn't stride through so arrogantly.

She put down her pencil and braced herself. He looked as dashing as ever, and much the angry pirate. His gaze snared hers and she couldn't look away.

Maybe she should have answered at least one of the phone calls.

"Your answering machine is broken," he said without any greeting. He stopped by her desk and glared at her. "Or you are ignoring my calls."

"Why would I do that?" she asked, licking suddenly dry lips.

"Good question, one I don't have an answer for. I've been trying to reach you since Sunday. Why did you leave so abruptly?"

"I didn't know how long you'd be, questioning your suspect. Was he guilty? Was he the one who pilfered the money?"

"He was. He's in police custody now, and a quiet warning has spread throughout the entire chain I won't tolerate theft."

"So Donny's days as bartender are over?"

He nodded, his eyes narrowed slightly. Flicking a glance at his watch, he said, "It's almost lunchtime, get your things, I'll treat."

Molly knew she should refuse, even opened her mouth to do so, when Justin strolled into view. He was finally working with Nathan on the delayed artwork, but he kept looking over toward Molly.

Pasting a brilliant smile on her face, she gazed lovingly at Nick. "How wonderful, darling, I'd love to." She covered the work on her drafting table, slid off the high stool and grabbed her purse. "It'll have to be casual, I'm not dressed for a fancy place." She slipped her hand into the crook of Nick's arm and almost batted her eyelashes at him.

A jaw muscle tightened in his face. "So glad, *darling,* that you can spare the time."

"I always have time for you, Nicky," she said, louder than needed. She wanted to make sure Justin got the message—she and Nick were still an item!

As they turned, Nick spotted Justin. He nodded once in the man's direction, then looked straight ahead.

"What's going on, Molly? Ignore me until you need reinforcements, then latch on to fool the opposition?"

"The opposition?"

"Justin?"

"Nick, you invited me to lunch. We're engaged, after all, why wouldn't I be delighted to see my fiancé?"

"You tell me first why you've ignored every message I've left."

She stalled for time, until they were in the elevator, when she dropped the adoring pose like a hot potato. The two other occupants in the elevator made conversation impossible. She'd wait until they had some semblance of privacy.

The busy sidewalk provided it. "I've been busy this week," she said as they walked toward Market Street.

"Too busy to call and say, I'm busy?" he asked. "To busy to return my mother's calls?"

"Your mother called?" She hadn't listened to the messages after the first day, suspecting they all were from Nick. "I didn't know."

"She wanted an answer to her proposal for a small dinner party this weekend."

"I'm going off."

"So I told her. That we would be going to San Diego to supervise the placement of your paintings."

Molly stopped. Ignoring the people who jostled her as they hurried by, she stared at him. "You did what?"

He took her arm, urging her along the crowded sidewalk. "We discussed it on Sunday, surely it didn't slip your mind."

"You suggested it. I never said I'd go."

"I made reservations for an early flight Saturday morning. We'll be home Sunday night."

"Of all the nerve. Nick, I'm not going off with you for a weekend. This is a fake engagement, remember?"

"Is that what has you worried? I booked a suite, two bedrooms. Your virtue is safe with me, Molly."

"No, that's not what has me worried." She closed her mouth suddenly, realizing what she had been about to say. The last thing she wanted was for him to have even a glimmer of an idea that her feelings had undergone a change. Instead of a business deal, she'd give her back teeth to have it change into a romantic affair.

Wouldn't he get a kick out of that bit of news.

"Then what?"

"I'm going to the spa this weekend. The one I was going to before." She sounded almost petulant in stating the fact.

"Another time. Come with me to San Diego."

His voice was compelling, making her wish for things that could never be. Intoxicating, like sparkling wine along her senses, awakening her to awareness and needs that were new and exciting.

She glanced up, and saw the intensity of his gaze. His dark eyes seemed to see through to her soul.

"Have you ever been to San Diego?"

She shook her head, mesmerized by the look in his eyes.

"I've heard it's lovely," she said.

"Mission Bay is especially enchanting, and the Magellan Hotel there was designed to enhance the enchantment. Say you'll come."

Molly looked away, trying to remember why she wanted to keep her distance. Surely a weekend wouldn't hurt—and it would give her a chance to see San Diego, see her paintings in the lobby of a famous hotel.

Give her a weekend with Nick.

See him in his element, the lordly hotel owner, showing off one of his hotels. Maybe she'd get disgusted with him and be able to easily say goodbye on Sunday night.

Reasoning took hold. "I can't go."

"It's that or the party at my mother's," he said shortly.

"No, it's not. Tell your mother we're going off, then just stay home and don't answer the phone."

"Like you've been doing all week?" he asked silkily.

"I've been busy," she protested, unwilling to concede defeat.

Nick paused by a doorway and ushered Molly inside a small sandwich shop. They joined the line waiting to order and she glanced around, recognizing one other person from work. The place was one she ate in often, and she knew was a favorite with many from

Zentech. When her coworker waved, Molly acknowledged her and turned back to Nick, hoping she looked like she was enjoying herself, and not provoked. If she ended things with Nick, would there be talk at work? She was tired of being the main fodder for the gossip mill.

"Friend of yours?" he asked.

"Someone from work." She stepped up and ordered, then waited while Nick ordered and paid for both sandwiches and drinks. They moved down the counter to wait for them to be prepared.

"Shall we eat outside?" Molly asked, not wanting to have a conversation in such a crowded place. Who knew who might be listening?

"It's a short walk to the Embarcadero. We can go there, if you like."

He was being accommodating, nice. She wished he would be as arrogant as he could get sometimes. It would make things easier.

Before long they were sitting on a bench in a quiet little park, dappled sunshine giving them respite from the sun. The breeze was slight, cool and refreshing.

Molly took a bite of her sandwich and looked at Nick.

"Now's when you bring in the heavy guns," she said.

"Meaning?"

"What threats are you going to use to make me go to San Diego."

A gleam of amusement lit his eyes. "Threats? Wouldn't a simple invitation do?"

She shook her head warily. "I don't want to go."

"Do you not want to go, or not want to go with me?"

That gave her pause. "With you."

"I told you, you have nothing to worry about."

"Just being with you makes me worry," she blurted.

"Ah, and that is because?"

She took another bite, unwilling to say anything more. Her tummy felt fluttery, her skin tingly and her heart raced. Just being with Nick. What would it be like to spend a weekend together? They'd get the best service, of that she was sure. And San Diego, renowned for its sparkling beaches, casual attitude and warm weather—outstanding even in California.

She'd never get such an opportunity again.

And get to see her painting put on display in the lobby.

And get to spend a few more days with Nick Bailey.

A wise woman would run in the opposite direction. Molly looked at him again, and jumped in with both feet. "Okay, early Saturday morning we leave for San Diego. How is your mother?"

"Recovering remarkably well."

"So we don't need to continue this charade much longer?"

Nick shrugged, for some reason unwilling to give Molly a date when they could end the charade as she put it. His mother's health was recovering quickly. He'd spoken with her doctor yesterday and been told the man was confident she'd regain her lost strength in a short while and be as fit as could be in no time.

Nick knew better than to believe his mother would go into a decline when he told her he and Molly were no longer engaged, but he didn't want any setbacks, either. It wouldn't hurt to continue a little longer.

"You don't have anyone in the wings, do you?" he asked.

"What wings?"

"It's an expression. Is there someone you'd rather be seeing?"

"Of course not. After Justin's trick, do you think I want to rush back into the dating scene? Not likely."

"Then what's the rush to end our arrangement?"

He watched her expression, wishing he could read minds. What was going on in that head?

He found a lot of benefit to the arrangement—Carmen had stopped calling, his mother was recovering, and he had an escort to social events, one with no expectations, and who wasn't constantly trying to impress him.

There was more to this than he'd originally expected. Maybe he should have thought to enter an engagement-of-convenience a long time ago. Found someone who was content to remain single, yet wanted someone to do things with occasionally.

"Actually, I'm in no rush to end the engagement," he said slowly, testing the waters.

"You're kidding?" Molly looked at him in surprise. "Why not?"

"Why would either of us? We have built-in protection against others, someone to do things with on occasion, and no strings attached."

She looked away, finishing the last of her sandwich and balling the wrapping paper into a tight wad.

"I can see the appeal to a man who doesn't want to get involved. But I do, at some point. Just not with someone like Justin. One day I want to get married, have some children, a dog. And have someone to grow old with.''

Nick frowned, not liking the image of Molly growing old with anyone. She was vibrant, young and beautiful. He could see her with children—knew her eyes would light up with delight. She'd be carefree and fun, and bring joy to each child she had.

He focused on the water, trying to forget that picture. But the image wouldn't leave.

''No one is saying you can't have that. But are you ready to do it now?'' he asked.

''Now, later, who knows when a person meets love.''

''Love is an overrated, romantic notion given by women to pretty up the basic instincts all humans have to mate.''

''Cynic,'' she teased.

''Dreamer,'' he retorted.

''Artists are allowed,'' she said, rising. ''Okay, you've accomplished your goal, we're going to San Diego. I need to get back to work. I'll see you Saturday. Should I meet you at the airport?''

''Oh no,'' he said, rising, as well. ''I wouldn't risk it. You might discover you're too busy. I'll pick you up at six.''

''In the morning? On a Saturday? That's my day to sleep in.''

''We have an eight o'clock flight. You don't want to waste the day. We can be on the beach in San Diego before lunchtime.''

Molly was not used to such casual travel. She rarely went on vacation beyond camping in Yosemite.

The thought of flying to San Diego to be lying on the beach by noon was fascinating.

As they ambled from the park, Molly dropped her trash in a container. Nick had achieved his goal—she was going away with him this weekend. How had that happened?

A lot could happen in a weekend.

Molly was enchanted with San Diego, just as Nick had predicted. The sugar-white sandy beaches beckoned, even when viewed from the airplane. The air was warmer, softer, than the crisp breezes she was used to in San Francisco. Palm trees swayed along boulevards as they took the hotel's limo to the hotel. Colorful bougainvillea covered walls and arched over doorways, deep red, bright purple, adding to the festive mood.

When they arrived at Magellan's San Diego, they were treated like royalty. Of course the staff knew Nick. He probably got that treatment everywhere—took it as a matter of course. But Molly was delighted with the warm welcome, and the fruit basket displayed prominently in the suite. She touched the cellophane wrapping lightly on her way to the large window. It overlooked the beach, in the quiet shelter of Mission Bay. Dozens of families were already enjoying the sun and cool water. The sparkling blue water was alluring.

Nick stood by the doorway to the suite, watching her, his hands in his pockets. "Want to go swimming?"

She turned, a bright smile hiding nothing.

"I sure do. It won't take me long to change once our suitcases arrive. This is a lovely hotel."

"Let's eat first, then we can spend the entire afternoon at the beach if you like. Later we can wander around the lobby and you can decide where to hang the painting. I selected the sailboats for this hotel."

She nodded, turning back to look at the water. They had a little more than twenty-four hours before the return flight, she wanted to make the most of every minute.

Once their bags arrived, Molly changed into her swimsuit, and then donned a loose sundress over it. Slipping on sandals, she pulled her hair up on her head, so it wouldn't get into her eyes once wet.

Going back to the sitting room of the suite, she waited for Nick, wandering around the luxurious room, admiring the furnishings, and the sense of elegance in every selection.

"Ready?" Nick asked from the door to his room. He was wearing shorts and a cotton shirt which was partially unbuttoned. She had the strongest urge to slip her fingertips into the opening and feel the warmth of his skin, test the strength of his muscles.

"Ready!" She turned toward the door, trying to get her thoughts under control. She had stipulated nothing physical between them, she couldn't change the rules to suit herself.

Nick led her to an outdoor café to one side of the huge hotel. Shaded by trees and strategically placed umbrellas, the tables provided a view of Mission Bay. Containers of bright flowers dotted the space, enhancing the feeling of dining in a tropical paradise.

"I have to have the shrimp salad," Molly said after

perusing the menu. "It's the only thing that would fit this setting. It's so pretty here. How do you stay away? I'm itching to paint—" She swept her hand in an arc, encompassing the entire setting. She would love to capture the different shades of blue that shimmered in the water, the reds and yellows of the flowers, the dark green of the trees. This was a feast for her senses.

"So come back sometime and paint it," Nick said casually. His eyes were hidden behind dark glasses. Molly wondered what he was thinking—maybe they'd come back together sometime? Or was he counting the days until his mother recovered and he no longer needed a fiancée-of-convenience.

When lunch was finished, they moved to the beach. It was crowded with families and couples, but walking along, they found a couple of empty reclining chairs and spread the towels the hotel had provided.

When Nick pulled off his shirt, Molly tried to keep her eyes on the water, but the pull of attraction was too strong. His skin was a warm honey color—not darkly tanned, but darker than her own. Obviously he took a few hours to swim in the sun during his visits to this hotel.

His bathing suit was tight, clearly defining his excellent physique. She swallowed, remembering how those muscles had felt when pressed against her. She had to get to the water to cool off—before she said or did something extremely foolish.

Slipping out of the dress, she almost ran to the edge of the bay. Molly stepped in, finding the water cool and refreshing. Soon she plunged in all the way, cooling her heated skin and trying to focus on anything but Nick Bailey.

But it wasn't easy when he joined her a second later, diving deep and then coming up beside her.

"This is nice," she said treading water, looking around. Time and again her gaze was drawn back to his. Daringly, she reached out and touched his shoulder.

"Glad you came?" he asked.

"Yes."

The afternoon was perfect. They splashed in the water, swimming the cool depths. Sunning for a while on the beach, they soon moved beneath a wide umbrella to avoid burning.

Talk was desultory. Molly knew she dozed part of the time, but it was so relaxing she couldn't help it.

Waking, she looked at Nick, he was studying her.

"Maybe you should have slept in this morning after all," he said.

"Oh no, I wouldn't change a thing about this day. I can sleep in tomorrow, can't I?"

"If you wish. There is a catamaran going out on an excursion run early in the morning, I thought you might like that."

She smiled dreamily. He was acting just like a real fiancé—looking for fun things for them to do on a weekend away. Would he ignore her rules later and kiss her? Push for more than separate bedrooms? Molly hoped not. It would spoil everything.

Or would it?

She closed her eyes again, still smiling at the memories of Nick's kisses.

"Nick Bailey, you son of a gun. What are you doing here? I thought you never left your office."

Nick looked up and then rose offering his hand. Sam Perkins had been a friend from college days. He hadn't seen Sam since he took over the hotels after his father died.

"What are you doing here?" Nick asked, gripping his friend's hand. "I thought you never left L.A."

"You knew I got married," Sam said proudly. "And when a man's married, he can't work all the time." Sam gestured to a pretty blonde playing with a toddler at the water's edge. "That's Stephie and our boy, Joel. I want you to meet her. I couldn't believe it when I saw you in the water earlier. I wasn't sure it was you."

Nick smiled and looked at the pretty woman. For a moment his gaze was captivated by the little boy, just able to walk on his own and fearlessly toddling into the water, only to be snatched up by his mother when he faltered. They both laughed, obviously enjoying the game. She'd set him back on his feet and again he'd head for the water.

He and Sam had been on the swim team at college together. Sam then started an import-export firm in Los Angeles specializing in Asian art. He'd been the last man Nick expected to marry. He remembered how surprised he'd been when he had received an invitation to Sam's wedding. Not that he'd been able to attend. That had to be three or four years ago.

Now Sam had a son.

Nick felt a tightening in his gut. He was thirty-six and not getting any younger. As his mother pointed out all the time, his own parents had had a school-aged child by the time they had been his age.

He looked at Molly who had sat up at the greeting.

"Sam, Molly McGuire. Molly, Sam's an old friend. We were in college together."

"Pleasure, Molly," Sam said, offering his hand. He glanced between the two of them, raising an eyebrow in silent inquiry.

"Molly and I are engaged," Nick said.

"Sonofagun!" Sam slapped Nick on the shoulder. "About time. This is great news. Congratulations! Molly, you're getting a terrific guy. Say, why don't you two join Steph and me for dinner. We can celebrate in style. At the Cove Restaurant, of course," he said, mentioning the five star restaurant in the hotel.

Nick nodded. "At seven?"

"Great, I'll see you both then." Sam smiled and headed back to his wife and son.

Nick watched for a moment, then sat back on the lounger. He looked at Molly who was thoughtfully studying the family at the water's edge.

Dinner with Sam would take the edge off dinner with Molly alone. She'd been clear it was to be a platonic weekend, but Nick had trouble keeping that in mind.

He suspected she had no idea how stunning she was in that two piece suit. Her midriff was slender, her breasts full and round. Her hips were perfection. He looked away again, wondering if he needed another dip in the water to cool down.

Closing his eyes, he tried to think of something else—anything else but Molly and her golden skin, hair piled up on her head, damp and spiky, yet tantalizing. He'd like to release it, let it spill across her shoulders. Bury his face in it and breathe in the very essence of her.

But he'd honor her request. Unless she showed she wanted it changed. And if he nudged just a little to make sure she knew her mind, knew if she wanted to change the rules, what could it hurt?

"You should have just said I was a friend," Molly said.

"What?" Nick rolled his head to the side to see her. "What are you talking about?"

"He didn't have to think we were engaged," she said, lying back down. "Now he'll have questions in the future."

"Easily enough handled," Nick replied.

"Of course," she murmured, her eyes closed.

Nick had known Sam married. But seeing him with his wife and child made it real. And changed how he viewed his old friend. He suspected if he asked Sam to go carousing like old times, he'd be turned down flat.

Sam's proud look when he spoke of his wife and son went to the heart of the matter. Sam *liked* being married. Liked linking his life with Steph and Joel. Liked being half of a couple, part of a family.

Nick wondered if he'd like something like that.

Molly didn't know if the dress she'd brought for dinner was dressy enough. She had thought she and Nick would just find a quiet restaurant. She certainly had not expected to have to play the role of adoring fiancée while sharing dinner with an old friend.

Not that she minded having dinner with the other

couple. She would learn more about Nick. Round out the picture a little.

To what end? She asked herself as she gazed at her reflection. Her cheeks and nose were just the slightest bit pink from the afternoon in the sun. Her arms and shoulders looked a shade or two browner. She clipped her hair up, in a slight variation of the way she'd worn it that afternoon. Now, a few tendrils here and there brushed across her shoulders. She was deliberately trying to look as seductive as possible.

Wouldn't a fiancée want to be sexy for her intended?

Eyes sparkling, she was ready. Let Nick eat his heart out for someone who was just passing through.

She just hoped her own heart would hold up!

CHAPTER TEN

HIS reaction when she stepped into the sitting room was all Molly could have hoped for. His gaze felt like a caress. Appreciation lit his eyes. Then a sensual sexuality seemed to arise between them.

Molly tilted her chin, she would not be daunted.

"I'm ready if you are."

"You didn't wear your ring," he commented.

"I didn't bring it. I didn't expect to need it."

"We'll stop in one of the jewelry stores before going to the restaurant and pick up something." He glanced at his watch. "We have time."

Molly blinked. They were going to stop off at one of the fancy jewelry stores along the hotel's shopping area and just *pick up something?*

"We can just tell them I didn't bring it."

He shook his head. "No sense giving rise to questions."

Molly assumed they would look at the expensive costume jewelry display when they entered the store a few moments later. But Nick steered them to the fine gems section. She blinked.

"A fake would work," she murmured. Just how far did he plan to take this?

"It would be just our luck Stephanie is a jeweler and would recognize a fake a mile away. Think of my reputation."

She frowned. "I doubt she'd say anything."

"Not to my face, but to Sam for sure. Then he'd mention it somewhere and pretty soon the entire West Coast would think I hadn't bought my fiancée a real diamond."

"By that time we'd have gone our separate ways."

"Humor me."

Nick spoke to the elegantly attired salesclerk and soon a display of lovely diamond rings was spread before them. Molly gazed in delighted awe at the selection. If only this was for real. If only they were choosing a ring to symbolize their mutual love. A ring that would last down through all the years of their life together. A ring to be passed down to a beloved son or daughter.

Molly's eyes filled with tears. This should be a special time between two people. She wished with all her heart it was a special time between her and Nick.

"Which one do you like?" His voice caressed her. He stood near, as if to protect.

"They are all lovely." She didn't ask the price. Not with one of his own employees there. A sense of relief swept through her. Of course. He would be able to return it once dinner was over. How stupid of her to think he was actually buying the ring.

"I like that one," she pointed to a solitaire on a plain gold band. It was simple, but to her stunning in its simplicity.

"Not this one?" Nick picked up one. It was showy and ostentatious. Perfect for Carmen, Molly thought waspishly. But not for her.

She shook her head, pointing to the one she wanted.

In only a few moments, the clerk had sized Molly's finger and checked the ring. It was a match.

"No wait for it to be resized," the clerk said smiling at them both. She handed the ring to Nick and waited expectantly.

He looked at her, at the ring and then at Molly.

She gazed up at him, pretending it was real. Pretending he loved her. That they were embarking on a life together.

Slowly he took her hand and gently nudged the ring on, never taking his gaze from hers.

"With this ring," he murmured softly.

The tears that filled her eyes threatened to spill. She blinked quickly and tried to smile.

When he leaned closer, she closed her eyes. His kiss was tender and gentle, his lips warm against hers, pressing as if a vow.

"Congratulations and best wishes," the saleswoman said.

Nick told her to send him the bill. She nodded, smiling broadly. He suspected she couldn't wait until they left to start telling the world he'd bought his fiancée's engagement ring at her store!

Molly was quiet as they headed for the restaurant. Nick glanced at her, wondering what she was thinking. The tears in her eyes had surprised him. Was she regretting he wasn't another man? Or that this was only a pretense?

He would have thought she'd be delighted to flaunt an expensive ring. Yet she'd chosen a simple one. It looked nice on her hand. Maybe when they were no longer engaged, he would let her have the ring.

Nick felt a sense of quiet satisfaction at the thought of Molly keeping his ring.

Nick spoke quietly to the maître d' at the restaurant and he quickly showed them to the table where Sam and his wife awaited. Introductions were made as Nick and Molly joined them. Soon dinner had been ordered and conversation began.

Sam was curious about Nick's engagement. When he learned it was recent, he flagged the sommelier and ordered champagne. He had a million questions, which Nick tried to answer as vaguely as possible. When the chance arose, Nick steered the discussion to Sam and his own marriage. On that, Sam was verbose. Stephie was friendly and amused by her husband's sweeping commendation for marriage, finally reining him in and deftly changing the subject.

Nick watched the interplay between his old friend and his wife. They were obviously well suited and enjoyed being with each other. The memories they already shared excluded others. Was that a part of marriage he hadn't considered? Being part of a team, a couple, who built memories only the two of them shared? Creating a world of their own?

He flicked a quick look at Molly imagining them over the months and years ahead. He was attracted to her on a very primal level. Yet he had never considered marriage. When he was ready, would he want someone like Molly? Want Molly?

The champagne arrived and toasts were made. Nick shook off the pensive mood and enjoyed the couple sharing dinner with them.

The evening sped quickly by. Making vague promises to get together before too long, the two couples said good night at the elevators. Molly and Stephie exchanged hugs. They had had plenty to talk about all evening, Nick thought. He was more wary about starting new friendships, not so Molly.

"They are nice," she said as they rode the elevator to their floor. "And Sam is so funny. I bet they laugh a lot in their household."

"He liked tonight's audience."

"Umm." She grew quiet.

"Tired?" Nick asked.

"Yes, a bit. I think that sunshine and fresh air really takes a toll. Not that I don't want to go to the beach tomorrow."

"Sleep in if you like. We'll hit the beach whenever you are ready. Our flight home isn't until late in the afternoon. Plenty of time to spend on the beach."

When they reached the suite, Nick opened the door letting her in before him. She passed so close, he could breathe in her sweet scent. He followed, shutting the world out when he closed the door.

If they were really engaged, he wouldn't let the evening end just yet. Did Molly want more?

She stopped in the middle of the sitting room and looked around at him.

"Thank you for today. I had a great time."

"I did, too." He came up to her, reaching for her. When she came willingly into his arms, he kissed her. He'd been wanting to touch her all night. Not the casual brushes of fingers against her arm, but hold her, touch her, kiss her until neither of them could think straight.

And for him, it wouldn't take long. She was a delightful armful of femininity that had his senses reeling. Her mouth was sweet and responsive. Her tongue touched his, mated with his, feeding the primal desire that built. Her taste was special, one he couldn't get enough of. The soft murmurings as she pressed against him were driving him crazy. She was hot and exciting and willing.

Slowly he moved toward his room. They could end the night together and in the morning—

Nick met resistance. He lifted his head and looked at Molly. Her cheeks were flushed, her eyes sparkling with passion. Her lips were rosy and slightly swollen from their kisses.

Her hand was pushing against his chest.

"I need to go to bed." There was no mistaking the determination and resolution in her tone.

"Come with me," he said softly.

She shook her head regretfully. "I can't. I can't."

Slowly Nick took a deep breath, wishing he could turn off his feelings as easily as she seemed to. He released her, spinning away, angry, disappointment, frustration replacing the hot passion of a moment ago.

"Good night," she said and fled.

He heard her door shut and with regret headed for the bar at the side of the room. It was going to be a long night.

Molly awoke the next morning and lay in bed a few moments remembering yesterday. She'd never been whisked away to a weekend before. And such a weekend. She glanced around the most elegant hotel room she'd ever seen. The furniture was French Provincial. The paintings on the walls were original oils, not mass reproductions. Even the carpet was thick and luscious. French doors led to the balcony that ran the length of the suite.

Rising, she crossed over and opened them. The cool morning air rushed in, billowing the lacy curtains, pressing her gown against her body. If Nick were awake, maybe they could have breakfast on the balcony. The view of the Pacific was stupendous, its deep blue waters stretched out to forever.

She grabbed a robe and went to see if Nick was awake.

Opening the door to the sitting room, Molly was disappointed when she didn't see him there. His bedroom door was opened, however. Maybe he was up and waiting for her.

She crossed the room, hearing his voice. Was there someone else here?

She paused at the door and peeked in. Nick was dressed sitting at the desk, talking on the phone.

"...thanks for the report. I'll leave the rest to the attorneys.... I haven't seen her, but I haven't even had breakfast yet.... I knew there was more to it than appeared on the surface, I never trusted her. You know I won't be bluffed by a trumped up breach of promise scam at some future date. She knew the rules going in. Let the diamond suffice in lieu of any other payment."

Molly stepped back, out of sight. Who was Nick talking to? Who was he talking about? Blood pounded in her veins as she suspected it was herself. He had never trusted her. Had questioned her motives more than once. Did he think she was going to try to bring some action against him to get money?

She leaned near the door, knowing she shouldn't be eavesdropping, but unable to help herself.

"Yeah, well that's Molly for you. Maybe you should just stay on the payroll and investigate every female I date. That way, I won't have to plan on a payoff each time I see one more than once. Diamonds aren't cheap."

Molly had heard enough. She turned and stalked back to her room. Her temper flared. How dare he think she wanted a diamond! She held up her hand and glared at the ring. Snatching it off her finger, she almost threw it out the French doors. But, prudently, she refrained. She tossed it on the bed and went to get dressed.

She hadn't asked to come on this trip, she muttered as she stuffed clothes into her suitcase. She hadn't asked to have her painting bought and displayed in hotel lobbies, she fumed as she dressed in record time. She hadn't asked to enter into some dumb engagement-of-convenience. She had only asked for one evening's pretense.

What she'd asked for, she remembered, was someone tall dark and dangerous. And Nick had proved all three. Especially dangerous to her heart.

She brushed her hair, gazing unseeingly into the mirror. He was too cynical to be believed. She had no intention of filing a breach of promise suit. Did people still do that? To tell the world someone promised to marry you and then reneged would be worse than Justin dumping her. How could anyone do that?

Maybe if they were mercenary.

Which she was not!

But maybe that's the way Nick saw her. She

paused, brush in midair. It was. Wasn't he always assuming he could buy this or that and get his way—like she was helping out just for what she could get? Slamming the brush down on the dresser, she almost went to confront the man. But she decided against it. Better to just leave. She remembered how fervently she had wished buying the ring symbolized something special—instead he saw it as payoff to buy her silence.

She had been doing a favor for his mother. But no, he had to think she was after more. Obviously Donny's preliminary investigation had not been enough, Nick had asked for more. Well he was welcome to his report. And his ring. And his stupid assumptions.

She glanced around to make sure she had forgotten nothing, picked up her small suitcase and the ring and headed out.

He was still on the phone. She placed the ring on the table where he'd be sure to see it. She didn't want theft added to the poor opinion Nick had of her.

Without hesitation, she left the suite and headed for the taxi stand. In only a short time, Molly was heading for the airport. She'd have to buy a ticket, but that was a small price to pay to leave immediately.

She felt as if she'd been slapped. She'd fallen for a man who thought she was a gold digger. She had offered to help out for the sake of a sick woman, and he'd believed she had something else in mind. How could she care for a man who thought like that?

Yet she did. The ache in her heart was almost overwhelming. She wouldn't see Nick again. And the thought almost brought her to tears. She loved him.

Molly took a flight to San Jose, and headed for her parents' home. They were still on their cruise. She'd check the mail, water the plants, and stay in her old room. It was hiding out, but she didn't care.

She'd call into work tomorrow and take a personal day. Or maybe use some of her vacation time and take the whole week off. And stay away from Nick Bailey!

CHAPTER ELEVEN

By Thursday, Molly was going stir crazy. She had weeded her mother's flower beds, dusted and vacuumed the entire house, caught up on some reading and visited with each of the next door neighbors. But she was unhappy and bored.

She dreamed of Nick at night and thought about him endlessly during the day. Keeping busy didn't drive his image from her mind. She had memories galore from the fun at the beach, to their day at the wharf, to meeting his mother, to seeing childhood pictures and hearing his childhood antics.

But she would get through this. She'd only known the man for a few weeks. In no time, she'd get over this silly infatuation and be back on an even keel. Every time the phone rang, she would not expect it to be Nick. Every time she heard a car in the street, she would not expect it to be Nick.

Maybe she was making more about this than warranted. Had he even tried to reach her once he returned to San Francisco? Or had he understood by her leaving the ring that their time was ended?

She wondered what he had told his mother. Or was he continuing to pretend so she would recover faster?

When the phone rang Thursday afternoon, Molly was tempted to let it ring. Her parents had an answering machine. But all their friends knew they were still away. And Molly had given this number to her boss.

"Hello?"

"Molly, this is Brittany. I do hope everything is all right."

Brittany! "They are, why shouldn't they be?" Why in the world would Brittany be calling her? And how had she gotten Molly's number?

"Well, you haven't been at work all week, which is so unlike you. And Nick has been here every day, looking for you. Obviously there's trouble in paradise. Is there anything I can do?"

Molly gripped the receiver tightly. As if! "Nick has been there?"

"Every day—but he does vary his times. He just left. I'd say he was desperate. I told him I'd see what I could find out for him."

"How nice of you to volunteer," Molly wanted to grit her teeth. She knew why Brittany had volunteered—more gossip! "Sorry, I've got to go." Molly hung up. She couldn't believe Brittany had called. Seeking information for the gossip mill, she knew. But was what she said true? Had Nick been to Zentech every day?

The doorbell sounded.

When Molly opened the door, she sighed. "I should have known. What took you so long?"

Donny smiled. "I do have other clients. But Nick's my cousin. He tried it on his own, but I had a hunch. Can I come in?"

Molly hesitated, then shrugged. What did it matter if Donny came in or not. He knew where she was. Her safe haven was gone.

She led the way into the living room, sitting on a chair and motioning to the sofa. Donny sat on the edge and looked around, then at her.

"Want to tell me why you ran out like that."

"Does it matter?"

"Not really, but it doesn't seem in character."

"From your extensive investigation?"

He narrowed his eyes. Despite the coloring difference, for a second, he reminded her of Nick. "I thought we were past that. We didn't want to introduce a total stranger to Aunt Ellen."

"I mean the recent one," she said.

He shook his head. "You've lost me. There was only the one, quick and dirty the day after the Zentech reception."

She studied him for a moment. Doubt came. "I heard Nick talking with you on Sunday."

"I brought him up to date on the embezzlement. Turns out there were two involved. Nick plans to prosecute both."

"There was more to the conversation—I heard him talk about a diamond."

Donny nodded.

"Well, then, that's why I left."

He frowned. "Why?"

"I just told you."

"You're mad because Carmen's keeping the diamond pendant he gave her for Christmas?"

"Carmen?"

Donny nodded. "Nick's looking for you. He didn't know why you left. He's tried Zentech, your flat."

"Then sicced you on my trail?"

"No, this is what you call taking initiative. If it didn't work out, I didn't want to get his hopes up."

Molly was confused. What hopes? Why would Nick care one way or another—except for his mother. And his own desire to be in charge, to make sure things were going just as he wanted.

She looked at her hands, then back up at Donny.

"It was a fake engagement. You know that. I never met him before that night."

"So? I think he cares about you. Maybe more than he knows. Your leaving shook him up."

"It wasn't intended to. Just to —" She closed her mouth before she could say too much.

"Well, for what it's worth, I think he'd sleep better at night if he heard from you. Or saw you. Give the guy a break, Molly. And see where it leads." Donny rose and gave a half salute. "I'm heading back home. This San Francisco living is too much trouble for an L.A. guy."

She watched him leave, wondering how long before he called Nick.

When the afternoon passed and no phone call came, Molly began to believe Donny had not told his cousin where she was. If he hadn't, why not?

I think he cares about you, Donny had said.

As she tossed in bed that night, unable to sleep, different images of Nick once more rose to mind. Then one scene crept in—when he'd bought her a ring. *"With this ring…"* he'd said. Just as if it were for real.

She sat up. What if Nick was falling for her? What if she was spurning the very thing she wanted more than anything in the world?

How could she find out?

She could ask him.

She plopped back on the pillows. Right, she had a life-size picture of her sauntering up to Nick and saying, "I love you, how do you feel about me?"

He'd probably laugh in her face, if he didn't accuse her of trying something to get his money. Honestly, the man was fixated about that.

And why not, if all the women he met were in it for one thing.

She wasn't, but did he know it? She'd wanted his help that first night. But that was all. And he'd asked for hers the next day. Which she'd given freely— though he was always talking about compensating her.

Except, he'd stopped that recently. Was he seeing her differently?

"With this ring..." His voice echoed in her mind. She had so wanted it to be real. But she had not imagined him saying that. Why would a hardened businessman be given to romantic fantasy? Just to play the part in front of a salesclerk? She didn't think so.

Molly sat up again, and looked at the clock. It was ten minutes after midnight. Too late to go anywhere tonight.

"He'd sleep better knowing where you are."

Was Nick having trouble sleeping, or was that Donny's way of saying he was concerned where she was.

More than concerned if he showed up at Zentech every day. How awful for him, to have to admit to people he didn't know where she was. He'd said once if someone wanted something enough, it was worth any risk. Was he taking a risk for her?

How badly did she want Nick Bailey?

She switched on the light and reached for the phone. Trying directory assistance, she struck out. Not that she really thought his number would be listed. And he had never given her any phone number. Wouldn't people who were interested exchange phone numbers?

Finally she tried the hotel.

"Nick Bailey," she said when the phone was answered.

"Whom may I say is calling?"

Molly blinked. She had thought of a voice mail or something. Was he still at work at almost twelve-thirty at night?

"Molly McGuire."

"Hold please."

"Bailey." His voice sounded the same. She closed her eyes, savoring it.

"Hi Nick, it's me, Molly."

There was silence on the other end for a moment. Then, "Where the hell are you and why did you take off like that last Sunday?" The harshness in his tone surprised her.

"I'm at home. I didn't mean to make you worry."

"What did you think I'd do when you weren't there? I thought at first you'd been kidnapped. Then someone said they'd seen you get into a taxi and head for the airport."

"I, uh, overheard your conversation on the phone and misunderstood."

"What are you talking about."

"It's sort of a long story. I'd be happy to tell you tomorrow. That is, if you still want to see me."

"Yes. Tonight. I can be at your place in ten minutes."

"I'm not at my flat, I'm at my folks' place. I'll return to San Francisco tomorrow. We could meet—"

"Where is the house? I'm coming there tonight."

"It's in Fremont. Good grief, you can't come all the way out here tonight. It's already after midnight."

"I'm awake and you're awake, what does the time matter? Give me directions."

As soon as she hung up, Molly flung off the covers and dashed into the bathroom. Nick was coming here tonight. She had forty-five minutes or so to shower and get dressed. She couldn't believe he wouldn't wait until tomorrow. She could have explained then. Or even over the phone.

But he insisted on seeing her tonight!

Molly was watching from the living room window when the car turned into the driveway. She ran to the front door throwing it wide as he got out of the car. Watching as he walked quickly up the walkway her heart pounded.

He saw her and quickened his pace.

"Don't you ever do that to me again!" he said, sweeping her into his arms and holding her so tightly Molly couldn't breathe. Before she could say a word, his mouth covered hers in a searing kiss.

Molly clung for dear life, feeling the anger in the kiss, but the relief and something else. Guilt assailed her. She had never meant to worry him.

She gloried in his embrace, relishing every inch of

him she could reach, holding on tightly as she returned his kiss, deepening it when he did, wishing the moment would go on forever.

It did not, however. Slowly he eased his hold until he pulled back enough to look into her eyes.

"Your explanation had better be plenty good."

She touched his cheeks, seeing the worry still lingering in his face. "You look tired," she said.

"I've barely slept since Saturday night. Why did you leave like that?"

"I thought I had a good reason. Want to come in and hear it?"

He glanced around the darkened neighborhood. No other people appeared to be up, but there was no reason to hold their conversation outside. "If you insist." He released her and stepped back. They entered the house and Molly led the way to the living room. She sat on the sofa, Nick right beside her.

"If you want something enough, it's worth any risk," she said. "Do you remember telling me that."

He frowned. "I may have said something like that."

"Sometimes risks can be scary."

"What does this have to do with San Diego? You were scared there?"

"No. I was happy there. I had a wonderful time."

"That's why you left like you did Sunday morning?"

"Actually I overheard your conversation with Donny. Or part of it, at least. And I thought you were talking about me."

"We were talking about the embezzlers."

"And Carmen, Donny said."

"You've talked to Donny?"

"He was here. I thought he'd tell you."

"When was he here? And why didn't he tell me?"

"He was here today and I haven't a clue why he didn't tell you. But he told me you two were talking about Carmen."

"And you got in a snit and left?" His look was incredulous.

"No, I said, I thought you were talking about me. That you expected a breach of promise suit or something and would pay me off with the diamond ring you'd just bought. I thought I'd been insulted and got mad and left."

He shook his head, anger flaring. He stared at her for a long moment, then slowly the anger began to fade.

"I thought we agreed to keep this engagement going."

"Until your mother was better."

"Or until we had a good reason to end it."

"Like you met someone else?" she asked. She didn't remember that aspect.

"Or you did."

Not likely, not any time soon. Nick filled her senses and her mind. She couldn't even see other men for him. Risk. Take a chance.

"I might never find anyone else," she said daringly.

"I might not, either."

She held her breath. What did that cryptic comment mean?

"So the engagement would never end."

"Or we could end it like engagements normally end," he said softly.

"Huh?"

"In a wedding."

She stared at him, hope blossoming in her heart. She was almost afraid to ask for fear he'd laugh and tell her he was just teasing. But she was feeling daring tonight.

"As in our wedding?" she clarified.

He nodded, his gaze never faltering.

"As in marriage?" she said, feeling as if the room was spinning. She reached out to touch him, to ground herself.

"As in I love you Molly. I want to marry you. I want this engagement to be real until your parents and my mother can see us get married. Then we'd live together forever."

"Oh wow."

"That's all you can say?"

"I'm shocked. I was taking a huge risk, you see."

"Seems like I took the risk. You haven't said yes or no."

She laughed and flung herself into his arms. "Yes, yes, yes. A thousand times yes. I was going to tell you I love you. I was going to risk being dumped again, being made a fool of, everything, to tell you. And you beat me to it!"

"You love me." He said it with satisfaction.

"I love you. Adore you. That's what you wanted, isn't it, adoration?"

"Yes it is. You have captivated me."

She gave him a sweet kiss. "I've never captivated anyone before."

"Since that first night, I've been captivated. I didn't recognize it, then fought it. But your leaving changed everything. After seeing Sam and Stephie together, I began to think I might want something like that. Before I could put two thoughts together about it, you were gone. And I realized what living without you would be like. Not something I want."

"Which reminds me, Brittany called today. She said you'd been at Zentech every day."

"You and Brittany are now friends?"

"Hardly. She was looking for gossip. I couldn't believe she had the nerve to call. Were you really there every day?"

"Looking for you. I thought I was being subtle."

Molly laughed. "I can imagine." She took his face between her palms. "I'm sorry I ran out like that. And for the wrong reasons, too. If I had had a clue how you felt—"

"How do you think I felt—I bought you an engagement ring."

She nodded. "I should have picked up on that. You said, with this ring…"

He reached into his pocket and pulled out a small box. Flipping it open, he held it out. "I brought it. Did you really like it, or was it for show for Sam and Stephie?"

She looked at it, and then at the man she loved. "The entire time we were there, I was wishing it was for real. And when you said those words, my heart melted."

"You were in tears. I'll always remember," he said. He took the ring from the box and placed it once more on her finger. Once again, he sealed it with a kiss. Once more she gazed at the man she loved through tears of happiness.

"I love you, Nick."

"I love you, Molly McGuire."

Tall, dark and dangerous had been the perfect thing to order!

MILLS & BOON

MEDICAL

On sale 1st June 2007

HIS VERY SPECIAL NURSE
by Margaret McDonagh

Dr Kyle Sinclair is devastatingly handsome – and nurse
Alex Patterson cannot help but be drawn to her new boss!
Kyle hasn't looked at a woman since his marriage fell
apart – could Alex be the one to heal his heart and
help him love again?

THE SURGEON AND THE SINGLE MUM
by Lucy Clark

City surgeon Trent Mornington has shut off his emotions –
until a howling storm sweeps him into the lives of rural
GP Aracely Smith and her little son. Warmed by the beautiful
seaside town of Port Wallaby, it's not long before Trent is
thinking of Aracely and Robby as his family-to-be...

THE SURGEON'S LONGED-FOR BRIDE
by Emily Forbes

Anaesthetist Abby Jackson has come home and is reunited
with her best friend, surgeon Dan Dempsey. Dan's a constant
in her life – someone to make her smile. She just hasn't
thought of him as anything more – until now...

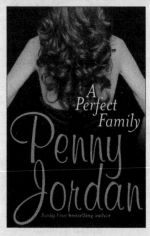